beneath *the* BURN

PAM GODWIN

Editor: Lesa Godwin, Godwin Proofing
Interior Designer: Pam Godwin
Cover Artist: Okay Creations

CONTENT WARNING

Visit my website at pamgodwin.com

For Amber
my Pamber
my bestie
my oyster

1

The aroma of rotting food crept in from a dumpster and clung to the humid air clogging the back of Jay Mayard's van. The brunette writhing beneath him smelled worse. Stale smoke and hairspray infected her gaping pores.

Facedown and arms spread over a speaker box, she nudged him with her bony backside. "Come on, Jay. You're so damn hot. I'm dying here."

He ground his dick against her. He wasn't hard, not even close. "I told you to shut up."

"But I want you." A husky, ashtray-laden whine.

He grabbed her neck, and she squeaked. Why was he even here? Maybe it was hope that sex would drown out the din in his head. Sometimes it worked. Sometimes it didn't. Dammit. His dick had been hard when they left the bar. Maybe he'd picked the wrong groupie.

He drove her face into the casing. "If you keep your fucking trap shut, I'll give it to you."

"Mmm." She relaxed, waiting.

He could do this. He needed this, as long as she didn't touch him. "Put your hands on the edge. Yeah, just like that. Now hold on and don't let go."

She panted and wiggled as he fished for the condom in his pocket and unzipped his leathers. *Come on, fucker. Get hard.*

The bastard lay limp against his thigh. He stroked it. Tried to drown out the body odor lingering in the band's lived-in van. Tried to tune out the metal guitar chords vibrating from the back of the bar. Tried to attenuate his thoughts to the one thing that could give him five mindless minutes.

Willing, wet cunt.

His cock half-woke. He wrapped it, positioned it, and worked it into her.

Numb. The hole encasing his dick offered nothing but empty, dead space. He might as well have humped the air. He thrust harder, deeper and felt nothing.

"Ahh, yeah, rock star. Give it to me." She pumped her hips and smacked her gum.

Could she not feel him shriveling? He fisted her ponytail. "Shut. Up." He released her hair with a shove of her head.

The pace of their thrusting increased, out of sync, but the finish would come. It had to. He kept his eyes open, focused on the music equipment stacked around them, the bed rolls he and his bandmates slept on, anything but the self-destructive thoughts prowling the edges of his mind.

Something moved over his thigh, clenched on his ass. He froze mid-thrust. His skin recoiled from the sensation. Fingernails raked down his leg, searing a trail of heat. Hurt. Burning skin. Oh God, too much burning.

He stumbled backward and knocked over his guitar case. "Never fucking touch me." His roar was harsh and clotted with spit.

Glittery black smudges caked her round eyes. She didn't know what was going on inside him, and she wouldn't be around long enough to find out.

The condom fell off in his hand. He flung it at her. "Get the hell out." His fingers shook as he stuffed himself in his pants and zipped up.

The clueless twat tried to rise from her squat on wobbly heels without bothering to pull down the skirt bunched at her waist. "You are one messed up motherfucker. What the hell is wrong with you?"

His memories were tearing open, spewing flickers of the shed, the rumble of the oven, the stifling darkness, the trudging footsteps, and the creaking door. Oh God, he needed to get out of there before he gave her a sampling of his madness.

He shouldered out the passenger door and jogged down the alley beside the bar. Boosting his pace, he left his bandmates celebrating their successful show with booze and girls. His sprint, however, put an effective distance from the bitch screaming after him.

"You're just a wannabe rock star. You and your limp dick."

He rounded the bend and slowed to plod along the main drag. He didn't want to be a rock star. He wanted to lose himself in his music, singing and playing guitar, town after town, night after night. Above all, he just wanted to forget.

Nightclub crawlers lingered in the south St. Louis streets, hanging on one another and howling with unrestrained laughter. He could be right there with them, immersed in all the trappings of a good time, if he figured out how to deaden his hang-ups.

He could go back to the van and write a song. He could find another groupie to screw. Or he could get high. Temporary distractions. He needed something permanent, something that would erase the hideous reminders that sucked sound judgment from his brain and his dick.

A tattoo could do that. A needle hammering ink into the second layer of skin was about as permanent as he could get. He'd wanted one for years, just couldn't work up the courage to expose his skin.

Fuck it. He'd spotted a shop on his way to the show. If it was still open, it was meant to be.

Another turn. Another crosswalk. He veered around the milling bodies, the parked cars, the huddled groups of smokers.

There it was, Kilroy Tattoo illuminated in neon overhead. It flickered then blinked off. Shit. He checked his watch. Midnight. The door knob turned.

A woman with a white-blonde pixie haircut backed out of the shop, and dammit if he could stop himself from gawking. She was slender but not in a bones-pressing-skin kind of way. She had a figure that could only be toned with good nutrition and rigorous activity. Oh yeah, she was built for stamina.

She locked the door and turned toward him, tipping back her head.

The bluest eyes he'd ever seen stared up at him. They were ringed with navy and glimmered with silver flecks. They were also wide with... Fear? No, that couldn't be true if her smile were anything to go by. Her beautiful face seemed to swallow up the glow of the streetlamps, the passing headlights, the goddamned moon.

"Hi." Her smile wavered. "You look lost. Can I help?"

Oh Christ, her voice. It was the complete package, like the full-bodied Fsus2 chord humming from the hole in his Martin Acoustic. Gentle, cool, hypnotic—

"You're lost, right?"

She had no idea. "Just found what I'm looking for." *Smooth, Jay.* What the hell was he doing? Shades of pink tinted the curve of her cheeks and parted lips. Distractingly adorable. He smiled despite himself. "I need some work done."

Those perfect lips formed an *O*. "Well, crap. I'm closed for the night. Come back tomorrow. I open at two."

"I'm only in town tonight." He dug out his wallet and held up his last bill. Small venues like Lewey's only earned a couple hundred bucks split between the band, the roadies, and the bar tab. "It's all I got, so it'll be a quick job." He would worry about his next meal later.

She chewed the corner of her lip, hand on the door knob, eyes on his twenty. "I'm supposed to be somewhere—"

"Fifteen minutes is all I ask. I really need this. Please?" He was a bastard for begging, for making her late, but he had to know if a tattoo would help. And now he had to know *her*.

The twenty was tugged from his grip. She pocketed it, unlocked the door. "Fifteen minutes." She pointed her key ring at him. "Since this is a quickie, don't expect much."

He smiled for the second time in two minutes and followed her through the door.

The lights flickered on, illuminating a counter, a workbench, and a padded massage table. Otherwise, the space was empty. Bare walls. No artwork. Nothing personal. Even odder, she didn't have a single tattoo on her toned arms, flat midriff, or the gorgeous swells of her tits, which were on display courtesy of her tiny tank top.

She plopped onto a wheeled stool and rolled before him. Her huge stunning eyes wandered from his neckline to his Chucks as if seeing through his clothes. He lengthened his spine, flexed a bicep. He didn't want her to stop.

"You're nervous. You must be a virgin."

His preening withered. "Excuse me?"

A dimple dented her cheek. "Your first tat, playboy?"

Oh. "Uh, yeah."

"Well? What are we doing?"

"Right." The thump of his heart sped up as he turned to give her his back. This would be the worst part. Would she try to hide her initial shock? Would she sputter in failed politeness? No one had seen him shirtless outside a doctor's office since he was a boy. Oh Jesus, could he do this?

He grabbed the back of his t-shirt, yanked it over his head, and waited for the gasp.

It never came. Instead, the spiked heel of her sandal tapped the tile floor. "So many options, so much we can do."

She must have been schooling her voice. Not a hint of sympathy or horror. He kept his back to her, avoiding the pity he knew she wouldn't be able to hide in her eyes. "Just cover it. One big sheet of black."

A sigh. "Please don't ask me to defile you. You should highlight these. Turn them into an artistic reflection."

What? His back was an atrocity. He didn't want art. He wanted eradication. "Cover what you can in the time we have."

"The scars look old. That helps, but doesn't guarantee all of them will take ink. What do you say we celebrate them? Not"—air brushed his back under her waving hand—"bury them under bullshit."

Every muscle in his body went taut. She knew nothing about him, the presumptuous brat.

"Whatever your reason for wanting them covered, you should ask yourself, really think about it." She shifted behind him, leaned over his shoulder, and spoke low in his ear. "Would the veil work?"

The answer hardened his jaw to the point of pain. "It's none of your fucking business. Either give me twenty bucks in ink or return my money and I'll be on my way."

Her silence was a heavy weight at his back. It prompted him to glance over his shoulder. There was neither pity nor indignation in the gaze glued to his scars. Her front teeth gnawed on a paint-chipped fingernail. What was going through that gorgeous head of hers?

Her ice blue eyes flicked up. "Fine. I'll do it."

Why did he have the sudden urge to prostrate himself at her feet? She wasn't some magic solution to his problems. Hell, women in general made his issues unbearable. "One more condition. Don't touch me."

She snorted. "You're kidding."

"You can only touch my back with the paper towel and heel of your gun hand."

Another snort. "Good lord, you're weird."

He chuckled, and the sound surprised him.

"Sit your happy ass on the table. Got to make a call then we'll get started."

She wiggled a phone from her back pocket. Sweet Jesus, she could fill out a pair of jeans. She tapped the screen and pressed it to her ear with a grin. "Hey, gorgeous...Yeah, running late...Umm, an hour...Yep." A bigger grin. "Overprotective much?...I know...You, too."

Her endearments penetrated his chest, lifting it in a way he didn't understand. He stared at his lap and imagined himself on the receiving end of that call. For the first time in years, he felt invigorated with a tingling sense that everything would be okay.

She pocketed the phone and gave him a beaming smile. Fuck him but he'd found a beacon of salvation in this gorgeous girl.

And lost his goddamned mind.

She sidled behind him to her workbench. “What’s your name?”

“Jay.” His voice cracked like a pubescent boy.

Plastic crinkled. Paper ripped. The snap of a rubber band. “And what do you do, Jay?”

“I’m—” He cleared his throat “—in a band.”

“In a band,” she mocked in a deep voice and laughed at herself. “What do you call yourselves?”

A damp cloth touched his shoulder blade. The contact sent a shiver through his body. *“The Burn.”*

“No shit? You guys sold out Lewey’s Uptown, right? I heard you rocked it hard tonight.”

Big deal. They sold a hundred tickets. After months of rockstarving on the road, they were still unheard of, but the truth didn’t stop her praise from sending a rush of satisfaction through him. *Play it cool.* “Yeah.”

The tattoo machine buzzed once, twice, and fell quiet.

“A big ol’ sheet of black, huh?” Her heel tapping resumed. “I really don’t think you should do this.”

“I’m not paying you to think.” Shit. That was a dick thing to say.

Her laugh filled the room with crescendo. “Don’t be hateful. I’m concerned about my safety. Your fan girls are going to trample me for defacing your perfect body.”

The compliment sifted through him and caressed vulnerable places. “Don’t worry about the fans.” They’d never see his back. No one did. No one but this tight-bodied little artist.

“I love your scars. They inspire me.” She softened her voice. “I’ve never met another person who has experienced pain like—”

A shiver raced over him, and he turned his head. She looked out the window, her eyes unfocused.

“Pain like what?” Hers? Had someone hurt this girl? “Does your boyfriend—”

“No!” She glared at him. “Of course not.”

He turned away, settled by the conviction in her voice, irritated he didn’t have an excuse to kill the boyfriend.

Her minty breath curled over his shoulder. “Done up with the right design, your scars would be a kick ass reminder.”

His spine snapped upright. He didn’t want a fucking reminder.

“You know, a reminder you survived.”

He wished he hadn’t. “You done with this speech?”

“And healed.”

He never healed, not where it mattered. This was a mistake.

"We're done." He stood to leave.

The sound of an angry hornet halted his forward motion.

She dialed down the machine's ohms, fidgeted with the rubber band hugging the dual-coils, and patted the table. "Sit down, you big baby."

The promise of spending fifteen minutes in the spotlight of her magnetic eyes snuffed out his unease with her trying to read him. "Can you keep your opinions to yourself?"

A shrug. The flicker in her icy blues should've sent him running. Instead, it wrapped phantom fingers around his stupid lonely heart and tugged him back to the table.

For the next fifteen minutes, the silence of the room was shared only with the vibration of the motor and her occasional humming. Off-key and erratic, most of her melodies were unrecognizable, though the one she frequently returned to sounded a lot like *Punk Rock Girl* by *The Dead Milkmen*.

Yeah, you're for me, punk rock girl.

Not once did she violate his no-touch rule. He tried not to think about why the stab of the needle was less painful than the touch of a finger. In fact, the discomfort was almost as pleasant as her whimsical tunes. It was exactly what he needed. When fifteen minutes spread to an hour, he held still, wishing time would too.

Her iron clattered on the bench. She flexed and relaxed her hand. "Have a look." She nodded toward the full-length mirror on the wall concealing the front door.

He jerked from the comfortable idleness he'd nestled into. Unease crawled over him, furrowing into his shoulders, tightening the muscles there. He tagged his shirt from the floor and pulled it on. "I'm sure it's perfect." Just like her.

"Oooh-kay. I need to bandage it."

He moved to the door. "Nah, it's good. I'm going to step out for a smoke."

The humid night air embraced him, dampening his tobacco and slowing the burn as he puffed. Why was he lingering? He already paid her, and the guys were probably looking for him. He needed to get back. He couldn't leave.

A few minutes later, she walked out, eyes scanning the street and settling on him.

"Thanks for the ink. It helped." More than helped. It was the best distraction he'd ever tried. Or maybe it was her. "I underpaid you, but I'll send you more money when I have it."

Her mouth fluttered between a frown and a smile, and she locked the deadbolt. "Don't do that, but if you decide to take a different approach with the ink, you know where to find me." Her lips settled into a smile. Then she walked away, taking all the air with her.

"Wait."

She paused, looked over her shoulder, lips still curved heavenward.

"What's your name?"

Her smile faltered then resurrected into a blinding vision. "Charlee. With two *e*'s."

Charlee. His future had a name.

He ground his teeth. She was on her way to see a man.

An unfamiliar pressure ballooned in his chest and boiled the blood in his veins. He locked his knees, forced himself to remain where he was. He knew where she worked. He would square his shit. Then he would come back and win her. "Charlee what?"

She shook her head. "Charlee of Kilroy Tattoo."

His anguish over letting her walk away was overpowered by his determination to make her his future.

Purpose girded his spine, gave him strength. "Catch you later, Charlee of Kilroy."

2

Why the hell did she give him her real name? Charlee practiced her alias daily, owned it for a year.

The tattoo was another stupid move. In the short session, she'd only started the outline, but the finished design would've been an unerring compliment to his masculine beauty. And exactly what he did not want.

An hour's worth of anxiety had whooshed out of her when he didn't check her work, and she wanted to get the hell away from him before he did.

Oh, he would catch her later. In a courtroom when he sued her ass for willful negligence. A problem she would've avoided if she'd turned him away to begin with. That was her first mistake. She never allowed a stranger in her shop after hours. She had been in St. Louis a year, the longest she'd stayed in one town, and she'd grown too comfortable with her business, with Noah. It was making her sloppy.

She'd always been good at reading people, and there was something identifiable about Jay. The perpetual dread that troubled his dark eyes reflected her own.

His eyes seared the spot between her shoulder blades, so she picked up her pace. She wouldn't look back. In her four years of running, always looking over her shoulder, there wasn't a single day she hadn't thought about the shackles, the servitude, and the beatings. But she thought of those things in past tense. Freedom was forward, and Noah was waiting.

She approached the corner of the building. Her rusted out Gremlin sat alone in the lot. She chose that lot for the lighting. Enclosed on three sides by tall buildings, there were no shadows. No hiding places.

Keys in her right hand, she slipped her left inside her bag and gripped the Bodyguard 380, finger beside the trigger. One more scan of the street, and she ran to the car, circled it, checked the locks, and swept the interior. All clear.

Safe inside and on the road, she allowed herself a calming breath and dialed Noah.

"Hey, you." Warmth flushed his voice.

Since the bars were shutting their doors for the night, the traffic closed in on all sides. She up shifted, building speed. "Hey. On my way. Still at the station?"

"Yep."

"See you in five."

"Don't speed. Safety first, sweetheart."

"Always." She opened the messenger bag on her lap, the strap tugging at her shoulder, and tucked the phone inside. Dozens of headlights bobbed in the rearview mirror. She couldn't distinguish one pair from another. Were any of them following her?

Did paranoia award safety? She wasn't paranoid. She was aware.

The police station emerged up ahead. The bleached brick facade glowed under high-powered flood lights. She slid her rust-bucket to the curb and tucked it between two police cruisers.

The rear and side mirrors reflected the well-lit terrace, the empty visitor lot, and more police cruisers. No loiterers. She hurried to the entryway and paused inside the protection of the alcove, staring at the door.

Noah would propose again. He'd become predictable in his resolve, and her defenses were thinning.

When she'd met him a year earlier, the excuses flowed easily.

The relationship's too new. I'm too young. There's no rush. And the time-honored*, It's not you, it's me.*

The proposals didn't stop until she suggested he let her go and move on. His broody silence lasted two days.

She should've run when she met him, but his occupation ensnared her, soothing her need for protection. Their year together hadn't been easy. He coaxed and wooed and devoted himself to earning her trust, and she let him. Must have been her bullheaded stand against victimhood. But she held that final wall in place for his own safety and kept their recent engagement debates trivial and remote.

Spend the rest of your life with me.

Don't need a court document for that.

Honor me by wearing this ring.

I'm allergic to jewelry.

Be my wife.

Not tonight, honey. I have a headache.

That morning, she was ready with her next retort. He sat her at the counter with a box of her favorite cereal and kissed her thoroughly. Then he walked out the door and drove away.

Stunned by his proposal-deficient retreat, she poured her cereal. A note tumbled out.

Dance with me at our wedding.

The longing that had been simmering inside her had burst, showering her oatmeal squares in tears. She was wrong, wrong, wrong for him. The stain inside her was deeply embedded. She couldn't scrub it off. If she accepted his proposal, it would taint him, too.

Dammit, Noah. Snapping back to the present, she turned the door handle and armed herself with the ugly truth. Marrying him was an expensive dream. If Roy found her—or worse, he found her married—the cost would be dear.

The station door swung open. Officer Blaire looked up from the screen on his cell phone. He tugged at the duty belt constricting his ample gut—that which followed his wife's good cooking—and stepped aside to let her through.

She smiled. "Good evening, Blaire."

The big guy's grin puffed his cheeks. Then, without warning, he dropped to his knees.

Shit. She reached for him. "Are you okay?" Was he having a heart attack?

He slapped a beefy hand over his heart. "Marry me."

Her shoulders shot to her ears. "What?"

His grin stretched wider. "Marry me."

What was he up to? Must've been a joke. She rolled her eyes. "I'll never make a fresh peach cobbler like your wife's."

His knees popped as he heaved to his feet. "Damn right." He turned to leave, flicking a finger over his shoulder. "Night, Sarah."

Sarah. Her alias. "Night, Blaire."

The squeak of rubber soles echoed down the hall. Officer Downing sprinted toward her and slid the last few tiles on his knees, panting. "Will you marry me?"

"Oh, now this is absurd." Was Noah behind this? Why would he want other men hitting on her?

"We're meant to be together." He shoved his coke bottle lenses up the bridge of his nose and sniffed.

"We hardly know each other."

Red blotches crept from his collar and spread over his face. "Love doesn't need to know. It just...is."

Sounded like something Noah would say. She crossed her arms and arched a brow. “Did Noah put you up to this?”

He squeezed the radio on his shoulder and barked ten-codes into the mic.

She cleared her throat.

“Got to...uh...” He spun, half-running, half-hopping toward the front office. “Got a...thing. Bye, Sarah.” In a blur of standard issue blue, he vanished beyond the door.

She approached the hallway cautiously, wondering which of St. Louis’ finest would fall upon her next. The path was clear until she reached the stairs.

Maurice Crane squatted on the bottom step, no doubt creasing his handsome black suit. She wasn’t surprised to see him. He worked for Noah’s brother, Nathan, who ran a private security firm two blocks away.

Nathan and his team spent a lot of time at the precinct, consulting, leveraging skills, or just horsing around. Noah and Nathan weren’t just brothers by blood. They were brothers in the Marines. Nathan’s entire firm was made up of their tightknit rifle squad.

“Hello.” Crane grinned then wiped it away with the back of his hand. His skin, dark as mocha, tightened through his face, relaxed, tightened again. He wouldn’t hold back that laugh much longer. “Will you—”

“Nope.” She bent and placed a kiss atop his silky bald head. “Sorry, Crane, but you did *not* have me at hello.”

He collapsed over his leather loafers, rolling with laughter. As she smiled with him, it made her want things. Things like friendship, good humor, and closeness that came with being part of a group.

Disillusion stripped the grin from her face as soon as she remembered the consequences of making friends. She stepped around him and climbed the stairs. She’d bet Jay’s twenty-dollar bill that Noah’s protective older brother would be waiting at the top.

On the third floor, she eased the door open to the corridor that led to the pit, where Noah would be holed up working on case priorities, analyzing leads, or plotting next steps with fellow detectives.

Just outside the pit door, Nathan sprawled in a chair, balancing on two metal legs, shoes planted on the opposite wall. He raised his eyes and watched her close the distance. “Sarah.”

Lean, hard, and soldier-boy handsome, he looked so much like Noah, it was discomfiting. “Nathan.”

The chair continued its two-legged poise as he stretched out his arms then twined his fingers behind his blond head. “Will you make me the happiest man alive?" The cheesy question belied his GI Joe stare down.

She shrugged. "That's a tall order."

"Marry him and you'll make us both very happy men."

Her heart gave a thump. Of course his happiness was dependent on his brother's. After Noah saved his life in Afghanistan and carried him twenty miles to safety, Nathan's loyalty to his brother knew no bounds. "He's happy now."

The chair dropped and, in the next breath, he towered over her. "He loves you, Charlee. Enough to help you carry that baggage you're dragging behind you."

He said her name. He said her name. He used her real *name.*

She stopped breathing. "What did you call me?"

He stepped back and reclined against the wall, frowning. "Charlee Grosky."

Oh God, oh God. Her heart rate spiked. "How?"

"It's not what you think." He swiped a hand over his whiskers and spoke in hushed tones. "I have a lot of questions, but this is neither the time nor the place."

"You investigated me?" Her knees wobbled. She should've guessed. Noah was a detective, and Nathan made his living in private investigation. But she'd covered her tracks, made it impossible. Apparently not impossible. Her lungs labored.

"Calm down. Here." He moved toward her, halted the fingers twisting at her belly, and pulled her to the chair. Then he crouched before her. "Listen. I'm working on an undercover case. One that *must not* attract attention from anyone. This morning, my client gave me a photo of a girl. I wouldn't have recognized her..."

Her hand shot to her hair, what was left of it.

"You've made drastic changes to your appearance since the photo was taken, but your eyes... No one has eyes like yours, Charlee."

Her heart plummeted, landing like a rock in her stomach. "Does he know?" She glanced at the pit door.

He shook his head. "Undercover, remember? My involvement must remain low profile." Strong fingers interlaced hers. "I haven't been working this very long, but I've gleaned enough to know you're linked with a very powerful, very dangerous man."

She swallowed, squeezed his hand. "My gut is screaming at me to run right now, Nathan. He'll hurt me. And Noah."

"Yet you lived with him."

He was diligent in his homework, but... "It's not what it seems."

"Because he didn't let you go. You escaped."

Memories of that night forced air from her lungs in shuddering waves.

"And the bastard's been hunting you since."

"He owns me—"

His eyes fired.

She winced. "He *thinks* he owns me, and his jealousy is a poisonous thing." The tremble in her voice made her sick. "I can't give him a reason to be jealous."

He sat back on his heels, his jaw working as he stared at their hands. Noah's safety would be his priority. Always.

After a few breaths, he met her eyes, whispered, "I know you care for my brother, which makes the decision you face an impossible one. You need to decide if you love him more than you fear for him." His thumb rubbed circles over hers. "No matter your decision, I'll pull my resources to hide you, protect you, whatever is needed." He released her hands and stood.

Could she trust him? Could he be working for Roy? Or could he be involved in some Federal investigation and drag her through court proceedings that would leave her vulnerable and exposed? "Thank you," she rasped through a dry mouth.

"Go on." He jerked his chin at the door. "He's been waiting long enough."

She didn't miss his double meaning. Noah's wait was over. She would marry him with full disclosure or she would slip away in the night.

Shoulders loose, chin raised, she choked back her heart and followed her proverbial gut through the door.

The pit exhaled an everlasting aroma of coffee, as if it were burnt into the walls and carpeting. Scribbled-up maps covered a central table. Mug shots and crime scene photos were taped to the walls. Paper containers and cups from various drive-throughs littered desks and overflowed trash bins. And amongst the clutter stood a beautiful man.

Hands tucked in the pockets of his suit pants, he leaned his butt against the table ledge. His smile was affectionate and unassuming, and it creased the tanned skin around his blue eyes. A picturesque blend of allure and good intent, he wasn't trying to charm her. He was simply happy to see her.

She went to him, quickening her stride with each step. A breath away, he stared down at her, eyes roaming her face. "Hi."

As reckless as it was, she wanted to sink to her knees and do the proposing. "Hi.'

"Good day?"

"Good day. Interesting evening." She narrowed her eyes. "You've been a busy man, plotting your little game."

He was unruffled, as always, in his commitment. "No games. Just trying to clean you out of excuses by the time you reached me."

If he hadn't already held her heart, he'd have it then. *Keep it physical, dammit.* "While you aced me on creative effort, Noah Winslow, my ever-growing list of excuses runs as long as..." She dropped her gaze to his pants. "Your cock."

A groan vibrated in his throat. He cupped her chin, lifting it. His other hand slid around her waist, down the crease of her butt and seized her upper thigh, slamming their hips together. Then his mouth opened over hers, and his tongue swept inside. Not an aggressive kiss. It was soft and doting, warm and giving.

Before Noah, she'd only known one kind of intimacy. The unwanted kind that held her down and wounded her flesh. Noah showed her the pleasure of a man's reverent touches, his humbled breathing no matter how hungry, and the respect in whispered words moving over her skin.

But his frustration over his inability to bring her to climax wedged between them. The problem wasn't his. There was something wrong with her. The things she wanted and couldn't ask for, the way she wanted them...her tastes tilted toward dark and sick.

The kiss slowed, and he breathed against her lips, "Let's get out of here. Yours or mine?"

Not the question she expected. Maybe he sensed she was nearing a decision and didn't want to put undue strain on her. She let out a breath. "Yours. I need to swing by mine and pick up clean clothes." She lived above Kilroy Tattoo, which was on the way. Had she known she would need her things, she would've just met him there. But he'd had a plan. "I'm curious. You talked your buddies into participating in this elaborate proposal tonight. I expected you on your knee when I came in."

His nose stroked the side of hers, up, down. "I saw the answer in your eyes, Sarah."

What he'd seen there was the lingering shock of Nathan's announcement. "Noah—"

"I'll meet you at the shop." He dropped his arms and leaned back, smiled. "We'll take my car home."

Home. Another disagreement he hadn't gained footing on. The amount of time they already spent together was too damned risky.

"Okay. See you there." She pecked his lips and fled for the door before he could gather his things. Being seen out with him, getting caught doing something as simple as holding his hand, could cost him his life. The station could be under watch at that very moment.

"Sarah." The soft tone stopped her at the threshold, turned her head. He raised his eyes, captured hers. "No more proposals."

Oh God, he'd had it. He was done with her. Her heart pounded out of control even as her gut told her the decision would save his life. Her gut was right, but her heart hammered to break out of her chest and fight.

"I'll make this loud and clear, sweetheart. We are not breaking up. You say you don't need a certificate to be with me. I'm holding you to that." His fists, buried in his pockets, flexed. "I want to give you everything." It was a heated whisper, and his throat bobbed. "I think this concession will make you the happiest."

The backs of her eyes inflamed. He'd already given her everything, and she hadn't given him so much as her real name. She nodded, a jerky movement. "See you at the shop."

3

Charlee swiped through the playlist on her phone until she found the song she wanted. Squatting behind the shop counter and plugging it into the sound system, her thoughts circled around Jay and his scars.

He wasn't intentionally dominating, but his aura exuded alpha, calling to her darkest desires. His mysticism only magnified the effect. She wanted to learn more about him, wanted to nestle deep inside and unearth the man who seemed all too familiar with pain. *Real* pain. Maybe he'd identify with her own.

She sighed. Damn her concentration. What she needed to be focused on was surviving Roy Oxford and making a clean break from Noah and Nathan Winslow. Leaving Noah was an excruciating necessity, and she had zero confidence in her ability to do it.

The lock jiggled, and the door scraped over the welcome mat. A chill tingled down her back.

Stop it. Noah was minutes behind her, and he had a key.

"Sarah?" His voice rumbled through the shop and breathed a flush through her cheeks. What would her real name sound like in that baritone?

Familiar footfalls closed in. So did her decision. The weight of it pushed against her chest and clenched.

Fuck Roy for making her so damned fearful. She hadn't signed up to be the girl whose father sold her as payment for his gambling debt. Yet that terrified girl endured. And she had escaped.

She closed her eyes and let herself want. She wanted to swing on front porches and cross streets holding his hand. She wanted to share her past and participate in his future. But did she want to marry him?

Her eyes flipped open and collided with his where they glittered over the counter.

A smile creased his face. "What are you doing down there?"

Was she trying to break down her options so she could fill her future with better ones? Her pulse pumped hollowly in her ears.

If she bared the ugliness of her two-year enslavement, would he respond as detective or lover? Would he go after Roy Oxford and inadvertently lead him back to her, catching a bullet in the process? Her musings of a normal future only delayed the inevitable.

She'd fought so hard to keep distance from Noah, to keep him safe from her and Roy. He was a Marine and a cop. Did he need her protection? Probably not more than she needed his.

She powered on the speakers. "I want to dance with you."

He arched a brow, and the side of his mouth kicked up. "Oh?"

Stooped over her bent knee, she picked at the black polish on her big toe where it poked through her sandals. Was he thinking about the note he left in her oatmeal squares, wondering if she was going to answer it? Her gaze floated back to his.

He smiled down at her, arms outstretched, waiting for his dance.

"*Swing Life Away*" she murmured and pressed play.

"*Rise Against*. Great band." His face transformed into sweeping bowed lips and white teeth and shining eyes. The beauty of it cartwheeled the distance between them, filling her with longing.

The instrumental intro carried her to her feet, around the counter, and toward the arms of the man who loved her enough to cease his proposals. In return, she wished she could give him her name, her story, and above all, a *Yes*.

A counter's length away, he stretched his arms wider.

She hummed with the vocals, etching the moment in memory, never looking away from his eyes. Freedom was forward. A freedom she couldn't have. Still, she reached her arms toward it, toward him.

A board creaked, paralyzing her. The walled entry way blocked her view of the front door. Oh God, did he not lock it? Was it a customer? She wouldn't wait to find out. Where was her bag? Her gun?

She lurched to move around the counter, and her gaze skidded across the room, slamming into hard eyes deeply set in a familiar face. The horror that bolted through her locked her legs, stripping away four years of freedom, every moment of happiness. The scrap of hope she'd harbored in the depth of her chest shriveled behind her galloping heart and fell away.

Toxic energy buzzed from his taut posture. He raised a pistol, a silencer extending the barrel, intent scorching from his glare.

Her heart stopped. "Noah!"

A pop whistled through the room. Noah's smile collapsed, as did his legs. She spun back, leaping, falling atop him as he dropped. He stared at his hand clenched on his stomach.

Blots of red stained his white button-up, blooming beyond his spread fingers. Her vision fogged. Blood roared in her ears. "Noooo. No, no, no. Oh God, Noah, look at me."

He writhed beneath her and wheezed through shallow breaths. She patted her pockets. Her phone… Where was it? Oh fuck, he didn't have much time. His eyes rolled to the side, and she followed his gaze.

A shadow fell over her, and the silencer pointed at his lolled head. She repositioned her body, caging him, shielding him.

The music fell quiet, signaling the song's end. Oh fuck, her fucking phone was plugged in behind the counter. Fuck, fuck, fuck.

"Kilroy Tattoo, Charlee? Roy doesn't appreciate your humor."

She loathed that rasp, the cruelty in his eyes, and the strength of his fist. She used to call him the Craig. She'd called them all Craig. This Craig was Roy's right-hand.

"Fuck Roy." Her shout was venomous, distorted with tears. "And fuck you."

Hang in there, Noah. Please, please. She kept her back to the Craig, blocking Noah's body, her hands moving frantically, searching pockets, front and back, his ankle holster, shoulder holster. Empty. Empty. Empty.

Her bag, which held her gun, sat behind the counter. Fuck, fuck, so fucking stupid.

Blood collected beneath them and filled the grout between the tiles. The stench of sewage and copper pervaded the air. His stomach was leaking, leaking…so much blood. Christ, it wouldn't stop.

She shoved a hand under his jacket, bumped into the weight of his phone in the inner pocket. *Oh, thank God.* She wrapped trembling fingers around it.

"Bad idea, Charlee." The Craig's boot shot out. A direct line with her head. Sharp pain stole her vision and darkness stole the pain.

4

The thrum in Charlee's head was a small thing compared to the agony crushing her heart. Oh God, Noah. She rubbed her eyes, her hands stiff with blood, though she was surprised to find them unbound.

Flashes of light passed the car window. The crunch of tires on neglected pavement vibrated the leather seat beneath her. The wide bench stretched across the black interior, a standard feature of all the SUVs in Roy's fleet.

She'd never successfully escaped one of his vehicles. The tinted bulletproof glass didn't roll down. The doors never opened from the inside. And they traveled in a procession of three. She would be in the center one.

An unfamiliar Craig drove. The other occupant—the Craig from her shop—tilted his head. With a phone pinched between chin and shoulder, he shook a water bottle with one hand. "Yes, sir." His other hand gripped her jaw, turning it. "She's just waking...I understand." He dropped the phone in a breast pocket and held out the bottle.

"I'm not thirsty." Not for Valium, Xanax, Ambien, or whatever sedative he was offering.

"We can do this the nice way or the Salvador way." The manner in which he whispered his name flared old wounds, surfacing memories of the flex of fingers, the whistle of parting air, and the crack of her jaw beneath his fist. The Salvador way.

She swallowed. "What's in the water, Craig?"

"Don't be 'Craig'ing me, bitch. I'm not your father."

Craig Grosky was the first and the worst in a long line of Craigs. She glared at the ear of the Craig beside her, the one missing the lobe. Last time he called her a bitch, Roy relieved him of that bit of flesh.

He glared back. "Rohypnol keeps you out of trouble."

Roofies. Roy wasn't taking chances. "Is Noah alive?"

The intensity in his gaze agitated. "If you want to live, you will not let Mr. Oxford hear you utter that name."

If there were a chance he survived the wound, reminding Roy and the Craig of that possibility was counterproductive. Anything could've happened after she lost consciousness. Perhaps Noah's gun was at the small of his back. Maybe the Craig tossed her over his shoulder and ran out with a volley of Noah's bullets at his heels. She grasped onto that thought, wrapped it around her, and nested into it. Then she grabbed the water, a promise to behave while she scrambled for options. "Where are we going?"

"Airport. We'll be at the tower when you wake."

Roy's private jet. Roy's tower penthouse. Back to San Francisco.

Fear, a living tangible thing, erupted in her stomach, grew in strength and size, and boiled through her throat. She folded at the waist and heaved. Bile splashed the floorboard, her sandals, and the door.

"What the fuck? You got that shit on my shoes." He yanked a Taser out of his pocket. "This or the water. Choose now or I'll choose for you."

Her stomach plunged. He'd choose both and would probably do so with a hard-on. She leaned back, wiped her mouth, and came to grips with her destination in three long, drug-laced gulps.

5

It had only been two hours since Jay watched Charlee walk away. Two *hours* wandering the empty St. Louis streets only served to echo his loneliness. What if it took too long to become the man she deserved? What if she got pregnant or married in that time?

A stab of pain shafted through his heart, and he stumbled on the sidewalk in front of Lewey's Uptown Bar. When would he be able to see her again?

Fuck. He was going to be on the road for the next couple months. He could call the shop, couldn't he? He could keep in contact with her under the guise of coordinating more tattoo work.

He pushed through the front door of the bar. Since his escape from the van earlier in the evening, the music had deteriorated into a repetitive din of mechanicalistic effects and distorted vocal synthesizers. He scanned the crowd for his bandmates and found them gyrating in a circle of women on the dance floor in front of the stage.

How could they stomach the noise banging from the speakers? *The Burn* could produce more rhythm pounding a hammer on a cymbal.

He weaved through the crush of half-naked, sweaty bodies, dodging the sweep of arms and swaying hips. Too many goddamned people. The sudden tightness in his chest spread to his neck and locked his jaw.

No way in hell would he pass through the crowd without a random touch. An elbow, hip, or leg didn't trigger his memories, but a purposefully placed hand, like that of the girl he was fucking in the back of the van, could bring out a catatonic meltdown.

What a shit idea. He considered turning around and escaping back outside, but he needed a bathroom and the bar was the only business open within walking distance.

A hand brushed his ass. He whirled and glared into the glazed eyes of a staggering brunette.

"Oh mmm, you're purrrtty." Hiccup. "S-sexy, too. Wanna fuu...cum?"

He jumped back from her waving hand and bumped into an entwined couple as they ground their groins together, damn near fucking each other to the *thump, thump, thump* of the bass notes.

A familiar clawing awoke beneath his skin. His shadows were digging out. He ducked his head and quickened his pace toward the restroom sign illuminated on the opposite side of the stage.

"Hey. Weren't you s-s-singing tonight?" The drunken woman followed him, scampered around him, and looked up out of beady eyes set in a rodent-like face.

"Get away from me." He sidestepped her and jogged around the dance floor.

The persistent gnawing inside him amplified. Chasing the dragon was one way to soothe it, and the brown powder in his pocket was prepped for smoking.

He raked a hand through his hair. Fuck that. No more drugs.

The bathroom door swung open, releasing the pungency from within. An older man strode out and clipped Jay's shoulder before he could spin out of the way. His heart raced.

Inside, fluorescent lights cast a bleached glow on the white tiles, the scuffed concrete floor, and the two men at the urinals.

They didn't look up as Jay sprinted into the private oasis of the only stall, latched the door, and leaned against the wall. After a few calming breaths, he fished the heroin out of his pocket and spun the small folded paper between his fingers and thumb.

The fix wasn't a daily habit, and he never used needles. He smoked it when his memories became too much to hold in, often before he went on stage or when he anticipated an encounter with a handsy crowd.

He wasn't an addict. He was a self-medicating nut job.

Deep breath. Another. He was about to find out the truth of his denial. Could his propulsion to be clean and deserving of Charlee bowl over any romance he might've had with chemicals? Could he be normal for her?

He dropped his head against the tile wall. *Normal.* His childhood hadn't created an affection for normal. He was young when his parents died. Too young to remember their faces, their voices, their love. In fact, he would never know if they actually loved him.

Sometimes, he would imagine what being loved felt like. It might feel robust and exotic like the harmonic minor in the key of *A* on his

Martin Acoustic. Or maybe it shared the beautiful monotonous strength of the glissando slide between short appoggiatura notes. Was it warm and soothing? Powerful and protective?

In his twenty-four years, he had never experienced closeness with another. Had his parents' death scraped the part of him worth loving right out of the marrow of his soul?

Their death might've hollowed him, but the years that followed their plane crash nearly killed him. In a way, that year in his aunt's custody had.

Enough. He unfolded the paper and held it over the toilet. He couldn't un-live his childhood, but maybe if he faced it, if he actually looked at the scars it left behind, he could overcome it.

What had Charlee said? Celebrate it, not bury it under bullshit? A smile stole over his face. Now that he wasn't overwhelmed with anxiety over her touching him, he let himself retrace her beauty.

She'd teased him about touching but had respected his physical space. Every time she'd smiled at him, she'd done so without intention, without wanting anything in return. Christ, she had navigated his freakishness with the patience and experience of an old soul. Perhaps she was the missing element of *his* soul.

Heat spread through him at the memory of her penetrating blue eyes. She'd looked at him as if she had the power to see through his clothes, his flesh, and his scars. Crazy how she didn't flinch at what she saw. Rather, she seemed to reflect it. Beneath her grin and her spunk, she carried a burden, a preoccupation, something that guarded her eyes and kept her focused outwardly.

His smile fell. And he'd been such a fucking dick to her. That would change, too.

He tilted the fold of heroin and poured the powder into the stool, his hand shaking. The condoms from his pocket were next. He emptied his half-full pack of cigarettes last.

As he stared at his self-loathing habits floating in the rust-stained bowl, he felt a purging rush through him, lift him. His shoulders sat a little higher, and his jaw loosened. Was it that easy?

Receding footsteps outside the stall were followed by more. The bathroom door swooshed opened, closed, and stillness settled through the room. Finally alone. He kicked the toilet lever, flushed the gear, and exited the stall without a twinge of loss.

On his way to lock the outer door, he caught his reflection in the mirror. Was he ready for the real reason he'd sought out the bathroom? He hadn't looked at his scars in years. Would an hour's worth of ink cover the worst of them?

He turned the lock on the restroom door and backed up to the mirror, angling his body to look over his shoulder. His chest tightened, and tremors gripped him. What if the sight triggered an episode?

If he didn't take this opportunity, he wouldn't get another one living out of a van with three other guys and no mirrors. Could he wait to look until they returned to L.A.?

"Just do it, you fucking pussy." He yanked his shirt over his head.

He choked. No, he wasn't seeing it right. He strained his neck. As the black outline took shape, a throb erupted between his ears and spread a burn behind his eyes. He backed up until his ass bumped the sink.

Flames traced the bubbles of his existing burns and danced around simulated scars. The edges of damaged skin, real and not real, were torn and charred and curling away from...

A sob escaped from deep in his chest. *Steel.*

The sketch was a rough black outline, but the new scars had a three-dimensional effect to match the old ones and were drawn as if to peel away from the illusion of steel plates and rivets beneath. She'd created the epitome of beauty and strength in pain. And yes, it fucking celebrated the freedom in survival. How incredible that she'd accomplished as much as she had in one hour.

He wiped his eyes with the back of his hand, shocked to find wetness there. It was cruel that art could be so exquisite and heart wrenching at the same time.

He wasn't sure how long he stood there, staring at the birth of so many possibilities and thinking about the woman who gave that to him. A pounding on the door eventually pulled his gaze away.

As he tugged on his shirt and strode to the door, he knew he didn't just want to be healed. He wanted to be healed by his own inner strength. Charlee had drawn the steel beneath the burns. And the next time he looked into her beautiful face, he would prove to her she had not misjudged him.

6

The scent of freshly oiled leather, the creak of bolts twisting in wood, and the sour taste of vomit coaxed Charlee awake. Cold metal rings collared her wrists, ankles, and neck, locking her to three horizontal bars. Each support hung from various heights, suspending her face down, staring at her knees, naked.

Sixty floors up. Down a long corridor. Last door on the left. Roy's stockroom.

Shadows clung to the walls on all sides and concealed the contraptions she knew intimately. She was confined in Roy's favorite restraint.

The steel bars connected to the ceiling by chains. The shackles locked her head and hands to one bar. Another bar hung near the floor, spreading her legs at the ankles beneath her bent waist, her feet bound to the ends. The third supported her hips, higher than her head, forcing her butt skyward and vulnerable to the movement behind her.

A heavy palm settled on the arch of one spread cheek. Violent shudders bombarded her body, making the chains groan against the wood beam above as she swayed.

"I missed you, Charlee." The voice, oily and pungent like octane, produced a rush of saliva over her tongue. She gagged, retching up water, stringy with spit, on the ebony hardwoods.

His touch vanished.

Slap.

A sting rippled over her butt. It was nothing. He was just warming up.

Anguish gripped her insides. Any semblance of hope she'd held onto shriveled with that first strike. It was only the beginning of the pain she would endure for the next few hours, perhaps for the rest of her life.

The palm returned to her hip, fevered and sweaty, sliding over her back, her shoulders, and dipped to cup her breast. "You've kept yourself beautiful for me, Charlee, my good girl."

She narrowed all thoughts on building her armor. She'd created the mental barrier at sixteen, and over the two years that followed, she thickened her skin with it, layer after layer, training her subconscious to unleash it. If she could figure out how to hold it through the worst parts, perhaps nothing would penetrate it. Not his words, nor his eyes. Not even the cut of his cane.

The stroking continued, down her breastbone, along her ribs, and backtracked to capture each nipple. Goosebumps trailed the path.

Her shield sparked in her mind's eye and shaped an ethereal coat over her body. The invading hand was still there, but the notional space beneath it buffered the sensation.

Oh God, she didn't want to be there. She trembled to be back in St. Louis with Noah, at his house, in his bed, just like they'd planned. He'd be wrapped around her, protecting her.

Her stomach bucked. Did he live? Was he angry at her for lying to him? Would she ever feel the tenderness of his touch again?

Finality coiled around her, constricting and choking. Her life with Noah was over, an unanswered wish. She couldn't think of him. Not in this place, where no one would be looking for her. Longing for him would destroy her.

"I'm talking to you. I expect an acknowledgment."

Smack. Smack.

"Unh." Fuck. Her armor shuddered beneath the sturdier strike, the lingering bite. The fucking paddle. She flexed the muscles in her backside, longing to rub out the sting. "Y-yes, Sir."

Smack. "Yes, Sir, what?"

He wanted her to say she missed him. Not just reciprocate but put her heart in the words. She could do it. She could look into his vile eyes and impart the words. She coughed, tried to clear the panic amassing in her throat. "May I... May I look at you, Sir?"

Einstein claimed that physical concepts were creations of the mind. The brain was power. She tried to focus on that, on her shield, and not on his shadow moving over her, around her.

Then he was there, nude from the belt up with his wool-stretching arousal an inch from her face. She'd watched clueless fucking women stare at his beauty, flock to him with ignorant desire. They wouldn't salivate over his strength if they were trapped beneath it.

The musculature in his torso stretched as he crouched to eye level. Despite the brawn on display, the pasty complexion gave him a sickly appearance. His eyes, violet in daylight, were as dark as the energy emanating off him.

Her armor rose from her skin and outlined her body. She kept herself safe beneath it where he couldn't see her or hurt her. On the outside, she arranged her mouth into a smile, her cheeks shaking with the effort, and held his gaze. "I missed you, Sir."

His pupils dilated, and his hands swung up, caging her face, fingers pressing into her temples. Then his mouth was on her, tongue knifing its way in, slashing, impaling. She held stock-still, mouth agape, and let his teeth scrape and pierce, his lips suck and yank. Puncturing her shield. Stealing her breath. Taking, always taking.

The kiss broke and his chest panted. "I own you. Say it."

Rehearsed and executed endlessly, she delivered. "You own me, Sir."

He jumped to his feet, hands tackling his belt buckle. Oh God, she wasn't ready. The shield. Harden the shield. It wavered around her, clinging, but not thick enough.

How had Jay survived his pain? If he were hanging in irons, what would he have done to guard his mind from splintering apart? How resilient he must've been to carry the weight of so many wounds. She wanted to borrow his strength, imagined it plated over her skin.

Roy's pants dropped. Boxers followed. His inflamed erection grazed her lips. Rigid fingers raked over the crown of her head, twisting and yanking the short strands. "I love this length."

She would never cut it again.

The fist in her hair tightened. The metal collar around her neck held her immobile. He punched his hips forward and slammed the head of his penis to the back of her throat.

Deep breath. No air. She gasped. Shit! No air. Relax the throat. Stretch the tongue. Swallow the thrusts. *Not working.* Her eyes burned, and her gagging was loud and sharp.

His pelvis rotated, burrowing in. Wiry hair scrubbed her face. "Oooh. Hot damn, Charlee. Mother...fuuuuck." Then the pounding began.

Tears clogged her nose and spasmodic bursts of air, noisy and wet, escaped her lips between pumps. She swallowed, slackened her throat, and fought for every shallow breath. *Please hurry. Oh Jesus, be done already.*

"Do you know how long it's been?" He panted and plunged.

No, no. Stop talking and finish. She shook her head, as much as his stabbing allowed. The metal bands around her ankles, wrists, and neck dug in, suffocating. Tears flooded her vision and seared her cheeks.

His pace intensified. "Four years." Thrust. "Two months." Thrust. "Seventeen days." He drove into her and held fast. His head fell back, and he roared to the ceiling, erupting down her throat. She choked, swallowed the bitterness of his release mixed with the salt of her snot and tears.

He pulled out, and she felt the relief in the sag of her body. He kicked off his shoes, the clothes at his ankles, and squatted to capture her eyes. "Last time I fucked you was in the backseat of the Expedition outside of Benu. Do you remember it, Charlee? Yeah, of course you do."

The restaurant. The night she escaped. Dread crept over her and raised bumps on her skin.

"I trusted you. I gave you that unsupervised moment. A gift."

And she'd seized it. Excused herself to the restroom, slipped through the kitchen, and escaped out the backdoor. She ran to the nearest motorist. She ran for four years.

"And you used it against me. Never again, Charlee." His anger was palpable, pelting her face in a mist of spit. "You won't leave the tower. Every action supervised. Every. Single. Breath." He twirled a finger above his head, indicating the walls, the ceiling, and the cameras. "Now, you owe me four years' atonement, but I promise..." His smile was diseased and more painful than what she'd just endured. "I'll go easy on you tonight."

From one rapid heartbeat to the next, he was behind her. He spread her cheeks and attacked her with his mouth, tongue digging and scooping between her labia. He shifted to her rectum and continued the assault. He spat, and the logy landed there, crawled down her crack, and clung to her inner thigh. The only lubrication he'd grant her.

It wouldn't be as painful as the first time, the night he took her virginity. She wasn't that sixteen-year-old girl anymore.

She put on her magic shield, pushed her arms through the sleeves, and wrapped it around her legs. The self-hypnosis prepared her, but when he impaled her ass, the shock of unbearable pain broke through her armor. She yelped, bit her tongue.

His teeth landed on her back, gnawing as he pounded into her backside. The shield absorbed some of it, but she still felt. Damn him, she felt it, and the realism was hell on her body.

He gripped her waist and punched his hips, in and out, again and again. "Did you fuck him?"

Her defensive haze convulsed. "What?"

The invasion in her body disappeared as he pulled out, but the relief was short lived.

Whack.

Agony annihilated the back of her thigh. Acute, localized, like a bolt of fire to the bone. Only one implement could do that.

"I do *not* repeat myself."

Whack.

Skin swelled beneath the cut of rattan.

Whack. Whack.

Sweat stung her eyes, and her limbs shook through the blows. *No more. No more.*

Whack. Whack.

What was the question? *Sweet mother, make it stop*. "Y-yes, Sir." She licked cracked lips. "Yes, I fucked him." She didn't even try to hide the self-loathing in her voice.

The cane clattered to the floor, and he plowed into her vagina, fierce and punishing. Pound after pound, he took from her. Flesh. Blood. Tears. It was disgusting. She was disgusting. Why did he want her? Why?

He grabbed her hair, yanked her head back, shooting pain down her back. "Your body was created for my pleasure."

She shuddered. Had she asked that out loud?

"No one bends to my cane or takes my dick like you do. No one feels as good as you do. I own you."

Tears clogged her throat, and he shoved her head away. Minutes blurred into hours. He violated every orifice, over and over without pause, and somewhere in the haze of anguish she panicked over his possible use of Viagra. He could go for hours on that horrible pill.

When her armor eventually crumbled, she tried to crawl away from her body, tried to project her mind and all its nerve endings to the corners of the room where the darkness stood still.

He spanked and caned, licked and bit, and spared no surface. Then he fucked her again.

Her breath wheezed through a parched throat. Dried stripes of tears burned her cheeks. When the blaze from his penetration dulled, she sunk into a listless fog of acceptance. The shadows crept in from the walls and guttered the lights until there was nothing. Nothing but the echo of his painful smile and the promise it imparted.

I'll go easy on you tonight.

7

Daybreak glowed through the expansive room. Mounds of bedding cradled Charlee's bruises and welts, and she buried her face in the foam mattress. The acidic stench of cologne scorched her nose.

Sixty floors up. Down a long corridor. Last door on the right. Roy's bedroom.

She'd dreamt of Noah. He'd busted into Roy's bedroom with guns drawn and nothing standing between him and Roy but a few dozen bullets. But she knew better. Dreams were dangerous in this place. She wiped it from her mind.

Quiet mantled the hollow space, but the atmosphere churned. He was near.

Beside her, the bed was empty, but a man-size indention remained. A muscle quivered in her lower lip. She bit down on it and shoved away the connecting thoughts.

"Charlee."

She flinched, a full body spasm, and tried to downplay it by stretching her arms and steadying her breath. Then she turned her head.

He stood before the dresser mirror, chin raised, knotting a blood-red tie. "I have meetings all morning, some things I couldn't cancel. I cleared my schedule for the remainder of the week."

The nerves beneath her skin rioted as he approached. He perched beside her hip, grabbed her throat, and used it to roll her body to face him.

Violet eyes sparked in the sunlight. "My beautiful girl. My bed. Perfection." He petted her hair, his gaze clinging to her face, fixated with obsessive longing. "I don't want to leave."

"Let me go," she said, quietly, swallowing against his fist.

He smiled, and it illuminated his eyes. "Never."

"Why do you hurt me?" His fingers dug in, pinching her esophagus. Where had her voice come from? Even when he wasn't choking her, she'd never had the guts to question him. But that was then. She'd grown a lot in four years. "Did someone hurt you?"

He chuckled. "Hurt *me*? No. My father was exceedingly wealthy and powerful. No one would dream of touching his son." He sighed wistfully, and the hand around her throat loosened. "He beat my mother regularly. Even she loathed to defy him." His eyes glazed over, faraway and heavy-lidded. "My father only needed to walk into a room and he owned it, its walls, and its occupants. He was a magnificent mentor."

His father had erected the cartel that was Oxford Industries. She shivered, grateful there was only one Oxford left to stain the world. As for Roy, the placidness of his current mood didn't delude her. Spoiled little rich boys could exhibit moments of good behavior. As soon as things didn't go their way, the tantrums ensued.

"I slept inside you all night." His whisper was a thousand crawly things skittering up her spine. "Your hot, tight cunt clung to me like a vacuum."

Delusional pervert. Thank God her weakened body had put her in a dead-like sleep. "Yes, Sir."

He reached around to her nape and pulled her face to his. The pain from the previous night was too fresh. If she fought him, it would only invite more. So she thawed her joints, molded against him, and tangled her tongue with the slug in his mouth. Cold and rigid inside, she gave him the silent, yielding response he expected. Whatever was needed to expedite his departure.

The door creaked. "Sir. Your car waits."

Their lips separated, and his eyes imprisoned hers. "Thank you, Salvador." His mouth, so close and pinched in a line, was a sanguine gash against the pale background of his face. Black hair and eyebrows intensified his complexion. He personified a macabre portrait of beauty and would look much the same frozen in death. The thought gave her strength, as did the lurch of the mattress and his parting words. "I'll be a while."

The door closed behind him, and she released a shuddering exhale. The tears in her rectum caught fire as she threw off the quilts. She flinched, froze. No clothes, but that wasn't what sent ice through her veins. It was the felt-lined shackle around her ankle. She twisted it, found the locking mechanism, and knew the key had just walked out the door.

She followed the attached chain, which was light-weight and wrapped in a tube of silk, down to the coiled pile on the floor. From there, it led to a steel ring bolted to the hardwoods beneath the bed. No sense in yanking it. He would've made certain it bolted securely to the floor joist.

Bruises speckled her hip bones and wrists. The welts on her legs tightened with each step toward the closet, and the chain unraveled to crawl behind her.

Nothing had changed in her absence. The spartan dresser at one end. Her easel, desk, and drawing boards at the other. A flat screen facing the foot of the bed was the only fixture on the wall.

The eyes in the ceiling followed her. The movement of tiny cameras wired in the recessed lighting might've gone unnoticed, but she'd had two years in her previous captivity to assimilate the room's every detail.

At the threshold of the closet, the chain jerked her leg mid-stride. All her old clothes hung in tidy rows beside his and out of reach. *Twisted prick.*

She limped toward his dresser. Half-way there, the chain strained again. Trapped and naked. Dammit. Her drawing supplies were twice as far. A classic Roy Oxford tactic. Nothing was carte blanche. Her favored pastime, her clothes, all of it kept in the room and out of reach as a visual reminder that everything had to be earned.

Four doors divided up the monotony of blank walls. The corridor, the closet, the bathroom, and the sliding panels that would open to his office. The exterior wall glared with floor to ceiling windows and a vista of the Golden Gate Bridge. The street below had a daunting view of Roy's fortress of mirrored glass. A view she had never experienced.

She walked the circle of the tether, her stiff muscles and sore bottom stinging with each step. Only the windows, the bed, and the bathroom were in reach. She emptied her bladder, used the toothbrush—the single item in the drawer-less, cabinet-less room—and skipped the shower. No toothpaste. No soap. No towels.

A tray of assorted pastries, berries, a pitcher of milk, and bottled water sat on the round table beside the bed. But it was the bowl of oatmeal squares at the center that made her heart skip a beat.

Dance with me at our wedding.

Roy wouldn't have known about the note Noah left the prior morning, but he did know what her favorite cereal was. Too bad he'd offered it so freely. She didn't want it, couldn't imagine ever enjoying it again.

She curled beneath the bedding and broke the seal on the water bottle. No sedatives in the water to erase the stockroom, the ride to the airport, the kick to the head. The gun shot. She rubbed her breastbone and breathed through the stinging in her nose. Not knowing was worse than the truth. Would the murder of a St. Louis detective make national news?

Every action supervised. Every. Single. Breath.

She glared at the ceiling. "Turn on the television."

Seconds later, the TV powered on. The screen showed a skinny woman huddled in a large bed, her spiky hair the color of L'Oreal Platinum #105. She'd worn the color for over a year, but she didn't recognize the woman beneath the disguise. Bit by bit, she was losing herself.

She tugged the duvet tighter around her nudity and raised a palm to the side of the room. On screen, her face disappeared behind the hand. "A news station. Please?"

She dropped her hand, steadied her breath, and waited.

Nothing.

"Turn it off."

The screen went black. The damned remote was another privilege to earn. Until then, she would let a fragment of her brain hold onto a still breathing, smiling, waiting Noah.

Over a selection of blackberries and miniature rolls, she rewrote the prior night. She replaced it with a dance, bodies entwined, a sway in their steps. The fantasy tormented her, burning her eyes and twisting things inside her.

Dread slithered over her and she shook it off, steeled her backbone. She would *not* let Roy break her. She needed to keep a measure of herself locked away from his keen eyes so when she did escape, she would have something left to help her mend.

But what did she have that he hadn't already taken?

She had a memory of a man with back full of scars. Beneath the superficial damage was a devotion to survival, an instinct to dominate his future. Most probably didn't see that when they looked at him, but she hadn't just recognized it, she'd felt it and wanted it.

She would lock his strength deep inside her, would mimic his steel undercarriage and make it her own. She recalled the unrefined charm in his retorts, the raw beauty of his expressions, and the way he looked at her when she turned to leave. As she replayed their hour together over and over, the pain dimmed, the bedroom bled away, and her eyelids sagged.

8

Charlee woke to the Craig's voice.

"Get up." He ripped off the covers. "Mr. Oxford is back, and you are requested in his office."

She wrapped her arms around her nudity. "Now?"

"Shower first." He wrenched the chain attached to her leg, and she tumbled to the floor.

"Dick."

The air hissed and a strike hit her back, ricocheting from her tailbone to her knees. She gasped. Fuck, her body would never hold up at this rate. She twisted her head and found him flexing over her and swinging a section of the chain folded in half.

He could go to hell. She pulled in her legs as if to stand, then reared back and shot a foot into his groin.

A grunt pushed past his lips, but rather than dropping the chain, he raised it for another strike.

"Hurt me again and I will beg Mr. Oxford to remove the rest of your ear." She matched his death glare with one of her own.

He worked his jaw and flared his nostrils as if sniffing for a bluff. Begging Roy would come with a high price, one she wasn't sure she'd be willing to pay.

The chain lowered. Sure, he was afraid of Roy, but he was more fearful of losing his grand salary, his swanky penthouse living, and the power that came with being the right-hand to one of the world's wealthiest men.

She hobbled to the bathroom, the twinge in her back adding to her frustration. In the brightly lit room, she found everything she needed to prepare for his summoning. Towels, shampoo, soap, lotion, toothpaste... A tactical folding knife to conceal in her ass? Well, almost everything.

The Craig leaned outside the door-less shower stall with the end of the chain handcuffed to his wrist. She turned her back to him under the spray of water and rubbed in shampoo. Even the follicles of her hair hurt.

Footfalls approached behind her. The steady, confident pace sent a shiver down her spine.

"Drop your hands."

Dread surged in her chest and ruptured into a struggle for breath. She lowered her hands, and her neck sank into her shoulders, unable to force her legs to turn. She didn't want to look in his eyes and see what was coming.

Water pelted her head, and the air thickened and charged around her. His chest slid over her back and his hands cupped her breasts, shifting lower and slipping through her slit. She held her breath. Maybe if she held it long enough, she would pass out.

He bit her shoulder, his teeth digging into bone, and a cry fled her mouth.

"Oh Charlee." He stroked his fingers between her legs, entering her. "I give you exactly what you need."

He didn't *give* her anything. He took. She shuffled toward the tile wall, wishing she could crawl inside it.

A smack scorched her ass, and his body wrapped around her, crushing her against the cold tile. "You like the pain. You need it, and I want to give it. See how perfectly matched we are?"

Hot acid hit the back of her throat. Fuck him. She twisted and swung her fist at his face.

He caught it and slammed her arm against the wall. "Salvador," he said softly, his tone at odds with the hard glass of his amethyst eyes.

The chain tugged at her ankle as the Craig gathered it and prowled to the shower stall. "Yes, Mr. Oxford?" His eyes wandered over her body.

"Hold her," Roy said, his voice relaxed, chilling. His stuffy suits tended to camouflage his physique, but it was in moments like this, when his naked body bore down on hers, that she was reminded just how strong and muscular he was.

And now it was two against one. She closed her eyes. Their weight alone quadrupled hers. But she had strength. Jay's strength. She gathered it from within and took refuge in the company of his scars, his pain. He would guide her, show her how to survive.

The Craig pinned her arms above her head and steam from the spray saturated his black pants and shirt, the chain swaying from one hand.

Roy lowered to a crouch, shoved her legs apart and traced her folds. His exploration followed the sensitive skin past her vaginal opening.

She clenched her butt. *Oh, please, no. Not there*. The ripped tissues in her rectum flared, throbbing. As if reading her mind, he shoved two fingers in the sore hole. The sting fired spasms through her insides, lifting her on tiptoes.

"No, please. It's too much. Please, stop." Her eyes burned, and she writhed against the hands trapping her arms against the wall.

Roy gripped her thigh, worked more fingers in her ass, and clamped his teeth around her clit. She gasped, shuddered.

The invasion pushed deeper, and she cried out, tears mixing with water. "Please, no more. No more." She sobbed and bucked uselessly.

"Your sweet pleading makes me so fucking hard. Ask for an orgasm. Beg me." He licked her clit and stretched her ass.

The agony of his pumping fingers eddied with a despicable surge of arousal. Her body remembered his ruthless touches, the way he could force her to orgasm. How could she come for Roy and not for Noah? She got off on brutality and not on tenderness? She was damaged. So fucking broken.

She pinned her lips and bottled the scream in her throat. She didn't want this. She didn't... Oh God, the sensations built in her groin and the stimulation from his tongue rushed the terrible desire higher and higher. Her body trembled, betraying her, and her eyes caught fire with the outpouring of her weak fucking tears.

Twisting her hands in the grip of the Craig's, she bowed her hips back, tried to escape Roy's mouth. All of it ineffectual. Her orgasm broke free, flooded every nerve in her body, ripping away her will and buckling her knees.

He removed the pressure of his fingers from her backside and cradled her pathetic body along the length of his. "That's a good girl. Your boyfriend couldn't give you that." He shoved her chin upward, his gaze boring into hers. "No, he couldn't make you come, but I can. You're fortunate I took you back. Don't worry, beautiful girl. I'll give you want you need."

Grief squeezed her throat with invisible straps. His mouth covered hers, and she yanked her head back, smashing it against the tile. The grip around her hands vanished, and the Craig slinked out of the shower. She flattened her palms against the clammy flesh of Roy's chest and pushed with no success.

He circled his fingers around her throat and pressed his weight into her hands. "I've tried with others. Four years of fucking trying. They're weak. All of them blubber and pass out from the lightest strikes. Their minds shatter within hours, and they never come." He stroked her face, and a sob dammed her throat. "I control you, dominate you, and your eyes spark for more as your juices run down your legs. You fight me because you know I love it."

She would not accept that, refused to consider his delusional psychobabble. Gathering the saliva pooling in her mouth, she spit it in his face and raised her chin above the collar of his hand.

A laugh burst from him. "Point made." His tongue darted out and caught the spittle sliding down his cheek.

Defeated, she slumped against the wall as he conditioned her hair and soaped her body. That done, he held his hand outside the stall. "Razor, Salvador."

Her spine stiffened. Could she wrestle it away and flay his pretty face?

He returned with a feminine razor, the blades shielded by pink plastic and moisturizing strips. Fuck. Impossible to do any damage with that wimpy thing, let alone gather enough courage to overpower him long enough to use it.

The Craig once again held her hands above her head as Roy shaved her underarms, pussy, and legs. Her skin crawled everywhere the razor touched. She fixated on a tile square, no longer able to watch.

She retreated into her head, marveling at how much she'd changed between captivities. She'd become Wendy, Tess, Sarah, always someone else and always acting. Her act had been a sticking point in her relationship with Noah. He never knew *her*.

But she hadn't acted with Jay, had she? How would she know? Held captive from sixteen to eighteen, on the run until twenty-two, she'd changed identities the way normal girls her age changed fashion styles.

Before Roy, she'd been a free-spirited liberal who hungered to help people, burned to take risks, and found pleasure in pushing buttons. How many times had she been issued a detention for sketching images of her high school math teacher's genitals? Yeah, Jay had unearthed the real her. How had he done that?

Finished with the shaving, Roy rose to his feet and pressed cold lips to hers. "Got to go, beautiful girl. Come to my office when you've finished priming yourself for me." He stepped out of the shower, taking the razor with him. A moment later, the whir of a hairdryer hummed through the room.

She twisted the tap to increase the temperature. The scalding water did nothing to burn away the previous minutes, but she lingered under the spray until his presence disappeared from the room.

When she finished drying off, the Craig stripped the towel from her grasp and tossed it on the floor. "Mr. Oxford requires your teeth brushed, hair dried, and every inch of your body lathered in lotion. Shall I assist you?" His leer sent her teeth crashing together.

He knew as well as she did he wasn't allowed to touch her intimately. As nonexistent as Roy's compassion was with regard to her, it was something.

She went about the tasks, taking her time. What did Roy have planned next in her never-ending nightmare of horrors? More caning in the stockroom? More forced orgasms? Maybe he would take her out of those rooms and into another part of the penthouse. Hope surged. Another room might present an opportunity for escape. The kitchen alone would be a warehouse of potential weapons.

At the office door, the Craig snapped the leash, and she skidded off balance, naked and irritated. "He's hosting a live teleconference. I don't need to remind you not to fucking breathe."

Her tongue darted to the porcelain crowns fused to her front teeth. No, the punishment from her last conference call misstep left a permanent reminder.

The door opened. With the Craig's shove at her back, she moved over the plush carpet in a soundless stagger. She understood then why the chain was wrapped in silk.

Surrounded by monitors on the walls and desks, Roy smiled at one of the screens. "You call it freedom, Nancy, but arming our civilians? Our youth? That isn't life, liberty, and the pursuit of happiness. Not when they're turning those guns on each other."

The leather-etched wallpaper created an ostentatious backdrop for his pinstriped Amosu suit and ebony hair groomed in thick waves off his face. His shoulders were loose, his smile charming, and his timbre was as smooth as his bullshit.

His billions per annum didn't come from his legit conglomerate of aerospace, defense, and software companies. She'd overheard enough of his conversations to deduce that arms-trafficking was the real money maker.

Not that he needed the money. She suspected his control of the underground firearms trade helped him strengthen his international connections and broaden his power in the defense business. Maybe his anti-gun falsehoods kept his political adversaries at bay. He seemed to thrive in deception and immorality.

The widescreen on the wall facing him broadcasted a CNN interview on mute. The separate locations of the people on camera were displayed side-by-side. A blonde woman, Nancy Davis, smiled in one of the picture-in-picture views. In the other view, Roy Oxford, Chairman of Oxford Industries, straightened his red tie...three seconds after he straightened it real-time.

The temperature in the room soared, and perspiration surfaced on her skin. This wasn't the first time he'd requested her presence during a live interview on CNN. She could yell, jump in front of the webcam, and announce her captivity, nudity be damned.

But the three second delay afforded him time. He could hit the safety switch and cut the transmission. Then he'd cut her.

"...it's a security, Mr. Oxford."

He smirked. "The Second Amendment doesn't make us safe from outsiders. It makes us dangerous to each other."

"Then what makes our neighborhoods safe?"

"Home Owner Associations should spend less time and money on their pools and landscaping and focus their resources on perimeter security. Digiford Solutions has a new line of digital neighborhood watch guards. They offer surveillance technologies..."

His voice droned on, but the words were absorbed by the roar in her ears. He smiled into the webcam, lips moving as his index finger stretched along his pant leg. It pointed at her then to the floor beside his leather loafers. Damn him. It was a test. A test she so often failed.

The same finger lowered his zipper and crooked between his thighs. *Come here.*

Inhale. Exhale. She dropped to her knees and crawled, her pulse cresting. Chills raced through her limbs. Silent and mouselike, she moved across the carpet on hands and knees like she'd done so many times before.

"Since Digiford is your latest acquisition, your argument sounds more like a marketing plug."

He tsked. "Nancy, I hardly need shameless advertising. Digiford stock tripled when we acquired it, and it continues to pressure the competition." Beneath the desk, he gripped the base of his length and wiggled it, bare and erect.

She swallowed back rising bile and knelt between his legs. *Get it over with. Don't fuck up.*

The chain at her ankle jerked, snapping her leg straight behind her. At the other end, the Craig fixed her with a warning in his eyes, prepared to extract her at the first sign of infraction.

Roy clenched a hand in her hair and guided her mouth.

Don't gag. Keep quiet. Oh please, don't gag. She inhaled without sound, and he shoved her face to his pubis. She stretched out her tongue to accommodate him, breathing shallowly and silently through her nose.

The grip on her head controlled the up and down motion, and the muscles in his thighs trembled and flexed beneath her clammy hands. He sped up his movements without faltering in his discourse on babies dying in drive-by shootings and marital arguments ending in gun-fire.

Could she yank open the desk drawer inches from her hand, the one housing a revolver, before the chain ripped her back?

At the edge of her periphery, the Craig waited a desk length away, feet braced apart and a double-fisted hold on the chain. His eyes were alert and locked on her hands, ever-loyal to Roy and the wealth she knew Roy shared with his guards to ensure that loyalty.

Her options were nonexistent, and the instinct to survive prevailed. She sheathed her teeth with her lips and sucked in her cheeks.

Without warning, he came. Stream after stream of ejaculate pumped against the back of her throat, and through it, not a hitch in his voice. "I'm not pro-gun control, Nancy. I'm anti-bloodshed."

"That's all the time we have today. Thank you for joining us. Roy Oxford, Chairman and CEO of Oxford Industries."

"Thank you, Nancy."

"Up next, we—"

The monitors blinked off, and his arm swung. The back of his hand hit her face so violently her body slammed against the desk cabinet. Fire shot through her nose, and the coppery taste of blood washed her tongue.

His lips twisted in a snarl, and his eyes promised more.

She curled into herself, protecting her core. What had she done wrong? "Sir?"

He jerked open the drawer she'd glanced at during the interview. Envelopes and stationary filled the space his gun once occupied.

Aw God, he missed nothing. She scrambled back, cowering.

He followed her, leapt on her, and squeezed her throat. "I meant what I said. I do *not* trust you, Charlee. You're as slippery as Craig Grosky and ten times as smart."

White bursts dotted her vision. She opened her mouth in a useless gasp and clawed at his hand, begging with her eyes.

"You will not share your father's end." He released her and

wrenched her thighs apart, renewing the pain in her ass. "I very much want you alive." Then he was in her, forcing himself into her dry opening, pounding her into the carpet, his tongue lapping at the blood on her lips.

Her father had been dead to her since the day he delivered her to Roy. The reality of his death meant nothing. The cause, however, was as jarring as the weight hammering her into the floor. "You killed him," she choked out.

He slapped her and resumed his thrusting. He of anti-bloodshed accepted a sixteen-year-old girl as a collection of debt. Then he destroyed all traces of the transaction, Craig Grosky included.

Something tore inside her, something beyond her vaginal tissues. It was the sensation of an emotion separating from the whole. To fear a man was to give him power. He had enough of that. So she let it go, and the chronic impulse to lock her joints and hold her breath ripped away.

When he climaxed, she felt limp, hollow. She knew, in that moment, the absence of fear was not synonymous with courage. She wasn't brave. She was numb. Was that how Jay felt when his scars were inflicted? Or had he always been courageous?

He stripped the chain from the Craig's hands and hauled her to her feet. "Don't misunderstand why I killed him, Charlee." He stepped close, and his rasp scraped against her lips. "I was furious. The fucker bet his daughter in a card game. He didn't deserve to live." His expression was as warped as his words, twisted way beyond normal. He seemed to catch himself and reached up to pet her hair. "Don't force me to get that angry with you. I would not live without you again."

Her head swam. He murdered because of the degeneracy of a father? The notion that he had some kind of paternal moral fiber stirred up all sorts of unsettling reflections, but one thought pushed away all the others. "Roy?"

His face slacked, his hand in her hair stopped mid-stroke, and she realized her mistake.

"Say it again."

Lack of fear was apparently equated to stupidity. To hell with it. She steeled her backbone, determined to challenge him, and looked him in the eyes. "Roy."

His mouth collided with hers, his tongue swiping in long strokes. "I love my name on your lips."

That would be the last time he heard it there. "My birth control shot will expire soon."

His eyes moved slowly, down, down, to her belly and his palm followed.

God, no. No, he wouldn't want that.

He yanked his hand away, and the skin around his mouth tightened. "I'll call the doctor." He glared at her midriff and walked backward, hand curling around the leash. "I won't share you with…a fucking kid."

He turned toward the door and dragged her down the corridor. "You didn't eat the oatmeal squares. There was a time when you never turned those down."

"People change." She plodded slowly behind him, spinning from his change of topics and navigating the untrodden territory of casual conversation with Roy Oxford.

"A challenge." He winked over his shoulder. "You'll teach me what you like now. You'll show me every new and fascinating fiber you possess."

"I'd rather not." Her pulse accelerated. Had she stepped too far?

He paused, waited for her to catch up. "I'll take that under consideration. You see? I'm not the tyrant you think I am." He yanked the chain and made her stumble. "But I do hold the reins."

Fucking dickhead. If he didn't want to be a tyrant, he could show her a little tenderness once in a while. She hungered for a connection to someone and if her only hope of ever receiving affection came from Roy, maybe it would've been better than none at all.

As they entered the last door on the left and walked to the center of the stockroom, she came to a realization. No matter what happened in the next few hours, her scars wouldn't be a fraction as gruesome as Jay's. If he were in her position, what would he have done to survive it emotionally?

He would've taken control the only way he could. She planted her feet.

The chain went taut and halted Roy's forward motion. He looked over his shoulder wearing a thunderous expression.

With a wipe of her nose, she pointed a bloodstained finger at the most confining implement in the room. "I want that one." She cleared her throat. "Sir."

His gaze snapped in the direction of her intent then narrowed on her. "The inverse chair?"

They stared at one another, a breath away. He could throw a fist, sweep a leg, or yank the leash and smash her head into the floor. She waited.

A muscle twitched in his cheek. His eyes darted between hers. Then the debate on his face settled. "Lead the way."

Thirty minutes later, he circled her, jacket and tie discarded. His shirt draped open, exposing a white expanse of torso that never saw daylight.

She hung upside down, doubled over at the waist, and arms and thighs squeezed to her chest by ratchet style straps. Her ankles were bound together and dangled below her face.

Choosing the punishment was not the same as choosing to be punished. The beating would've happened with or without her consent. There was no power exchange. No safe word. Choosing the method gave her an illusion of control, and in the monster's lair, illusion was better than reality.

The whip of the flogger caught her labium. She loosened her muscles, held her expression sedate, and embraced it.

Another strike. Upper thigh. A burn flared her sinuses. She breathed through it, and for better or worse, said in her toughest voice, "Again."

He stumbled mid-lunge, and the lashing fell short. His expression was so openly bewildered, it drew his brows inward over dark eyes searching hers. Here he was, Master of the Dungeon, and he seemed unsure of how to proceed.

Then he smiled, and it chilled the air.

"Whatever you're up to..." He raised his arm. "It's making me hard as hell."

The flogger swung down. She held his eyes and adapted to the pain, in all its twisted faces.

9

The van pulled off the interstate and parked at a rest area in Alabama... Mississippi... Hell, Jay didn't know where. He hadn't looked up from his acoustic and notepad since they left Georgia that morning.

The heat of the summer sun baked the windows, and the A/C cranked on high. With his guitar cradled in his lap and his socked feet on the dash, he was too comfortable to move. Laz and Wil were out of the van before Rio killed the motor. The tight quarters and endless driving must have been wearing on them.

Rio lingered, as did his stare.

Jay didn't look up from his scrawled lyrics. "Don't you need to hit the head?"

A huff. Rio wadded up his envelope of flavored candy sugar he'd been licking out of for the past hour and threw it at the windshield. The crumpled ball bounced off the dash and fell amongst the litter on the floorboard.

A smile pulled at Jay's lips. "Who took the fun out of your Fun Dip?"

"You did, Jay. That's who."

Rio's glare eclipsed Jay's periphery. Was the big guy seriously pouting? Jay twisted in the seat to face him. "How did I do that exactly?"

"You've been strumming funeral hymns for five-hundred miles. I'm about to off myself emo-style."

Friggin' drama queen. And it wasn't a funeral hymn. "Just don't do it while you're driving".

"Which song are you working on?" Rio arched his neck to look at Jay's notes, his tanned bald head catching the glare of the sun.

Jay angled his lyrics out of view just to be a dick. "Whichever one I want."

"You can work on whatever you want...as long as it's *Cuntapus*."

How could Rio say that ridiculous word without busting a smile?

Yet he maintained his unflinching glare.

Jay tucked his pencil behind his ear and dug his phone out of the console. "I will never write a song about cunt, pussy, or any other term for the female anatomy." He wanted to be taken seriously as a musician. Not sell out with shocking song titles.

Rio's half-growl, half-groan was a heavy, continuous reverberation as he stretched his ogre-ish biceps toward the roof. The dude was big and carried his intimidation the way he carried his muscle mass. Viscerally and without force. It just sort of clung to him, much like the rough-hewed women who made up a good portion of their fan base.

"I want high energy." Rio glowered and stressed every syllable. "Lots of aggressive, wet dripping beats. I want *Cuntapus*."

Said the drummer who could tap out a mellow ride with more dynamism than the fast double strokes of a punker. He met his glare. "No."

The sudden tilt of Rio's lips cracked his stony mask. "I guess you can't write about cuntapus when you aren't getting cuntapus."

Whatever. After a month of celibacy, he was used to their taunting. Especially as the sexual offers heightened with *The Burn*'s skyrocketing notoriety. Hot girls, too. As in big-tittied, tight-bodied, wild-in-the-sack kind of girls. They cornered him after shows, in parking lots, and followed him into the fucking bathroom. He moaned inwardly.

Just made him want Charlee more. And dammit, he would come to her as a clean and deserving man. Thank Christ the clinic in Florida confirmed he was free of STDs.

With all his focus on seeing her again, his neurotic episodes and bouts of depression had become less frequent. How was that possible?

His youth counselor had used terms such as *PTSD*, *internal and external triggers*, and *cognitive behavioral therapy*. It was difficult to identify what cued his internal trigger. Sometimes all it took was the recollection of a memory. His external trigger was simply a hand, intentionally placed on his body. When he was unable to manage his environment, rather than turning to drugs like he used to, he simply thought of Charlee.

He tried not to think about what might've been going on with her and her boyfriend or if there would be any room for a rising musician in her life. The possibility that he could win her on the other side of their tour was enough. One more month.

Gah. *Another month.* Impatience buzzed through him. "How about we make St. Louis our next stop and I'll write your damn song."

"You know we can't do that. We're booked every night along the

Gulf until we return to L.A."

Disappointment sunk him into the seat. They were opening for some of the biggest rock bands in the business, and concert goers had begun to take an interest in them. If he bailed out, he'd be bailing on his friends. A venue cancellation would void thousands of ticket sales, and the penalties would be monstrous.

Rio's grin widened. "I guess if you're going to compose while you're hung up on a girl, just try to save your menstrual tearjerkers for your jerk off sessions."

"Where's the faith?"

"I have faith in you, but we're not a soft rock band."

"I'm not writing soft." He traced a finger over the fret of his guitar. "It's a rock ballad."

The stare returned. "As good as *Huntress*?"

He'd composed *Huntress* the night he met Charlee, and the fans loved it. "It's better. Now go change your tampon or whatever it is you do in the bathroom, so I can make a phone call."

A laugh burst from Rio's barrel chest. "I like this."

"Like what?"

"Straight edge, pussy-whipped, jolly Jay." He jumped out of the van and leaned in the open crack of the door. "Just don't let that faggoty shit anywhere near our music." He slammed the door.

Jay shook his head as he pressed *Redial* on his cell and put it to his ear. "Please pick up. Please pick up."

Ringing blared down the line. Once. Twice. He sucked in a breath. *Beep.*

Fuck. He squeezed the phone to keep from throwing it through the windshield. Then he did what he always did when he heard her voice over the recording. He closed his eyes and visualized her gorgeous blue eyes and blinding smile.

"You've reached Kilroy Tattoo. I'm either inking or sleeping. Leave your deets and I'll holler back."

"Hey, Charlee. It's Jay Mayard again. I really need to talk to you...uh...about finishing the tattoo. You should have my number." He'd only left it a hundred times. "But here it is again."

He rattled off his digits. What else could he say to convince her to call him? "You know, I realize I might've come across like a dick the night I was there. If I did, I'm sorry. I...um..."

Christ, he was fucking this up. "The tattoo...it...well, it changed a lot of things for me. Made me look at things differently, and I'm anxious for you to finish it. I'll be there in a month, but I would really like to talk to you about it ahead of time. Just... Just give me a ring, okay?"

His voice was dripping with desperation. Time to shut it down. "Well, I'll...uh...catch you later."

He pressed *End* and stared at the phone with an ache in the pit of his stomach. He left messages every day. Several times a day. At all hours. How could she not answer the phone for thirty-three days?

In the back of his mind, something murmured. Deep behind his longings, buried beneath his Charlee dreams, his greatest fear whispered.

Heat flared through his face. No, he hadn't lost her. Her voicemail box was never full. She was picking up the messages. She was just busy. Or annoyed.

He'd give his Martin acoustic for her cell phone number. Hell, he'd give his soul for her returned call.

10

Cross-legged and naked on the cold hardwoods, Charlee leaned her forehead against the floor-to-ceiling window and waited for the sunrise to cast its glow on the Golden Gate Bridge. But it was the sensual voice humming through her ear buds that held her frozen to the glass, as though under a spell.

The music player was the first thing she'd earned in her two months of perfect obedience. Roy allowed her one song. When she requested anything by *The Burn,* he gave her their only hit single. *Huntress.*

She closed her eyes and let the deep, velvety voice she remembered from that night in her tattoo shop wrap around her. "Huntress of the room in my head. Fearless and knowing." The melodic voice hit the high notes and sent a shiver through her. "Your blue eyes plunder the depths of my song. Tonight is only the beginning."

A flutter unfurled in her chest. Then his voice dove so low she felt it in her belly. "Nothing can stop me. To be who you saw. To be the steel. To be yours."

His words... God, his words stole her breath.

The instrumental change in rhythm seemed to lead to a close, but it didn't. His whispered baritone sent a chill down her spine. "You showed me beauty in survival. I'll show you strength in healing."

She sucked in a breath. *Blue eyes*. *Steel*. *Survival* and *healing*. He was singing to her, about her, about his tattoo. She looked down at the leather-bound sketchbook in her lap, the only other thing she'd earned during her captivity. Flames leapt around the sketched scars and bled off the page beneath her pencil.

Jay was the only memory she allowed herself to linger on. He was alive, and *Huntress* confirmed he hadn't forgotten her. The power in that was fortifying. She could suffer another two months, hell, she could endure years beneath Roy's whip knowing someone out there thought of her and maybe even missed her.

"Come back to bed!" Roy's shout bellowed over the music.

The lead tip of her pencil snapped and rolled off the paper. She lifted her head from the window, yanked out her ear buds, and blew the graphite dust from her drawing. The graphite that had enabled her to hold onto the vividness of her memories. "What time is it, Sir?"

"Five in the fucking morning. Bring the book."

She hugged it to her chest. *Not the book. Please, not that*. She ate with it, slept with it, staved off insanity with it. She'd drawn the same flames over and over again, perfecting the illustration. Someday she would finish Jay's tattoo, and her conviction in that was often the only thing that got her through another day.

"Now."

If she disobeyed him, he would destroy her music player. She set the device aside and rose from the floor, an effort that sent her molars crashing together. The hours spent hanging from the ceiling the prior night had torn something in her shoulder. Just thinking about it sprung tears in her eyes. She swiped them away, kicked the chain from her path, and trudged to the bed.

The pencil was plucked from her hand and flung outside the reach of the tether. Didn't matter. A few practices on her wrist confirmed it wasn't strong enough to pierce his trachea.

He gripped her hips and pulled her over to straddle him. Then he opened the book to the last drawing. His customary callousness blanked his expression as he studied the page. "Always fire. Why?"

"A couple months without clothes." She shrugged. "I'm drawn to warmth, Sir."

He set the book aside, stared at it, then swung his hand and struck her face. The force of it whipped her head back. "That was your only warning."

Perfect obedience hadn't warded off daily beatings. His strikes still hurt like hell, but her body had grown pliable. When the hand reared, she didn't stiffen. She bent with it. "It was the last tattoo I did when I was free." Truth, yet it meant so much more.

"Whose?" His voice was calm, eyelids half-mast.

Lying wasn't an option. Perhaps because it took a liar to know a liar. "A walk-in. Some musician." With a beautiful voice, a steel determination, and a body rendered for art.

"What do you know of your mother?"

Her shoulders drooped even as her brain scrambled to keep up. Her mother? All she knew was the woman died of health-related issues a few months after giving birth to her. "I don't have a mother." Had Roy tried to find her?

He watched her in his calculating, unblinking style that made her want to look away. "I searched for her when I lost you four years ago. I thought maybe you'd seek her help."

She'd had no one until Noah. If she had a mother, Roy would've killed her, too. A lonely ache swelled in her chest, and more damn tears burned down her cheeks. Would she ever run dry?

"You had no money. No family. No skills. And no education beyond tenth grade."

She didn't like the direction the conversation was headed, and she wanted to flail on him for the last part. Not worth another strike to the face.

"Rather than succumbing to drugs or prostitution, you leveraged an impractical talent in the most efficient way." He wrapped his hands around her waist and ground her groin against his. "I made you who you are. I gave you the strength to survive."

Even as he boasted his perverse pride, he was trying to unbalance her, weaken her emotionally. He could try all he wanted. Her tears were involuntary, but she was *not* broken. Her strength was her own. She gave him her weight and her eyes.

There was a self-interested air about the way he regarded her. "You tattooed to earn money. Yet you have none yourself." He smirked. "Money, nor tattoos."

Another one of his games. Whenever his dick wouldn't harden from his physical lashings, he turned to humiliation and verbal fighting. Fuck him for being such a cruel, sadistic bastard. "No, Sir. I was the payment for a gambling debt, remember? Not the heir of a billion-dollar monopoly."

His fingers dug into her waist, and his eyes narrowed. "Tell me why you aren't covered in skulls and flames." He smacked the sketchbook, sent it flying off the bed. "I want to hear you say it."

His dick swelled beneath her, and the need to draw into herself strained her voice. Fuck that. "A girl on the run needs plain looks to go unnoticed. No identifiable marks." Someday, she would have a tattoo.

The room held still, and his eyes didn't stray from hers.

"Tell me, girl-on-the-run, what are you planning now?"

She could lie and get the truth beat out of her. Or she could tell the truth and maybe learn something from his reaction.

"You should remove the chain." She rotated her ankle. "Because I intend to strangle you with it while you sleep." She kept her muscles relaxed, prepared to absorb the next strike.

If he were another man, the stiff prod of his groin would've been at odds with his words. "I would kill you if you tried."

Knowing he fed on her rebellion, her question rolled out anyway. "Would you survive my death?" He would either hit her or fuck her, but maybe, just maybe, he'd give her an answer.

The torso between her thighs rose and fell with his breathing. A cyclone of emotions stormed over his expression.

Eventually, his cheeks smoothed, and his eyes cleared. "You belong to me, beautiful girl. I retain what is mine, even if I have to retrieve it from hell myself."

As he flipped her to her back, she wasn't sure if his response reassured her or terrified her. Knowing her death might bring about his was an option to consider, but if one were to believe in afterlife, would she never escape him?

He moved over her and entered her in one urgent stroke, hammering his hips and slamming her head into the headboard. "Not even death will separate us." He reached beneath her ass and shoved a dry finger into her rectum.

The pressure was horrible and wonderful. She bit her tongue and bottled the cry bubbling in her chest, her hands wringing the bed sheets.

"I own you." His hot breath curled around her ear. "Now come for me."

Two months of training pushed her over. He'd mastered his strokes, knew how to balance the pleasure and pain to perfection. As with all the orgasms before it, her body shook, and her tears flowed.

His attempts at humiliation had bounced right off her, but the manner in which he'd degraded her sexually might've been beyond repair. What kind of person climaxed while being raped? She wept, limp beneath the weight of his body, as he grunted and thrust his way to his own finish.

When he caught his breath, his tongue roved over her cheeks, collecting her tears. "I'm meeting with my security staff in the dining room tonight. You'll be joining us for dinner."

A dinner party. Her stomach bottomed.

11

Jay strode out of the airport terminal and choked on the humid Missouri air.

"Damn, dude. Seriously." Laz zigzagged behind him, veering around the flow of pedestrians. "Slow it down a notch. Or ten."

"Didn't ask you to come." He whistled at an approaching taxi, and it stopped at the curb.

"And miss watching you try to romance the girl who's turned you into a faggot?" Laz held the cab door open and waved Jay inside, smiling like an asshole.

"Fuck off." Jesus, he was wound tight, but he hadn't seen Charlee in two months. How would she react to him seeing him? After all the unanswered voicemail messages, he could guess.

They slid into the cab, and Jay directed the driver to Kilroy Tattoo.

"I'm just here for the tat." Christ, he needed to see her. "We'll barely have enough time to finish it and fly back to L.A. for tonight's show." The ink on his back tingled. For the first time in twenty years, he *looked* at his scars when he took his shirt off. Not only that, sometimes he took his shirt off *just* to look.

"You flew eighteen hundred miles on a redeye to get a tat?" Laz's eyes danced. "Come on, man. Just admit you're a lovestruck chump."

Jay stared out the window but could only see her pearlescent blue eyes. He wasn't lovestruck. It went so much deeper than that. Somehow she'd managed to dig her needles into his scarred-up mind and leave them there where he couldn't stop thinking about her. Maybe it was infatuation that first night, but all the nights since had burned into a heartsick, soul-saving kind of love. The kind of love chumps like him wrote songs about.

"Listen." Laz shifted in the seat beside him. "The guys and I have been talking."

He groaned. It was his preface for the lay-off-the-drugs speech. "Save your breath. I've been clean for over two months."

Two months without his unhealthy coping strategies. Two months without setting off emotional triggers. Two months living clean, normal, and deserving of Charlee. And along the way, he'd decided she wasn't just a cure. She was the secret fucking ingredient to happiness.

"That's just it," Laz said. "The smack, the self-loathing lyrics, the angsty sex... Don't look at me like that. The girls talk. The point is it's all mellowed since you met Miss St. Louis. Since you won't let me see the tat, I got to know. Was it her soul-piercing artwork or her brain-sucking pussy—"

"Jesus. I didn't fuck her."

"That might be true, seeing how you've lost your will to fuck at all."

He stared at the roof of the cab. He hadn't had sex since that night in St. Louis, and he couldn't blame it on a limp dick. No, that organ worked just fine. When he thought about the pixie with huge blue eyes.

"I didn't tag along to scold you, man. I'm here to help you catch your girl." Laz's hair stuck up every which way, and his eyebrows hopped behind his aviator glasses. Laz couldn't scold if he tried.

"My girl? My encounter with her was so brief, I'm not sure I could even consider her an acquaintance." He hoped his eyes impressed the words his heart rejected.

"Bullshit. What about *Huntress*?"

A prickling sensation stiffened his spine. "What about it?"

Laz clutched his chest, cleared his throat, and belted, "Huntress of the room in my head. Fearless and knowing. Your blue eyes plunder the depths of my song. Tonight is only the beginning."

And that was the consequence of having no separation between his soul and his lyrics. "Don't knock it, douche bag. It's our bestselling single." The song he wrote the night he met Charlee. Lucky fucking break. A record promoter caught wind of it, came to a live show to hear it, and ran with it.

"That song is carried by the brilliant guitar solo, my friend."

He smiled. There wasn't a musician on the planet who could shred a diminished chord in lowered fifth as drugging and eerie as Laz Bromwell. "Ah yes, the charms of the devil's note."

"And someday soon, women everywhere will cluster in overcrowded arenas chanting *Bromwell note*." He cupped his mouth. "Raaaaah. *Bromwell note*. With their shirts off, of course."

"Of course."

They shared a look, one born in high school where they met over a clutter of scrawled lyrics in a clichéd garage. Neither of them hid their expressions, their smiles overflowing with equal measures of excitement and uncertainty.

The driver slowed the cab. "Kilroy Tattoo."

Laz paid the fare and twisted on the seat to look him in the eye. "Let's go get the girl. And try not to fuck it up."

He gripped the door handle. "Tone down the battle cry. I'm pretty sure there's a boyfriend."

Laz smiled, all teeth and mischief. "There's two of us and one of him. I'll hold him while you show him how it's going to be."

Yeah, that would win the girl. "This is why I never ask you for advice."

He jumped onto the sidewalk beneath the neon sign. A thrill fluttered through him and settled in his gut. He wiped his sweaty palms on his jeans, sucked in a deep breath, and pulled the door knob. It didn't budge.

A knot clotted in his throat. Maybe she took the day off. He peered through the dusty window between cupped hands.

No furniture. No supplies. No Charlee. His heart pounded, and his stomach dropped. "She's gone. Fuck, her shit's gone." His greatest fucking fear.

Laz mirrored his pose beside him. "What's with the police tape?"

He followed Laz's point at the floor just inside the door. Pieces of yellow tape stuck to the tiles and nearby wall. A suffocating dread fell over him. He couldn't move. Laz was running his mouth, but his voice was so far away. What the fuck happened in there?

He unlocked his muscles and scanned the neighboring businesses. "There." He jogged toward the bar across the street. A car honked. At him? At Laz? Who the fuck cared? He quickened his pace.

Inside, the woman behind the bar slung a towel over her shoulder. "Hey, boys. What can I get you?"

His body buzzed with adrenaline as he moved toward the bar on autopilot. "What happened at Kilroy Tattoo?"

Her brows knitted, and she looked out the front window.

"Sorry." Laz shouldered past him. "My buddy left his manners in L.A. He'll have Johnnie Walker Black. Neat with a water back. Same for me."

She poured the whiskey. "So you're from L.A.?"

Laz nodded as they settled on the stools at the counter.

"Then I guess you wouldn't have seen it on the news. There was a shooting a couple months ago. Double murder. The owner and her boyfriend."

A dark tunnel engulfed his vision. He flew to his feet, and the stool tipped back, crashing to the floor. "The owner? Who was the owner?"

"I-I don't know. A young girl. Mid-twenties maybe. Real pretty—"

"Charlee?" A red-hot burn kindled in his throat and choked his voice. "Was her name Charlee?"

"I'm sorry." She licked the hoop piercing her lip. "I don't know. She was a quiet little thing. Kept to herself."

No, that didn't sound like her. "Blue eyes? Hair cropped short?" He scrubbed a hand over his own short hair.

"Yeah, that was her."

Was. The fire in his throat burst into an overwhelming helplessness that spread through his body, sent him pacing in a circle. He felt dizzy, sick. He was going to be sick.

"Jay. Jay, you need to sit down." Laz stepped in front of him, tried to guide him to a stool without touching him.

"Sir, I don't know if this would help, but one of the investigators left his contact info." She pulled a business card from a drawer and slid it across the counter.

He fumbled his phone from his pocket, scanned the card for the number, and dialed.

"Winslow Investigations. Maurice Crane."

He glanced at the card, his hand shaking violently. "I'm calling for Nathan Winslow."

"I'm sorry, sir, but Mr. Winslow is unreachable. Who's calling?"

"I understand he was involved in the Kilroy case. I'm looking for one of the employees. Charlee..." He swallowed back the anxiety piled up in his throat. "I don't... Fuck, I don't know her last name." The silence on the other end was stifling. He could've really used some fucking C-dust to clear his head. "You there?"

"Sarah Teves was the shop owner and only employee."

He blew out a shuddering breath. "No, there was a tattoo artist there. Couple months ago. Name's Charlee."

"Who am I speaking with?"

"Jay. Jay Mayard."

"How are you affiliated with Kilroy Tattoo, Mr. Mayard?"

"I'm a customer of Charlee's. Is she okay? Where is she?"

"One moment. I'm connecting you with Mr. Winslow."

Click. A long pause.

He was vibrating out of his skin. "What the fuck is going on?"

"Easy, man." Laz flanked him, almost touching him. Definitely hovering too goddamned close. Jay paced away to the far end of the bar.

Click.

"Jay Mayard?" The voice was deep, hushed.

"Yeah. Is this Nathan Winslow?"

"Speaking."

"I'm looking for Charlee. There was a double homicide at her shop?"

"Where did you hear that name?"

Strange fucking question. "She gave it to me. I came in for some ink—"

"When was this?"

"Couple months ago. Where—"

"What day?"

"Uh...night after Independence Day." He palmed his nape, tried to slow his breathing. "July fifth." The line went deadly quiet. "Hello? Mr. Winslow?"

"Yeah. Hang on a minute. I'm stepping onto an elevator. If we get disconnected, I'll call you right back."

A series of dings echoed down the line, followed by silence.

He wore a path on the hardwoods in front of the bar, sweat beading on his forehead.

Revving motors and car horns barreled through the phone, breaking the silence. "Jay? You still there?"

"Yeah. Where is Charlee?" The fever in his cheeks paled and flushed, and his chest tightened. He was not going to pass out.

"So you came into the shop on July fifth, and she told you her name was Charlee. Describe her."

He ground his teeth. "White-blonde hair. Slender frame. Mouthy. Strangely perceptive. And eyes so blue you'd never fucking forget them. Now tell me, dammit. Tell me she wasn't one of the victims." His voice was raw.

"Your description matches that of Sarah Teves. She and her boyfriend were murdered in Kilroy around two in the morning on July sixth. I'm sorry. I'm transferring you back to Crane to take down your information..."

Anything else he said was lost to the pounding in his ears. He couldn't breathe. He couldn't think. His phone hit the counter he didn't realize he was leaning on.

He sought out Laz's eyes, anchored himself there. "She's gone."

"Oh, man. I'm sorry."

"She was just a girl." He covered his mouth. His lips were numb. His fingers, numb. "She was just a girl. I didn't know her. She was just some girl."

"I know, Jay. I know."

"Just a fucking girl." His voice was thready, broken.

12

The walk down the long corridor that night was harrowing. Charlee's body trembled with waves of nausea, made worse by her nudity.

The security staff had monitored her for two months. They'd seen her raped, beaten, and brought to her knees. But she hadn't seen them, didn't know who remained on the payroll from years earlier. She preferred faceless Craigs. Somehow, they seemed less real.

She followed the chain and the man holding it around the corner, through the massive den, and into the dining room.

The table seated ten. Two empty chairs waited. The men, all dressed in suits, stood when Roy pulled her through the archway.

She shifted behind him to hide her nudity then thought better of it. She stepped around him and stared right back, taking in each Craig, pausing on each face in turn. Salvador, new Craig, new Craig, familiar Craig... She locked on the last one and froze. Beneath the bushy beard and extra weight, she marked the Marine with eyes so much like Noah's.

The room fell away. She grabbed the back of the chair, seeking support. Damn, damn, damn. What was he doing?

Undercover, remember? My involvement must remain low profile.

Shock tried to wheeze its way out. She swallowed, smothering it. How long had he been there, in the same building, a shout away? Was he on a job for a client or a rescue mission? How did he know where to find her?

She concentrated on leveling her breath. No way would she make it through dinner and dessert. *Son of a bitch, the dessert.*

As was Roy's custom, he would command her to perform during tea and sweet bread. A way to make her vulnerable and test the loyalty of his team at the same time. He would force her to entertain them, emasculate them as they watched. As Nathan watched. No. No, she couldn't.

Engulfed by an overwhelming need to puke, she felt her legs move, and sank into the chair Roy held out for her.

He took his seat beside her and slithered a palm over her thigh. "Good evening. As you can see, we have a special guest tonight. Say hello, Charlee."

She coughed her hysteria into cupped hands and stared at her placemat. "Hello."

"Don't be nervous, beautiful girl. These are the men keeping you safe."

Safe? She thrashed in the padded room of her mind while she smiled outwardly. "Yes, Sir."

Seeing Nathan flooded her with memories of Noah until all she could think about was him bleeding out on her shop floor. Nathan held the answer to the question she'd ignored for two months. Just a jerk of his chin or a subtle shake, and she'd know.

Every face at the table volleyed leers and smirks at her. Every face but Nathan's. Why wouldn't he look at her?

A parade of white jackets moved around the room carrying platters of steaming dishes. Bowls of Miso soup were placed on the utensil-free table. The servers kept their eyes down. Well-trained and probably highly overpaid.

Two seats down, Nathan kept his eyes on Roy, who slurped from the rim of his bowl and prated on about surveillance and FBI investigations. *Dammit, Nathan, look this way.*

She coughed. She yawned. She feigned choking on fried eel. The conversation circled around security briefings, and Nathan didn't spare her a passing glance.

Midway through the battered Tempura, she set down her water glass and spilled it in his direction. Finally, she snagged his eyes, and pleaded with hers. *Is he alive?*

His attention flicked back to Roy. "I have an update on the detective who's been sniffing around for the girl."

The detective? The girl? Shivers tore through her.

"Go ahead, Matthew."

Matthew? Of course. Nathan was undercover.

Nathan reclined in his chair. "He's been hushed."

A throb lit in her head, and her heart beat erratically. The detective on her case could've been one of Noah's friends. She didn't think for one minute Nathan would've hushed his own brother, but if the detective on her trail wasn't Noah, that meant... No, she wouldn't follow that train of thought. She wouldn't make assumptions about Noah's life.

"Very good." Roy squeezed her leg.

Her mental plate ran over with what-ifs. She felt like she was the only person in the room who didn't have a clue what was going on. It didn't add up. Who was the detective? And who did Nathan really work for?

"Sweet Red Bean Bread, ma'am?"

Dessert. She rocked her chin left to right, a mere reflex. Maybe Roy would test the new recruits another night. Maybe they'd worked for him long enough he didn't need the dessert test at all.

"Charlee."

She clutched her stomach and willed herself not to be sick. "Yes, Sir?"

"Hop up on the table. Show these boys how pretty you are." He popped a battered morsel in his mouth as if he just asked her to pass the salt.

The servers flowed around her, clearing dishes and pouring green tea. *Delay it. Distract him.* What could she do? She stole a glance at Nathan beneath lowered lids. His eyes, aimed at Roy, flickered. Too late.

A hand chopped across her throat and knocked her out of the chair. "Put your ass on that table."

She coughed—blinded by the pain, overwhelmed by the looming humiliation—and climbed over the ledge.

"Spread your legs and let them see your cunt."

They say animals react to threats by fighting or fleeing. With Roy, the triggered stress response was to follow. And follow without delay.

She lay on her back and stared at the ceiling. They were simply resting their eyes on her. Fear gurgled inside her. Fear *for* them. She knew Roy was monitoring every breath and shift of their eyes. One wrong move would be the last.

She swallowed past the sore spot in her throat and let her knees drift apart. Chilled air brushed the insides of her thighs. She trembled, no matter how hard she tried not to.

Roy rose from his chair and walked alongside the table, bathing the room with the stench of his almighty power. The chain tightened between her ankle and his hand, knocking over bowls and glasses in its path. He paused behind a new Craig, grabbed a fistful of hair and yanked the man's head back. "Eyes on Charlee. You will not look away again." He released him with a shove.

During her time in the penthouse, she'd tried to reason what it would take to willingly work for Roy. Did he deliberately hire people with no morals? She'd heard whisperings of their extraordinary salaries and special benefits, such as women, drugs, firearms, and admittance to the most prestigious clubs and casinos. She also suspected many were in his employment out of debt or obligation. If her father hadn't bartered her, would he have become a member of the staff?

"Pleasure yourself, beautiful girl." Roy stepped back and settled against the wall.

A fresh wave of shudders pummeled her. She lifted on her elbows and scanned the voyeurs, certain their job interviews didn't include his fateful disclosure. *Look at his property, envy it, but never ever touch it.* No, he wouldn't have warned them, because he took too much pleasure in baiting them. So she met each pair of eyes in wordless caution and placed sweaty fingers between her legs.

Around the table, bodies shifted, hands dropped to laps, and lips twitched. Nathan selected a sweet bun and chewed indifferently.

"Convince us, Charlee." Roy's pose, with hands in his pockets and the wall holding him up, was not in agreement with the turbulence rotating in his eyes.

Her head fell back, and her fingers massaged the way Noah's would have. No way would she get there unless Roy interacted. She breathed deeply, circled her clit, and staged a good act.

Without warning, a hand brushed her breast and returned for a squeeze. She jerked, slapped it away.

Chair legs screeched. The table wobbled, and teacups tipped in their saucers.

"Don't, Wes." Nathan's command reverberated in her chest. Oh no. Was his reaction the right one? No, he should've stayed out of it.

Wes smiled, oblivious to his fuck up. "My God, how could I resist? She's a sexy little thing."

He was dead. He was so fucking dead. Her fingers froze as the pressure built in the room, seeping from the corner Roy occupied.

"Salvador." The one word held finality. Salvador's exit through the kitchen door confirmed it.

"Sir? What's wrong?" Lines etched Wes' forehead. A heartbeat later, his face paled. His brain must have caught up.

The kitchen door swung open, and Salvador walked through clutching a meat cleaver. The men huddled together, backing up and forming a wall of death, all eyes on Wes.

She slid off the table and panted through uncontrollable tremors. "Sir, don't do this. He didn't know."

Roy leveled her with a look so menacing, she regretted opening her mouth. "One more word, Charlee, and this time, I will not replace your teeth."

He grabbed the cleaver from Salvador, his other hand circling Wes' wrist. Salvador slammed the man's arm onto the table, stretching it as Roy pinned Wes' bucking body and heaved the ax-like blade in a downward arc.

Wes' screams shook the chandelier crystals. Blood soaked the white linen. He stumbled to the floor, convulsing and pawing at his fingerless hand.

Roy turned, his expression terrifyingly blank. His movements were so fucking methodical as he wrapped his fingers around Nathan's arm.

No. No way in hell. She moved to them, driven by sheer purpose. Holding her mouth and cheeks slack, she tried like hell not to let him see how concerned she was.

For a fleeting moment, Nathan's eyes narrowed on her. Disapproval? Then it was gone, replaced by a Marine with a raised chin, hardened jaw and rolled back shoulders. "You hired me to protect her."

Wes let out a long, lamenting cry from the floor.

Roy pressed the cleaver beneath Nathan's chin. "And you failed. What do you think, Charlee?" He didn't want her to defend the Craigs. He wanted her to fear them. "I gave you permission to speak. Do so."

She traced the edge of the table. "The truth, Sir?" His glare struck her like a fist in the chest. Deep breath. "I don't give a shit about your Craigs. Do whatever you want. You're going to anyway." She sniffed for effect. "Sir."

His laughter drowned out Wes' moaning. Then it cut off and his dark eyes pinned her. "Apparently, my time would be better spent beating the impertinence out of my beautiful girl."

A rush of air punched from her lungs.

He passed the blade to Salvador and gestured to Wes. "Take care of this." Then he coiled her chain around his arm and prowled over to her. Hooking his arms beneath her thighs, he lifted her to straddle his hips and carried her out.

She looked over his shoulder. Nathan bent above Wes, talking to him, but she knew he was aware of her gaze. It was in that moment, clarity struck. The dinner, the maiming, it was all recorded. Roy would revisit the video feeds and scrutinize every detail, every glance. Nathan knew it and ignored her deliberately.

She dropped her head on Roy's shoulder. Had she sabotaged Nathan's efforts? As far as punishments went, maybe she deserved this one.

He carried her into the stockroom, and she assembled her shield. This time, she did it with hope, and all the messy emotions that came with it.

13

The crowd roared. “Encore. Encore. Encore.”

Jay clung to a shadowed corner behind the drum kit on a makeshift stage. His body trembled from exhaustion after playing a two-hour set. Or maybe it was from the everlasting misery he struggled to mask.

They were somewhere in rural Texas, compassed by endless fields and a low hanging ceiling of clouds. The muggy atmosphere clung to his skin and the exhalation of cigarette smoke vied with the earthy aroma of loam and dug up peanuts.

Several hundred fans congregated on the acreage, keyed to a state of crazed anticipation. Sexy people. Ugly people. Posers. Punkers. All ages and stages of life rocked and bobbed beneath the temporary field lights and the haze of smoke. The atmosphere was buoyant, hearty, and energetic. All the things Jay was not.

The Burn’s popularity cast a blinding light on his future. Their impassioned fan base grew virally. Their newly signed record deal loaded their pockets. Their upcoming album promised more recognition, more fans, and more money. And after this show, their nights of playing in bowling alleys, bars, and peanut fields were over.

Yet the bright light also pitched shadows. A celebrity lifestyle didn’t lend itself to someone who fell apart under large crowds and intentional touching. For that, there would never be a treatment as effective as the two months he’d spent reforming himself for Charlee.

That remedy had died in St. Louis two weeks earlier. He remained committed to being the man she would’ve wanted, but he couldn’t ignore the terrible loneliness in never being able to hold her. That ever-growing chasm inside him consumed him more and more every night.

He turned, facing the nylon backdrop behind the stage, and struck an *Fm7* chord on his Les Paul electric. The amplification pealed into the dark wall of night, and the crowd rallied with such thunder and force he couldn't hear himself think. Didn't matter. For this last song, he only needed to feel.

When they calmed down, Laz switched on his mic. "You fucking rock, Lubbock, Texas."

The screams waxed with ear-stabbing intensity.

"One more song." Laz waited for the hush. "This is the first time we've played this one live. And since Jay locked himself in his room for ten hours writing it, I think he should sing it front and center. What you guys think?"

Shrills and roars echoed hollowly in Jay's chest. He scrunched his neck farther into the shelter of his shoulders. He respected what Laz was trying to do. The relentless nudging was backed with nothing more than good intentions. But Jay's reason for performing from the isolation of the dark corner was beyond a sane person's understanding. Triggers and traumas and murdered dreams. He was a walking manual on mental disorders.

"Welp." Laz laughed. "Jay must be getting a blowjob back there. Guess we'll hear how he sings while he's cumming."

More screaming. "Jay. Jay. Jay." His name rolled into a chanting staccato.

Jay blew out a ragged breath. Laz teased him about blowjobs, knowing he'd committed to abstinence from alcohol, smoke, drugs, and sex. Laz also knew he had been teetering precariously on that straight edge ever since he learned about Charlee.

The burn in his throat spread behind his eyes. She was gone, but she could never die. She was alive in him, guiding his thoughts and holding together what was left of his heart.

He strummed the beginning chords. He didn't hear them. He felt them. In the stretch of his chest. In the heat of his blood pushing through his veins. In the burning around his eyes. He felt *her*.

He cleared his throat and turned on his mic. "This is called *You Weren't Just a Girl*."

The drugging tones of Laz's guitar joined his own through a slow-building chord progression. Then the instruments fell silent for his vocal solo.

"When I walked into your eyes, I saw tomorrow." He swallowed. "I saw you sleeping next to me. I saw you holding me." He licked cracked lips. "I saw you loving me."

He pushed heavy breaths through the mic. "You weren't just a girl." His heart ached, bending with the refrain. "You were a vision. And without that vision, I would perish."

Laz eased back in with a crawling tempo, accompanied by Rio's *tap-tap-tap* drum beat in 4/4 time. Wil's pulsating bass guitar brought the measures together with a deeper modulation.

As Rio opened up the hats and played quicker, Jay moved the chords up the fret in a fast, even legato and raised his voice. "I know something about pain. I have enough to liberate. I don't know how to let it go." His vocals cracked. "I don't know how to let you go."

His throat was on fire. Not from the strain of his vocal chords, but from the mass of grief simmering to escape. He sang the refrain hushed and pained. "You weren't just a girl." He choked, and Rio threw a concerned expression over his shoulder.

"You were a vision. And without that vision, I would perish."

The harmony of instruments began the complex climb of the song. Jay grasped at the next verse, couldn't feel it. So he altered it. "In my vision you hear me. You hear me say. There's no metal. No rivets. No man of steel."

The guitar pick in his hand shook and screeched the chords. His heart pounded painfully. "Take me to your grave. You weren't just a girl."

Sudden vertigo quaked his knees. He sang an improvised verse. "It's getting dark. So dark. I can't see you." His fingers locked up. "I'm losing you."

The pick dropped to the stage. His guitar followed, and the music crashed to a deafening silence.

He walked away. Down the metal stairs. Across the field. Away from the lights. Away from the crowd.

He walked until the burr of cicadas drowned out the distant roar of people. Then he dropped to his knees and pressed his fist on his sternum as if it could hold in his sob. It couldn't.

Footsteps crunched the dried grass behind him. A moment later, a slender shadow fell over him. He looked up into blue eyes. They weren't exquisite or unforgettable. Just...blue.

"You have a beautiful voice." She knelt before him. "In fact, you are an incredibly beautiful man. And I think you could use a little lift. Allow me."

His cloud of grief labored his breath, squeezed his chest, and fogged his mind. He wasn't alone in the fog. There was a spark. His beacon in the dark. "Charlee."

She smiled. "You can call me Charlee." She pulled on the chain around her neck and a small vial appeared from between her breasts with a tiny spoon attached. She dipped it in the vial and held up a scoop of powder.

Her plain features blurred, fading in and out and morphing into the visage of his dreams. His fantasy raised her little spoon to his nose and blinked huge inimitable blue eyes. "Sniff, baby."

Charlee wouldn't tell him to sniff. She would never be able to tell him anything. Looking into the face before him, she was all he could see. Christ, he needed to let her go. He needed to forget.

He sniffed. A zing pulsed through him. His senses opened. The sky deepened. The soil smelled richer. And the powder-coated finger sliding over his gums and the roof of his mouth trailed ice.

His mind fractured in memory. *Don't be so cold, little boy.* The shed loomed against the night sky, waiting.

A tongue replaced the finger. It stabbed in his mouth and his own lay limp and numb. "Charlee?"

"Mmm." She purred and rubbed her tits against him.

The numbness trickled down his throat and enveloped the chasm in his chest. The ache at the center melted away.

He fell upon his back, arms stretched out above him, and gave into the high. Gave into the hands in his pants. Gave into the mouth around his cock.

The loneliness lost its grip. Charlee was all around him. Her smile, her body, her mouth, her hands.

Hands. Petting his thigh. Squeezing his dick. Dragging him to the shed. Shoving him into the belly of hell. Oh God. He pushed her off him and jumped to his feet, swaying through a wave of dizziness. "Hands flat on the ground."

Blue eyes stared up at him. Then she smiled and turned on her knees, bending at the waist and offering her ass.

Nausea turned his stomach. He pushed it away. "Move your hands from where they are, and we're done. Clear?"

She nodded.

The girl he'd spent one eternal hour with was gone. Yet she wasn't just a girl, and she could never die. Submerged in the haze of hallucination, he visualized her skin beneath his palms, her pussy wrapped around his dick, and her strong-willed voice filling his ears. She was alive in him and always would be.

He dropped his head on his shoulders and shouted his release. "Charrrrleee."

14

In the two weeks that followed, the penthouse had taken on a kind of tense stillness. Maybe because Charlee's perception was limited to the confines of the stockroom, bedroom, and office, with Roy and Salvador as her only visitors.

She perched on the floor beneath Roy's desk, her back pulled against his leg where he sat in the chair above her. She tried to tune out his conversation and focus on the drawing in her lap. If she could recall Jay's scars better, she could perfect how the sketched flames should lick and curl around them.

What she did remember, however, had bound her to Jay those long painful months. Her mind remained whole, strengthening even, amidst the flames and steel of a man she hoped had gone on to fulfill his dreams. She clung to the vision of someday finishing his tattoo and seeing it displayed on stage for thousands of worshipping eyes. He deserved no less for saving her.

"I don't care how long the company has been in your family." Roy's hand settled on her head and stroked her hair.

She leaned into the touch, craving the affection, despite the source.

"Sentimental shit is why you are drowning in debt." Roy coiled a finger in her short strands and yanked, making her eyes water. "Take my offer, sell me the business, or I'll make sure your competitors push you into bankruptcy."

"I didn't want to resort to this, Mr. Oxford." The voice on the speaker shook, coughed. "Does the name Craig Grosky ring any bells? How about his daughter Charlee?"

The hand paused, stroked again. "I don't hear any bells, Henry."

"I hired an investigator. I know what that girl looks like, and I know what you did to her. I have proof."

She stared at her sketchbook, hid behind her calmest expression, and tucked all her nerves deep inside.

"Are you attempting to blackmail me, Henry?"

"Yes."

The stillness in the room convulsed. "Show me the evidence. This pointless conversation is nothing more than a poor attempt to weasel out of the hole you've dug for yourself. Until you have something useful to say or *prove*, we're done here." His fist hit the phone, and it flew off the desk.

She held herself immobile, invisible.

"How the fuck does he know anything about the Grosky's? Charlee doesn't even look the same."

The air crackled with his bellow, and she wasn't sure who he was addressing.

He rose from the chair and sent it wheeling into the bookcase. "Unless he used *my* facial recognition software, *my* fucking design when she was out fucking around for four years."

She curled into herself. His fury would seek her out, eventually.

He paced the room. "No, that's not it. The evidence he's insinuating would've come from inside the penthouse. A witness." He stopped, whirled. "We have a mole, Salvador. It's the only explanation. No one has access to the video storage, so it must be one of the men monitoring the cameras."

I'm working on an undercover case...My client gave me a photo of a girl.

Dammit, Nathan. Was he leaking information to this Henry guy? How would she get a message to him when she hadn't seen him since the night in the dining room? Could she signal something to the cameras? But how would she know who was watching? Roy didn't miss anything.

The Craig shifted his weight. "Yes, sir."

"I won't cancel our trip to Newark tomorrow." Roy approached her, hands in his pockets, eyes boring into her. "That worthless Russian running the Dinmore shipment cannot be trusted with this job. There's too much on the line with this one. I have to be there."

"Understood, sir."

"Charlee will go with us." He patted her head. "How's that sound, beautiful girl. A trip to New Jersey?"

Like she had a choice. Leaving Nathan's vigilance rammed her heart to her stomach. She suspected he'd watched her on the cameras over the previous two weeks and that knowledge alone had made her feel protected and less lonely, despite the depraved situations he must've witnessed. "Yes, Sir."

"Very good. Salvador, make the preparations and find that fucking mole."

15

That night, Roy caned Charlee harder than ever before. Perhaps because he anticipated little opportunity to beat her on the trip or maybe it was punishment for Henry and the mole. She limped to bed on heavy feet, nursing even heavier thoughts. The reason for his brutality didn't matter. Nathan was in danger, and she didn't intend on leaving him.

As Roy showered, she gathered the chain beneath her pillow, one link at a time and hoped the movement wasn't caught by the cameras.

He joined her in bed and wrapped his body around hers. She lay still. *Please don't stretch an arm beneath the pillow.*

He settled, and she stared into the dark, listening as his breath slowed into the rhythmic pulse of sleep.

Thirty minutes passed. If she waited any longer, she'd wimp out. She could do this. *Do it now.*

At least one of the cameras would be infrared. They would see her but wouldn't reach the room in time.

She clutched a length of chain, her hands concealed under the pillow, her movements slow and precise. He was on his back, his chest rising and falling with even respiration.

The garrote was ready, taut between her fists. *Breathe, Charlee.* Three...two...one...

She slipped it from the pillow, shoved it beneath his chin, and crossed her fists behind his head.

Sirens blared, and the overhead lights flickered on. Damn it to high heaven. She hadn't thought of that.

His eyes popped open, and his hands shot to hers. "Charleeeeee." His roar was a bad sign. Very bad. It meant she hadn't yanked hard enough. He could still breathe. And scream.

He wrestled her for the noose, and the stomping of footfalls exploded through the door.

Pull tighter, dammit. He was gasping, hacking. His eyes rolled back in his head. It was beautiful.

A fist shot through her periphery, slammed into her eye. Then another. And another.

She couldn't breathe. She clawed at her throat. The chain. Oh God, the chain was wrapped around her neck and a heavy weight crushed her chest. Roy stared down at her, his face a manifestation of hell itself. Even if she survived, she wouldn't recover from this.

"Your eyes," he whispered. "That's the first thing I noticed about you the night Craig Grosky brought you to my doorstep. Big open windows."

She couldn't speak, couldn't take a breath. Her lungs burned. The dark crept in from the edges.

He cinched the noose tighter, his face raging above her like a wall of nightmares closing in. She swiped a hand at him. He grabbed her flailing arm, bent it backward. Something cracked, and pain jolted through her shoulder and chest. Another blow landed in her side, and her lung burned as if stabbed.

She couldn't scream, couldn't moan, couldn't inhale. Her eyes throbbed. She blinked through the wet darkness, tried to open them as wide as possible and fill them with her words. *Would you survive my death?*

He stared at her. His brows slanted in a *V*, the angle of his clenched jaw severe. She wasn't getting through to him. He was going to kill her. It was there in his glare.

The part of her brain capable of processing her own end grasped onto a thread of optimism. He wouldn't survive her death. She was certain of it, and the thought made her smile, as much as her contorted face would allow. *Do it. Kill me.* She was so fucking ready.

His eyes widened, but he wasn't looking through them. They were glazed and far away. Had he come to the same realization?

He flung himself off her, and the sound of his footsteps marked his clumsy retreat.

She gasped for air, her throat on fire, her lungs straining. No punctured lung? Broken rib, maybe. She could no longer see through her swollen eyes.

"Everyone out. Salvador, ready my plane. I'm leaving now."

She pulled the noose from her neck and gathered her useless arm close to her body. She cried out, miserable with pain.

"Now, Mr. Oxford? It's two in the morning."

A body thumped against the wall, followed by a gasp.

"I don't give a fuck what time it is." Roy's voice bellowed from down the hall. "Get me the fuck out of here. She stays. No one goes in that room while I'm gone."

The door slammed shut, and the quiet crept in. The prior minutes settled over her in a heavy fog of pain.

She made a mental perusal of her injuries. Swollen eyes. Broken arm. Possible broken ribs. She still had her teeth. She might've laughed at that if her throat wasn't so damaged. Her body throbbed and burned as if on fire, and the sad thing was, the pain was beginning to feel just a little bit normal.

Maybe she should worry about her injuries being left untreated in Roy's absence, but the buzz in her head weighted her eyelids. So fucking tired.

16

Charlee awoke to the bed jostling, lurching. How long had she slept? Darkness shrouded her vision and nausea rolled through her gut. Why couldn't she see? She was so damned tired, drifting in a furry sort of haze. Or was it fuzz? Yeah, fuzzy.

Something pulled on her ankle and her leg felt lighter.

Free.

"Shhh. This might hurt."

That voice. She knew that voice. She'd made it to heaven.

Steady hands tucked her arm next to her body. Stabs of pain skated through her shoulder, and she moaned.

Bedding wrapped around her, chin to feet. The mattress fell away, and her body was lifted, cradled against a hard chest. Was she going somewhere?

"I…" She swallowed past the hurt in her throat. "Can't…see. Book." She jerked her chin in the vicinity of the table.

The forward motion stopped. "Got it." He walked through the room. "We're heading into the hall now. Don't make a sound, sweetheart."

Sweetheart. "Noah." She melted into the arms holding her so gently and pressed her face into his neck. "You came."

He tightened his grip and shifted into a sprint. Just like her dream, he'd come to save her. She wanted to kiss him. She wanted to bawl like a baby.

Footsteps emerged behind them. He jerked right, stopped, and pressed her mouth harder against his neck. A warning to keep quiet?

Where were they hiding? She pictured the penthouse's layout. A closet, maybe?

"Aren't you supposed to be in the monitoring room?" The unfamiliar voice was far enough away she was sure whoever it was couldn't see them.

"Matthew let me step out for a smoke." Another voice she couldn't mark.

Her exhales were coming out so loud. She couldn't help it. The damn injury in her chest was igniting with her panic. Could they hear her? She couldn't stop shaking.

"Where's Matthew now?"

"He's still in there. It's fine, man. Mr. Oxford put him in charge."

The pain in her shoulder hammered. The trembling grew more violent, reaching deep in her bones. *Please, leave. Shut the fuck up and leave.*

"Mr. Oxford also said two guards should man the cameras at all times. And don't forget. While you're monitoring her, he is monitoring you. Get the fuck back there."

The voices faded. He inhaled deeply. Then they were moving, around a corner, and...climbing? Stairs? What was up? The roof.

Metal rattled. Crisp outdoor air washed over her. In the distance, the *whump, whump, whump* of a helicopter approached. Fast.

"This might go to shit. Just hang on, okay?"

She tucked in, her body paralyzed with shock. Noah, the rescue, it was a dream. She was dreaming.

The wind picked up, and the whine of the helicopter's rotor announced its descent.

He ran. She held her breath, tried not to pass out from the agony of her injuries battering against his sprinting body.

A gun fired. More followed. Behind them. In front of them. Footsteps and shouting rang out in every direction. She couldn't see, couldn't fight, and her consciousness ebbed and flowed with his ducking movements.

Clutching her to his chest, he lowered to a squat. The gun fight waged. Minutes felt like hours as she tensed against the pangs gripping her body. She soothed her nerves by picturing them concealed behind a wall, out of the path of the whistling bullets.

How much time had passed since Roy left? Was he turning his plane around that very moment? A barrage of questions piled up her damaged throat. Holding herself as invisible as possible, she waited.

Finally, he shot to his feet and dashed several paces, zigzagging left to right, setting her teeth on edge with pain. "Get this thing in the air." He panted. Skidded to a stop. Twisted them, leaping forward, and landed on his back. "Go, go, go."

The sheet unraveled enough to free her good arm. She tried to sit up, but he held her tight. The floor shifted below them, wobbling with the shift of the helicopter. The gunfire died down and fell quiet. A collective sigh released through the cabin.

"How?" She swallowed, flinched. "This rescue?" He'd accomplished the impossible, and if she had the strength, she'd pinch herself.

He lifted her and settled them into a seat, tugging straps around them, stabbing pain through her chest and arm. "Marines. I called in a favor."

The helicopter vibrated, and she gasped against the agony. "Nathan okay?"

His body tensed and caused hers to do the same. His hands were on her, but she could no longer feel them. A terrifying anticipation of something ugly and awful curled her fingers into a fist. She unclenched her hand, forced it to reach up and brush over his face.

Her touch met wiry hair from cheek to cheek. She didn't understand at first. Her hand raked back and forth through the full beard she knew Noah couldn't grow. If she rubbed it long enough, maybe he would pull her hand away and tell her it was fake. He didn't. Instead, his chest began to buck, and a sob escaped his throat.

She jerked her arm away and choked, "Nathan?"

He grabbed her hand, pulled it to his chest. "I'm sorry."

"No. Where's Noah?" She covered her mouth, couldn't smother the horrible sound coming out of it.

"I'm so sorry, sweetheart."

She didn't have to see the pain in his eyes to hear it. She felt it throughout her entire body. She wanted a different answer. He couldn't give her one. "When? How long…?" Her voice was ugly. Choked. Dead.

"He didn't suffer long. He passed within minutes of the shot."

She'd lived two months without knowing, hoping he'd survived, yet girding herself for this likelihood. But as it pressed down on her, she couldn't bear it. It hurt too damn much. "No. He was still breathing."

Four Marines chatted quietly around her, voices she didn't recognize, men who'd risked their life for hers. Nathan kept her clenched against him, careful of her injuries, and stroked her face. "I'm so sorry. I'm so sorry." He chanted it, over and over.

The whir of the passing wind, the vibration of the rotor, and the men's chatter fell away. She was in such wrenching misery, she could only lay there in his arms and press her face against his cheek. Every sob pained the injuries. Tears burned her swollen eyes, mixed with his. She wept and didn't stop until they reached their destination.

He gathered the sheet around her and carried her off the

helicopter.

"Where?" It was all she could muster.

"The where is nowhere. We're going to disappear, Charlee. And once we've regained our footing, we'll get him. I promise."

17

Three years later...

The clinking of silverware and the drone of whispered conversations sifted through Charlee. She bounced her leg against her seat in the vinyl booth and let the atmosphere feed her incessant need to crawl out of hiding.

The stiff presence across the table did not share her sentiment. Nathan perched on the edge of his chair, the seatback shoved against the farthest corner of the room where he kept an invariable yet subtle eye on their surroundings.

A server bustled by, trailing fumes of garlic from his raised tray. Her mouth watered. "I'm starving."

He glanced at her. "You need to eat more." His focus returned to the crowded dining room. "And you should cut your hair."

She rolled her lips between her teeth and bit down. He could bitch all he wanted. She told him daily to go live his life. Not that she wasn't grateful for his protection and his company. He was the brother she never had. With his parents long passed and Noah... All they had was each other. And he was going to blow his fucking top when he found out her agenda for choosing that specific restaurant.

"Dammit, I know why you won't cut it." He scrubbed a hand across his eyes as if wiping away images. "God, I know. It's just..." He looked at the mop stringing around her shoulders and whispered, "With all that red hair, you're too noteworthy."

She twisted a finger around a lock. She hadn't dyed it, hadn't cut it in three years, and had no plans to. A small rebellion against the fuckhead who liked it short.

Their server approached the table and slid vibrant colored plates of elote and carne asada tacos between them. She flared her nostrils, inhaling the aroma of chili and lime. "I love New York City. Where else can you get authentic Cuban food?"

"Miami," he said with a smile in his voice. "Or Cuba. Why don't we go there?"

She'd chosen New York for a reason. What he didn't know was she'd spent three years stalking *The Burn* on the Internet. She analyzed every song. Maybe she was nuts—was probably certifiable—but the lyrics seemed to be written about her, for her.

By the time she left the isolation of the penthouse, the band had reached stardom. They weren't just popular. They were untouchable. Jay, Laz, Wil, and Rio were each iconic in their own right. They monopolized the cover of every magazine and *Tonight* show with miniscule activities about where they ate, vacationed, and who they slept with. Given their short careers, they should've been ranked among the rising stars, but *The Burn* had become legendary.

Jay was the least public of the four. No gossip or pictures of girlfriends. In fact, photos of him were difficult to dig up.

The band lived in L.A. but visited New York monthly. A couple days earlier, she tattooed a guy who had a friend who knew a roadie for the band. This roadie claimed that *The Burn* frequented the *El Sabor Outpost* restaurant on Friday nights.

It was Friday night, and her hope was as bright as the neon *El Sabor Outpost* sign above the bar. Oh God, Nathan was going to kill her.

She bit into a corn cob and the kernels squirted with sweetness. "So good." She raised her eyes, watched him watch her eat. His lean frame, defiant posture, and bright blue eyes consumed her with painful nostalgia. She shook it off with a roll of her shoulder. "Why do you hate New York so much? We've only been here a couple months. Give it a chance."

Another glance around the room. "He owns too many businesses in this town. Hell, he might even own this restaurant."

"Bullshit. You'd know if he did, and we wouldn't be dining here."

He ran his private investigation business remotely, though most of his time was focused on gathering evidence against Roy. He'd made little progress in three years, and his frustration radiated from his pores. It seemed Roy Oxford's payroll extended to members of the FBI and law enforcement in most major cities.

"Fine. He doesn't own this one." He squeezed a lime over a taco and dug in. "Yet," he amended around a mouthful of shredded beef and dragged his sleeve over his clean-shaven chin. "We need to stay hidden until I can gather enough evidence to nail him."

Screw hiding. She longed to confront Roy on the street and oust him where the oblivious world could bear witness. "I used to be a girl with ambitions and fanciful dreams, you know?" Her dream of teaching children to paint might not have been fanciful, but the notion still caught in her throat. "He took that from me. Now my only aspiration is running as far and fast as I can. I'm tired of it." Damned tremors crept into her voice.

"Shh. I know." He reached over the table and patted her hand. "I need more time. We have to be smart about this, and I'm regretting this move to New York. Three thousand miles doesn't make us safer, sweetheart. He's buying up corporations from coast to coast. He's everywhere." He dropped his voice. "And his arms-trafficking activities are headquartered on this coast. Please be mindful of that."

She slunk down into the seat. He was her voice of practicality and her only comfort. He was also an ever-present reminder of the man she lost.

Despite her pleading, Nathan refused to return to his life in St. Louis. Roy was looking for an overweight, bearded man named Matthew Linden, not a thin, clean-shaved private investigator and Marine. And Nathan excelled at his job, covering his aliases and securing his connections. He was certain Roy hadn't connected Matthew Linden to Winslow Investigations, which meant he didn't need to be on the run with her. Yet here he was, taking care of her in some kind of noble dedication to Noah.

He picked up his fork. "How much money did you make today?"

Two tattoos. Not much, but inking out of his temporary PI office in the Village didn't exactly tantalize would-be customers. "A hundred and fifty dollars."

Laughter barreled from across the room and stole his attention. His eyes cut back to her, and they were stone-like in resolve. His you-don't-need-to-work lecture was imminent.

She held up a hand. "Don't say it. I earned this money to see Duke again. I made an appointment for tomorrow. Will you take me?" She straightened her backbone and waited for his disappointment. Just saying Duke's name brought out his overprotective tension.

His face paled, and he pushed his plate away. "There are other kinds of therapy."

The deadness in his tone raised her hackles. "The normal kind, you mean. And what exactly would I talk about with a psychiatrist?" She lowered her voice to a whisper. "That I was held as a slave and I'm on the run because my captor is too powerful to bring down? How many red flags would that raise? How much bribe money would it take for the therapist to turn my confession over to the man hunting for it?"

A swallow bobbed in his throat, and his eyes darted between her and the rowdiness across the room. "Then *talk* to *me*."

She leaned over their plates and closed the distance between them. "I do talk to you. I tell you everything. And goddammit, you've seen it all firsthand."

He closed his eyes, no doubt remembering the night in Roy's dining room. Or his two months of monitoring the cameras in the stockroom. Or maybe he was reliving her first appointment with the Dom in Shreveport. He'd been adamant about remaining in the room during the scene. She was certain he regretted it, because he never attended another one, and her bondage *therapy* continued to be a driving wedge between them.

His eyes were closed for so long, she kicked his shin under the table. "Look at me."

He did, with torment-glazed eyes, and their hands joined at the center of the table. Her relationship with him was a complex tangle of revenge and preservation. She suspected he loathed her and cared about her in equal measures. Noah saved his life in Afghanistan, and now Nathan had found a way to repay him by protecting her. Nothing she could say would deter him.

She rubbed a thumb over his. "I have so little control over my life. I need this." She needed to control when to be shackled, to name the limits, and to speak the safe word to stop it. So she paid the Nathan-vetted Doms to give her that. "I need those few hours of power. I know you understand this."

He let out a breath. "You're resilient, you know that?"

"I'm a survivor." If she kept telling herself that, maybe she would be at the end of this.

"I look at you every day and wonder how you do it, how you don't break down under—" He squeezed her hands, swallowed "—under it. So if these appointments help you hold it together..."

She nodded. He understood the reasons she gave. What he didn't need to know was she used the physical pain to push her past her emotional barriers. When arousal tormented her, relief could only come from a choking restraint, the cut of a cane, the dry penetration of a cock. The notion was shameful, but each visit with a Dom guided her closer toward acceptance of her fucked-up desires.

"I need to run a full investigation on this Duke guy again."

"Of course." She straightened his fingers in her hand, tried to smooth out the tension there.

"And I'll be there. Right outside the room." His mouth twitched, and it could've been mistaken for a smile. She knew it was nerves.

The front door swung open and the whoosh of motoring traffic filtered in, followed by the footsteps of multiple people. The restaurant broke out in excited screams.

"We need to go." Nathan dug out his wallet.

Her pulse spiked as she twisted in the booth. A crowd had gathered around the new-comers, blocking the view. Was it them? Had to be. A chill spread through her, and perspiration surfaced on her breastbone. How would she approach them without showing her face? Her plan hadn't gone further than steering Nathan to the restaurant.

A man climbed atop the table at the center of the commotion, his head rising above the throngs of women. Chunks of hair spiked over his large sunglasses. He shoved two fingers in his mouth and whistled. "Good evening, wonderful patrons of *El Sabor Outpost*. My buddies and I have a wager going, if you'll be so kind as to oblige us. You see, they are questioning my mojo."

Women hooted around him, hiding his lower half, but the jerk of his shoulders implied he was thrusting his hips.

She bent around the high back booth, craning her neck. "Let's just wait it out."

"No fucking way." He ground his teeth, flicking his eyes in every direction, and waved at the server. "Check, please."

Laz Bromwell, lead fucking guitarist, bounced on the table to peek over the crowd. "My friends don't think I can get a date with the most beautiful woman in this restaurant. My manhood demands I take that bet. What do you say?"

The women screamed and jumped up and down. Charlee's heart mimicked in kind.

Camera phones waved in the air. Dammit. Fuck. She flattened a hand beside her face to hide her features and met Nathan's wild eyes. "This isn't so bad." Holy shit. Oh fuck, he was never going to forgive her for this.

"We're going to slip down that aisle on the far side and out through the kitchen." He threw a wad of cash on the table, grabbed her hand and hauled her from the booth. "Do not look at him."

Shit. She couldn't leave. Not without making contact with Jay. Where was he? She arched her neck, couldn't see through the horde of people.

Nathan tugged her toward the door. "Look. The. Other. Way."

Laz surveyed the room, making a show of eyeing each woman

with his charming smile. Two others joined him on the table. The bald drummer, Rio Ketch and surfer boy bassist, Wil Sima. Where the hell was Jay?

She dragged her feet, her heart sinking.

Three pairs of well-known eyes locked on hers. Her heart sprinted into a marathon, urging her to run, but her legs were paralyzed. She didn't know what had led Jay Mayard into her shop three years earlier, but this possibility of seeing him again might be the only one she'd ever get. She couldn't walk away.

18

An arm wrapped around Charlee's midsection, lifted her, and carried her toward the kitchen.

"Wait." She bucked against the unbreakable hold. At twenty-five years old, she could behave like a swooning fan just like the squealing girls across the room. He didn't need to know her true intentions. "I want to meet them."

He growled in her ear. "I know you know the singer."

"What?" How the hell would he know that? She elbowed him in the ribs. "Put me down."

"Hey, Red. Wait. Don't leave." Laz pointed at her, jumped from the table, and pushed past the grabbing arms of the crowd. If she continued moving toward the back exit, would he follow? She hoped, because escaping the camera phones that would soon be turning her direction was the priority.

A team of stiff, plain-dressed men held back the fans as Laz closed the distance.

Nathan reached around her waist and pulled her through the kitchen doors. "This is the worst scenario imaginable. What if the paparazzi show up?" He spun them in a circle, likely scanning for an exit. "Great, just great."

"Hey there. Don't hide." A few feet away, Laz's smile filled his adorable face, the doors swinging behind him and muffling the screams. She dropped her hands.

"Sweet God in heaven, you are undeniably—"

"My wife, Maylynn." Nathan held out his hand, his jaw clenching in her periphery. "I'm Hank, the guy who cost you a bet. And we were just leaving."

Hank and Maylynn McGraw. Nathan's ridiculous aliases made her fist twitch.

"Is Jay here?" She couldn't keep her anticipation from pitching her voice.

Laz ignored Nathan's hand and dropped his smile. "No. Why is he always the ladies' first pick?

"Where is he? Is he in New York?"

"You're wounding my pride, babe." He spread out his arms. "What do you say? A date with Laz Bromwell? Since you're married, I'll do you both." He shrugged. "I'm magnanimous like that."

The body pressed against her back turned to stone, pushing her to the side and out of view if the door opened.

She patted Nathan's hand where it clenched on her arm. "I think we'll pass on the date."

Laz hung his head, shuffled to the door and poked his head into the dining room. "Shut down, folks. This bet is going to hurt like a motherfucker."

They responded in a roar of boos that rallied into "Pick me. Pick me."

Nathan grabbed her hand and moved them deeper into the kitchen, weaving around cook stations, his eyes probing the hallways and doors.

Laz ran behind and skidded into her path, stopping her. "Just my luck I find the most beautiful woman on the fucking planet, and she's taken." He brushed a strand of hair from her face.

The bold gesture made a slow curl through her stomach. She was such a glutton for tender touches. "What did the bet cost you?"

His face flushed. "A tattoo."

A thrill kicked through her. "Any tattoo?"

Nathan's hand pulled her elbow. "We need to go. Now."

Laz laughed, and it had a nervous hitch to it. "The tat has to be a ruler."

"Like a king?"

"Like a standard unit of measurement."

Weird. "Where?"

He looked pointedly at his groin and back to her. "Know a good tattoo artist?"

Nathan squeezed her hand. "Absolutely not." He stopped a passing server. "Which door leads to the access road out back?"

Charlee snorted. "A ruler on your dick?"

Laz lifted his shoulders. "Marked off in inches. Or feet." He grinned. "My friends are sick, I know. Change your mind about that date?"

She needed money, but more than that, she needed to see Jay.

"I'd consider doing the tattoo for the right price."

"Maylynn." Nathan's warning tone.

"No shit? You do tattoos?" He pushed his hands through his hair and the spikes bounced back. "Five grand."

A *Hell Yes* tried to jump out of her gaping mouth. She caught it with a snap of her jaw. Think first. Then leap.

He misread her expression. "Fine. Ten grand. I'd pay that just to stare at you for an hour with my cock in your hand." He flashed a spread of white teeth. "I'll double it to twenty grand if you'll do it with your shirt off."

Nathan put his mouth next to her ear. "I don't like this. They're fucking media darlings."

"Twenty grand. Shirt on. In a private, secure area. No media."

He threw his fist up. "Done. How do I reach you?"

She waved over a hovering waitress and borrowed a pen and a napkin. "Here's my address." Nathan's office address.

He stuffed it in his jean pocket and blew her a kiss as he walked backward toward the doors to the dining room.

She snapped herself out of the surrealism of meeting Laz Bromwell and realized she'd never hear from him again. He didn't have to pay for a tattoo. He'd have busty artists lining up to do it for free. And stroke him off while they did it. "Laz?"

He put his hand on the door and raised his brows. "A parting kiss?"

Since she hadn't been able to find on photo of Jay without his shirt, she had to ask. "What did Jay end up doing with his tattoo? The one on his back?"

A strange expression fell over his face, and he stared at her as if he were staring through her.

Nathan blew out a loud exhale. "Fuck."

Fists banged on one of the doors behind them. A clamor of voices shouted on the other side.

Nathan jerked his head toward Laz, his face red. "Paparazzi?"

Laz lifted a shoulder. "Probably."

Shit. If their only way out was through a barrage of snapping pictures, Roy's facial recognition software would find her.

A kitchen rag landed on her chest, and she caught it. Nathan grabbed another one and pushed her toward the banging door. "Keep your face covered with that. Head down and away from the cameras."

She unfolded it and draped it over her nose and mouth as they swerved around a steel counter.

"Wait." Laz's voice chased them. "Maylynn, is it? That's your name?"

"Keep going." Nathan shifted them around a tiered rack of pastries.

The back of her shirt caught and pulled taut, halting her forward motion. She looked over her shoulder, around the edge of the towel, and met Laz's green-eyed glare.

"There's only one person who knows about that tattoo besides Jay and me, and her name was Charlee. Her eyes were so blue you'd never forget them. I know this because we have three hit songs written about those damned eyes."

Hers widened.

"So tell me, *Maylynn*, what the fuck is your real name?" His jaw was set, his tone more forceful than she thought him capable.

Nathan grabbed his wrist and squeezed. The fingers in her shirt flexed, released.

"His tattoo artist must have talked." Her voice was thready, dammit.

Laz tsked. "I'm not an idiot. You disappeared three years ago. Now you're…" He flicked a hand over her body. "You're undead and running from the press faster than we do." He leaned against a shelf of can goods and shoved his hands in his jean pockets. "Our limo is waiting at the side entrance. There won't be paparazzi there."

"Stay back, stay back." Voices shouted in the dining room, just outside the kitchen doors.

The air in her lungs cut off. Were the fans pushing in?

"That's our guards." Laz grinned. "Sounds like the party wants to move to the kitchen."

Nathan shuffled backward, taking her with him. "Get us out of here."

"Right this way." Laz jogged toward a pantry.

19

Charlee couldn't tamp down her pulse as she followed Laz through the small room crowded with food supplies and into a hallway on the other side. The silent sentry at her back was in as much danger as she was if their faces were posted on the Internet. With all those camera phones, it was probably too damned late.

A sea of fear sloshed in her stomach and robbed the strength from her legs. She stumbled, caught the edge of a shelf.

Laz pushed the bar on an exterior door and stopped at the black limo waiting in a narrow alley just outside.

The cool night air stirred with the rustling of litter. Cars rumbled somewhere around the corner, and there was not one flashbulb in sight. She strained her neck left to right and discovered why.

Tall privacy gates blocked both ends of the alley, each guarded by a man in head-to-toe black. She released her breath in a puff of steam. How many bodyguards did they have?

A woman with a stiff posture and hair combed into a severe bun opened the passenger door for them. "Good evening, Mr. Bromwell."

"We're in a hurry, Tony. To the hotel, please. You'll have to come back for the guys and the rest of the security team."

"Yes, sir."

Nathan placed his hand over Charlee's Bodyguard 380. The pistol was seated inside her waistband at the small of her back. She crawled inside the limo, the leather seat aiding her slide to the far side.

Nodding at Tony, Nathan followed her in with Laz at his heels. He settled beside her and pressed his phone to his ear. "Need a full run on the band *The Burn*...Yes...The musicians, promoters, managers, producers, security detail, everyone... Yes." His arm tightened. "I've got her. And Crane? We might've been exposed. Reassign someone to 24/7 facial searching."

They didn't have the recognition software Roy's company was

developing, so their effort was manual and inefficient, but they looked anyway. If they found her photo on the Internet, they'd rip it down with the hope they caught it before Roy did. Her gut clenched. What a royal fucking conundrum she'd steered them in.

Across the aisle, Laz eyed him, his lips flattened in a harsh line. He glanced at her, and an uncomfortable tension vibrated through the cabin.

"Sorry," she mouthed.

"Yes...Keep me posted." Nathan pocketed the phone and returned Laz's glare. "Where are we going?"

"The Plaza Hotel."

Nathan swung his head, looking out the windows. "Just drop us ten or twenty blocks up the road. We'll take the subway back."

The hotel would be a cluster of fan girls. Didn't stop the too-curious-to-be-rational part of her from speaking up. "Is Jay there?"

"Depends." Laz leaned into his arms bent on his spread knees.

"On?"

A battle of who-has-the-fiercest-glare launched between the men. She snapped her fingers in front of Laz. "On?"

He didn't unlock the stare down. "On if this guy is FBI or DEA or any of the other acronyms that would cause a rash in my ass."

Nathan blew out his cheeks and tapped his fingers on his knees.

"Also depends on how much more damage you plan on doing to my best friend."

"Let us out." Nathan thumped a fist on the divider behind the driver.

"I want to know what the fuck is going on." Laz scowled at her. "You're dead. Then you're not dead. Do you have any idea what you did to him?"

Was she responsible for Jay's damage? By leaving an unfinished tattoo on him? Had she made his pain worse by giving him a design he didn't want? She hadn't meant to hurt anyone, but a wanting need to fix it pulled at her heart.

She clasped Nathan's chin and made him look at her. "He just saved our asses from a media nightmare. A nightmare I led us into."

His jaw hardened beneath her fingers.

"That's right. I picked the restaurant knowing I might run into them. I *will* see this through."

"No. No fucking way." He shoved her hand away, twisting in the seat and eyes flicking over the surrounding buildings and streets.

She sucked in a breath. "You're smothering me, Nathan. I didn't ask you to be here. In fact, I've begged you to back off."

His gaze swung to hers, and they shared a moment of unspoken communication. She knew he walked a razor's edge between controlling her and protecting her. His obligation revolved around repaying his self-imposed debt to his brother, and in the process, he imprisoned himself as much as her.

Three years earlier, she'd put up with a paranoid life on the run. What did that get her? A dead boyfriend and two months in Roy's penthouse. No more overbearing men.

She dug deep to not buckle under Nathan's confining eyes and filled hers with a silent command. *Stop controlling.*

He closed the pregnant gap between them and patted her cheek. "Fine, but next time you'll warn me before you parade us into the public eye."

She nodded and turned to Laz, swaying toward him as if her nearness would convey the prudence of her words. "I think you've already worked out that I met Jay in St. Louis three years ago when I gave him his first tattoo."

Laz leaned back and let out a long-resolved breath. Then he jerked his chin at Nathan. "And him?"

"Nathan owns a private investigation firm, but he spends most of his time keeping us under the radar."

The flicker of passing lights illuminated Laz's sudden stiffness. "Private Investigation? Are you the asshole who—"

"Yes." Nathan scooted closer, crowding her.

She tensed against him, preparing herself. "What is he talking about?"

An explosion of fists pummeled the driver's seatback. Then Laz turned and pointed one of those fists at Nathan. "That bastard told Jay you were dead. Jay went to St. Louis more hopeful than he'd been in his life, only to find out you were fucking murdered."

"Be careful, Mr. Bromwell." Nathan's voice was low, deadly. "The man who *was* murdered meant the world to us."

His face paled. "The boyfriend?"

"And Nathan's brother." She squeezed Nathan's hand as her words, and the guilt that came with them, pulsed in her chest.

"Shit." Laz pressed the heels of his hands against his eyes, then lowered them and looked at her. "They didn't catch him, did they? The murderer? That's who you're hiding from?"

Her jaw was clenched so tightly, she had to focus to unlock it. "It's more complicated than that, but yeah." She shifted to face Nathan.

"When did you talk to Jay?"

Nathan's gaze was elsewhere, searching the passing streets. "I was at the tower when I got the call."

So he was deep undercover within Roy's ranks. "And you took the call?"

"Crane said Jay Mayard knew your name. I was afraid..." He rubbed the bridge of his nose, shifted his attention to her. "When one of our detectives discovered there was never a body for Sarah Teves, he dug in and connected your real name with Roy. He was hushed. At least, that's what Roy thinks. The detective is in the witness protection program now."

Her nod was taut with guilt. Roy would've put a hit on anyone looking for her.

Laz's chest rose and fell, watching their exchange.

Regret over Jay's involvement simmered through her. "Laz, if Jay was asking questions and using my real name, he would've become a target. Nathan shut that down the best way possible and saved his life."

The air choked with his harsh laughter. "I assure you, you did not save him. He's been in a three-year walking coma."

"Why? He didn't know me." Her voice sounded as uneasy as the conversation.

"I don't know." Laz bent toward her. "Whatever you gave him made him look at things differently, made him want to get better. He wanted to explore it... The tattoo, you, I don't know. But your death meant he would be forever incomplete. Unfinished."

She cleared her throat. "What's his story? How did he get the scars?"

His eyebrows slammed together. "Scars?"

Just cover it. One big sheet of black.

Oh God. Jay had really wanted to keep his back covered, even from his friends. "Yeah."

A wretched kind of silence fell between them. She tried to ride it out, but after an idle debate with her heart-shaped conscience, she couldn't convince herself to walk away. "I want to talk to him."

Nathan sighed, and Laz swung out an arm and pounded on the divider. "Come on, Tony. Can't you make this thing go any faster?"

The smile he directed at her danced at the corners of his mouth, betraying his nervousness. "When we get there, try to see the man beneath the surface. Whatever you saw in him three years ago, look for that, okay?"

"I didn't—"

"You did. The proof is permanently inked on his back, and he cherishes it more than life itself."

20

The limo stopped in a private underground garage a few feet from the hotel's service elevator. The ride to the top floor pulsated with impatience. Laz tapped the toe of his boot against the steel walls, sputtering Charlee's heart more than it already was. Nathan clenched his fingers along with the Musak jingle trumpeting from a hidden speaker.

What would she say to Jay? The notion that he cherished his tattoo sung through her veins. Maybe he'd ask her to finish it.

The bell dinged, and they jerked in unison. The doors opened to an austere landing lined with more doors. She welcomed the stark privacy, but it surprised her. "Do you always take the sneaky way?"

Laz swiped his card key on a solid-looking door. "Jay prefers to be removed from the view and presence of strangers, and he hires the best security professionals in the business to ensure he gets that."

"He chose the wrong damned lifestyle then." Nathan held the door for her with a smirk on his face.

They walked through another service door, and... Oh, wow. The entry engulfed them in another world. Marble pillars, gold-leafed mirrors and red velvet settees adorned the space. A heady reminder of how famous Jay was. Would he give a shit about a nobody like her? What if she'd misinterpreted his songs and she'd built up some ridiculous fantasy about him in her head? Her heart pounded, and her hands trembled.

Laz led them down a hall. "Jay didn't choose this life. It chose him. And to answer your question, Charlee..." He looked at her over his shoulder. "When our security personnel suggest we use the service elevator, we use the damned service elevator."

Good to know. The lackluster elevator seemed like a small concession as she passed a junior suite, a grand elevator foyer, another long foyer, a second bedroom. The scale and quantity of the rooms floored her. "This is all part of your suite?"

An oval foyer opened to a powder room, a study, and a gym. He stopped them in the center. "For thirty thousand dollars a night, we should have our own fucking pool." He smiled with a tinge of red in his cheeks. "And you've only seen the entrance."

She'd lived with one of the richest men in the world and never experienced extravagance on this level. None of it was visible from her *cell*. She'd been nothing more than a pet. No, not even that. Rich people pampered their pets. She stared at her Doc Martens in a harrowing moment of clarity, and fuck her, but it stung.

Nathan scanned something on his phone and returned it to his pocket. "Charlee?" He narrowed his eyes.

Damn him and his awareness. "Just having a little awed moment. Sheltered girl, you know?" She pointed at herself.

His eyes narrowed. Yeah, sheltered was a nice way to put it.

Laz moved to the double doors. "We took the security team out with us tonight, which means Jay's been in there without a chaperone for a few hours. Mind waiting here for a minute?"

What, was he twelve? She rubbed a sweaty palm on her jeans. "We'll wait."

When the doors snicked behind him, she leaned against the wall and tried to still her racing heart.

Nathan mimicked her lean beside her. He seemed strangely calm as he eyed her.

She rolled onto her shoulder to face him. "Why aren't you lecturing me about my bad decision-making?"

"Maybe I'm impressed with their security." He nodded his chin to the ceiling. "Cameras at every bend and doorway, the high-tech security gate at the garage entrance, and the preparedness of the bodyguards when we left the restaurant blows me away." A shrug. "Crane just sent a text. He hasn't found anything on the band or their staff to cause suspicion." He smiled. "Enfolded in all these safety measures is a nice change."

Oh, the things money could buy. The relief in his words melted over her. "The way to Nathan Winslow's heart is through impressive protection."

"True story."

Their smiles were interrupted by the whoosh of the doors. Laz stuck his head out and looked at Nathan. "Can you...uh...help me a minute?"

She moved with Nathan and Laz blocked her entrance. "Just Nathan, okay?"

Her teeth sawed together. "I can handle it, whatever it is."

"Maybe." He pinched the bridge of his nose, took a deep breath, and met her gaze. "Jay wouldn't want you to. Man's ego and all that."

Nathan wedged himself between them. "I prefer she stays with me."

"The suite is locked down—"

"Let me in, Laz." She stepped to the side and held his weary eyes.

A moan rumbled from behind him. A woman's moan. It hit her like fingers digging around in her innards, stirring up feelings she didn't have the right to act on.

Laz glanced over his shoulder and back at her. "You sure?"

Was she? She'd only met Jay once and had been through hell and back since that meeting. And how screwed up would it be for Jay if she walked in on something embarrassing? Depending on what she saw, he may not ever want to talk to her again.

Dammit. She needed to wrangle in her self-doubt. Famous Jay Mayard held an all-you-can-eat VIP pass to the pussy buffet, good for every night in every town. At least she wouldn't have to worry about entangling her emotions in whatever waited on the other side of the door. Images of his feasting chased her heart far, far away.

She jerked her chin in a stubborn nod and followed him through the door.

21

Charlee strode through the suite, head high, shoulders back, and stomach rolling. The moaning grew closer and laughter joined it. Her ankle wobbled, and she righted her gait without slowing.

"Jaaaaay." A second woman.

Another foyer opened to a dining room set for a royal court. How many damned foyers were in this place? The gold-plated light fixtures, hand-carved mahogany chairs, and tinkling crystal glasses made her want to hold her breath for fear of breaking something. She *wanted* to break something.

She was thankful they skipped that room until they arrived in the living room. It exuded the same stuffy air with marble fireplaces and silk embroidered couches too sumptuous to sit on.

Her focus narrowed on the grand piano and the two naked women tied to the top of it.

"Holy guacamole, it's Laz Bromwell. Untie us, Laz."

"Or fuck us." The other one laughed.

Did Jay restrain them? Whether they were willing or not, if that kind of thing turned him on, what else was he into? Would it be a scene like the Doms she played with? Or something more comparable to Roy's breed of kink. She tensed against a shiver.

The first one jerked her hips. "Jay left like an hour ago. Come on, baby. We're dying here."

She couldn't see the mouths that were polluting the air. She couldn't see anything beyond the spread legs and the gaping vaginas. The light from the chandelier illuminated their glistening slits. Cloudy-white globs drenched their crevices from knees to hips. Oh, God. Jay had been there, in there, all over there.

A wave of disgust swept through her. The kind of disgust that seeped from open sewers. Maybe his dick would rot off.

Where was her sense of ownership over him coming from? What

the hell was wrong with her? She couldn't stop her cheeks from heating, her body from shaking, or the progression of vicious thoughts storming through her head.

"Charlee?" Nathan's hand touched her back.

She startled. Was that normal behavior for women? Did they all look that debauched? She'd never witnessed another woman in a sexual situation. "Did I look like that?" she whispered for his ears only.

"No, Charlee." It was a repulsed response.

She wanted to believe him. She also wanted to power wash those vaginas with a fire hose. Inside and out. Then hold them down in a tub of bleach.

Jesus, that was a hell of a thing to wish on someone. Why was she so appalled? Was she ashamed for them? For herself? How many hours had she spent tied down and wearing come just like that? She was no better than they were.

Despite her unraveling justifications, she knew her reaction was driven by jealousy. How important were those women in Jay's life? Was he writing songs about them? She clutched her gut and circled, scanning the room. Where was he?

Nathan grabbed her shoulders. "Charlee?"

"Why do you keep calling her Charlee?" The woman struggled against the ropes. "I'm his Charlee tonight."

A shiver chilled her spine. She pushed around Nathan and glared at the woman. "What did you say?"

"Whatever, bitch." The other one tried to kick a tied foot. "He called me Charlee right before he ejaculated."

Bile bubbled in her gut. She wasn't sure what her expression held, but Laz ducked out of a bathroom and turned her toward the connecting bedroom. "Don't pay attention to them. While I'm looking for Jay, can you just..." He nudged her forward. "Go turn down his bed or something."

She twisted her head, searched his eyes, driven by a need for answers. "He calls them Charlee?"

His face tightened as he shifted his gaze to the piano. "Girls, where did Jay go?"

"He wandered off." One woman giggled. "Didn't look so good. Hey there, sexpot. Who are you?"

Nathan bent over the piano, untying the knots in the rope. They could stay there for all Charlee cared, but in the eyes of her benevolent protector, a restraint was a restraint, no matter how willing.

With a sudden need to be out of the room when the women

were free, she trudged to bedroom. The maid service had already turned down the bed, but what caught her eye was a doorway in the furthest corner of the room. A walk-in closet? She moved toward it and flicked on the light.

A center island dominated the space. She walked around it and froze.

Jay sprawled on the floor, nude from the waist down, his face planted in the rug. Lines of white powder dusted a square plate beside him.

How many times had Laz warned her? She understood Jay had issues, but seeing him prone and pathetic on the closet floor squeezed things in her chest. "Laz!"

Should she check to see if he'd overdosed? Her experience with drugs was limited, as in nonexistent. She screamed louder, "Laz!"

Stomps pounded through the bedroom. A moment later, Laz dropped beside Jay, lifting his head up and to the side, and prodding his lips. "Lips aren't blue. Still has his annoying bronze *glow*." He rolled his eyes, hovered his mouth over Jay's ear, and roared, "Faggot!"

A flinch rippled over Jay's body, and his eyes opened and squeezed shut.

"He's just high, not OD'd." Laz grabbed a wadded towel from the floor, spread it over Jay's very sculpted, too naked ass, and raised his eyes to her. "Remember what I said, Charlee. Look for the man beneath the—"

"Towel?"

He smirked. "You're twisted."

She shrugged, and it was stiff and forced. "When it fits the bill."

"Fair enough. Any pants up there on the counter?"

She tagged a pair of workout shorts from the island where she leaned and tossed them. As Laz shoved them up Jay's long legs, she tried not to watch, let alone think about how toned his calves and thighs were. Those legs were wrapped around piano sluts. Her cheeks heated and sparked. "I thought cocaine made a person jittery and excited. Why is he so out of it?"

Laz tugged and twisted the shorts over his friend's ass and removed the towel. "Doesn't look like he touched much blow tonight. He was probably drunk off his ass before he invited the girls up. I bet he hurls before he wakes."

Here he was, rich and famous with the world salivating at his feet. Yet... "What a sad and lonely life, drinking, fucking wanton women..." She waved a hand over the bed. "Vomiting in his sleep. Is it a rock star thing?"

With a heave and a grunt, Laz threw Jay's body over his shoulder in a fireman's carry and carted him to the bed. "Is it a rock star thing to drink, fuck, and vomit? In the nineties, maybe. You won't find much of that among modern musicians. Our schedules are hell, the media slaughters us for bad behavior, and most of us are businessmen in this industry."

Laz rolled him into the bed facedown, and Jay bounced with a moan. Then he kicked a trash can with his foot until it bumped the bedside. "No, this is a Jay thing."

A Jay thing? *He's been in a three-year walking coma.*

With his hands hooked under Jay's armpits, he pulled until Jay's chin hung off the side of the bed and over the can. That done, he stepped back and stared down at her. "Be patient with him, and please, *please*, wait till he wakes up. Talk to him." He softened his eyes, put the meaning of his words there. "It would kill him to learn you were alive without seeing you for himself."

Despite the drama, there wasn't a chance in hell she would leave without talking to Jay. She crawled across the bed, settled beside him, and hovered a hand over his shirt-covered back. "Can I touch?"

"Only when he's comatose." He studied her as if a sudden move might scare her off.

"I'll stay with him. Go help Nathan with the leaking vaginas."

A laugh burst out of him. "Jesus, you're a hell of a woman." His laughter cut off, and he stared at her, resolute in his stillness. "I see it now. I totally get what he saw in you."

He didn't see shit. Neither of them did.

She lowered her hand, tested the feel of his back with a finger, right over the ink. "Have you seen the tattoo?"

He shook his head, watching her. "No one has."

"You think he wants me to finish it?"

"More than anything."

She was too stunned to respond. It wasn't shock. It was the echo of her longing. She saw her drawings. The sketches of charred skin made to look like it was curling away. The flames. The steel plates and rivets beneath the hurt.

She wanted to finish the tattoo, but it wasn't all. There was something deeper, something vibrating beneath, begging her to unveil. It was the strength of the man that had kept her alive during those long two months with Roy.

Footsteps approached, sped up, and one of the piano girls

skidded into the room, flippant in her nudity. "We're staying in here tonight. Jay invited *us*. Not her."

Nathan charged in after her dragging the other woman by the arm. "Laz?"

Laz scooped up the one on the loose, tossed her over his shoulder, and smacked her butt. "Party's over ladies. Let's go."

The woman pounded on his back. "Nooo. It's not your decision. He didn't fuck us yet. He promised this time." Her voice faded as Nathan and Laz moved them through the suite.

Nathan left her alone? Apparently, he just needed a woman to protect and control, any woman—or two—would do. Not that she cared. It was a rare moment to be out of his watchful gaze.

She leaned over Jay's back. *Please, wake up.* Thick lashes fanned his sculptured cheekbones.

If he hadn't fucked the women, what was the white shit between their legs? A shudder barreled through her. Roy loved to jerk off on her and watch his come drip down her pussy. But why did the notion of Jay stroking off *on* them rather than *in* them soothe some of the boiling in her blood?

She fell on her back with a sigh. How often did this kind of thing happen in his life? Jealousy surged anew, gripping her insides. She hated the feeling. It was a needy weakness, and she wasn't weak.

She stretched out on the bed beside him while he slept and wondered how he felt about her, wondered *if* he felt anything. Maybe the only way he thought of her was in some bondage fantasy that he jerked off to?

What about his song *Charlee*? The title was convincing with two *e*'s, its passionate lyrics aching with love and regret. Was it written for her? If it was, she wanted the opportunity to try to free him from the pain woven into those words.

She rolled to her side and studied his face, where it cocked awkwardly over the side of the bed. A shadow of whiskers darkened his jaw. The curves of his lips looked as though they had been drawn on, every crease sketched to perfection. He was so devastatingly handsome, it hurt to look at him. No wonder he was the ladies' first pick.

The masculine angles of his face begged to be gentled. Would his taut tanned skin be warm?

She crawled off the bed and crouched beneath his face. Reaching out tentative fingers, she brushed his eyelid. It was soft and twitchy. Yes, there was life in there. She traced the arch of one cheek, stroked through the thick brown hair that curled over the tip of his ear, and followed the sinews in his neck. Could she lift his shirt and peek at his back without waking him?

He opened his eyes. Glazed and dark, they blinked at her. And blinked again. "Emb I dea...iiidth?"

She jerked her hand back. "Are you dead? No, but you're headed there at the rate you're going."

He swallowed. "I muth be dead. You're...you're..." His jaw stretched open, his chest heaved, and he reared back.

She dropped to her ass and rolled as a wash of vomit hit the can on the floor. After a few heavy exhales, he lowered his head to the bed and mumbled, "Charlee."

He remembered her.

Whatever, bitch. He called me Charlee right before he ejaculated.

She sucked in a breath and with it the rancid stench of puke. A few splatters had hit her chest despite her efforts. She fought her gag reflex and ran to the closet, stripping her shirt on the way.

As she shrugged on one of his t-shirts—*a vintage* Dead Milkmen *shirt? Yes!*—she told herself that he was every bit as fucked up as she was. The only thing they could develop beyond friendship was a madness shared by two.

She wanted to be supportive. She wanted to finish his tattoo, but she had to be careful with her feelings, and most definitely with his. More than that, she had to make sure Roy didn't learn about her interest in Jay Mayard.

22

Charlee returned to Jay's bedside, wearing his t-shirt instead of his puke. He hadn't stirred. The sheets appeared clean. There were a few drops on the carpet, but the can caught most of it. A practiced move, no doubt.

She rinsed out the bucket in the bathroom and scrubbed the carpet with a towel that probably cost more than her entire wardrobe. Then she stood beside his head, staring at him. Should she move him?

Stop staring at him. Stop thinking about him. She should find out what was keeping Laz and Nathan, but she didn't want to leave him. What if he needed her?

That was when she knew she should leave the room. Her longing for a man she'd met three long years ago was surfacing and she didn't know what to do with that. Panic flooded her. She tucked her ridiculous feelings away and fled the room.

A few empty foyers led her to the hush of voices in the suite's library. Nathan and the driver—*what was her name? Tony?*—sat on velvet chaises amid the shelves of leather-bound books. It wasn't the company Nathan kept that surprised her, so much as how close they leaned toward one another.

Nathan laughed at something the woman said, and he turned his head. Their eyes caught. "Hey Charlee. Everything okay?"

She crossed the room and settled in the closest chair. "Jay's out for the night. I'll talk to him tomorrow if he's not busy."

The woman stood with her shoulders kicked back. "This is a pleasure trip. They don't have anything booked."

Nathan rose. "Let me do some introductions. This is Master Sergeant Maryanna Tony, U.S. Marine Corps. She leads the protective team for the band." He actually puffed out his chest. "Master Sergeant. Meet Charlee Grosky."

A fellow Marine. This would be interesting. "She outranks you."

He stared at his feet with a smile playing on his lips.

"Nice to officially meet you, Master...er...Tony... How should I address you?"

"Tony is fine. And I'm retired, Nathan." Her rigid posture mirrored his, but her teasing expression softened her pretty features.

He shifted his weight from one foot to the other. "We were just discussing escort formation techniques for protection while on foot. Their area security procedures for traveling and the perimeter barriers at their L.A. home are—"

"Impressive?"

He grinned. "Yeah."

Oh, yeah. Tony had nuzzled right into his heart. He'd never get it back. "Sharing trade secrets then?"

They looked at one another with blank expressions. Must have been some kind of Marine language. But beneath his usual stiffness, there was a phlegmatic feel to the way he observed—and didn't observe—his surroundings. He trusted the pretty Marine. "Did you tell her?"

He palmed his nape. "Some of it. She knows who Roy is. In fact, he recruited her for his VIP protection personnel."

Jesus, Nathan really did trust her. She looked at Tony and felt a little intimidated by the air of competence exuding from her. Her crisp black pants suit, alert eyes, and fierce set to her jaw were enough to act as a deterrent to would-be celebrity maulers. "Turning down that job was probably the smartest thing you've ever done."

"So I hear." Her face gave away nothing. "My sidearm is useless without fingers to fire it."

A chain of memories coiled its way around her. It tightened when Nathan asked, "You ready to go?"

Until that moment, her nerves had been less sensitive since they arrived at the suite. "You know, I haven't thought of Roy once since we've been here."

He squatted before her and enveloped her hands with his. "I feel safe, too. It's nice, huh?"

"Then stay."

She turned toward the voice behind her.

Laz leaned against the door jamb, hands in his pockets. "Stay the night. I've already tucked the guys in. You can have my room."

When did the guys return? Another guard must've gone back for them. A laugh bubbled out of her. "Did you read them a story before you tucked them in?"

"Yeah, it was a picture book. Lots of boobs."

She shook her head, smiling at the image of him caring for his drunken bandmates. “I don’t want to kick you out of your room.”

“It’s yours. Stay.” He batted his eyes. “Please?”

How could she say no to him? Why would she want to? For once in her life, she could wake up surrounded by luxury without being held as a prisoner.

She looked at the man perched before her. “Well?”

23

Charlee shimmied out of her jeans, slid the Bodyguard 380 under the pillow, and fell back into a cloud of luxurious bedding. "This is the life."

Nathan said something to the guard in the hallway and closed the door. "We have a bodyguard." He scratched his head, his voice flattened with disbelief. "He's going to stand out there all night."

She pulled the blankets up to her chin. "Maybe we can sleep with both of our eyes closed tonight?"

He perched on the other side of the bed and tugged off his pants. Then he clicked off the light and lay on his side to face her. "Crane still hasn't found any connection between these guys and Roy, so yeah, we're sleeping well tonight."

She smiled, and it was bitter sweet. "The one night you could sleep alone, yet here I am. You're stuck with me as usual."

They'd shared a bed for three years, too concerned about the other's safety not to. The worst part of that had been the way Nathan just accepted his celibacy in this life with her, making her his responsibility and giving up everything for her and his revenge.

He shoved her shoulder. "I'm not stuck with you and have never felt that way. Besides, how else will I trap Roy? You're my bait."

It was her turn to shove him. "Ass."

He might've been driven by revenge, but three years of simply trying to exist without being caught left him frustrated and without a plan to bring down Roy. Moreover, if anything happened to her, he would see it as failing his brother. Again. In truth, if Nathan wanted to use her for his own end, he would've been justified in doing so. She was the reason Noah was dead after all.

A burn torched her throat, and she swallowed through it. "I might be doing a couple tattoos tomorrow, so I'll need to get my supplies from the apartment, okay?"

"A couple? Laz and..."

"Jay." Hopefully. There was so much hope in that name.

"Be careful with him, Charlee. The last thing you need is another obsessive man."

She tensed. There was a lingering fear in her that she might somehow attract compulsive men. If she could entice a monster like Roy, it might happen again with another man. Jay wasn't a monster. He wasn't Roy. "He's different."

"Yeah, he's a whole other breed of messed up." He kissed her brow. "Sleep well, sweetheart."

That he could count on.

24

Jay woke up shaking. Charlee had invaded his dreams again, but this time was different.

The blue-eyed beauty had been haloed in flames of red. Her fiery hair swept over her tiny shoulders and cascaded in curtains around her. He clutched the bedding. She was so fucking beautiful.

He closed his eyes, tried to push himself back into the dream. He found her, and she saw him, saw into him. He could hear the happy tune of her humming. Her tattoo gun was buzzing against his back. She touched his shoulder with her fingertips, with her sweet lips. She actually touched him, and it was the best sensation he'd ever experienced. He turned his face to capture her mouth.

Gone. She was fucking gone.

Fuck. He punched the pillow. *Fucking let her go*.

He rolled out of bed and nausea fisted in his gut. He plodded through the room in a hangover daze on uncoordinated, hundred-pound feet. At least there was a bright start. He didn't have to chase any clingy strangers from his bed.

In the bathroom, he shed his shirt and shorts and turned his back to the mirror. Why did he torment himself everyday by staring at something that would never come to fruition?

He looked over his shoulder and saw the finished illustration the way she might've seen it. He saw the blaze, the heat, the passion in the detail. She didn't cover the scars. She added more, the edges burning and twisting away from the flames. It was the steel etched beneath the melted skin that fortified him. He wanted to be that iron man underneath. She'd seen something in him he hadn't been able to see himself.

Before Charlee, he couldn't look at his scars without hurtling back to the weather-worn shed with no light, no food, and no toys or human contact. The sooty insides of the cast-iron cooker and the rumble it made when it fired up still made him ball his fists so hard his nails left indents in his skin. And the woman with the empty eyes who kept him in the shed and forced him in the oven…

The room tilted sideways, and he caught the edge of the counter. His breath pushed through his teeth in a wet hiss. He fumbled through the medicine cabinet. Bottles and soaps tumbled out. Where was his snuff box? He removed the toilet lid. Son of a bitch. His vials were gone. Fucking Laz.

He grabbed his toiletry bag and dug out the nasal spray bottle. He shook it to mix the coke with the water and ethanol he'd drizzled in it. A few sprays in each nostril, and ahh…

His body awoke. The tingles lifted him, and the pull of gravity released. He smiled. The world was his happy place.

He buzzed through his shower, rubbing soap over his defined chest, his hard abs, and… Jesus, look at that massive cock. My God, he was a virile man. Women wanted him. Men wanted to be him. He needed to get out there and fuck the world. That was what he'd do. New York City was waking, and it wanted to spread its legs for Jay Fucking Mayard.

Showered, shaved, and dressed in his tightest leathers, he strode through the bedroom. His heart pounded to do…something.

He swung open the door and tripped, catching himself on the jamb. A bundle of blankets lay at his feet. Chaotic chunks of gelled hair stuck out of one end. Why the hell was Laz sleeping on the floor?

He looked like a cuddly little kitten curled up in a ball. He kicked it.

"Ow. Fuck."

"Why are you sleeping outside my door?"

"My bed is occupied." The bastard pulled the blanket over his head.

He kicked him again.

The blanket went flying in a cartwheel of fists hitting air. "Fuck. Quit fucking kicking me."

"Tell me you did not let those girls stay in your bed."

"No." Laz glared at him. "Piss off. The sun's barely up, and you're already fucking high."

"No you won't tell me, or no they didn't stay?" His teeth sawed the inside of his cheek.

"No, they didn't stay."

The sawing stopped but only for a heartbeat.

"Someone else stayed." Laz smiled up at him, and he didn't like the look of it.

"Who?"

The fucker stretched like a lazy cat, his smile turning more Cheshire by the second. "Guess."

Okay, he was up for the challenge. His dick twitched. Yeah, he was definitely up. "A woman?"

The grinning cat nodded.

"Is she hot?"

"You're seriously asking me that after the strays you let in last night?"

Ugh. He didn't remember what they looked like. All he remembered was tying down their wandering hands.

Screw the Q&A. He moved through the suite, fueled to fuck. He didn't care if she was a Laz leftover. He vibrated with a sense of health and vitality. It was the blow, he knew, and he was about ten minutes from crashing. Fuck it. In that moment—*"Raaargh!"*—he felt fucking great.

Edison stood post outside the junior suite wearing his spiffy suit and even spiffier com device sticking in his ear. He had no business standing there. "What are you doing here?"

"Tony's orders."

A sudden surge of paranoia rocked him on his heels. No, it was too soon to crash. Just a few more minutes. "You're relieved of your post. Go away." He grabbed the door knob and stormed toward the bed.

Red hair filled his horizon. Just like his dream. It flowed in sheets over her back, her petite arms, and curled around her pillow. He crept forward and knelt on the floor beside the bed. His fingers shook as he brushed the soft strands from her face.

His breath caught in his throat. His chest burned. Oh God, the coke must have been cut with something. He was hallucinating.

It was the best trip of his life. He held himself motionless, savoring the fantasy, afraid if he touched her again, his fingers would wisp the phantasm away.

A man-shaped lump moved in the bedding behind her. Then its head popped up and glared at him over her shoulder.

What the fuck? "Who the hell are you?"

"Lower your voice."

Charlee's ghost stretched her arms over her head and rolled to her back. Was that his *Dead Milkmen* t-shirt? Holy hell, the girl was real. His stomach dropped. Did Laz find and fuck a Charlee-look-alike? "I really want to fuck you."

She opened her eyes. Blinding spheres of blue hit him in the chest just as the man's fist slammed into his face. His back hit the floor, and he stared at the garish gold scrollwork on the ceiling, smiling. Those eyes couldn't be cloned. Charlee was alive.

The euphoria evaporated into a murderous cloud. She was in bed with a man and the fucker was standing over him, shooting daggers as if he owned the place and the girl. Fuck that. "Get out."

The man's arrogant chin lifted, and he stepped back, eyes on Charlee. "Come on, sweetheart."

No way in hell. He jumped to his feet and swayed. The sudden loss of his high only added to his irritation. "She's not going anywhere."

"Are you kidding me right now?" She sidled between them with her hands on her hips. "I think you both need a timeout. Nathan, why did you hit him? And Jay, you don't get to decide if I stay."

Goddamned adorable. "You're wearing my shirt."

"Yeah, well, you puked on mine."

He groaned. *Smooth, Jay*. He dropped his chin on his chest. Shit, what had she witnessed last night? "How did you get here?" he asked her bare feet.

She snapped her fingers in his face. "Quit sulking."

Her gorgeous eyes were intense and aimed at him. Jesus, that one look from her was a punch in the groin.

"I ran into Laz in the Village. What's wrong with you?"

"He's crashing." Laz's voice drifted from the foyer and crawled under his skin.

"Scram, Laz. I've got this."

Disappointment dominated her glare. He'd let her down. A blurry fog of doom closed in on him, drawing him toward its center, but the man hovering too goddamned close to her incited him to fight through the haze. "Who is this guy?"

"Jay." Laz was wearing his stern face. He hated that face. "Listen, buddy. Nathan is Charlee's husband."

The whole fucking world crashed down upon him in a turbulent sea of red.

25

The room broke out in maelstrom of tumbling bodies, save for Charlee, who refused to participate in a wrestling match of male egos. But maybe she could nullify it. "I'm not married. We're not together."

Jay swung an arm at Nathan's head. His fist overshot and cracked the leg of a baroque table. The misfire seemed to surprise him, and he sprung from the floor. Shuffling backward, he edged the room. His face transformed from rage to despair and back to rage as he looked from her to Nathan.

"Don't do anything crazy." Laz held up his hands, circling him. "Think of Charlee, man."

"Don't bring me into this. I'm trying to stay the hell away from crazy." She was brimming with enough of it herself because all she wanted to do was kiss that stricken look off Jay's face. "Is cocaine doing this to him?"

Laz nodded. "He's hardcore crashing. He'll be restless and bad-tempered for a couple hours."

She exhaled a fog of frustration. Dammit, she needed to talk to him.

"Great." Nathan rubbed his jaw and rolled back on his heels in a squat. "Maybe we should move him to the punching bag in the gym."

Jay hissed through clenched teeth, his eyes aflame and locked on Nathan.

Nathan climbed to his feet. "Don't look at me like that, motherfucker. Stop swinging at me, and I'll stop hitting you."

"What happened to all the voicemails?" Jay ground out as he looked between her and Nathan. "I called for two months."

Voicemails? Her head throbbed. "What voicemails?" And why did Nathan's face slack?

Nathan raked a hand through his hair. "I kept the landline number active and picked up the messages. It was the easiest way for me to keep track of you. To make sure you weren't going to interfere or give away Charlee's identity. I didn't want to engage you, but when you placed that call to my PI firm, I made the decision to lie about her death. A guaranteed solution to your relentless inquiries."

He called her for two months? She glared at Nathan. "Why didn't you tell me?"

Jay charged him. They collided in the doorway and rolled through the foyer, punching and grunting.

"Laz," she shouted as he ran after them.

He skidded through the door and looked back at her.

"Tell him we're not married. We're not together like that at all. If he'll even listen at this point."

Lines formed around his gaping mouth. "You're not?"

She shook her head. "Hank and Maylynn McGraw were aliases."

He slapped a palm on his forehead. "Aw shit. I just assumed the marriage was real. You slept—"

Glass shattered. The walls thumped and vibrated. More breaking glass.

"Oh shit. The dining room." Laz took off.

Where were the guards? Was it not one of their jobs to breakup fighting? She trailed him through the foyer and passed a half-awake Wil Sima, scratching his ass in his open doorway.

He yawned. "Let me guess. Jay's crashing?"

Laz didn't stop to answer him, so she did. "Yeah."

Plaid pajama pants sagged from his narrow hips, and he blew a curl off his boyish face. "You're the foxy lady from the restaurant. That sucks."

"I'll try not to take offense to that."

"No, it's just that I really wanted to win that bet."

She patted his cheek. Wow. Wil was standing right in front of her in his pajamas. "No dates with Laz. I'm an old friend of Jay's. I think that means you won the bet."

Shouts erupted down the hall, and the crystal teardrops in the chandelier overhead clinked on their gold hoops.

She and Wil shared a look and raced to the dining room. When they reached Jay, he was tearing around the table.

Beside her, Nathan and Tony clasped their hands behind their backs, feet braced apart, and watched the show.

Laz stood at one end of the table, eyes wide and finger pointing at him. "Don't do it, Jay. Don't—"

Jay swept his arm over a placemat and sent more crystal glasses crashing into the wall. "Get out of here, Laz." He picked up an ornate candlestick and chucked it through the air. It landed somewhere in the living room.

"Dude. You're not listening. They. Are not. Married."

"I don't give a shit. They're fucking sleeping together." He kicked a wood-engraved chair into the wall.

Should she jump in? Try to talk to him? Would she get hit over the head with the brass centerpiece? She looked at Tony. "You're not going to do anything?"

"I only interfere when he's hurting himself or someone else."

Jay looked around the room with wild eyes. Then he locked on Nathan and rushed toward him.

Tony ran to block his attack, but Laz jumped on his back, pinned his arms, and brought him to the floor. Jay flailed his arms, yelled incoherently, and dragged his legs forward, his knees buckling, taking Laz to the floor with him.

Charlee's heart stopped, her body frozen in horror. Jay threw back his head and screamed, "Burning. It's burning." He ripped free of Laz's embrace and scrambled backward until he hit the corner of the room.

His head hung between his knees, and he wrapped his arms behind his neck. His body shuddered, and he let out one muffled sob. It was small, lonely, and more than she could bear.

26

A miasma of burning flesh emanated from him. It was pungent and smoky and everywhere. Jay couldn't move, it was so cramped in there. No light. The walls were hot and growing hotter. "Turn it off. Please, Aunt El. Turn it off."

Stop it. Not real. He proved it by rooting himself into the wall at his back and staring at the swirly designs in the rug. He dug his bare foot into a splinter of glass. If the slivers pierced skin, he didn't feel it. The dirt floor flickered in, the thin boards of the shed rattled. The room darkened.

Then he saw feet next to his. They were tiny and naked with black painted toenails, wiggling, bringing him back to the dining room in the New York suite. It was only a few moments before she spoke.

"Will you come with me to your room?" Her voice was so delicate, so sweet. "Just you and me?"

He loved the sound of those words, but her feet were in danger. "Don't move."

A pause. "Why not?"

"You're standing in glass."

She curled a toe.

"I said don't move." He raised his head and dove into the crystal-blue pools of her eyes.

"I guess you'll have to carry me then."

What a silly thing to suggest. He was barefoot, too. He knew she was trying to redirect his emotions, and damn, it worked.

She didn't give him space as he rose to his feet. The top of her head came to his throat. The perfect height to tuck all that red under his chin.

He shimmied around her in an awkward dance of bending and standing. How would he do this? Scoop under her legs? Where would her hands go?

She put her arms up, waiting, and dropped them back to her belly. "How about a piggyback ride?"

A laugh escaped his chest. A laugh? What a strange sound in his voice. "Yeah, piggyback is totally rock-n-roll." He turned his back. "Hands—"

"No hands. I remember." She leapt, arms up and over his shoulders, legs squeezing around his hips, and laced her fingers together in front of him.

She weighed nothing. Not sure what he expected. He'd never carried a woman, let alone allowed someone to ride on his back. She was childlike in her bone structure, though the thighs beneath his hands and the curves of legs wrapped around his waist were deliciously mature.

She kept her fingers away from his body and tightened her clench around his hips. "You've never held anyone this close before."

He was stiff, he knew, but was he that obvious? Maybe she'd gathered that from his no touching rule.

Her breath circled around his ear. "Your heart's knocking against your chest."

It sped up. "I might be nervous." As in a thrashing maniacal ball of nerves.

"I think there's a little of that happening on both sides right now."

The misery-loves-company thing didn't usually work for him, but he knew without a doubt his misery loved Charlee.

His friends stared at him with their mouths and eyes gaping as he left the dining room full of echoes and broken glass and strode to the bedroom in long urgent steps. He kicked the door closed behind them, and instead of releasing her, he pulled her legs tighter around him.

The hopelessness piled on his shoulders weighed so much more than she did. Now she'd seen him at his worst. "You thought I was made of steel. Now you know."

There was a pause as if she were debating the answer. She was probably glaring at the back of his head.

She dropped her cheek on his shoulder. "No, it's still in there. You just haven't found it yet."

His hands curled into the flesh belonging to the woman who strengthened him by merely opening her mouth. She was his ghost of dreams, his backbone, his everything.

He realized she was struggling to get down, and he released her immediately. "Sorry. I'm sorry."

She smoothed the borrowed shirt over her bare thighs and

stepped back. "We have a lot to talk about."

In a strolling circuit around the room, she traced the curvature of the King Louis furniture, fidgeted with the knick-knacks, and sniffed the bouquets of fresh flowers. How extraordinary it felt to have her there, in the same room, sharing the same air. He could watch her for hours, the graceful way she moved, the elegant arch of her throat, the flicker in her eyes when she looked at him.

She paused in front of the sheer ivory curtains. He could tell by the way she stared out at the gray-stone architecture of Fifth Avenue that her mind was in another place. Her words confirmed it.

"Three years ago, you walked into my tattoo shop. An hour after you left, my lover and dearest friend, Noah Winslow, was killed." She turned to face him. "And I was kidnapped by his murderer."

He reached out for the bed and sat, his pulse at full throttle. "Who took you?"

"I'll get to that, but first you need to understand Nathan's role in this."

Noah Winslow had been the boyfriend. There was a worn card in his wallet with the contact info for Winslow Investigations...for Nathan Winslow. A brother? "He's the fucker who told me you were murdered."

She snapped up her chin, her eyes hard as aquamarine glass. "Insult him again and I'm out of here. Do you understand?"

He needed to know who abducted her and what the soon-to-be dead motherfucker did to her, so he focused on that instead of the man she so vehemently defended. He nodded.

"Good." She took a deep breath. "Noah and Nathan were brothers, and I'm the reason Nathan lost him. The fact that he hasn't killed me himself speaks volumes."

"How—"

She held up a stiff finger, but it was her glare that shushed him.

"Nathan saved your life by lying about my death. The man who enslaved me put hits on anyone looking for me. Though there was no one. Friends or family, that is." She paused as if to let that set in.

Yeah, he had definitely stopped looking for her.

"I think you're beginning to see, but here's the big one, Jay. Nathan sabotaged his mission, at a great financial cost to himself, and risked his life to carry me out of a prison where I was shackled, beaten, and raped by a man. The man I've been running from since I was eighteen. The man I'm still running from."

27

Charlee watched as the gravity of her situation settled over Jay, contorting his face and tightening the muscles in his neck and arms. That was the moment she realized he'd fully perceived she was in danger.

She didn't regret telling him truth, but worry slid through her and knotted in her stomach. Would he reject her? Would he compare her to the piano girls? Or would he go ballistic again? "What I tell you cannot be repeated. You could endanger my life, and yours."

He jumped to his feet. Given his sudden tenseness, she'd anticipated his rage. What she hadn't prepared for was him moving toward her in three ground-covering strides and enfolding her in a crushing embrace. "Oh God, Charlee. You've lived that nightmare since you were eighteen?"

His arms pinned hers at her sides, and his face pressed into her neck. A warm, low crackling fire kindled in her core and spread through her body. Roy had never held her that way, which meant he hadn't stolen her capacity to trust hugs, and return them.

"Since I was sixteen. Nine years ago." She held her breath, the explanation sticking in her throat. She steeled her spine against the images of memory. Nathan told her rape victims blamed themselves, but she wasn't a victim. "He imprisoned me for two years." A smile twitched her lips as she recalled her proudest moment. "I escaped on my own that first time."

When he raised his head, she wanted to wrap her arms around him and squeeze him as tightly as he squeezed her. Since she couldn't do that, she held firmly to his eyes. Their brown depths were murky, but the emotions swimming in the deepest parts begged for answers, for help, and for things she didn't want to address.

He saved her from the painful questioning. "Are you okay?" His breath pushed against her lips. "Can I hold you like this?"

Life was jaded like that, throwing them together when he

couldn't tolerate affection and she was desperate for it. "Yes. I really like it."

He dropped his forehead to hers. "Thank God, because—" A shuddering inhale. "This is going to sound really forward, Charlee, but I want to kiss you. I've dreamed of it for three years. I've enacted it in my head so many times." He straightened. "Jesus, I sound creepy."

Creepy? Maybe a little. It was a harmless creepy. His hard body pressed against the length of hers. Not a forceful weight. Instead, it propped her up, supported her. "A fantasy, huh? I can't compete with that."

He removed his hands from her back, cupped her neck, and slowly tilted her head back. "Let me show you."

The first kiss touched the hairline at her temple, and the muscles in her face relaxed. The next brushed her eyelid. She smiled, remembering the way his had twitched under her fingers the night before.

A kiss landed on the corner of her smile. More trailed along her cheek to the spot below her ear, and he lingered there with nipping lips.

She laughed and buried her ear in the crook of her shoulder.

"Tickles?"

"You're a tease. I thought you were going to kiss me?"

He stared at her mouth, his own parted with increased breath. His chest rose and fell, moving against hers. When his tongue wet the top corner of his lip, she felt it on her skin from her lips to her toes.

"Jay—"

He swooped in and took her mouth. It began with a sip, then nibbles, a little at a time. Soon he was sucking every inch of her lips, sending the beat of her heart spluttering through her veins.

She fell into a trance, yet she could mark every perfect second of his mouth opening hers, and the precise moment their tongues touched.

Oh, to run her fingers through his hair, or over his ribs and around to the rise of his backside. As it were, her hands were useless weights hanging on her thighs. She didn't want to move them, afraid she'd startle him and ruin the moment.

He seemed to sense her distraction and joined their fingers without breaking the kiss.

She pulled on their hands to bring them around to her back, but he tugged them the opposite direction, over his hips, and settled them with the backs of his hands over his ass. The position brought their hips together, and she felt the strength of his arousal at her belly.

"Is this too much?" he breathed against her lips.

She arched into him and chased his tongue, entangling it with hers. She moved to his bottom lip, drawing it in, tasting it, and slowly let it go. "Not enough."

Beneath the solid rock of his chest and arms, she felt him shaking. With restraint? Anticipation? She rose on tiptoes to deepen her strokes, leaning into him, bolstered by the musculature of his body.

They began to gasp for air, and the roll of their tongues slowed. The intensity faded into lazy doting licks and the wet slide of swollen lips. When their breathing returned to normal, she dropped her heels to the floor and searched his eyes. "How did reality stand up?"

"Incomparable." His eyes glimmered. "The fantasy was an opening act. You just flattened me with a show-stealing encore. I'm ruined for all other performances."

Her pulse fluttered in that girly draw-hearts-around-his-name kind of way. Was she an idiot? She needed to pull up before she drowned. "I was hoping for a more explicit answer."

His dark eyebrows crept together, and he tugged her closer by her hands held at his back. "I was one thrust against your cunt away from busting a nut. That explicit enough for you?"

The lewdness of his words stiffened her spine. She asked for it, deliberately forced the sentiment from the moment. Emotional distance was safer for them both. So why did she feel so sick?

"Shit. I'm sorry, Charlee. I shouldn't have said that."

"Don't be. It's better that way."

He dropped her hands and stepped back. The absence of his body was as discomfiting as his expression. "You don't get it, do you?" The brackets around his mouth deepened with his scowl.

She could feel his disappointment because it was hers, too, and the air was thick with it. "I came here to talk, not...this—" She gestured between them. "You're forgetting the last time I attempted a relationship, my boyfriend was murdered."

He touched her shoulders and guided her backward until her legs hit a chair. With a nudge of his hands, he sat her in it. Then he dropped on his knees between her feet and pulled at the hem of her shirt at her hips until it covered her thighs. That last gesture made her want to yank out her heart and hand it to him. She was an idiot.

"And you're forgetting I lost you once. I won't let you out of my sight again. I have one of the highest trained security teams in the country. The safest place for you to be is at my side."

The suggestion was noble. And ridiculous. "Will I stand on stage with you in front of thousands of people while you perform?"

He glared at her and she realized the crater in her argument. Jay Mayard didn't stand on stage. He sang from the shadows despite his fans' dismay.

"I owe Nathan Winslow an apology. When I scrape up what's left of my ego, I'll give him one." He interlaced his hands with hers. "He's a fucking hero."

Her hackles went up. "Don't—"

"I'm not being flippant, Charlee. I mean it. He rescued you, and as much as I want to kill him, he's my fucking hero, too. I got to tell you that's hard to compete with."

Why wasn't he badgering her with questions about Roy? Maybe he wasn't ready to ruin their reunion by grounding them in her ugly reality. "There's nothing romantic between Nathan and I."

Little lines fanned from the corners of his squinting eyes. "I saw you in bed together."

She sighed. "We've been sharing a bed for three years. We're on the run. We're scared. We don't leave each other's sight, okay? Not even to sleep."

The disbelief was still there in his eyes.

"As far as I know, he hasn't been laid in a long damned time." The reminder squeezed her chest. He deserved so much more than what she'd condemned him to.

"Then I really find it hard to believe that he sleeps next to you without feeling something."

Her heart tripped. "When we share that bed, Noah's there between us. Always."

The tightness in his face ebbed. "Did you love him?"

An ugly mess of emotions balled in her throat. "Not enough."

28

Jay looked down at their joined hands, his pulse a fuzzy squish in his ears.

Not enough.

He knew Charlee carried guilt over Noah's death, but if she'd loved him, she would've known.

In the years that separated them, he'd written dozens of songs. Every creation bloomed from his memories of her and the emotions those memories stirred. "You can't control love. It's like creating music."

That brought her eyes up to his. "How so?"

"Love is like a series of improbable, lonely notes landing together in meaningful chaos. Where every channel carries a rhythm that conveys an expression of emotion. It doesn't feel flat or fake or hollow. It's not exaggerated with overtones. The complexity might feel organized, but the creation is never controlled."

Her eyes were huge blue portholes. She untangled her hands from his and reached a tentative one toward his face. The movement was a slow climb, allowing him time to welcome it or intervene.

The thought of her touching him produced a clash of feelings in his gut. He wanted to get fucking lost beneath the slide of her hands, but his reaction to touch was involuntary. His trigger would scare her away, even as he wished more than anything it would be different with her.

He caught her hand inches from his face, turned it, and pressed the backs of her fingers to his cheek.

She leaned into his hold, accepting the compromise. "What are your demons, Jay?"

A prickle lit his skin. "That's a limit."

"Talking about your demons is a limit?"

For a moment, he couldn't shake the grip of the old shack. He saw his aunt's deserted eyes and felt the stiff way she touched him.

The fingers against his face nudged him, pulling him back to the present. "Yeah." His voice cracked. "That's a limit."

"What are your other limits?"

How could he convince them both they could be together when they couldn't share the simplest thing? "No hands."

"No hands where?" Her eyes flicked to her own hand resting against his cheek.

He sighed and lowered their arms to her lap. "Anywhere."

Her auburn brows gathered. "Then how—"

"I had control of the touch. I put your fingers on my face and kept hold of them."

She sat there, taking it in, becoming infected with it. She was probably jumping to the next logical question. What would sex be like with a man she couldn't embrace?

She blinked. "Can I touch your toenail?"

He stared at her in stunned silence.

"Or your nose? Can I touch the tip?" She squinted, and her lips bowed downward.

So fucking cute. "I don't know how to respond to that."

She was so still, studying his nose, her hands cupped in his. "How do you not know?"

His laugh stumbled out, as awkward and confused as he was. "No one has ever tried to touch my nose."

"You're making fun of me."

"Maybe."

"Then let me touch it. The teensy-weensy tip."

The challenge in her tone suspended him in a moment of lucidity. Wonderful things were going to happen with this girl. She would push him. Maybe even fix him. If his nightmares chased her away, though, if she ran out the door, his existence would go up in an inferno.

He shook his head. "It could flip a switch. I don't want to chance it."

Women fixated on him all the time with intense wide eyes, wanting things from him. Never had a woman stared at him like that, as Charlee did then, wanting things *for* him.

"What would happen if we tried it?" She wiggled the finger laced with his.

He knew she was testing him with that minute movement against his hand, but his trigger was unpredictable. "Remember the guy curled up on the floor in the dining room?"

She pursed her lips. "Yeah. Okay, better not then." Her eyes lowered to his nose as if she wasn't ready to let it go.

That decided it. He would confront the thing that made him like this. He would become a man she could hold, despite his tattered and worn edges. First, he needed to know more about the man who hurt her. "Who took you, Charlee?"

She withdrew her hands and squared her shoulders, but the abused girl emerged in the falter of her breath. "Roy Oxford."

Did he hear her right? "Roy Oxford?"

She slumped in the chair and let her head fall against the upholstery, turning to look out the window. Maybe to watch the haughty metropolis bustling below. Maybe to avoid his eyes.

"Not the Roy Oxford of Oxford Industries?"

"The same."

"What?" He leapt to his feet. "He's like the most powerful man in the world. How is that even possible?"

"That's exactly how it's possible."

He walked the circumference of the room in an attempt to work off his overloaded nerves. With the band's fame and money, he was accustomed to getting whatever he wanted. But Roy Oxford? Fuck.

Heat swelled through his face. He wanted to hit something. He wanted to destroy the dickhead who raped and hurt her. Deep inhale. Focus on the facts.

He turned to her to ask why a billionaire would kidnap a woman, but looking at her, he had his answer. A man could lose himself in those eyes, those sinful lips. He could become, not a man at all, but a thing controlled by possessiveness and desire. Hadn't he decided himself only moments before that he'd never let her go?

He yanked on his hair and strode to the door. Nathan stood post on the other side.

Fuck him, but he admired the man even more for watching over her like that. "Will you join us? I'd like to have a word."

"You've calmed your cocaine-fried spaz attack?"

He ground his teeth. In truth, the crash should've lasted hours. "Charlee might've helped with that."

Their glares collided, and Nathan's arrogant chin hardened beneath the stubble. "Charlee is a remedy for many of life's problems. The people in hers have taken advantage of that. If I find you're one of them, I will kill you."

The comment hurt, but it was honest and heartfelt. "I expect nothing less."

"Tell me, Jay, what is it exactly you do expect?" Nathan crossed his arms. "She's not the kind of girl you fuck and forget."

A rash of anger pumped through his muscles as he stepped into

Nathan, toe-to-toe. At comparable heights, they might've touched noses, but Jay seemed to rise an inch taller with indignation alone. "I didn't have to *fuck* her to never forget her, and you better hope to God you can say the same."

A flinch jerked Nathan's head back. "No. I mean yes. Jesus, she's like my sister." He dragged his fingernails up and down the back of his head. "You should know that she's relationship-ignorant. If that's what you're after, you're wasting your time."

Jay held his position in Nathan's face. "Insult her again. Do it." His fists clenched at his sides, his voice shaking. "I fucking dare you."

Nathan looked away, pushed past him through the door and went straight to her.

Jay tried not to lose his shit when she rose from the chair and they bowed their heads together, whispering and nodding. When Nathan removed a small handgun from his boot and positioned it at the small of her back, Jay's tolerance pulsated at the end of an unraveling rope. He appreciated the necessity for the gun, but the man didn't have to shove it down her pants.

The territorial tension taking hold of him didn't dissuade him, but he worried how she would perceive it.

Nathan studied her hands, her expressions. Not her mouth as Jay would've done. There was a measure of closeness between them, united in their suffering and in their need for revenge. He also knew with certainty, as Nathan clutched her arm and patted it, the threshold of intimacy had not been crossed. Finally, their eyes shifted to him.

Jay released a breath of conflicting emotions. Confident their relationship was platonic, his stomach twisted over where he would fit in. Dipping his head, he palmed his nape, unsure how to begin. *Just fucking say it.* He found Nathan's eyes. "I owe you an apology. I misjudged you. I was an asshole and I'm sorry." Sincerity softened his voice.

Nathan's eyebrows shot to his hairline. Then a mask fell over his expression. He nodded and released Charlee's squirming arm.

She walked toward Jay, her eyes like still lakes, glassy and fathomless. She blinked, and they rippled, smiling. She was stunning in her approach, holding her hands out to him, a gentle sway in her hips.

He caught her fingers, pulled her close, and didn't miss the devilish twitch in her cheek. "What?"

"Come here." Her gaze dropped to his mouth.

His heart skipped, and he lowered his head. A breath away, she shifted her lips up and planted a wet one on the tip of his nose.

She didn't give him time to recover, spinning out of his arms and disappearing in the closet. The sneaky little—

A cabinet door slammed. What was she up to? "What are you doing in there?"

"I'm commandeering some shorts." A drawer squeaked. "Oh, for pity's sake. You wear tighty-whities? With superheroes?" She was louder than she needed to be, and so full of shit.

A chuckle rolled across the room. Nathan reclined in the chair, arms crossed over his chest. Then his smile retreated, replaced with a watchful mien. "You wanted a word."

Jay bowed his head and looked toward the closet, toward his purpose. "Tell me about Roy Oxford."

29

Charlee lingered in the doorway of the closet, calling to mind a history lesson in her short high school career. The lecture on the Thirteenth Amendment to the U.S. Constitution hadn't meant much to her then. She'd been too young and naive to appreciate the abolishment of slavery. Yet, the conversation circulating around her was laden with references to a runaway slave, indentured servitude, and ownership. Nathan and Jay didn't use those terms, but the connotations were there, forever haunting her waking and sleeping existence.

Hiding her story from Noah had been a detrimental mistake, one she wouldn't make again. When Jay's questions dug in, she nodded at Nathan to field them. She tuned out most of it as he unfolded the ugliest details. Craig Grosky, Noah's death, the maiming of Roy's henchmen, the stockroom, the surveillance, and Henry Munt, who was Nathan's client and Roy's blackmailer.

The whites of Jay's eyes glowed out his taut crimson face. "How did Roy Oxford find you in St. Louis?"

She looked at Nathan. "We think the man who issued my fake identity documents connected me to Roy, or maybe Roy tracked him down. Either way, he sold Roy my Sarah Teves identity." She shrugged. "Nathan hasn't been able to locate him."

He turned to Nathan, his anger whipping around him. "How did you kill off Sarah Teves after she went missing?"

"I leveraged Noah's connections on the force. I was at the crime scene and my employees were involved in every step of the investigation, flubbing paperwork along the way. I knew who had Charlee and closing the case on her alias prevented government red tape from slowing down her rescue."

Jay prowled along the windows, back and forth, his nostrils flaring tension through the room. "Is that why the FBI isn't involved?"

"The bureau isn't involved for the same reason they're not

patrolling his arms trafficking activities." Nathan kicked a foot over his bent knee. "He owns too many inside."

"There can't be that many corrupt public officials. How do you know this?"

She stepped in his path. "Roy has been in and out of my life for nine years. I spent every minute with him from age sixteen to eighteen during my first captivity. I ran for four years after that. Until the night I met you." Her voice rasped. "Three years ago."

The red around his eyes mirrored her grief over the long separation.

She cleared her throat. "Roy was more lax with me before my first escape, careless with his conversations. I don't know names and doubt they would be authentic anyway, but his connections are deep. He owns a lot of people, Jay."

"Stop using that word. He doesn't own you. He never will."

Her chest tightened under the weight of his assertion, but her voice remained light. "This isn't your problem."

He went deadly still. She couldn't see it or hear it, but she could feel it bump over her skin and raise the hairs on her neck. A storm was coming, and she needed to calm it. "What are you doing today?"

"Whatever you're doing." He glared at her.

Crazy obsessive man. His unwavering focus should've been choking her oxygen. Instead, it enveloped her in a warm blanket. There was well-meant intention beneath his brand of crazy, the kind she would survive and possibly even savor. "I've got a tattoo to do."

The storm rotated around him and settled on his face, swishing in his eyes and parting his lips. "*My* tattoo."

She grinned. "It's three years overdue."

He fisted her hair and covered her mouth with his. She could feel his excitement in the hard pushes of his tongue. She captured it, responded to it with rolling thrusts in his mouth, and felt her own excitement curling her fingers. What would it be like to grab his ass and pull him closer? She dug her nails into her thighs.

The door snicked with Nathan's retreat and reminded her that she was wobbling on unsteady ground. She broke the kiss with a lick of his upper lip and smiled up at him. "Wow. I didn't want that to stop."

He stroked a thumb over her lips, his own puffy and wet. "Then why did you?"

Because her emotions were running loose and entangling dangerously with those of a world-touring rock star. Because she didn't know if he still meant to keep her at his side, and she didn't know how she felt about that. “Because Laz said you were heading back to L.A. tonight, so we should get started on your ink.” Her face began to fall at the thought of him leaving, but she tried to keep it blank.

“Why are these here?” He traced the vertical lines between her eyebrows.

Her heart thumped as she looked at him. His beautiful talented lips turned down at the corners. The canvas of his body called to her artist’s fingers. And within all that tanned skin contained an artist too, a brilliant musician and singer. “I’m feeling a little clingy. It’s embarrassing. I don’t want you to go yet.”

He grinned, popping a dimple through the shadow of his whiskers, and turned toward the door. “Clingy is perfect because you’re coming home with me.”

So he meant what he said. She ran to catch up with him. “I can’t just—”

“I’ll work out the details with Nathan and Tony.” He opened the door and hollered, “Where’s the butler? Charlee needs her clothes.” He looked back at her. “Where are your tattoo supplies?”

“At our apartment in the Village.” Could she just pack up and go with him? She and Nathan moved every few months, and he hated New York. But L.A. was so very close to San Francisco—

“Anything else you need to bring with you?”

How dangerous it was to consider going with him. “I can’t just leave. I’ll have to discuss this with Nathan.”

“He’s coming with us.”

“He has a business here. If he wants to go, he’ll have to close it and I’m not leaving without him.” Her excitement to stay with Jay battled with her fear of being so close to the penthouse.

“Trust me.” He was still smiling, but his eyes were quiet and sober.

“I don’t know.”

The smile vanished. “You will.”

Tony knocked on the open door, holding a stack of folded clothes. “Looks like he got the vomit out.” Not a smile cracked.

“I’m going to ignore that comment. Who’s on duty right now?”

“Colson and Vanderschoot.”

“Send Colson to Charlee’s apartment. Tell him to pack what he can.”

Was he nuts? Even if she agreed to go, she’d do her own packing. Besides, he didn’t have her address. “Jay—”

A finger slanted across her lips and pressed. His hand at the back of her head reinforced the gesture. Then his eyes twinkled. Oh, fine, but shushing her like a child? Seriously?

Tony narrowed her eyes. “Are you extending your stay at the Plaza Hotel?”

“No, she and Nathan are accompanying us to L.A.”

She wanted to smack his hand away. Since touching him was off limits, she darted out her tongue and licked the finger at her lips. When his head swung around, his eyes wide on her, she bit down.

“Ow.” He yanked his hands back, holding his finger, his expression wounded. “I’m beginning to grow wary of that mouth.”

“Now that I have your attention, you big baby, here’s my terms, my…constitution.”

His jaw hardened.

“*I* am going to go pack up my tattoo kit and bring it back here. *We* can discuss next steps over tattoos and crumpets.” She accepted her clothes from Tony. “And I’m using your shower.”

“Can I pass two amendments to the Charlee Constitution?” His face molded into starchy formality despite the teasing in his voice.

“I’ll hear them.”

“First Amendment. I join you to collect your supplies.”

Could they get in and out without a celebrity circus? He did have a top-notch protective team on his payroll. “The fourth clause in the ninth section of the first article states that at no time will paparazzi or screaming women waving camera phones accompany me in on this mission.”

“Done. Second Amendment. Can we have pizza instead of crumpets?”

A snort escaped before she could catch it. “Approved.”

He called after her as she shut herself inside the bathroom. “What the hell is a crumpet anyway?”

“A tasty little muffin.”

Silence. Then his voice muffled through the door. “Does it have red hair and blue eyes?”

Her cheeks puffed with contained laughter. The cheesy bastard didn’t need encouragement.

Something thumped the door. Was that his head?

“I’ve changed my mind.” His voice vibrated the wood between them. “I want a crumpet.”

Her laugh escaped, echoing around her, and for the first time in a long time, she felt free.

30

A survival skill Jay picked up early in his stardom was his efficiency in quick disguises. He adjusted the long blond wig over his short brown hair until the fake bangs brushed the top of his big plastic framed sunglasses. A frayed Alice Cooper ball cap completed the concealment.

The bathroom door opened with an exhale of steam. Charlee padded out, straightening her black top over the waistband of her jeans. "I'm keeping your *Dead Milkmen* tee—" She tripped, staring at him with a slack jaw. "Shit. Garth Algar?"

"Who?"

"Never mind." She inspected his body from hat to Chucks with an amused cant to her eyebrows. Then she circled him, wrapping him in a sweet natural scent that was uniquely Charlee.

When she came back around, she was grinning and chewing a fingernail. "Jay Mayard's sexy ass is still back there, but the rest of him is incognito."

Just thinking about her noticing his ass made his dick jerk against his zipper. "This disguise hasn't failed me yet."

"Then you haven't tried to pick up women wearing that wig."

A laugh erupted from deep inside him. Dear God, it was so easy to want her. The way her cheeks glowed. The challenge in her eyes. The catch in her breath when he returned her stare. All the countless fucking reasons he never stopped craving her after she was gone. He dipped his head and brushed his lips over hers. "I've only tried to pick up one woman."

A wall of silence descended between them. He searched her eyes, unsure how to interpret her mute response. "Has it failed me?"

"Not yet." The level of resistance in her voice only fortified his resolve to scale her walls. He suspected she wanted to fight it, but maybe she was as drawn to him as he was to her.

A fist rapped on the door. "Charlee?"

"You can come in, Nathan." She didn't unlock her eyes from his glasses.

Nope, he was certain she couldn't ignore the pull. *That's right, baby. Don't fight it.*

Nathan strode in and dismissed the disguise with a brief smirk. "Tony and I worked out the drop-off and pick-up points and the best evacuation routes at the apartment. We're ready when you are."

The absence of bulges in Nathan's nondescript pants and button-up shirt meant his weapons were hidden. That kind of unobtrusiveness combined with his constant awareness of Charlee and her surroundings made him an ideal bodyguard. No doubt he'd piss in a store trash bin before he'd leave her unattended.

However, it was the instinctual way he placed himself between her and everything else that made him the only man Jay wanted leading the team he would hire to protect her. "I want to offer you a job."

Nathan glanced at her and back at him. There was no surprise in that gaze. "I have a job."

"This one would be the same. Just better paid."

Nathan's current income from odd PI assignments couldn't possibly be enough to fund his crusade in revenge.

The tic in Nathan's cheek confirmed it.

A toe poked the back of Jay's knee, her nudge teetering his balance. "I know what you're up to, Jay Mayard. The *three* of us will discuss this later."

Small, sexy, with her honeyed lips pouting, she refused to be managed. He tried not to think about the events that made her so defiant, but he respected the hell out of her for standing against him if he slipped in his efforts to *not* control her.

"Mr. Mayard." Tony poked her head in. "I summoned the car. It's waiting at the elevator in underground parking."

A ripple of panic bit along his spine. Time to leave his safe environment. His disguise hid his face, so there wouldn't be any grabbing and touching.

What if a gusty wind disheveled it and someone saw through? The mobs would rain down upon them and endanger her.

Would it be safer for her if he stayed behind? Too many things could happen to her. What if she didn't return?

Nope, she wasn't going anywhere without him. Still, the urge to sneak a couple snuffs off the inhaler in his pocket consumed him. Could he face the clutch of the crowds and the lurking unknowns without the numbing lift of coke?

Charlee clapped her hands and sashayed her heart-shaped ass to the door. "Let's go get some ink."

Yeah, he could do it.

For her.

31

The SUV stopped at the entrance of Charlee's building and sent Jay's heart hammering into the red zone. He squeezed the warm anchor in his hand.

Charlee curled her fingers around his, returning the squeeze. "You okay?"

A woman on the sidewalk slowed her gait to look at their car. He stopped breathing. Could she see through the windows?

Moments later, she turned her head and strode into a boutique two doors down.

Gah. The windows were blacked-out, for fuck's sake. He needed to calm down. "Everything will be fine."

"Is that response for me or you?"

"For you." His worries, his hopes, his fears were all for her. "Always, Charlee."

She opened her mouth and he muffled it with a quick kiss, surprising a smile from her.

Nathan twisted in the front seat to face them. He glanced at Tony, who perched on Jay's other side then rolled his gaze to Charlee. "Just like we discussed, okay?"

The protective team's extensive security precautions would be implemented first. Nathan would sweep the flat for intruders, tampering, and bugs. Once he deemed it sterile, he would radio to Tony to escort Jay and Charlee to the residence.

Charlee tapped the heel of her Doc Martens on the floorboard. "We should go in together. We always go in together." Her nerves pulsed through Jay, echoing his own.

Jay settled his hand on her knee and quieted the bobbing. "You have three times the bodyguards right now. After your exposure with the paparazzi last night, the danger is heightened. We'll follow protocol. They know what they're doing."

Nathan smiled his thanks and stepped onto the cracked pavement with Tony on his trail. She split off and traversed in the opposite direction to clear the rear and side entrances. Her jeans were meant to help her blend in, but they did nothing to conceal her alert and professional air.

Storied buildings lined the veritable Greenwich Village thoroughfare. Commercialization occupied the street level flats and residents inhabited the floors above. Jay had never visited this end of the city and his unfamiliarity with the area didn't help his anxiety.

Her building was four stories, veneered with laddered scaffolding, and surrounded by enormous old trees. Without much traffic, it should be a seamless in and out. Yeah, he'd keep telling himself that.

Colson, his secondary driver and bodyguard, parked in the side lot and stepped out to stand by Charlee's door.

She turned to Jay. "Is this how life is for you? Bodyguard formations and perimeter sweeping every time you want to go somewhere?"

One of the many reasons he never wanted to leave his safe zone. "I should ask you the same question."

"Point made." She looked out the window, her eyes darting between Colson's post and Tony's movements around the building. "Though my excursions are a bit more economical."

Not anymore. She would have everything needed to stay safe.

He patted his wig, hat and sunglasses. Everything was where it should be. The street was calm. The security team was thorough. Then why was his pulse racing?

"You have a look about you."

How could she see anything behind his sunglasses? "What kind of look?"

"The kind of look your fans have at the ticket booth when they find out your show is sold out."

Disappointment? Indifference? He shook his head.

"Fear and aggression."

Jesus, she was perceptive. "I don't like public places and crowds."

"Ah. Crowds with hands." She gnawed the corner of her thumbnail. "How do you deal with concerts and public interviews and red-carpet stuff?"

"I avoid them when I can."

Stillness settled over her. She stared at her hand in his, her eyes weighted with thought. "When you walked into my shop three years ago, you didn't have security to protect you. How'd you maneuver the crowds then?"

Very carefully. His mouth crooked up. "No one knew or cared who I was then."

She nodded. "When you came to me that night, you brought me a hopeful vision. Want to hear it?" She looked at him beneath her lashes.

He tucked a lock of hair behind her ear to see her face. "Very much."

"This might sound silly, but I envisioned you on stage in a crowded arena proudly baring your tattoo. The tattoo I hoped you'd grow to appreciate. The one I hope to finish."

A collision of emotions accumulated in his throat.

"I lost so much the night I met you, but I hung onto that image. It got me through some of the tough parts, you know?"

"Jesus, Charlee." He cupped her jaw and lifted her forehead to rest against his.

"Someday soon, I want to see you singing at the center of the stage instead of from its darkest corner."

Could he do that for her?

"With your shirt off."

He bit down on his tongue to stay the refusal.

"What about the live shows? How do you deal with it? Even if you aren't visible, you're there, singing and playing in front of thousands."

Admit it and fix it. She deserved nothing less. "I use blow, Charlee."

She removed her forehead from his and replaced it with her lips. "Getting lit on stage is not cool." Another kiss to his brow and she leaned back to meet his eyes. "I guess we both have our fucked up self-therapies, huh?"

A shudder gripped him. This woman survived slavery and untold abuse and rape. "How did you escape hell with no mental or physical damage?"

She let out a mirthless laugh and released his hand to mime swinging a baseball bat. "Ol' Roy was proficient at caning. He knew how to hit without scarring." She dropped her hands and a cold deadness hollowed her eyes, her voice. "And he brought in a plastic surgeon to erase wounding cuts when he slipped." She touched a spot under her thigh and leaned forward to drag a finger over one butt cheek.

The muscles in his face and neck became painfully tense. Calm the fuck down. She was speaking openly about it. He needed to openly listen.

"And these—" She tapped her front teeth "—are porcelain crowns."

A red fog clouded his vision and he clenched his hands.

"There are scars you haven't seen. From the vaginal and rectal tearing."

His fist slammed into the seat in front of him, again and again.

"Jay, stop." She twisted her head toward the door where Colson stood, facing the lot and ignoring Jay's rage like a good bodyguard.

He couldn't hit hard enough, couldn't obliterate her words or the images ripping out his heart.

"Stop, stop, stop." Her voice chanted through him.

He reared back for another hit and glimpsed her out of the corner of his eye. She curled against the door with her eyes closed. Oh, Charlee.

He shoved his hands beneath her thighs and back and dragged her into his lap.

Her arms hugged her belly and her face lowered to his neck. "I didn't mean to upset you."

"*You* didn't, Charlee. *He* did."

She burrowed her shoulder into the curve of his and pressed her lips to his throat. "My instinct is to bury it all, but I know how damaging that is." She leaned back, narrowed her eyes at him. "So I've disciplined myself to keep it exposed, with Nathan anyway, since I can't talk about it with anyone else. I guess I just unloaded on you."

He wanted to be her confidant, not hero-fucking-Nathan. The urge to demand that from her tensed his muscles and tangled in his throat. "Does it help? To keep it on the surface?"

"Sometimes."

He envied her. She was incredible. If he freed his shadows from their hiding places in his mind, they would devour him.

"I have other...therapies."

"Tell me."

A deep breath. "Are you familiar with the fetish communities?"

Fetish? Like leather crops and ball gags? He wasn't aware of wearing a meaningful expression, but it incited her to lean away and look out the window.

"Shouldn't Nathan be radioing in by now?" She chewed on a nail and tapped her boot. Her eyes fixated on a car parked across the way, but they were unfocused, lost in her head.

He gathered her closer in his arms, cradling her small frame with his thighs. It was an impregnable feeling, like hugging his Martin hollow body guitar, only this sensation was fuller, warmer, and to his surprise, more complete. She was meant to be there. "Their perimeter preparations take thirty to forty minutes. They usually arrive ahead of me to do it." He raised her chin with his knuckle. "Tell me about the fetish thing."

She glanced at the dents in the seatback in front of them. "Promise me you'll let me finish what I have to say before you react."

A swell of adrenaline surged through his veins. Fuck, this was going to piss him off. "I promise."

She reached up, careful not to let her fingers brush his face, and removed his sunglasses. "And no more fists. Got it?"

He nodded, unsure.

"I hire professional—"

Knuckles rapped on the window and the door opened. Tony ducked her head in. "We're ready."

A shout seethed in his throat. He drew it into his lungs with a deep inhale and leveled his voice. "Wait outside."

"Yes, Mr. Mayard." She shut the door.

Charlee bent forward to move off his lap, and he stopped her with an arm across her waist. "We're not done."

A frown wrinkled the sweet little spot below her lips. "We should—"

"They'll wait. You hire professional..."

She slumped against him with a sigh. "Dominants." She raised her eyes, holding his captive. "I pay experienced BDSM players for sessions in private and rented dungeons."

His heart rammed against his ribs. *Let me finish what I have to say before you react.*

He had a damn good idea what dungeons were, but he wanted to be very clear what they meant to her. "What happens in *your* sessions?"

"I pre-negotiate the boundaries each time."

His face heated, and his breathing sped up. "And those are?"

"It would be easier to list the limits, but if you're not familiar with the lifestyle..." Her smile quivered then fell when he didn't return it. "My typical scene includes shackles, crops, paddles, whips, ch...chains, clamps, and oral and vaginal intercourse."

Every word stabbed his heart anew, slicing away piece by bleeding piece. "You let these...men have sex with you?" The question tore from his burning chest.

She held his gaze. "They're simulated rape scenes." Her voice was so soft he tilted his head to hear her, wishing he hadn't.

His composure was slipping, his volume elevating. "Why would you do that?"

She closed her eyes and pressed her face in his neck. "To reenact the things Roy did to me. I set up the scene and have control of it every step of the way. I know I'm damaged, Jay. I get that, but—"

"Charlee."

"Let me finish." Her jaw hardened against his shoulder. "Those scenes help me restructure my feelings about what happened. They allow me to be in charge of the things he did, the punishments. The rapes. I always end the scene before the Dom does." She let out a breath, warming his throat. "I use my safe word like a weapon."

It was a harsh and penetrating moment of comprehension. How many times had he relived his first trip back to his land in the Canadian Boundary Waters, when he burned down the old shed and the cruel shadows within? Contracting a cabin to be built in its place, one with sunny rooms and walls of windows, had given him a sense of control over his memories. Someday, he'd have the strength of will and mind to live there.

Hired bondage was Charlee's cabin. In a fucked up way, her methods made sense, but the risks were glaring. "How do you trust these people? I can't believe Nathan would—"

Her head shot up, her eyes like blue flames. "He doesn't like it, but he's supportive. He investigates every person I hire. And after three years and a dozen cities, I've accumulated a very reliable portfolio of references."

Images of calloused kinky men beating and fucking her corroded his ability to identify with her solution. She had options. She had *him*. "I get it, Charlee. I do. And I want you to trust me."

A startled look softened her jaw.

"Hang on. I know for that to happen, I need to prove to both of us that *I* trust *you*." He removed his arms from her waist and stretched them along the back of the seat. Maybe he was delaying exiting the car. Maybe he was out of his mind, but he wanted her wrapped around him in a way he'd never allowed anyone before. "Straddle me."

32

Silence. So dense it weighted the air in Charlee's lungs. Straddle him?

Jay's palm slid up her spine, raising bumps there, and returned to the back of the seat. A pulse of reckless want built up between them. Looking at his beautiful face, feeling that momentary comfort of his hand along her back, it was a glimmer of promise that left her burning for more.

Roy had stolen so much from her, but her desire to touch and be touched was still embedded deep within her. She hungered for physical closeness, in friendship or otherwise. "This will be a much more intimate position."

His brown eyes clung to her like slow-moving molasses. "Exactly."

Good lord, his sexiness issued from the purr of his voice, the dimple in his cheek, the lazy way his Adam's apple nodded in his throat, and his vulnerability with touching. Hell, even wearing the stupid wig, he was tempting. She closed her eyes to break the trance.

"What are you thinking?" Warm exhales steamed against her lips.

She opened her eyes and found him watching her from inches away, stealing her breath. "Your security team is waiting for us."

A flex rippled through his arms. He didn't spare a glance at Colson and Tony, their backs to the SUV, keeping a vigil on the empty parking lot.

"We're safe and in no hurry." He bit his bottom lip, staring at hers. "Whenever you're ready. My arms will stay here." He patted the headrests on either side of him. "To prove to myself I don't need to restrain you from touching me."

The discussion about moving her to L.A. waited for them at the hotel. If she was going to consider his offer, they should feel comfortable enough to trust each other in this small thing.

Besides, he was so inviting, sitting there, chewing his lip, she wanted to close the distance just to lick where his teeth were.

She tossed his sunglasses on the seat and slid off his lap. He wasn't a big man, but his presence was formidable, exuding potency and overwhelming the space around him. He moved his legs closer together and kept his arms outstretched, watching her, waiting.

Slowly, she placed a knee on the seat beside his hip and reached overhead, bracing her palms on the roof.

Curiosity nudged her. She wanted to pursue this connection with him, had to know where it would take her. She swung her other leg over his and hugged his narrow lap with her knees. A foot of emptiness separated their groins. Almost there.

He was motionless beneath her with his head tilted back and his eyes on hers.

The strength of his gaze tingled her cheeks and prodded her to close the distance. Would he trust her if she put her hands behind her back where he couldn't see them? Could she trust herself to leave them there?

"Closer, Charlee." He stretched his neck and opened his mouth for hers.

She pressed her hands to the roof and dipped her head. The gap was too great for a full kiss. His tongue stretched, and the tip teased hers, coaxing a quiver in her inner thigh. The touches slid into licks and their tongues tangled through wet greedy pants. They arched toward one another, and her hands on the roof became fingertips, slipping.

He nipped at her bottom lip and missed. "You taste so fucking good. Come here." He bucked his hips, but the space between them prevented contact.

Straining toward him as she was, her fingers teetered on the ceiling. Her noisy breaths matched his, making her question her sanity.

In the confines of Roy's penthouse, she experienced sexual desire against her will. But Noah taught her how to want it and the professional Doms showed her how to develop it.

She craved affection above all, and despite Jay's limitation on touch, he gave tenderness in the dance of his tongue, the softness of his tone, and the way he looked at her as if he adored her. Even more, he was stretched out beneath her, willing her to explore with anything but her hands.

She lowered herself onto his lap until her fingers lost their hold on the roof. The contact of his arousal against her pussy stole her breath. She wanted to cup his gorgeous face and bury her tongue in his mouth, but she held her palms up and away. “No hands, but arms are okay, right? Just like the piggyback ride?”

A raw unquiet stirred in the cab. His body hardened and vibrated around them. His voice hushed through the tension. “I’ll keep my shit tight. I promise.”

The steadiness in his eyes chased away any doubt she might’ve had. He would probably chew off his fist before he used it against her.

She draped her arms over his shoulders and dangled her hands behind the seat. “This okay?”

“Yeah.” He arched his hips against her and the leather creaked. “Fuck, I want you closer. Relax your legs.”

She let gravity press her down, mold her body into his. The warmth of his chest soaked into hers and she knew in that moment, it would kill her to let him go.

33

Their heartbeats paced the stillness between them. Charlee savored the dips and cuts of Jay's body against hers, his heavy-lidded eyes, and his breath panting through parted lips.

Sunlight filtered through the tinted windows. The silent sentries stood motionless outside the car, watching the traffic on the street and surrounding buildings. Apparently, when Jay told them to wait, they did so with patience.

Beneath her, his muscles began to relax. She traced her nose along the hard line of his throat, rousing a low-pitched rumble in his chest. He tilted his head to give her more room and a spicy, earthen aroma flavored her inhales. She retraced the path with her tongue, continued the lazy tour over his jaw, and into his waiting mouth.

His sharp inhale stole her breath, and he crushed their lips together. The kiss was hungry and jaw stretching, and her heart thudded as if it would burst from her chest. He chased her licks in his mouth and curved his body into hers as much as his arms on the seatback would allow.

She moved her mouth to his nose and he flinched. She laughed. "I won't bite." The bright white of his smile and the intensity in his eyes made her chest ache to move closer. "Still good?"

His pupils dilated, and his shoulders strained toward her. "Never been this good, Charlee. Come back here." He raised his mouth in invitation.

Wow. It really was just the hands he had a problem with. Groin to groin, chest to chest, she shifted her boots from the outside of his knees to the inside, using her toes to open his legs. She rubbed her body along his, sliding her tongue over his bottom lip. It *did* feel good. "I think we passed the test. You trust me not to put my hands on you, and I trust you not to take my control."

The erection trapped in his leather pants jerked between them.

He seemed oblivious to it as he regarded her with dark unsmiling eyes. "To be trusted by you is the greatest compliment I've ever received."

She melted into him and his body pulsed against her. She wanted to free him from the confines of his pants and work them both into a mindless fog where boundaries didn't exist. "I feel the same way, Jay, and all I can think about is..." She caught his ear lobe between her lips, drew it into her mouth, and released it with a pop. "How I could fuck you like thi—"

His hands flew off the seatback, grabbed the back of her head, and yanked her mouth to his. Rough and penetrating, he ate at her lips, his teeth scraping and nibbling, his hips grinding. She opened for him and met the thrusts in her mouth and the rocking of his body, trembling against the fervor bolting through her.

Despite his aggression, there was a measure of restraint between kisses. She pulled back to test it. He allowed the slack, his gaze tracking the roll of her swollen lips as he gasped through his own.

The freedom to stop and start ignited something inside her. She wanted him, wanted to surrender to him. A slow throb kindled and warmed between her legs. She dove at his mouth, submitting to the strength of his jaw and the urgency of his tongue.

The car filled with his breathy moans and the squeak of leather. His hands shook as they traveled to her neck then her shoulders, and separated. One moved up to tangle in her hair as the other pushed down her spine to rest over the crack of her butt. "Where's your gun?"

Arousal trembled through her limbs, cranking her hips, and curling her fingers. "Moved it to my messenger bag." She peppered kisses on his wet lips, the sculpted contour of his jaw, and the arch of his fevered cheek. She lingered over his eyelid, brushing her lips along the delicate skin. He was so soft there, so unlike the rest of him. "I want to touch you so badly."

A low groan escaped from deep within him. He dropped his head back and stared at her with his mouth hanging open. "I want that, Charlee. More than anything." He shoved his hands through her hair and gathered it off her face. "Do you have any idea how beautiful you are grinding on me and looking at me like that?"

Only a man would define grinding as beautiful. Holding his eyes, she rotated her hips once, twice—

He gripped her thighs and the sinews in his neck bulged against the skin. "Christ. Okay, stop. I'm about to embarrass myself."

"I'd like to see that." She smiled, and the blissful feeling panicked her. How could she let herself want someone so unobtainable? He was a celebrity and she was on the run. He had some kind of fucked up tactile defensiveness and drug issues, and she didn't have the background or expertise to deal with it. Yet, all the shitty circumstances faded away as he leaned in and took her mouth.

A vibration buzzed in her pocket. Creases bracketed his scowl as she slid off his lap and tugged out her phone. "It's Nathan." She gave him a shaky smile and hit *Answer*. "Hey."

"Everything okay? Tony said you haven't left the car yet."

Jay slipped his fingers into the neck of her shirt and caressed the outline of her collarbone. A chill raced up her spine and she sighed. "Are we in a hurry?"

"I'm packing our shit. I assumed you'd be helping."

What? They were there to grab her tattoo supplies only. "You're packing?"

"Yeah, Charlee. I'm packing. We're going, if not to L.A., then somewhere. I just got the call. Photos of you and Laz have started popping up faster than my guys can delete them."

The folly of the previous night flashed through her mind, suffocating her with replays of the restaurant, the cameras, and their overnight at the hotel. Roy controlled Craigs all over the country. She knew without a doubt he had thugs in New York. The photos linked her to *The Burn,* and if Roy knew where the band stayed, Jay would not only be targeted... "We could've been followed from the hotel."

"We watched for tails, didn't see any. But, yeah, we could've been followed. I'd prefer you stay in the car. I just wanted to check on you."

She didn't want him in the apartment alone. Not with their whereabouts broadcasted all over the Internet. Damn. Double damn. That restaurant was only a few blocks away. She should've been up there with him, watching his back. "I'm on my way up."

She hung up on him, pocketed the phone, and faced the deep dark night of Jay's eyes. It was so fucking painful, having to distance herself from people she cared about to keep them safe. A familiar loneliness spread out around her, cold and harrowing. Pushing Jay away would propel her further into that cavernous pit. Her hatred for Roy tunneled through her like poison, seething in her gut, tightening muscles, and burning her eyes.

She met Jay by chance the first time. Destiny brought them together a second time. If one were to believe in such a thing, perhaps they would find each other again. She needed him alive for that to happen, and the best way to ensure that was to stay the hell away from him. She had to believe it wasn't too late. If she separated herself from the band immediately, Roy would leave them alone.

Goddammit, this was going to hurt. "I'm heading up to meet Nathan." A red-hot burn seized her throat. "Alone." She grabbed her messenger bag, slipped his sunglasses inside it, and opened the door.

He reached for her, crawling after her. "Wait. I'm coming—"

"*You* are going back to the hotel, back to L.A." She stepped away from the door and put as much toughness as she could gather into her glare. "*That's* my decision." All the yearning of their moments together swelled inside of her, weakening her knees, making her stumble.

"Bullshit." Spit sprayed from his shout. He shoved his hand over and between the seats, searching for the glasses. "Something happened. Who followed us?" He punched the seat. "Tony!"

Tony jogged from around the car and stuck her head in the door. "Yes, Mr. Mayard?"

"What the fuck is going on?" His yell rolled across the lot.

Backing away, Charlee strapped the bag across her chest and reached under the flap where she'd moved her Bodyguard 380. She secured her fingers around the grip and trigger guard. Colson watched her from his post by the car, but didn't follow.

A car motored by. Two young men exited a pizza shop across the street and walked the opposite direction. Rows of trees shaded the lot and furnished a living wall. They also provided an abundance of hiding spots.

"Colson," Jay shouted. "Stay with her."

The lot spread over what must've been two blocks. Charlee covered it as fast as she could run, flying over the concrete to the side of the building and putting the safety of its brick foundation at her back.

Four stories up, the roof was a stark flat horizon against the glaring sun. Heaps of leaves and garbage lined the back alley. There were so many places to lie in wait. The urge to run back to Jay's car made her legs tremble.

The alcove for the back entrance to her apartment was around the corner. She side-stepped along the building, back to the wall, paranoia spiking her heart rate. Jay would come after her as soon as he found something to cover his face. What could she say to convince him to leave? Think, think, think.

34

Jay pushed off the seat, shouldered past Tony, and sprinted across the parking lot. The endless pavement, the streak of passing cars, and the gathering crowd dimmed away.

Charlee huddled with her back against the corner of the building, her eyes on the trees that lined the back fence.

Someone moved behind the building, just feet from where she stood, but the angle of the corner probably shielded the movement from her view.

Jay rubbed his eyes, his legs burning. The profile of a man shifted toward the corner where she lingered. The man's walk seemed off, unnaturally stealthy, and too zeroed in on that damned corner.

"Charlee! Behind you." Jay's wig shifted sideways as he dodged a parked car.

The stalker reached inside his jacket. A black metal barrel flashed.

"Charlee! Charlee!" Jay ripped off the wig and tossed it, where it hit the man flanking him as he ran. "Goddammit, Colson, I told you to stay with her."

"The perimeter's not safe." The older man gasped, maintaining Jay's pace.

Charlee slipped around the bend and out of his sight.

"Charlee, no!" The scream barreled from his chest, and he ran harder, faster.

The race to her building was the longest moment in his life, one in which timing and speed could change everything. His heart thundered, his muscles heated, and his legs wouldn't move fast enough.

Footfalls pounded after him. "Mr. Mayard," Tony shouted from his other side. "Go back to the vehicle."

The concrete blurred beneath his Chucks. He neared the side of the building and was slammed into it with the force of Tony's body.

Her chest pressed against his back, and her hands and gun on the brick caged him in. She bent her neck and shoved her face in his. "The threat isn't neutralized." Her gray eyes became steel cannons. "I need you out of the kill zone. Back. In. The vehicle."

Any other time, her look alone would've had him checking his pants for his balls. He bucked her off his back and skirted around her.

She shoved an arm out to block his forward motion. The downside of a top-notch bodyguard was her over-the-top-fucking-notch guarding.

"There's someone back there *with* Charlee. Move." He spiked the last word with venom.

Her lips peeled back in a snarl. "Argh!" She spun ahead of him and put her back to his chest, positioning his body behind the cover of hers. Her left hand hovered a wobble away from his hip. Her right aimed a Glock up and out in front of her. "Stay behind me."

Ahead of them, Colson led with his raised pistol, his other hand on the device in his ear as he spoke low into a mic. "This is Colson. Possible gun threat. The principal will not leave the kill zone. Need a mobile support team yesterday."

They inched forward, and Tony's hand brushed his leg. It was a haunting presence of his aunt's hand on tattered little boy briefs. He recoiled and grabbed his head against the images of the shed, the soiled mattress, and Aunt El's cruel smile.

He stumbled toward the corner of the building. Fight it. Focus on Charlee. Reaching into his pocket, he fingered the nasal bottle. A lift would sharpen his concentration, numb his trigger, and nourish his strength. Fuck, his grip on the present was spinning, darkening.

Tony crowded him, her nearness invading his focus and conjuring pollution from the sewer of his mind. He could taste the soot in the oven. He could hear the hollow reverberation of his aunt's mewling. *You'll stay in the Bolo until you warm up to me, little boy.*

A wall of hot ash and rust blackened the sun. Not now. Stop. Fucking stop. His fingers scraped uselessly on the brick building, on the Bolo oven's door. Charlee could be struggling, hurting, and he was fucking trapped, couldn't reach her. He fumbled with the inhaler from his pocket and huffed two burning squirts into each nostril.

The rush tipped his balance, and Tony caught his elbow. The sensation from her hand rippled over him, through him, like water. He was sailing, driven by the wind.

"Mr. Mayard?"

A strong sense of buoyancy sighed through his body, and the

mist of scared boyhood evaporated into the cloudless sky. Vigor pumped through his limbs and strengthened his spine. He broke away from Tony, racing past her. Urgency flogged his thoughts, pushing him faster, harder.

At the corner of the building, arms wrapped around him from behind and the ground dropped away from his feet.

The same old shit rose in him, but he was fueled now, his senses were armed to fight it. He threw his head back, colliding with Tony's. She grunted and released him.

He needed to catch up with Colson, who had already vanished around the corner. He held his fear tightly within him and burst into the rear alley.

At first, all he saw was the stiff back of Colson's shirt. Tony positioned herself in front of him, panting and steadying her gun. "Stay behind me."

Fuck that. He ran around her and froze.

At the farthest end of the building, a man faced Charlee where she stood with her back against the wall, the barrel of a handgun pressed against her jaw.

Rage buckled through him and dread knotted in his gut. He blinked against the sun beating down on him, whirling under weight of the sky and the buzz of cocaine.

The man looked his way, met his eyes. The wind beneath Jay's high dispersed and his nervous system crashed. Sweat slicked his palms and panic rode in on a wave of tremors.

If he ran toward them, would the fucker shoot her? Even with Tony and Colson aiming their guns behind him? Not a chance he would take.

Charlee's hand twisted in her bag. Was her hand on her gun? His heart panted with indecision.

The bag shifted. If she adjusted the angle right, could she point at the kneecap? Jay sucked in a breath. Not without the gun at her face going off.

The man jerked his head back to her and wrenched the bag strap from her chest, the barrel of his gun sliding over her cheek.

Jay ran toward them, air heaving from his lungs, and tension straining his muscles. Tony and Colson shouted his name, their footfalls trailing.

The man wrestled the strap over Charlee's head and Jay's panic unfurled in a roar. "Get the fuck away from her."

Wrinkles marred the unfamiliar Asian features. The barrel

twisted against her cheek, but his gaze turned to Jay.

The bag flew up with Charlee's hand wedged inside and paused at the man's chest. Jay's heart rate skyrocketed.

Boom. Boom.

35

The double gunshots stunned Jay in mid-stride, shattering his pace into a stumbling stagger. The man dropped to the ground, as did Charlee.

The echo of the blasts lingered in alley, ringing in Jay's ears. A river of red seeped from beneath her face where it lay on the man's chest. Not her blood. No, it couldn't be hers.

Hands shaking, heart roaring, he skidded beside them, fell upon his knees and pulled her into his arms. Was she hit? Breathing? Other than the spots of crimson dotting her chest, her shirt was free of bullet holes. Yet, she hung lifelessly in his embrace, eyes closed.

Blood caked one side of her face. It also puddled on the pavement. Streams of it trickled from the hole in the Asian man's chest, who lay on his back, unmoving.

Colson squatted and touched the meaty neck. "Dead."

The validation did nothing to soothe Jay's hammering heart. He let her legs drop to his lap as he groped for a pulse in her throat, uncertainty resonating in his constricting chest. Then he felt a steady thump against his fingers. He choked, exhaled.

Hand on her chin, he turned her head, wiped the blood from her cheek, and searched for injuries. There. A graze marred her earlobe and another at her hairline behind it.

Life was made up of a series of defining moments, but the instant his eyes rested on those wounds, the very second he realized how fucking close that bullet came to killing her, every harrowing moment of his life before it burned away.

Her lashes fluttered, and she looked up, squinted. "My head hurts."

He ducked his head and kissed her cheek. "Because you just used up another one of your nine lives. Problem is, I don't have nine lives and I fucking die every time you do. No more near-deaths, okay?"

A small smile shook her lips. "'kay."

Momentarily paralyzed by her eyes drifting closed and the memory of the gun in her face, he blinked through the shock, and alertness snapped back in a painful spasm. He needed to get her the fuck out of the alley.

Gathering her close, he climbed to his feet and whirled in a circle, marking an overfilled dumpster, parked cars, an iron fence peeking through wild vines. Were there more men with guns out there, watching?

Around the corner, the parking lot woke with approaching footsteps and excited voices. At his feet, the blood was drying beneath the sun and breeze. And somewhere Roy fucking Oxford was orchestrating his next step.

Colson nodded to Tony and took off toward the lot and the growing crowd. Tony moved to Jay's side with her gun hand out between them, muzzle pointed skyward. She tilted her head with a finger on her ear piece and glanced up at the top of the building.

Jay followed her gaze. Did the curtain move in one of the fourth-floor windows? Charlee and Nathan's apartment? If he couldn't move her to the car, her apartment was the next safest place. "Which one is hers?"

Tony held up a finger. "Copy." The way she continued to listen to her wireless com while wildly scanning their surroundings kept him rooted where he was, his heart beating a furious rhythm.

Her gaze flicked to him. "We're on our way."

"Was that Nathan?" He tucked Charlee close to his chest, her slight weight a comforting presence in his arm.

She nodded and spoke low in his ear. "He doesn't believe the gunman would be here alone. Their apartment is secure, so we're moving there until the rest of the team arrives."

Charlee tensed in the cradle of his arms. Her eyes were closed, but a tremble rippled over her body.

The chatter in the parking lot grew louder. Multiple footsteps shuffled closer. Colson whirled around the corner and ran toward Jay and Tony. "Cover the principal. The shots drew a crowd."

Jay's blood heated and hairs on his nape bristled. Another gunman could be mingled in with the approaching crowd.

Colson and Tony shifted into their protective formation, pressing their backs to his flanks, closing in tightly with their gun hands at their sides.

Eyes sweeping the fence line, rooftop, windows, and blind corners, Tony applied her usual pressure signal—tapping her elbow beneath his—to set the pace and direct him to the back entrance of the building.

As dozens of wide-eyed, slack-jawed spectators filled the alley, all he could think about was holding Charlee as close as possible and how incredible it would've felt to have her arms wrapped around him, holding him back.

36

Charlee hadn't moved from the couch in their studio apartment since Jay carried her in from the rear alley. She couldn't shake the hammering buzz in her head. If she were to guess, the gun firing beside her face had ruptured her eardrum.

What happened behind the building had registered a want she'd harbored for years. She'd been more than willing to squeeze the trigger and kill Roy's man. But when it came to Roy, she didn't just want to kill him. She wanted to destroy him.

With one hand on a towel at her ear, she shoved the other beneath her thigh to stop the violent trembling and blinked back the tears that thickened her throat. Neither Jay nor Nathan should have to deal with her fragility. They were suffering enough of her drama as it was.

The risks were riding her hard. How many Craigs prowled the property, waiting for them to emerge? Roy had caught up with them, but Nathan was still solidifying connections with Roy's business adversaries. No one was prepared to stand against him yet.

Nathan prowled the room, cell phone to his ear, strategizing with his team in St. Louis.

Everything they owned filled half a dozen duffle bags and waited by the door. This time, they didn't have a Marine chopper to carry them away.

Jay's low tones drifted from the kitchen nook. His head bent toward Tony's, lips moving, eyes hard as he glared at his bodyguard. Was he scolding her? Were they arguing over how to exit the building? Or was he just raging over the hell Charlee had led them into? Given his flushed cheeks, white-knuckled fists on his hips, and the heated way they whispered back and forth, Charlee guessed it was all of the above.

The heat in her graze wounds pulsed with the din in her eardrum. She removed the towel from the side of her head, relieved to see the flow of blood had slowed.

So fucking lucky. If Jay hadn't distracted the Craig at the perfect moment, she'd be on her way to San Francisco. She wasn't sure who fired first, but she knew she owed Jay her life.

"Keep pressure on it." The cushion bounced with Nathan's weight. He stooped down to meet her eyes. "Looks like you're going to live."

The dull throbbing pain was nothing compared to the up close and cutting wrath of Roy. "Yeah."

He kept himself relaxed as he regarded her, but the strain of unleashed anger glazed his blue eyes. "You're a pain in my fucking ass. Why didn't you just stay in the car? Yet one more bad decision that's landed us in a heap of shit."

Ouch. She'd left the car because she was worried about him. No sense vocalizing that. "This is my shit, my problem. I never asked you to dirty your hands with it." A tired argument, one he always ignored.

Nathan's eyes hardened. "Let me have another look." He turned her chin to examine the graze of the bullet behind her ear. "I don't know if this one will scar." He shifted his gaze to her ear. "Your earlobe..."

"Please don't say it looks like Salvador's."

He swallowed.

Super. "Better than a hole in the head."

He sucked in a breath and looked away. "I should've protected you better."

Of course, he would assume personal responsibility. The burden he shouldered was so misplaced and undeserved. "You didn't do this, dammit." She returned the pressure of the towel to her head and gnashed her teeth against the burn.

They stared at one another through the swelling tension. What was going on behind those stony eyes? He'd told her for three years he didn't blame her for Noah's death, but she knew it was eating at him. How could he even look at her?

"I need to check in with the team." He twisted to kneel against the back of the couch and parted the curtain behind her. A flood of daylight spilled in from the window that overlooked the rear alley.

"This is Nathan," he said slow and crisp in the wireless headset. "There's a stiff in the rear alley." He moved to the window facing the side lot. "And there's a crowd around our vehicle. Colson's not going to be able to contain them."

In the kitchen, Jay shoved his hands through his hair, the muscles in his biceps twitching. He'd risked his life to save hers, and he didn't do it out of debt. The thought sent sticky tendrils of attachment wrapping around her. For once, they were coming from her. It was careless and selfish, but she didn't want to fight it. And if he stuck around through gunshots and getaways, maybe he was more than just crazy. Maybe he was attached, too. She wouldn't take that for granted.

The faint and undeniable blare of sirens pierced through the walls.

Jay shifted, found her eyes. Hair disheveled, strong shoulders lolling forward, eyes wide and glued on her, he wore an intense look on his face. The way he just stood there, not moving toward her, pulsing waves of emotion around him prompted her to rise from the couch. The distance suddenly felt wrong, discomfiting.

A flash of heat shot through her ear from pressing too hard. She lowered the towel to check for bleeding.

That broke through his stupor. He raced to her side and swung her into the cradle of his arms. "Jesus, Charlee. I'm sorry. I needed to work out a plan with Tony, amongst other things." He hugged her face to his neck and, in a few strides, had her in the bathroom and sitting on the counter, back to the mirror.

His breathing was wild, and a measure of him flinched at the sight of her injuries, something only present in the twitch of his scowl. Still, watchful caution remained in his eyes.

"They're just graze wounds." She raised the towel to cover it.

"Don't. I haven't had a chance to look at them." He wrapped firm but gentle fingers around her hand on the towel and lowered it. "Fuck, you need a doctor."

"It's fine. My eardrum isn't ringing so bad and—"

"A fucking bullet cut through your ear." He flew backward and slammed against the wall behind him as if to keep her distanced from his anger. He swiped a hand over his face, sucking in air and staring at her out of feral eyes. "Fuck, fuck." He punched a fist backward and dented the sheetrock. "Fuck, I should've stopped it. I should've been there."

"You were there. Calm the hell down. You're not helping."

More punching. More dents.

What was wrong with him? He seemed fine in the kitchen. Did she look that bad? She turned toward the mirror.

37

A small gouge separated the cartilage high on Charlee's earlobe. Following the path of the bullet, a strip of skin the length of her thumb was flayed behind her ear at the hairline. It could've been worse. She'd survived worse. Although she wouldn't be wearing earrings for a while, what bothered her was Jay's reaction. Why was he punching the wall?

The bathroom wall propped up his back. His ready fists curled at his thighs, his head bowed, and his eyes were raised and clinging to hers.

Tanned skin smoothed his face, giving him a calm expression, but there was a restlessness in the way his eyes shifted between hers. She recognized that look from that morning, and it twisted her gut. "You're high."

Her words hung there between them until movement drew their attention outside the bathroom. Nathan stood in the doorway, arms crossed over his chest, glaring at Jay.

Jay pushed off the wall and formed the other half of the deadlock with an identical stance. They bandied hostile looks, flexing their jaws and issuing so much testosterone the small room choked with it.

She sighed. "Nathan."

The only thing Nathan moved was his lips. "He's high."

Protective till the end. "He's harmless. Is there a plan? We need to leave, right?"

Nathan glanced at the dents in the wall. "Backup's here. So are the cops." He met her eyes.

"And we can't trust them," she said, softly, miserably.

Jay swung his head toward her. "Why not?"

"They're probably on Roy's payroll." She chewed a fingernail. "The officers outside are probably here to ensure this ends according to Roy's directive."

"Roy's directive? Fuck that." Jay's eyes blazed. "Do we know who these corrupt cops are? Why don't we just call in different ones? He doesn't own the entire NYPD."

"That's what I'm trying to do." A tic bounced in Nathan's jaw. "But officers protect each other. I can't penetrate the blue code of silence with a couple of phone calls. It takes internal affairs and special investigations a long time to unearth who's on the take and who isn't. We're on our own." He raised his hand and stared at the screen on his phone. "The security team is sweeping the perimeter. Could take a while, but once we get the all clear, we move out. Be ready." He and Jay shared another stare down, and he left the room.

Jay closed the door and turned to her, eyes on the floor.

Where was the battle glare now? "Jay?"

He looked up, the richness of his gorgeous brown eyes loaded with uncertainty. "I'm not high...at the moment, if that helps." He rubbed his neck and shifted his weight from foot to foot. "I'm pretty much back to fucked up, angry, and vulnerable."

A sudden influx of feelings for him welled up, filling her with a perverse sense of intoxication. His admission was the steel that made the man. He had no idea how courageous he was. "Everyone has vulnerabilities. A strong man isn't afraid to show his."

He chewed the inside of his cheek, making his adorable dimple more pronounced. "I don't like feeling this way, Charlee." His body drew ever closer, and she realized she was doing the same.

"Putting your trust in someone is the most vulnerable thing you can do." She placed her palms flat on the counter behind her and spread her knees in invitation to stand between them.

The shadow of Roy's forceful hand coiled around her, inside her, strangling her. She shook it off and focused on the man before her. "Dare to be vulnerable with me." Was the quake in her voice as noticeable as the trembling in her legs?

A vibration seemed to ripple over his body. She might've been relationship handicapped, but she knew what arousal looked like on a man. It was evident in his sharp gasp, the softening of his gaze as it lowered to the apex of her thighs, and the way he carried himself through his pelvis as if all energy and thought were concentrated there.

Desire resonated from him as he followed his hips into the triangle of hers, holding her eyes until their faces were close, so close his breath became hers and their lips brushed through their exhales.

Wedged between her legs, he smoothed his palms along her jeans from her knees to her thighs, around her waist, and hooked his fingers beneath her butt. Then he yanked her to the edge of the counter until the zipper of her jeans was flush with the strain behind his leathers.

It was hard to remember not to touch him as his lips fell over hers and his tongue caressed back and forth, taking over her mouth and stealing her breath. She tasted the familiarity growing between them and savored the potency of it.

His fingers grazed her jaw and he rolled his brow against hers, panting heavily as he caught her licks and deepened them with the flat of his tongue. Her own fingers were locked, curling against the countertop.

They came up for air, slowly, breathlessly, and smiling like fools. His body was rigid. Pulsating. Ready. And at that moment, it was all hers. She rubbed her chest against the chiseled wall of his, her nipples hardening through her t-shirt.

He groaned and floated a hand over her breast, holding her eyes in silent question.

The imploring way he looked at her and the caution that preceded his actions made him someone she wanted to place her confidence in. She dropped her head back on her shoulders and pushed her breast into his waiting hand.

He chased the swollen nub with his thumb, flicking and squeezing. Then he went after it with his mouth, swiping his tongue against the fabric and dampening it with his gasps.

The hard muscle embracing her produced a kind of tranquilizing effect. His arms supported her. The pillar of his body was her strength. Without lifting her hands from the vanity, she loosened her limbs and let her butt slip off the edge and into the waiting cradle of his rocking hips. The sculpted surface of his stomach contracted against her, invading her headspace and simmering heat in her pussy.

Too soon, he raised his mouth from her breast and nipped at her chin with a grin on his beautiful face. He brushed her hair from her ear with a gentle hand and checked her wounds. Satisfied, he moved to her lips, tracing them with a finger, watching her steadily. "You build me up and turn me inside out. I've never felt so defenseless and yet...so daring at the same time."

Wasn't that what intimacy felt like? She smiled, her skin hot and flushed. "Mission accomplished."

He curved his upper body around her with his hands on her hips, seemingly oblivious to how desperately she wanted to hug him back. His voice whispered over her cheek. "You said everyone has vulnerabilities. What's yours?"

Slick with sweat, her hands slipped on the counter behind her. She adjusted her grip and straightened to sit. If she were going to trust him, she needed to do it in the most important way. "Do you know what happens when you open up?" She looked pointedly at her legs, spread around his.

A smile danced on his lips. "You get laid?"

She snorted. "If you're lucky." She placed her lips against his, held them there for a long moment, drinking in the spice of his breath. Then she leaned back to look in his eyes. "There was a time when I wouldn't have willingly sat like this with an aroused man between my legs."

His body turned to stone, and hers hardened in kind. His nostrils flared, but she pushed on. "I've been raped sixteen times in this position."

The hands on her hips curled into fists. He closed his eyes, and his chest rose and fell through rapid breath. His body shook against hers. Was he going to explode? He looked like he might puke.

"Hey." She squeezed his hips with her thighs. "Don't shut me out. If I can't talk to you, this stops. We stop." She wanted him to have access to the place inside her she never showed Noah. A mistake she wouldn't make again.

He opened his eyes, and they were haunted and cloudy. He dropped his forehead to hers, and she could feel the tension sparking from his body. "Sixteen times?" A whisper.

"I stopped counting after that." The truth was empowering. It opened her chest and released the toxin. It also exposed her heart. Maybe Jay would crawl in and rip it to shreds. Or maybe he would fill in the cracks. "When I learned how to open up, do you know what happened?"

He wrapped his arms around her and buried his face in her neck. "It made you incredibly fucking strong."

She smiled and kissed the soft skin below his jaw. "It made me strong enough to enjoy the feel of you between my legs."

His shuddering breath bathed her in warmth. He kissed her neck, nuzzled it, and kissed it again. "Please don't run off on me."

She cringed. "Your sunglasses are in my bag. I'm not sorry about that. You know why I did it."

"Yeah, Charlee." He straightened, rubbing his hands along her spine, fingers circling her back. "It was brave and... Romantic." His eyes glimmered. Then they turned to brownstone. "And it nearly cost you your life. Until we bury Roy Oxford, you'll be wearing a bodyguard."

Until *we* buried Roy. The *we* sounded dreamy and brash. But his hell-bent expression dissuaded her from arguing. She wasn't sure the bathroom wall would survive another Jay Mayard tantrum. "Shouldn't your security team be done sweeping?"

"They'll turn over every stone within a ten-block radius before they let us out of here." He kissed her lips and explored her face, her neck, her shoulders with his mouth and hands. Her fingers tingled to touch him back.

"Can I put my hands on you?" she whispered when he returned to her lips.

A struggle of emotions swirled in his eyes and tightened the muscles in his cheeks. Maybe she was pushing, but pushing was what he needed.

His flawless complexion glowed beneath the loose strands of his dark brown hair. After a few thudding heart beats, his deliberation settled into smooth skin and a soft gaze. "Hold your hands up, palms facing you."

She remembered how strong the angles of his jaw felt beneath her fingers the previous night as she held up the backs of her hands. "I touched your face last night when you were sleeping."

He widened his eyes, but they were smiling. "Next time, I'll be awake." He interlaced their fingers, palms to palms and brought the backs of her hands to his chest. "Baby steps, okay?"

With all that thick brown hair curling around the tips of his ears, his dark round eyes and clear golden skin, he was way too beautiful to not be touched. She strained toward him. "Baby steps."

He moved their hands from his shoulders to his cheeks, flinching as her knuckles stroked his velvet skin. Then he gathered her fingers at his mouth where he nuzzled and kissed each one, sending trickles of pleasure over her hands and up her arms.

What he did next, cut her breath. He let go briefly to turn her wrists, pressed her palms against his cheeks, and dropped his hands. He stared at her out of penetrating eyes, pinning her in place.

A fever bloomed beneath her fingers, and his facial muscles bunched and lolled. His breath sped up, quietly at first. Then the whoosh of air pushing through his nose carried noisily through the small space.

There was something pulling at the edges of his eyes, twitching the skin there, stretching from the corners, and spreading through his face. It settled on his mouth, twisting his lips away from his clenched teeth.

She jerked her hands back. "Jay?"

He was looking at her, but he didn't see her.

"Jay, talk to me."

Not a blink. Not a twitch.

Dammit, she wanted to wrap her arms around him. Since she couldn't, she tried to warm her voice with the comfort of a hug. "I'm here. Please, talk to me."

He closed his eyes and cupped his ears. One hand dropped to the front of his pants, rubbing whatever the bump was in his pocket.

Fucking hell. Holding her arms out and away, she circled her legs around his hips, hooked her boots behind his knees, and closed the gap between their bodies, trapping his hand against his pocket.

No response. He was lost in his head. Could she climb in there with him and pull him out?

She stretched her neck to reach his slacked jaw and kissed his bottom lip. "Where are we, Jay?"

He stopped breathing. He held his breath so long, she filled her lungs to shout for help—

"The shed." he exhausted in a shuddering gasp.

Her heart slammed against her ribs. The shed? "Who's with us?"

"Alone. So dark." His voice sounded small, younger. He brought his arms up between them and hugged his chest, rocking.

Oh God, what memories was he hanging onto? "What are we doing in the shed?"

"Hiding."

The childlike whisper chilled the room and coated her spine with ice.

"I'm with you, Jay. I need you. I need you to hold me."

His eyes shot open, and his breath released in gulping waves. "Charlee."

"I'm here." With useless fucking arms hanging at her sides.

The sculpted cuts of his gorgeous face sharpened as he dropped his hands in her lap. "Put your hands back."

No way. She shook her head.

He bent until their brows touched. "We're so close. Please?" His timbre was stiff, forced.

Shit. Shit. Shit. She clenched her fists at her sides. She'd wanted to push him, but not like this.

Without warning, a hum vibrated in his chest. What began as a purr, warbled into quivering notes. The first inflection of his voice sent a shiver through her. "Cut me open. Dipping deeper." More soughing notes. "Heart in hand."

The pitch of his voice and its reflection of meaning wrapped around her, lulling her into a trance.

He licked his lips and sang the next verse against her mouth. "With you, I float."

The effect his lilt had on her was visceral. Immediate. Erotic. His voice stroked her body, saturating her pussy and seducing her into a dripping wet puddle. So hypnotized, she didn't register his arm moving until he gripped her wrist and placed her palm over his heart.

His humming broke when her hand made contact, and his heart pounded against her touch.

He began again. "It's the only way to swim." He held her eyes, his hand over hers, and murmured the rhythm as he sang. "In your blue seas."

Gasps broke through her parted lips.

Nestling closer into the triangle of her legs, he brushed his lips over hers. The low melody of the song vibrated through the press of his lips and the thrum in his chest. Her heart pounded, and she returned his kiss while he hummed.

He leaned back and looked into her eyes. "That's where I'll be," he sang. "Don't disappear on me."

The tune reverberated through his closed lips. "Come to L.A. with me." He ended with a sultry hum.

Her chest tightened. She wanted more of his sexy voice, wanted more of this beautiful man. "When did you write that?"

"Just now."

Wow. Music had always had an effect on her but… "Your voice… I've never heard you sing live. It was…" Dark. Deep. Panty-soaking. "Profound."

"You inspire me, Charlee."

She kissed him, and he answered it, led it. The thrusts of his tongue were as enthusiastic as the beat of his heart against her palm. The sensation was overwhelming. She was spinning, falling. She pulled back. "This is crazy. What is this between us?"

It was dreamlike, this moment, amid of the chaos and dangers around them. On the heels of such a frightening and death-facing experience, they seemed to fall so easily into one another. Yet, wasn't that what she'd done in the penthouse? In the threat of Roy's presence, she'd focused on her memory of Jay, exploring it, growing it.

"I don't know, but it feels incredible." He squeezed her hand on his chest to punctuate his words.

A fist rapped on the bathroom door.

They broke apart. The moment was interrupted but not lost, if the promise in his eyes were anything to go by. They had opened a window, one they would never close again.

Nathan's voice muffled through the door. "We have a problem."

38

Nathan's interruption kicked Jay off his Charlee cloud and into the dregs of reality. If his protective team wasn't able to secure a safe evacuation route, the crowd must have swarmed out of control.

He clasped Charlee's hand and followed Nathan out of the bathroom.

"You need to get rid of those clothes, Charlee." Nathan glanced over his shoulder, his eyes flitting from the stain on her jeans to the smears on her shirt.

She lowered her chin and picked at a splatter of dried blood as if it were something she saw every day. She shrugged. "Yeah. Good call."

What kind of shit had she seen in her life to be so nonchalant about wearing a dead man's guts? Jay tucked the question in the back of his brain. He needed to focus on getting them out of there. Where was everyone? Other than his team leader, none of his guards were there. Not a good sign.

Tony didn't say anything as she left her post by the door and strode toward him. The lines etching her frown spoke for her.

Had someone recognized him? Did they know he was there? Tingling invaded his body, accompanied by the usual feeling of a loss of control. Some of that was the lingering effect of the coke. The reminder of his drug use bubbled guilt through his gut.

But he had Charlee's hand in his and her strength by his side. "How bad is the crowd?"

Tony was so exacting in her posture as she looked between Charlee and him, she could have been mistaken for a statue. "The crowd is gone. As is the body."

The crowd was gone? They obviously didn't know *he* was in the building. Wait. "What do you mean the body's gone? How does a dead man disappear?"

Charlee sighed and released his hand to squat beside one of the duffle bags and rifle through it. "What about the sirens we heard? Did you uncover anything about the cops that arrived?" She tugged out a black footless stocking thing and climbed to her feet. "I guess I'm not surprised the Craigs cleaned up that fast." She unbuttoned her jeans and pushed them down her thighs.

"No." Nathan paced a circuit in front of the curtained windows. "Since the police aren't banging down the door looking for a murder suspect, it's safe to assume they work for Roy."

The sight of her little red panties shot blood straight to Jay's dick. Heavy warmth pulsed through his genitals and heated his face. What in the hell was she doing? "Craigs?" he croaked.

Nathan stepped in front of him and blocked his view. "She calls anyone loyal to Roy a Craig."

Craning his neck, he could feel Nathan's glare, but fuck, Jimi Hendrix's 1968 Stratocaster wouldn't have pulled his eyes away from the leggings sliding up her toned legs. "Why Craig?"

"The Viet Cong were Charlie. Roy's adherents are Craig. That's all you need to know." Nathan cleared his throat in a useless effort to distract his eyes. "And the body disappeared in the time it took Colson to escort you up here, search the area for snipers, and return to the alley."

She gripped the hem of her shirt. "So the Craig dispatched the crowd, the dead Craig, and the police? The latter would've been a phone call from Roy to an inside guy on the force. I've watched him do this too many times to count." Her voice trailed off, quivering. "Now what? His thugs are out there waiting, without anyone to witness them attacking us when we come out?" She pulled off her shirt, unleashing waves of red hair tumbling down around her.

Sweet suffering Jesus. The trembling in her fingers nullified him somewhat, but he could see her nipples shadowed behind the lace. Heat surged through his dick. He was mindless with the need to pull it out and stick it in her.

Nathan droned on about blah snipers and blah blah tampered police reports and who the fuck cared? Her tits overflowed their red laced prison as she dug through the luggage. Any moment they would spill out in perfect servings for the cups of his hands.

His dick hurt. Could he slip a hand beneath his leather pants and make an adjustment without being obvious?

She stood, fumbling for the neck hole in a drapey-shaped shirt. Her leggings hung low on her waist, highlighting her fuck-me curves. With all that sleek skin stretching over her flat stomach and the arches of her tits, yeah, the chubby in his pants required some realigning. He reached for it.

"Charlee." Nathan pinched the bridge of his nose. "Please hurry. Your rock star's about to rip through his thirteen-year-old-slut pants."

What was wrong with his pants? Besides the painful nut-hugging?

Her eyes flew to his hand on his dick and widened. Then she looked down at her bra and tensed as if just realizing she was baring her assets to everyone in the room.

She righted the shirt and shoved her head and arms through. The ivory tunic hugged her ass and hips and hung loosely off her shoulder and around her tits. She was a fucking knock-out, which did nothing to cool his erection.

Face red, she scooped up her plaid Doc Martens and strode toward the kitchen nook. The apologetic look on her face shriveled him right up. She hadn't been teasing him on purpose. Something was wrong.

He side-stepped Nathan to follow, but the bastard blocked him again and leaned in.

"She was stripped of her modesty a long time ago," he whispered, low and stern. "Two months without clothes. She's immune to nudity."

Slivers of what Nathan had shared that morning about her captivity pierced through him, stabbing his heart. A lesser person would've hidden her pain in shame, but she bared hers with a grace that outshone everyone. "She's so fearless; it's easy to forget."

"I know." Nathan let out a sharp huff, but a smile twitched at the corner of his mouth. "Don't beat yourself up too badly. I've had three years to get used to it, and sometimes..." He glanced over his shoulder and watched her rummage through the refrigerator. "I'm still a man."

That pissed him the fuck off, but the tension retreated when Nathan's eyes strayed to Tony. It was a lingering look he hadn't seen on the man before. Okay, Nathan wanted to fuck his bodyguard. That he could live with.

"What's the plan?" Charlee asked around a spoonful of yogurt and leaned her butt against the counter. Her posture exuded a deliberate calmness, but the way her jaw stiffened around each bite exposed her fear.

He closed the distance and rested his palms on her hips, emptying his face of his own fears. There could be men on the surrounding buildings with sniper rifles, hiding in dumpsters, riding by in passing cars. Hell, they could've been waiting in the apartment across the hall. If they couldn't trust the police, they truly were on their own.

"The protective team will be ready to move us soon."

Charlee rubbed her temple. "How many bodyguards?"

"When we're traveling, they're a five-man team." He had another five on reserve at home. Lot of good that did him. He pulled her against him and a quickening buzzed through his body, making him gasp. Maybe it was the stressful energy bouncing between them. Maybe it was just Charlee and the pulse of life itself.

"So there are three of us? We're principals?" She glanced up at him, arms folded behind her. "That's what your bodyguards call us?"

He nodded.

"Three principals and five bodyguards." She unlocked a hand from her back to chew a fingernail. "That's doable, right? I mean, there are four in your band with five bodyguards."

He tugged her finger from her mouth. "Guarding the band means holding back energetic crowds and photographers, not snipers and kidnappers." He thought back over the worst scenarios he'd been in. "I've had moments, trapped at the center of closely packed crowds, when I thought I would die, actually thought I would keel over and stop breathing, but my team always escorted me out unharmed."

What a coward he was, buckling under something as benign as an enthusiastic mob. How many times had she held her shit together while looking in the eye of a rapist and murderer?

At that moment, he realized he could change their current situation by changing himself. There were no easy solutions. But there was an obvious one. "Tony, contact the paparazzi agencies and tell them where I'm at."

Tony glared. She didn't like it, but she would follow his orders.

He looked down and floated in the depths of Charlee's huge eyes. "You've been hiding for a long time. You ready to start living?"

"When you have to hide to live, you're ready for anything." Her jaw set.

Damn, he loved her fire. "Good, because Roy Oxford knows where you are, and he's going to watch you walk out of here on whatever camera shit his men have set—" He faltered when she closed her eyes. Fuck, he forgot about the cameras in the penthouse. He raised her chin and waited for her to look at him. "He's going to watch you walk out of here and there's not a damned thing he'll be able to do about it."

Her lips pinched in a line and the wheels spun behind her watchful eyes. Then she sucked in a breath. "The Craigs can't nab me if we're at the center of paparazzi attention."

"That's right." He nodded to Tony.

She pulled out her phone and dialed. She'd called them before, giving them false locations so they could move around effortlessly. This time would be legit. He stood taller, lengthened his backbone.

A frown scrunched Charlee's face. "You'll be mobbed. Exactly the kind of thing you avoid."

He knew she was thinking about his trigger. It was a valid concern, but she would be there to help him transform his stardom from oppressive to useful. "Avoiding isn't living. I want to live, Charlee, and I want to do so deeply." With her.

"You don't have to battle the shit in my life to live yours."

He pushed the hair from the side of her face, careful of her injuries, and settled his hands on her hips. "Won't I be battling my own shit at the same time?"

"Yes, but—"

"Do you know what happens when you open up?"

She closed her eyes and inhaled through her nose. "It makes you strong."

He kissed each lid and whispered against them, "Dare to be vulnerable with me?"

She opened her eyes, looked up into his, and smiled so brightly, he knew the glow from it would stay with him forever.

He decided to push his luck. "Come to L.A. with me."

She rolled her eyes to Nathan, who was rubbing his jaw, watching her. His reaction was pivotal. Better be the right one. Jay didn't want to beat the shit out of the man who had protected her for three years.

Nathan chewed on his lip, stared at his sneakers, glanced at Tony, and sighed. Then he raised his eyes to Charlee. "You might be free of your chain, sweetheart, but we both know you aren't really free. Your life is yours to live your way. If Jay is offering you that freedom…" Nathan glared at him. "Under the protection of his security team…"

No wonder she listened to him. The dude knew how to woo her. Jay wanted to hate him for it, but he couldn't. And of course, Jay would protect her with the best security money could buy. He nodded his agreement.

Nathan looked back at her. "Then nothing else matters."

She smiled and mouthed, "Thank you." Then she directed that smile at Jay, and it was pure vibration in his body. "Let's go battle some crowds and Craigs."

If he had a fraction of her courage, he could battle anything.

39

Unseen commotion bumped and rattled the apartment door. Charlee stood before the looming thing, fingering the bandage on her ear, waiting to be escorted into chaos.

Dread gurgled in her stomach and tried to rob the strength in her legs. Her outlook wavered by the minute, so she distracted her nerves by perusing a mental checklist.

Five-man protective team plus Nathan? Check. Bodyguard 380 wedged in her butt crack? Check. Paparazzi vultures gathered outside? Check. Hot rock star with more balls than sense?

She bent her neck to look at him. He rocked on his heels beside her, clutching her hand and humming the tune he'd written in the bathroom, though the undercurrent to this rendition was darker, more subdued. His hand was sweaty and trembling, but his balls were present, outlined in his spray-on leather pants. Check.

What else would she need to accompany an agoraphobic-ish celebrity into the sights of cameras and sniper rifles?

Courage? Any bravado she was trying to hold onto would be left behind with their luggage in the melee of the evacuation attempt. "I can't believe you called in the paparazzi." Her voice choked on a mass of fear. She swallowed. She understood why exposing her to the paparazzi might work. The public eye would protect her a hell of a lot better than the dark corners she'd been hiding in. But as she stood there, preparing to walk into it, she was shaking in her Doc Martens.

He kissed the top of her head. "Yeah. I'm starting to second guess myself. How will I be able to protect you while they're blinding me with flashbulbs? Especially when the beautiful girl at my side works them into a frenzyfuck." He flashed a cheeky grin.

Beautiful girl. How many times had she recoiled when Roy called her that? Yet as it filled her ears in Jay's deep timbre, it recreated itself. "Will I have my own Wikipedia page after this?"

The sexy rumble of his growl lifted her up on tiptoes and into the solidarity of their joining lips. She drew the flavor of his mouth into hers, drinking him in, and whispered against his exhales. "Thank you for doing this."

Eyes round and thoughtful, he shook his head and stroked his thumb over her jaw. "I don't know what you're doing to me, Charlee, but whatever it is melts everything else away. It's the best feeling in the world." A quiet seemed to collect around him. He straightened to his full height and his hand in hers stopped shaking. "Tony?"

"We have alternate evacuation plans lined up if riots break out." Tony positioned herself beside Jay. "And the chartered jet will be ready for our arrival. We're waiting for your visual signal."

Jay captured Charlee's lips in a quick kiss and patted his left shoulder with his right hand.

The sudden formation of bodies boxing them in wound up her nerves to the utmost point of tension. When the forward two bodyguards—Tony called them Vanderschoot and O'Neil—moved to the door, she thought her veins might snap from over-pumping.

He put his mouth at her ear. "Deep breath, baby." Then it was gone with the push of the door and the flashing of bulbs.

Click. Click. Click.

Vanderschoot, the guard in the lead, held back the mob for O'Neil to exit. In the next heartbeat, the two bodyguards barreled through the throngs in a choreographed attack, each pushing back photographers and carving a path through the crowd.

The vultures bumped into one another. Equipment clanked together. "Watch it. Back up. Back up."

"Clear." Tony held the door for Jay.

He released Charlee's hand, locked his arm around her shoulders, and guided her into the hallway. Edison, Colson, and Nathan brought up the rear.

"Go. Go. Go." The mobs shuffled with them, squatting to snap pictures and tripping over themselves.

"Jay Mayard. Look over here."

Click. Click. Flash. Flash.

What kind of hell had she walked into? Paparazzi crammed every inch of the hall. What if the Craigs prowled amongst them? How would the guards spot them? Her heart drummed a frenzied rhythm.

"Is that your girlfriend, Jay? What's her name? What happened to your ear, miss?"

She cupped her injury and blinked against the assault of blinding lights. Man, oh man, if he dealt with this every time he went out, no wonder he never wanted to leave his hotel room. She pressed closer into the mantle of his body, and his heart knocked against her cheek.

"Give them space. Give them space." The photographers' questions never slowed.

The cameras darted in and out of her face. There were so many of them. No way could the bodyguards hold them all back. Remarkably, the photographers didn't reach out, didn't try to touch.

She kept her eyes on her Doc Martens, scuffing them slowly along the concrete landing to the stairs. Jay's Chucks dragged alongside hers.

A photographer shoved another into the wall and shouting interrogations pursued.

At the top of the stairs, she and Jay waited behind the bar of Tony's outstretched arm while Vanderschoot and O'Neil cleared a passageway. Their eyes swept up and down, passing over the paparazzi as if they weren't there.

"You're doing well," Jay whispered in her ear.

"I don't know about that. How are you doing?" His smile was small and sad and held her heart hostage in her throat. "Do the paparazzi ever touch you?"

"It's generally against the law to touch someone without their consent. They're a nuisance, but they rarely break that rule." His lips brushed the shell of her ear, and he hugged her closer to his chest. "The fans are the law breakers."

A reminder that the worst was yet to come. The herd trailing them was mild, relative to the shouts thundering from the parking lot.

"Clear," one of the guards shouted from below.

Down the stairs and around the landings they went. Tony and Nathan flanked them. Every time their eyes flicked upward, Charlee's pulse spiked. Edison and Colson kept their positions always a floor behind.

The paparazzi leading the slow parade walked backward, scuffling while snapping pictures, some falling down the stairs and climbing their way back up. Jay ducked his head under his free arm, squinting against the invasive flashing.

She dug into her messenger bag and handed him the sunglasses. The way he hurriedly fumbled them on made her wish she'd never taken them.

The closer they came to the ground, the thicker and louder the crowd grew. The security team tightened their circle and the air clotted with unease.

They stepped off the bottom stair at the front of the building and a chorus of shrill screams rode in on the crisp breeze. Six rigid bodies backed into her and Jay, squeezing them in a tight box. Her breath came out in noisy pants. She couldn't see a damned thing around the wall of guards.

Jay rose on tiptoes, peering over the crowd. "Fuck. The road's been barricaded. The SUV won't be able to pick us up here."

Christ, could this get any worse? The mayhem was closing in on her. Tremors weakened her body. How close were the Craigs? Could they see her? Was one sneaking up now, only a bodyguard's length away?

He folded her into the *V* of his legs, chest to chest, trapping her hands between their bellies.

She tensed. How would she walk like this? "Jay, my hands."

He rubbed his whiskers against her cheek, his body drenched in sweat. "Shhh. We're good."

His voice and proximity suspended her. Strange how peace could be found at the most inopportune moment. Cocooned in the orbit of guards, pressed tightly against him, her breath began to normalize. She imbued the intimacy of their private little world. Beneath the eye of the blue sky, it was just him and her and the thunder of their hearts.

"Doing okay?" she asked at his ear.

"It...wa...ot."

The high-pitched chanting of frantic women calling out his name drowned out his response. She leaned back to read his lips. "What?"

"I said it's just a walk in the parking lot."

"Clear," Tony said above the shrieking.

Clear of what? Weapons? Bad guys? They certainly weren't clear of crowds.

The guards spread out and her private world came crashing down.

Jay turned her back to his front and hooked his forearm across her chest. She gripped the bag's strap at her hip to keep from grabbing him for balance. He held his other hand out in front of her to block some of the camera shots and ward back the posters, pads, and markers shoved through the guards' line.

Shutters snapped from every direction. Bulbs flickered against the sunlit sky. Paparazzi barked out questions, but it was submerged beneath a flood of girly piping.

"Aaaaaah. Jay Mayard!" At least twenty women of all ages pressed against the bodyguards, screaming and sobbing. Yes, sobbing.

Actual tears streaked down the make-up-smeared faces that were twisting behind the camera phones. Jay Mania had gripped the Village.

"Oh my God. Oh my God. You're so sexy." Twenty women grew to forty or fifty. Others were running through the street, some dragging small children into the fray. Cars honked, and people shouted from the windows in nearby buildings.

She scanned the hustle of bodyguards, looking for Nathan. Too much movement. Too many identical black shirts. She'd spent three years avoiding scenes like this to evade Roy's watchful eyes. Now, she was certain he could see her, through a camera lens or a Craig.

Her muscles were so tight, dizziness surged over her in waves. The hard, metal weight at the small of her back was a false sense of relief. Shooting a Craig in the crowd would've been impossible without endangering a bystander.

A sense of urgency, bordering panic, took over the guards and their pace picked up. By the time they reached the corner of the building, the number of screaming fiends had doubled again.

They bounced, covered their mouths, and fanned themselves. Where did they come from? Tony had alerted the paparazzi. Not the entire state of New York.

The arm around her held its position, despite the jostling of the guards and crowds. Jay dropped his head, his shoulders hunched, and hung his mouth open to accommodate his rapid breathing. He didn't want this. He held his gut with his free arm as if the attention were actually hurting him. She was thankful for his sunglasses. She wasn't sure she could've handled seeing pain in his eyes.

Selfish, invasive cows. An ugly aggressive hate for these women buried its roots in her heart. If she could bargain with the devil, she would trade places with Jay. She would suck the hurt away, inhale it deep, and make it her own. Anything to ease the misery that was wrenching his body.

And he was doing this for her.

"OhmyGod, you're haaaawt, Jay Maaaaayard."

Click. Click. Click.

Head down, Jay led her through the masses and into the parking lot. The car wouldn't be far, would it?

The roar of the crowd bounced between the buildings. The guards kept a two-foot space cleared around them, but the perimeter wavered, straining inward.

The sea of writhing people spilled into the street and to the other side. Upstretched arms held huge-lensed cameras over the push and pull of bodies. The front line reached out with wiggling fingers and blinking phones.

Did a boob just flash in his face?

"I love you, Jayeeeeeee. Looking good. You're so handsome."

No, several boobs. Huge naked boobs. The girls elbowed each other to bend over the barricade of the guard's arms. How far away was the damned car?

"Can I have your autograph, Jay?"

He kept his head sheltered beneath his arm. His other arm was a vise around her neck.

"I want a picture. Please take a picture with me." More crying. More bouncing nipples. And the crowd grew. Pounding footsteps and distant screaming announced more coming from the street.

Was that the diversion they wanted? The paparazzi seemed to be losing their footing to the tizzy of desperate women, but the cameras didn't stop clicking.

Without warning, Tony spun toward Jay, slamming her back against his chest and dislodging his arm from Charlee's neck.

Oh God, no. What was happening? Charlee chased him, only to be yanked back by the shoving current of bodies.

Tony's mouth moved, and her eyes flicked between the roof and the crowd. What was she shouting? One word over and over. Gun?

Charlee's legs locked up and her mouth went dry. Something hunkered on the roof. Impossible to make out details with the sun's glare.

Jay swung his head back and forth. "Charlee?"

More people rolled in, pushing her further back, blocking her view of Jay. She elbowed and kicked with the best of them, but the force of the frenzy swept her more feet away, bumping her into the grill of a parked car. "Jay!"

She glimpsed him through the crack of bodies, five...six car lengths away. The sunglasses on his face pointed in her direction.

His lips stretched from his clenched teeth. "Charlee!" He struggled against Tony's grip, but something paralyzed him. He choked, curled in on himself and cupped his ears.

Oh Jay, no. Charlee's heart skipped, helplessness curling her nails into her palms.

Tony bolstered most of his weight with hands on his chest and shoulders. No! Not her hands.

Charlee doubled her effort, punching and body slamming through the crowd.

A young girl broke from the melee. She flung herself at him, shackled her arms around his neck. Charlee watched, unable to move forward, as the girl smothered his mouth with hers.

The swarm devoured her view. Her blood boiled, fueling her muscles and propelling her forward. An arm shoved her back. She grabbed the bitch's ponytail and yanked her to the ground. Too many fucking people. *Come on, come on, let her through.* A few more elbows and she gained half the distance to him.

Through a break in the rocking heads, she glimpsed Tony release his arms and punch the girl clinging to him. The girl went down, and he stumbled back, gripping his chest and chanting something. His entire body seemed to lock up. What horror was tearing him apart inside?

Her heart sprinted. He needed her, goddammit. "Get out of my way." She launched herself into the wall of bodies and closed a few more feet.

The crowd rippled behind Jay. A moment later, his SUV pushed its way through. The passenger door opened, and Edison reached out, pulling Jay inside.

Where was Nathan? Charlee whirled, probing the sea of heads. No Nathan. Oh God, anyone of those heaving bodies could be a Craig. Her heart raced.

Jay arched his back and screamed two syllables. The distance and the shrill of the fans drowned out his voice, but she felt it in the marrow of her soul. He was suffering, buried by his nightmares. She felt him say her name, so close no matter how far. She was there. She willed him to see her.

The remaining bodyguards climbed in on the opposite side of the SUV. Tony pushed Jay into the seat and climbed in after him. As she reached for the door, he jerked his head in Charlee's direction.

Were they going to leave her? Yes. She swallowed. They couldn't wait for her to reach them. Tony had clocked a gun on the roof. She was doing her job, getting Jay out of there. "I'm with you, Jay. I'm here," she whispered.

The door slammed shut, and the vehicle backed out toward the street. Her heart collided with her ribs. Caged by the crowd, she was powerless to get to him. She knew he was incapacitated by his guards, and more so by his nightmares. Would he come back for her?

Women flung themselves on the hood and against the windows, but he was safe inside. Good. That was good. His security did the right thing, her need for him be damned.

Suck it up. Jay was safe. She felt it in the slump of her shoulders and the looseness of her neck. She rolled her head back and glanced at the roof of her building. The hunkered shape was gone. Where was the sniper? *Find Nathan.*

The mob of fans and photographers thinned, spreading out as they chased the SUV down the street.

Heart pounding, face burning, she scrutinized the lingerers for blond hair, blue eyes, and a white button-up. Where the hell was he?

A gentle hand cupped her shoulder from behind and traveled over her collarbones to settle on her other shoulder. Oh, Nathan. She wanted to sag against him. "We need to get out of here."

As she turned to face him, an unmoving figure caught her eye on the far side of the lot. Blond hair. White button-up. The man beside him held his hand beneath the cover of his jacket, pointing the bulge at Nathan.

A shiver swept through her. She lowered her eyes to the hand on her shoulder. Pale. Manicured. Cold. Her heart stumbled, and her lungs seized all the air in the sky.

A chilling whisper snaked around her neck. "We'll be out of here soon, so I can show you just how much I've missed you, beautiful girl."

40

Charlee was an impulse away from stuffing Roy's cold black heart with lead. The pistol at her lower back would do a bang-up job, but her revenge would have to wait until she could assure Nathan's safety.

Two years of slavery. A combined seven years of running. He stole nine of her twenty-five years. And he stole Noah. The burn to retaliate pumped as naturally through her veins as her blood.

She turned in the hook of his arm, rolling her hips forward to keep the bump of the gun concealed under the drape of her shirt, and looked up.

The baseball cap, oversized leather jacket, and jeans made him difficult to recognize. Roy Oxford did not do casual, but his countenance was its usual color of death. Icy. Bloodless. She wasn't sure he was even breathing as he stared at her. Then he opened his mouth. "How convenient that I was only a four-hour flight away when your photos went viral." He tsked. "I thought better of you than to keep company with a litter of lowbred musicians. Though I'm not surprised to find the traitor, Nathan Winslow, amongst the trash."

Furious dread balled up in her throat. *Traitor* meant he'd connected Nathan Winslow to Matthew Linden, which also meant Nathan had little chance of surviving the next few minutes.

"Tell me, Charlee." The mouthwash on his breath was as aseptic as his expression. "Has he stuck his dick in you?"

Nathan's odds of survival dropped to zero if Roy didn't believe her. She raised her chin and held his suffocating gaze. "No. You murdered my one and only lover." Her body pulsed with the desire to watch his eyes empty of life.

One of the few dependable forces of good in her world stood a parking lot away with his cover blown and a bullet pointed at his gut. She was too far away to shoot the Craig threatening Nathan. And where there was one Craig, there would be more spread out around her, their guns trained from their hiding spots.

Though the bulk of the crowd had scattered into the street to chase Jay's SUV, some milled about as if waiting for him to return.

Two police officers lingered at the entrance of the lot, directing the streams of foot and motor traffic. They glanced at Roy and turned their backs. So much for serving and protecting.

"*I* am your only lover." Roy pressed his nose against her cheek and inhaled. "It's been three years and I can still smell you on the pillow next to mine. Three years, Charlee. My life is hollow without you."

She laughed and found her courage in the sharp intake of his breath. Found it and fortified it with the realization that this was the first time she faced him without shackles. The first time she could address him in any manner she wanted. "You're not my lover. I've never loved you. You're my abuser, my ball-and-chain, and you'll be hollow when I'm standing over your dead body."

He dug his fingers into her shoulder and flicked his eyes over the bystanders. Oh, he wanted to beat the shit out of her.

Weaving through the cars and people was the ever-dependable Craig, Salvador. He strode toward an SUV and unlocked it. There were two other lone men prowling opposite corners of the lot with bulges under their jackets where shoulder and hip holsters would be.

Nathan was too far away to read his eyes, but the set of his shoulders and raised chin said he was ready to prove there was no worse enemy than an avenging Marine. His handgun should've been in the inside-the-pant clip holster on his hip unless the Craig had confiscated it. Maybe he didn't need it. Given his military combat training, he could disarm the gun aimed at him. She knew he was waiting for her to do something. For the right moment to take his eyes off her. What could she do?

She swallowed, her throat dry. The smallest mistake would cost him his life. And any threat to Roy's life would beckon the nearby cops.

"Mr. Winslow is just an incentive for you to leave quietly." He wrapped a hand around her throat, pinched her airflow, and dragged her to the vehicle. "If you draw attention, he's dead."

If she got in that SUV, Nathan was dead. She thrashed against him and screamed with burning lungs. Nothing came out. No sound. No air. There were a few stares in her direction, but no one moved to intervene.

He wrenched her through the vehicle's open door by her neck. She grabbed the roof, bucked against him, and tried to make a scene.

The Craigs corralled. Her fingers slipped. The agony from the vise on her throat tapered her thoughts to one. Kill him. She released the roof and reached for the gun at her back.

Tires squealed and an engine rumbled, approaching from behind. More Craigs? The cops? Brakes screeched. Roy let go of her throat and spun toward the commotion.

Oh, thank God. Gulping for oxygen, she turned just as Roy shifted back. Face-to-face, she yanked the gun from her waistband. Flicked off the safety. Lined up the sights on his chest.

Inhale.

He looked at her gun. Looked at her. Then the monster smiled.

Exhale.

41

Crammed in the backseat between three of his bodyguards, Jay covered his head with the hood of the sweatshirt he'd borrowed from O'Neil and pushed the sunglasses up the bridge of his nose.

"*Never* separate us again." The directive exploded from deep in his chest and echoed in the small space. He lowered his voice. "From this point on, Charlee is your principal. Her safety supersedes mine. And hurry the fuck up."

With all the people in the street, it was taking an eternity to make their way back to the parking lot. He stared at the nasal spray in his hand, needing it to numb the rage that sent his jaw into enamel-grinding spasms.

"Yes, Mr. Mayard." Tony held his gaze. "I'm aware of this as you advised me of your priorities before we left the apartment. I made the mistake in assuming a sniper aiming for your head superseded Miss Grosky's security. I apologize. It won't happen again." Her glower didn't look sorry.

Colson slammed on the brakes. Jay's knees smacked into the console and his blow flew under the seat. Fuck the drug. She was out there alone. Every second counted. "Let me out."

Too many bodies blocked his view. Bodyguards inside the car. Lollygaggers outside. "Can you see her? Let me the fuck out."

A gunshot cracked the air and, for the second time that day, heart-stopping fear ripped his anger asunder.

Tony jumped out first, hand at the gun at her hip. Everyone but Colson followed.

In his hurry, Jay stumbled onto the pavement and slammed into a wall of fleeing people. They parted around him, spun him the wrong way, and holy shit, they were running *away* from him. He turned back and jerked to a stop a few feet short of Charlee.

She stood over a man, who lay face up on the ground. Roy

Oxford? He looked paler in person than on TV and a lot less put together. Maybe because she pointed a gun at him as he pawed at a dime-sized hole in the chest of his leather jacket. His breath was ragged yet he longingly stared at her as if oblivious to the gun she aimed at him or the bullet she'd already delivered.

Red clouded Jay's vision. This was the piece of shit who had raped her more times than she could count. His thirst for blood swelled at the epicenter of his rioting emotions. "Pull the trigger, Charlee. Finish him."

Three men emerged from a break in the crowd. They wore common clothing—jeans, t-shirts—but the guns they pulled from their open jackets were big, scary, and probably illegal. The hostility in the air that followed them emulated their bloodthirsty eyes and hard features.

The parking lot exploded in a frenzy of screams. Not the squeals of fan girls. These were the oh-shit-save-yourself kind of screams.

The mayhem of the bolting crowd crested as two officers sprinted across the lot with guns aimed at Charlee. "Drop your weapon. Hands in the air."

Shit. Jay locked his legs in an attempt to stop himself from lunging for her. "Don't do it, Charlee."

The gun didn't twitch in the cup of her hands as she glared at Roy. "Don't drop it? Or don't shoot?"

She was wielding a gun in public, and the cops weren't shooting her. Nor did they spare a glance at the three gunmen, which meant Roy was lining their pockets. They were still NYPD and, Christ almighty, she'd already killed one person. The last thing she needed was a prison sentence for killing another in front of the police. "Don't shoot, but don't drop it either."

The cops jogged closer and one shouted, "Sir, do not engage the shooter."

Roy's goons closed their triangular formation around him, Charlee, and Roy until they were about six-feet away. Jay vibrated with the need to move behind her and wrap her in the shield of his body. If he reached out and stretched his arm, he might've been able to touch her, but there were too many fingers on too many triggers. The slightest movement would endanger her.

Something caught his eye on the far side of the lot. *Oh Shit. Nathan*. Jay kept his gaze on Charlee but could make out the movement in his periphery. Nathan head-butted some guy and chopped his hand at the throat. Jay refocused on Charlee. "Talk to me."

She didn't shift her eyes or the gun from Roy. "I shot him in the chest. Why aren't you bleeding, you...you bloodless monster?"

Roy rolled his head back and released a laugh that tumbled into a hacking cough.

Maybe the blood was pooling unseen beneath his bulky jacket. *Bulky jacket.* He would bet his Martin Acoustic there was a bulletproof vest. "Take off your coat."

A gunman with a missing earlobe angled his barrel at Jay. "How should we precede, Mr. Oxford?"

Roy's exhale whistled past his clenched teeth. He unzipped his jacket and pushed back the sides to reveal a black tactical vest rising and falling with his wheezes. Sharp edges protruded from the dimple left by the bullet. "What are you waiting for, Charlee? You can still shoot me in the head."

Fuck. Jay wanted to grab the gun and do it for her.

She shifted her aim from his chest to his face. "If I shoot you, your Craigs will shoot me. If I don't shoot, I get to ride down to the police station. Except we both know that ride will take me to San Francisco and I'll end up chained to your bed by morning."

Roy scraped his curling fingers along the pavement. "Oh, it'll be the stockroom for you, darling. I'm hard just thinking about it."

Jay's adrenalin rushed to murderous boil.

"I choose death." She squared shoulders.

Not going to happen. Jay forced a calmness he didn't feel into his voice. "Give me the gun, Charlee." He would start with Roy's nutsac. A bullet in each testicle. Then he'd shove the barrel in his rectum and pump it with enough lead to shred his innards from sphincter to esophagus. "I'm going to fucking kill him."

"I earned that privilege." She adjusted her finger on the trigger.

The sudden rigidness of the gunmen strained the tense atmosphere to the edge of snapping.

Jay needed warp speed to shield her in time. Even if he had the speed, the firepower that would unleash from the surrounding gunnery would tear through him and hit her anyway. "Wait."

She glanced up without moving her head or her trigger finger. Looking into her eyes was like watching a storm roll over the horizon and devour the blue skies. It was magnificent. Unstoppable. And deadly. "I have to end this, Jay."

"There's a better way." He hadn't worked out what that was yet, but he'd make damn sure it was a solution she would walk away from.

Colson remained in the driver's seat with the engine running. The bodyguards had spread out, but not one was in sight. Where were—

Nathan poked his head around the SUV nearest to Charlee.

Jay tried not to fidget or make eye contact. No one looked in Nathan's direction. Was the rest of the team hiding? Planning an attack from concealment?

His muscles tensed in readiness. His pulse fired with purpose. An idea played out in his head. It could work. Adrenaline flooded his body with instant energy.

Roy shifted to a sitting position in a cautious stiff movement. His breathing was quieter, steadier, as he looked between Jay and Charlee. "You lied." His eyebrows lowered over his narrowing eyes and his nostrils flared. "You're fucking this lowlife?"

Jay's fist clenched. "That's rich coming from a rapist."

Charlee snorted. "There's a hell of a lot of horny girls willing to *lower* themselves for Jay Mayard." She shrugged. "He's a wet-panty dream. I'd do him."

Was the casual disregard in her voice and posture enough to convince Roy? The man's blank face revealed nothing. Jay burned to put a bullet hole in it.

"Put your guns on the ground." Tony stepped from around a parked car. Nathan, O'Neil, Vanderschoot, and Edison rushed in from nowhere and everywhere. Five on five, each of his team covered the three thugs and two cops.

Jay released a breath, but anticipation billowed in the wake of relief. With her gun leveled on one of the officers, Tony looked at him out of the steely eyes of a Marine and waited for his signal. She was prepared to fight this with muscle and gunfire.

And Charlee stood at the center of the web formed by the projectile paths of ten guns if they went off.

Jay's plan would ensure her safety. He was used to being the coward, the social retard, the pain in the ass. That was his go-to. He would fight this with evasion and bullshit. "Roy. Got some bad news for you. My team leader just gave me visual confirmation that you are being recorded." He jerked his chin at the SUV they arrived in that morning and at the backup vehicle they had returned in. "They activated video and audio equipment on the dashes when we arrived. The recordings are fed live to my team in L.A. If anything happens here, it will be broadcasted." He held Roy's glare and made sure he didn't miss a single word. "Charlee will *never* see the inside of your stockroom again."

Unease rippled through the gunmen. Roy rose to his feet and held up a hand to stay them. "Miss Grosky shot me. Did you record that? Are you recording the weapon she's aiming at me now?"

"Of course, she *wants* to shoot you, you rapist motherfu—"

"When we pulled into the lot," Tony said, "we logged Miss Grosky defending herself during an attempted kidnapping."

A shiver ripped down his spine. If that was true, how close had he been to losing her? "This ends now. Charlee is going to holster her gun, and I am going to escort her to my car." He captured her huge eyes. "Go ahead. They're covering you."

The cop at the business end of Tony's Glock kept his own gun trained on Charlee. "We can't let you leave, Miss Grosky."

The pressure in the air was going to pop. Any second, someone was going to pull a trigger.

Tony was the calm in the eye of the storm. "What's it going to be, Mr. Oxford?"

Roy watched Charlee with an infatuation that consumed his entire demeanor. "Stand down, officers." When they lowered their guns, he said, "Your turn, Charlee."

She inhaled through her nose, flicked the safety on, and tucked the gun at the small of her back.

Jay wiped a sweaty hand on his shirt and offered it to her. She grabbed it so quickly a thrill rushed through him. He waited for his shadows to crawl out of their holes and chase her away, but as Nathan joined them and they walked her to the SUV, he only felt her hand. Her essence. His Charlee.

"You want to know how it feels?" Roy's query tingled over Jay's shoulder.

His gait faltered. Would Roy call his bluff on the recording? How many guns were pointed at their backs?

He pulled Charlee closer and picked up his pace. Nathan positioned himself behind them.

Roy let out a mirthless laugh. "Imagine losing your fame, your money, your drugs, your band... Whatever it is filth like you values."

Determination powered his strides. His blood pumped with one intent. Get her the fuck out of there. Ten more feet...eight...six...

"Imagine watching the most important thing in your life walk away." Roy raised his voice. "When I find out what that thing is, you'll know exactly how it feels."

Don't engage him. Keep walking. The backs of his ears burned. His teeth ground. He held his breath until Charlee was safely inside the armored vehicle. Then he turned and looked Roy in the eye. "She's not a thing, you fucking prick."

42

She's not a thing.

Jay's words resonated, loosening the knot coiled in Charlee's belly. She wanted to crawl into his lap and envelop him with comfort. But the tic in his cheek and his wooden posture suggested he might need more than a handless hug.

Nathan followed Jay in, putting Jay in the middle, and Tony climbed in the front seat. When the last door slammed shut, the knot unclenched.

She met Nathan's eyes over Jay's slumped head and saw her relief reflected there. "So you disarmed that Craig in the parking lot, I assume?"

He held the gun on his lap, his eyes glassy and locked on his fingers as he clicked the magazine in and out, checked the safety, went back to the magazine. "Had to time it right." He glanced at her. "I didn't want to force Roy's hand."

"Nothing *forces* him to do anything." Recalling the things Roy had done to her produced a dull ache in her chest, but watching Nathan avert his eyes at the memories sucked the air from her lungs, strangling her.

As Colson merged the SUV into traffic, the gravity of Roy's threat knocked her in the gut. She turned to look out the rear window. At the center of the standoff between his men and Jay's remaining bodyguards, Roy stared directly at her as if he could see through the dark tint.

A shiver penetrated deep in her bones. On its heels was the incessant hum for vengeance. Did she just walk away from her only opportunity to kill him?

If she had the penthouse camera footage, she might've stood a chance against him in a courtroom. But during Nathan's undercover sting, he hadn't been able to crack the firewalls to copy the recordings or pinpoint where they were stored. The photos he'd snapped of her injuries the night he rescued her didn't incriminate Roy as the abuser. Without proof in court, it would've been her word against a powerful billionaire and his infinite team of lawyers.

If Jay's video cameras captured Roy forcing her into the SUV, maybe they finally had something. Something they could use. She lowered her finger from her mouth, the nail ripped to the quick. What a disgusting habit. "I know you made a verbal agreement back there, but what's stopping us from using your recordings against him?"

Tony glanced over her shoulder and shared a look with Jay. He lowered his gaze. His fists clenched, flexed, shook, and clenched again.

Charlee felt his silence. Why wouldn't he look at her? She rubbed her temples as his non-answer ripened to realization. "You were bluffing."

"Yeah." He scrubbed a hand over his mouth.

The remorse in his voice pained her. She leaned forward, tried to snag his gaze. "You know what? We didn't run away from him. We *walked*."

He cut his eyes to her.

"I've *never* walked away from Roy Oxford. You gave me that." Just thinking about it made her blood sing through her veins. She glanced up and found the corner of Nathan's lip twitching. Yeah, she was certain he shared her sentiment.

She returned her attention to Jay. "Roy knows where I'm at, who I'm with, and what I'm doing. Which means he's lamenting the fact he can't just pluck me off the street anymore." She grinned. "Not with the parade of media following you. And not with the level of security you employ. The cameras were a bluff, but the threat is still there. He won't risk it."

"Charlee's right." Nathan holstered the gun and leaned back. "We've been running so hard for so long, we've been in nonstop defense mode. Now that we don't have to run, we can finally focus on our offense."

Her head swam. "Since he can no longer force us physically, he'll try to outmaneuver us. He'll blackmail your PI business, Nathan." She looked at Jay. "And he'll dismantle your band. He won't be above using your loved ones as leverage to force me to him."

Jay stared at something on the floorboard, his tone flat. "I don't have loved ones outside of the band."

She would ask him about that when there wasn't an audience. She followed his gaze to... A nasal spray bottle? She bent to pick it up, and his body jerked to stillness. His eyes locked on the bottle in her hand,

and he leaned toward it even as his expression seemed to draw away. What the hell? She turned it over. The label was worn and peeling.

"This isn't allergy spray, is it?"

He snatched it from her grip, eyes hard, and dropped it over Tony's shoulder and into her lap. "Get rid of this."

Twisting toward Charlee, he grabbed her waist and dragged her across the seat to straddle his legs. With his arms crossed behind her back, he pulled her hips to his and nuzzled his face in her neck.

She held onto the seat on either side of his shoulders and angled her head to look at Nathan. A small smile touched Nathan's lips but bypassed his eyes. Grooves crept over his forehead as he watched her with Jay.

Was he thinking about Noah? Did he think she'd given more of herself to Jay in one day than she gave Noah in their one year?

But she had, hadn't she? She didn't love Noah enough to lay her broken life at his feet. She'd wanted to. God, she thought maybe someday she could've. It had taken her six months just to let him steal a kiss. Would she have ever let him know her beyond their physical connection? She never even gave him her real name.

Her chest cramped. She dropped her eyes to her hand, clenched on the seatback, shamed by the direction of her thoughts.

After a moment, Nathan pinched her chin and gave her head a little shake. His gesture chased away a fraction of her guilt, but his narrowed eyes promised an imminent conversation.

She nodded.

The angles of Jay's face sharpened as he leaned back and shifted his hips away from the other man. The subtle movement put distance between her and Nathan as if Jay were trying to break their exchange.

Jay's flushed cheeks glowed against his tan complexion, his hair tousled and trenched from his fingers. His natural beauty alone could shackle the heart of any woman who laid eyes upon him. Yet, he looked at her as if she were the only one. An unfamiliar feeling swelled in the back of her throat.

He kissed her neck and pressed his brow against it. "I'm so sorry."

The remaining guilt she'd hidden in her silence echoed in the pained whisper of his apology and the beat of his heart drumming against hers. "Why are you sorry? I'm the one who should be apologizing."

His breath grew heavy, intensifying her own. He raised his head and met her eyes. "I lost it out there with the fans and the guards and...

My fucking issues—"

He looked away, worked his jaw, and dragged his gaze back to hers. "Won't happen again. I will *never* walk away from you." The resolve in his tone enthralled her.

With all the hands that had been on him and the distress that rocked his body when Tony shoved him in the car, she knew he had been in the grips of his own demon. "You didn't bail. When I needed you..." She placed a kiss on his hairline, breathing in his masculine scent. Kissed his nose, his parted lips. "You were there. Thank you."

The circle of his arms cinched, pressing their bodies together. "I don't just want to be *where* you need me." His tone was deep, sharp. "I want to be *what* you need."

Something pulsed between them. Perhaps it was the rhythm of their shared breath. Or maybe it was the vibration of some invisible boundary falling away. She inhaled it and let it tremble through her body as she rested her cheek on the brawn of his shoulder.

For nine years, she didn't know who she could cling to, or if she would ever be able to take that risk, but clinging to Jay felt elemental. As if deep within him lay the map to emotions she'd lost and maybe some she never experienced. She wouldn't let go. No matter how contagious his pain. If she were tough enough to endure hers, could she shoulder his too?

He brushed his lips over her jaw and pointed his chin toward the front of the vehicle. "Tony, I want training immediately." His voice barked through the cabin with an air of dominance. "Self-defense. Firearms. And I want to carry my own gun."

"What?" Blood rushed to Charlee's cheeks. "What about your protection team?"

His fingers stroked up and down her spine. "I will never be in a situation again where I can't defend you. We'll start tomorrow, Tony."

"Self-defense?" Tony asked with a smile in her voice.

"Yeah." He lifted a lock of hair from Charlee's shoulder and twisted it around his finger. "Charlee will help me get through the hand-to-hand stuff."

The nerve endings in her fingers itched to touch his face. "I will?"

He smoothed her hair behind her ear and held his hands palms up on either side of her. A perfect brown eyebrow rose as he waited.

She slid her hands into his, and a jolt tingled up her arms, the urge to strip him bare and explore his hard body overwhelming. But she couldn't touch him. Didn't stop the thought from materializing into a warm throb between her legs.

"See?" He kissed her bottom lip. "You're already helping."

The heat from his fingers soaked into hers. She blinked against the sensation. "If helping means upending your entire life."

He shifted their linked hands behind her, settling them at the small of her back and pulling her hips closer to his. "Christ, Charlee. I needed upending. Do you have any idea how much progress I made today?"

Her body buzzed with the excited pulse of her heart. She shook her head.

"I think you've gathered by now I have some fucked up shit corroding my head." He looked at her imploringly.

She nodded.

"And you probably saw that shit stir up when I had my pathetic fucking break down in the parking lot."

"It's okay—"

"No. Listen. I *always* need narcotics when it hits that hard. Smack, blow, pills, weed, any or all of it. Every. Fucking. Time. And even then, it takes me hours to resurface."

His words squeezed her heart.

"Today, I was so damn crazed to get back to you, I shut it down in record time. *Without* drugs. Know what that means?"

She had watched him shatter twice that day. Both times he picked up the pieces and put himself back together. "*You* fixed it. Not drugs. Not me."

"You're wrong. It's you. You make me want to rake up the shit just to dissect it. Figure out what I'm made of, what I'm not, and who I am." A dimple flashed on his cheek, its appearance endearing him all the more. "Got to say, Charlee, that's an undertaking I've never cared to attempt. You make me want to care about a lot of things."

Intensity saturated his brown eyes. He appeared completely unconcerned about the presence of Nathan and the others listening in, until he touched his mouth to her ear. "More than anything, I want to learn how to bend to your touch without breaking." He stroked his cheek along hers, the rise and fall of his chest intoxicating her. "I want you to touch me inside and out." He straightened to look at her.

The heat from his words left her breathless.

He squeezed their hands at her back. "You saw strength in me once. Do you think you could find it again?"

He was a man like any other man, draped in a net of memories. But it seemed like his memories were suffocating him, as if his scars whispered and burned and tried to dominate his life. Only the man trapped beneath could do something about that.

"You stood up to Roy. You called him a fucking prick." She let out a laughing snort. "Do you know how many times I've witnessed someone confront him?"

The skin around his mouth softened, giving him a gorgeously exposed look. He shook his head.

"None. Never."

She fell into the deep waters of his eyes. They held the opening between her past and future. "To answer your question... For two years and two months, I stared at the Golden Gate Bridge from Roy's penthouse window. I watched it weather the strongest storms, rise above the thickest fogs, and buttress countless commuters with unbending steel. I used to fantasize that one day, it might carry me to a place Roy couldn't touch me." She held his gaze. "When I look at you, I see that bridge."

His lashes lowered, fanning his cheeks. Holding her hands at her back, he curled his upper body around her and spoke low into her ear. "Then I promise not to buckle beneath you."

43

Charlee followed Jay up the portable airstair to the door of the rented jet. The exhausts of shuttle buses, private planes, and fuel trucks added to the heat wafting off the tarmac.

Could one of the bustling vehicles have a Craig in it? Not that she was in a position to notice something like that. She couldn't seem to tear her eyes away from the black leather stretching over the back of Jay's thighs and cupping his ass with each lift of his muscled legs.

As he cleared the last step, he glanced over his shoulder and winked. "Like what you see?"

She pulled her lips between her teeth to suppress a grin. "You know I do, you arrogant ass." She nodded to the oval doorway in front of him. "Watch your head. It might be too swollen to fit through."

Turning toward her, he looked pointedly at his groin and pursed his lips. "You might be right."

Warmth spread across her chest and threatened to reduce her to girlish laughter. She filled her lungs with the dusk air and anchored herself to his beautiful smile. She hadn't been this relaxed in... Well, never. If only she could tuck the feeling away in a place no one could steal it.

He squatted to eye-level and she felt his gaze in the spike of her pulse and the sudden desert in her mouth. He leaned in. "Keep looking at me like that and we're going to spend the next six hours in the lavatory." He chewed the inside of his cheek. "Actually, I think we'll do that anyway."

A shiver swept through her and her hand faltered on the railing. "Is the rest of the band onboard? I thought these jets had bedrooms."

His head dropped, and he groaned. "Fuck, Charlee." He scrubbed a hand over his scalp, mussing the thick strands. "Yes, the guys are boarded." He looked up at her out of smoldering eyes. "You can count on a bedroom in all our future rentals."

They were staring at one another, ensconced in their own cosmos, when Tony's voice floated up from the tarmac. "We're on a schedule, Mr. Mayard."

He rolled his eyes and grabbed Charlee's hand, walking backward and leading her into the cabin. "Welcome to the Rolls-Royce of the sky. This twelve-passenger jet will whisk us at a speed of Mach .80 for four-thousand nautical miles—"

"Twenty-three hundred nautical miles." The man in the captain's chair turned from the dash of blinking screens. "That's our flight distance from New York to Los Angeles."

Jay shrugged. "Fine. For twenty-three hundred naughty miles—"

"Nautical miles." She laughed.

He bit his lip. "Who's giving this tour?"

She forced a straight face. Clearly, he was unconcerned about Tony's time schedule. "Right. Go ahead."

Pulling her a few more steps forward, he cleared his throat. "To your right is the full-service galley." He stretched out an arm to indicate the built-in wet bar, a grin accentuating his full lips as he opened drawers and lifted rollback covers.

Behind him, a leather couch, convertible tables, and swivel recliners sandwiched the cabin. Not much smaller than her Village apartment, the space easily accommodated the four band members, her and Nathan, and the two bodyguards.

At the rear, Laz's gelled-up spikes sprouted behind the headrest of a backward-facing recliner. Beside him, two guitar cases were oddly seat belted into their own chair. Wil and Rio perched across the aisle, wearing ear buds, eyes glued to the devices in their hands.

"To your left is the cockpit. This cloud craft features a..." Jay flicked a finger at the high-tech digital control panel. "What's running this thing?"

The pilot beamed. "An Oxford Romulus 2000 avionics system."

The blood drained from Jay's face, and his hands dropped limply at his sides.

She took a step toward the heaving wall of his chest and looked up into his wide eyes. "Get over it. Oxford Industries owns everything, especially in the aerospace industry." She lowered her voice. "And it's not like he can control the system from afar and send us hurtling to our deaths."

A sweaty pallor cast over his skin. Something beyond Roy's avionic systems was unsettling him. Unease coiled up her spine. "What's wrong?"

He looked at his Chucks, lips a thin line, and shook his head.

The silence stretched on, fraying her nerves. Standing against him, she leaned back and raised her chin. "So that's how it's going to be? Soon as something bothers you, you're going to close right up? You might as well walk away."

Without looking up, he bent an arm around her waist and pressed her body to his. His mouth grazed her jaw, her cheek, and settled over her ear. "Told you I'll never walk away."

That was probably true. She seemed to attract self-adhesive kind of men. With Jay, she didn't just want him to stay. She wanted something she didn't understand. "Will you walk *to* me? Will you move so close that the ground wobbles, the walls between us crumble, and your thoughts rip open until we're melding our fears and hopes as easily as we share air?"

He parted his lips and calmness drifted out with a sigh. "Just...just show me how." His hand trembled as it combed through her hair. "Jesus, Charlee. Nothing in this world compares to the way you make me feel."

His words bore into her heart, filling it with so many hopeful emotions, she thought it might explode.

He pressed his lips to her temple, his voice soft. "My parents died in a plane crash when I was six. It caught me off guard thinking about Roy sending you to your death in this plane."

Not the answer she was expecting, and it turned her thoughts soft and sticky. She wanted to hug him so badly it hurt. She released her grip on the countertop behind him, wedged her arms between their bodies, and hugged herself instead. "Thank you for telling me." She leaned against him. "Someday, I'd like to hear more about it. *While* I'm holding you. Okay?"

"Okay." Color flowed back to his face, but his smile was shaky. He released her, though his fingers seemed reluctant to let go of her waist. He reclaimed her hand and let her lead him through the cabin.

The drummer, Rio, glanced up and yanked his ear buds out. "Well fuck me, you old menstruating recluse." He rose and strutted down the aisle, tapping a beat on the ceiling with his knuckles and grinning at Jay. "The rumor is true? This is her? The Huntress?"

Huntress. A flutter awoke in her chest. That one word sucked her back to a time when all she had was Jay's voice singing to her through her ear buds from outside her prison. She held out a hand. "I'm Charlee."

Creases formed on Rio's bald head as his mahogany eyes roamed every inch of her except the hand she offered. "Too fucking sexy for a handshake." He stretched out his beefy arms. "Come here, baby."

Tension steamed from Jay's body as his muscles turned to stone against her back. He reached around her, stabbing a finger at Rio's chest. "No fucking way."

"Aw, come on—"

Gliding footsteps approached from behind the drummer's huge frame. Wil Sima leapt over the nearest chair, knocking Rio's arm down to get around him, and landed in a crouch on the cushion. He blew his bleached bangs out of his eyes. "Charlee. You made it."

Jay's hand tightened in hers, pulling her back a step. The narrow aisle didn't allow much maneuvering, but he managed to wiggle himself between her and his bandmates.

"Did you bring your tattoo stuff?" Wil cocked his head, his boyish grin matching his lanky body and shaggy hair. "Laz is anxious to pay his debt."

In the rear of the cabin, Laz knelt against the back of his rear-facing chair with his arms folded on the headrest. He gave her a chin lift and a grimace.

She was surprised he hadn't found a way out of the bet. "My things didn't make it." Everything she owned remained in the duffle bags at her apartment. "Maybe I could have my tattoo supplies shipped." She couldn't afford to replace them unless Laz gave her an advance on the twenty grand.

Shaking his head, Jay stared down at her. "No need, Charlee. You and Nathan will have all new things by the time we arrive. Tony's already arranged it."

A fit of objections coursed through her, but her shock by how quickly he'd solved their immediate problem of no clothes led the questioning. "When did you coordinate that?"

"She made some calls before we left your apartment. I have personal assistants and shoppers on call." His tone softened to a careful lull. "Did you leave anything behind you can't put a price on?"

Like photos? Keepsakes? Family heirlooms? A pinch of pain twisted in her chest. The only sentimental thing she owned was her sketchbook of tattoos. She rubbed a hand over the canvas of her messenger bag where it hung at her hip and felt its shape safe inside. She shook her head.

He stroked a thumb over her cheekbone. "Are there prescriptions or anything specific you need?"

"No, but the tattoo gun... You can't just—"

"Do you trust me?"

More than she should. She nodded.

Static crackled the overhead speakers. "This is Captain Hugh. We're ready for departure, so if you'll take your seats and get those seatbelts on, we'll push off in about three minutes."

As Jay guided Charlee to the two side-by-side chairs in the middle of the cabin, she looked for Nathan. A silver-haired woman in a black skirt suit plugged the exterior door. Nathan stood behind her, scanning the cabin. When he locked eyes with Charlee, he slid into a seat in the front row.

Tony moved from her post at the cockpit door and advanced up the aisle, steely eyes on Jay. "Need anything before we take off?"

He lowered into the seat beside Charlee and laced his fingers with hers. "The rest of the security team is returning commercial?"

"Yes. They followed Mr. Oxford to ensure he wouldn't obstruct our takeoff. Your L.A. team will be waiting for us when we land."

He let his head fall back against the seat. "Thanks, Tony."

The lights dimmed, and the engines whirred. The leather seat cradled her backside, and the gorgeous man beside her hummed a mellow tune.

What an indulgent way to travel. If she stayed with Jay, could she jet set all over the world with him? What if he and his band lost their lifestyle because of her? Her smile slumped, as did her shoulders.

Damn. Thinking about what-ifs was such a buzz kill. Instead, she concentrated on the hand in hers, the hypnotizing cadence of his soft humming voice, and tried to suspend the moment forever.

44

During the long minutes of taxiing and takeoff, Jay's proximity was so heady, it rubbed against Charlee's erogenous zones. He stared at her in silence, his thumb circling the top of her hand. The simmering energy between them multiplied with her heartbeats. The recycled air blowing from the ceiling did little to cool the heat searing from her skin. He appeared just as flushed. In fact, he looked like he was about to crawl out of his clothes.

Once the plane was airborne and the captain turned off the seat belt sign, he released her hand. "I need to talk to Tony for a few minutes, okay?"

"Yep," she breathed.

Leaning into her, he cupped her jaw and raised her mouth to his. The first touch sent a thrill vibrating through her body. As he deepened the kiss, wildfire spread from his lips, his breath moist and hot, and his tongue coaxing a flame of sensations. He pulled back, drank her in with his eyes, and dipped his head again, kissing every inch of her lips, her cheeks, her eyebrows, and returning to her mouth.

Their tongues, teasing and receiving, stroked warm exhales and muffled moans. She gripped the armrests, gasped for air, and squeezed her thighs together to mollify the ache between them.

One of his hands retreated from her face, sliding down her neck, over her collarbone, lingering along the outside of her breast, and lowered to clutch her waist and pull her closer. The seat belt halted her movement. He released her mouth to glare at the offending obstacle.

Fingers aching in their locked position, she uncurled them and freed the belt. "I want to touch you."

As she leaned toward him, she glimpsed the guys through the crack between their seats. Rio slumped in the last seat in the rear, head bent on his shoulder, mouth open and eyes closed. On the couch, Laz strummed a guitar in his lap, the sound piping to his large headphones.

Beside him, Wil's face pinched in concentration as he restrung his bass.

Jay removed his hand from her waist, redirecting her attention. He clenched his jaw and gripped the bulge in his leathers. Then he fell toward her and buried his moan in her neck. "Let's go to the lavatory."

The charged pulse between her legs dulled. What would Nathan think of her if she snuck off to the bathroom with Jay? Her lungs deflated. She couldn't risk his judgment without first venting her guilt. "Thought you needed to talk to Tony."

He put his hands on his knees and frowned at his erection. "Um... Not with this." The leather pants seemed to magnify his arousal.

"I could shoot it with a rubber band."

He barked out a strained laugh. "Where the hell did that come from?"

"It's worked for me in the past."

His smile crashed into a frown. "What do you mean by that exactly?"

"It's not what you think. I was just a kid."

"Jesus." He stared at her, the whites of his eyes glowing in the dampened light. "That's even worse."

"No, this is good story. Want to hear it?"

"I don't know." He rubbed a hand over his thigh, distractingly close to his erection. "Do I?"

"Yeah." She curled up in the seat with her legs beneath her and twisted to face him. "When I was little, Craig used to leave me at the neighbor's house all the time. Nice lady, but she had five boys. Bigger and older, the bastards liked to gang up on me."

His hand clenched on his leg. "Where was your mother?"

"I didn't have a mother. Just listen." She leaned back in the chair. "They cornered me in the basement, the backyard, the bathroom, anywhere Linda wasn't, and tried to bully me into taking off my pants. You know, the *I'll let you touch mine if you let me touch yours* thing?"

"No." He ground his teeth. "I don't know." His hand flexed and his eyes clouded, so she hurried to the good part.

"I was finding it difficult to fight them off. I could've tattled on them, but their retaliation would've made things worse. Instead, I made a deal with them."

"Please tell me this deal did not involve the removal of your pants. How old were you?"

She tapped her lip. "Ten. Yeah, I was ten. And the deal was, whoever's dick I could hit with a rubber band from fifteen paces away would never be able to bother me again."

He groaned.

"They agreed to one attempt each."

"Fucking hell, Charlee. And if you missed?"

She grimaced. "He would have unrestricted access below my waistband."

His hand flew to his hair, tangling and yanking with his fingers. "That was a hell of a risk." His voice rose. "You were only ten, for fuck's sake."

"Calm down. What they didn't know was I had spent the entire summer collecting rubber bands and shooting them at the bagworms that covered the big spruce behind our apartment building." She grinned. "I tagged a lot of bagworms."

His hand dropped to his lap and his lips twitched. "You hustled them."

Just thinking about it made her smile. "They lined up along the basement wall with their briefs around their ankles." She let out a happy sigh. "Nothing like watching five hard little pricks shrivel with the delightful sound of snapping rubber."

He shook his head. "That's fucked up."

"I don't know. I earned their respect, and they never messed with me again." She laughed. "It's one of my fondest memories." She glanced at his lap. "How's the hard little prick?"

"*Not* little, but definitely shriveled. Thankfully, without a snapping sound." His mouth descended toward hers.

She angled away, smiling. "Sure you want to do that again?" She pointed at his lap.

"Argh. I'll be back in a minute." He stole a quick kiss and jumped from the seat.

She leaned into the aisle to watch his ass flex through his strides. The confident way he carried himself, especially in his tight pants, made her cheeks heat and her body tingle. Good lord, she would have to cool off before she attempted a conversation with Nathan.

Too late. Nathan gave his seat to Jay and headed her way. She took a few calming breaths, looked up and smiled. "Hey."

He held out his hand. "Give me the gun."

She flinched. "Why?"

"Because it makes you too brave, too dangerous, and even more of a pain in the ass than you already are." His hand waited.

Bastard. She yanked her bag from the floor, pulled out the gun, and dropped it on his palm, meeting his glare with one of her own.

Checking the safety, he tucked it in his waistband, dropped into the chair beside her, and rubbed at a scratch on the metal arm rest. Silent seconds ticked by. She told herself she was just letting her arousal dissipate, but he was strangely reserved.

They never had trouble talking to one another, but she'd stirred up a lot of shit in one day, in addition to whatever was going on between her and Jay. Her relationship with Nathan was navigating new territory.

The awkwardness between them ballooned into a heavy pressure in her lungs. Reaching for his chin, she gently turned his face toward her. "I'm not sure when this started, this guilt I'm carrying. I need to know—"

"It's good, Charlee."

She lowered her hand. "What's good?"

"You're moving on." He turned sideways in the chair to face her and rested his head against the seatback. "I know you're still grieving over how you think you handled things with Noah, and I wish you'd stop."

A violent mess of emotions clogged her throat.

"I've looked at things from Noah's perspective a million times in the past three years. He knew something was up. Hell, *I* knew, even before I took that PI case. He was ignoring all your signals and forcing a connection that wasn't there. Can't say I blame him, though." His eyes flicked to the front of the cabin and back to her. "You're easy to love, Charlee."

She stopped breathing and the air chilled the perspiration on her face. "What are you saying?"

Sitting up, he met her with an unwavering stare. "Not what you think I'm saying. I love you, but not like that. You're my best friend, my sister, and the only family I have."

The mounting tension seeped from her body and she breathed deeply through her nose. She reached for his fingers and traced his knuckles. "You're those things to me, too, but I don't understand why you don't hate me."

He stared at their hands. "How the hell could I hate you? You gave my brother what you were capable of giving him. He didn't die brokenhearted. He died happy."

She looked away with burning eyes. "He died because of *me*." Her whisper ended on a croak.

"Bullshit. You didn't kill him. Salvador did that."

Grief pummeled her insides, but she kept it bottled, held her expression empty. She would not break down.

He cupped her cheek. "Jesus, I know your face so well. Let it go.

Don't you see? You've given me things, too. Without you, I'd be consumed by revenge." He dropped his hand and looked out the window at the passing clouds. "All those times you suggested we go our separate ways, I considered it. Believe me, I did. I want revenge, and I can accomplish it easier on my own." His eyes locked on hers. "Protecting you gives me a second chance, a kind of absolution. I didn't save him, but I can still save you. Call it a self-righteous pursuit to build my hero complex."

"Oh, please. You're the epitome of a pure heart. And I'll tell you the same thing you tell me. You aren't to blame for his death."

His lips quirked, but sadness weighted his eyelids. "No. And I sure as hell wouldn't have left my damn guns in the car that night. Wish I could beat his ass for that."

Pressure swelled in her sinuses and faded just as quick. It *was* getting easier to let him go.

"I want you to be happy. And if a guitar jockey in slut pants does it for you, who am I to judge?"

She cocked her head. Yeah, the pants definitely did something for her.

"Noah's happiest moments are kept here." He tapped her temple. "And I get to relive some of them when they shine through in your smile. I'd like to see that smile more often."

She tried to give him one, her lips quivering with the effort, and failed. "I'll see what I can do."

"All I ask is that you don't close off my part of your life, okay?"

"Never." She tackled him in a hug, and his arms enveloped her.

He laughed and pulled back to look at her. "You really like the rock star, huh?"

She reclined against the window. "Yeah." Her smile appeared suddenly and without effort. "You really like the bodyguard, huh?"

A shrug. "She's a Marine. What's not to like?"

"Whatever. We both know there's more to it."

"Maybe." His whiskered cheeks crawled to a grin. "We good?"

For the next few hours, they were outside of Roy's reach, shooting through the air at—*What did Jay say?*—Mach .80. And she had a date with a beautiful man in a bathroom.

She gave Nathan another effortless smile.

45

"We're all set then?" Jay nodded at the e-mail on Tony's laptop, tapping his fingers on his knees, the heels of his sneakers bouncing with his excitement.

"Yes. The machines will be ready in a week, but the customized engravings and the rush job quadrupled the price. Do you want to look over the bill?"

"I don't care how much they cost. Just make sure she gets them as soon as possible."

The tattoo irons served him as much as they served Charlee. There was such a thing as wanting something and someone beyond the edge of sanity. He wanted his tattoo completed, but not nearly as much as he wanted the artist. It was an all-consuming desire, unlike any he'd experienced. It lived in his blood and fed on his heart.

"You're in my seat."

He looked up to find Nathan glaring down at him. "Everything okay with Charlee?"

"She's good." Nathan bent over him, his voice lowering with palpable hostility. "If that changes and I find you're the reason, I will hollow out your dick with a butter knife."

Nathan's protectiveness surpassed Jay's instinct to defend himself. He made a hell of a trustworthy bodyguard.

"Tell you what." Jay hardened his tone, punctuated each word with conviction. "If I hurt her, in any way, I'll cut it off myself and give it to you."

Nathan straightened, his eyes smiling. "Excellent." He jerked his chin toward the rear of the cabin. "If you're done here, I think she's waiting for you."

Jay jumped to his feet and turned.

Charlee leaned her back against the lavatory door, hands behind her, laughing at something Laz was saying. Her red hair curled around her toned arms, bouncing with the shake of her head. A pink flush tinted the curve of her cheeks and glowed against her milky skin. Her smile was as full of life as her bright eyes.

Seeing her there, waiting for him, combined with the feelings he had for her, delivered the ultimate in sexual fantasy. He moved toward her, picking up his pace, driven by the memory of her satin skin beneath his fingers. He wanted to kiss every part of her body. Wanted her hands covering every inch of his. What kind of noises would she make as he lost himself inside her?

"Need a condom?" Rio kicked up his feet on the chair across from him. "Or five?"

Jay growled. Knowing his buddies were squatting feet from the bathroom dampened his arousal. He closed the final few steps and captured her gaze.

She half-turned, eyes firmly fastened to his, and fumbled with the door lever.

"I've got it." He nudged her hand away and opened the door.

"I think the couch folds into a bed." Laz leaned back in the seat, hands behind his head. "Wouldn't that be more comfortable?"

Charlee looked at the couch and back to Laz. "The couch would be preferable." She grinned. "For the boring missionary type." With a snort, she turned and vanished behind the door of the lavatory.

Jay's body hummed with anticipation as he followed her in and shut the door on the barrage of whistling and laughing. He turned the lock and tumbled into her amused eyes. "You weren't hoping for discreet, were you?" He brushed a thumb over her upturned lips.

The space was twice the size of a commercial jet lavatory and included a narrow shower stall at one end. She hopped up on the tall vanity counter and lifted a shoulder. "I haven't had discreet sex in a long time."

Her monotone statement wrenched the air from his lungs. What the hell was he doing? He couldn't just screw her like a groupie in a bathroom, much to his erection's dismay. "Charlee, I'm not going to—" Bang her? Too vulgar. Have sex with her? Too casual. Make love to her? She'd laugh. "—do this with you for the first time in a bathroom."

Some of the light dimmed in her eyes. "By *this*, you mean slam me against the wall and fuck me until I can't walk?"

Alarms screeched in his head. So much of her sexual history was tainted with Roy's abuse. What he didn't know was if she'd ever willingly given herself to another man for love. He didn't think so.

He braced his hands on the counter, caging her hips, and leaned over her, his face inches from hers. "That's the second time you've tried to cheapen us with crude language." He softened his voice, his eyes searching hers. "Why do you do that?"

A swallow nodded in her throat. "You're right. It's a defensive habit." She stared up at him and her expression opened. "I came in here with one expectation. To touch you. Will you take off your shirt?"

The air thinned, and his pulse sped up. He was desperate to be wrapped in her embrace, her body, but what if his reaction scared her? "Charlee—"

"You asked me to trust you. I do. Your turn."

She had asked him to walk to her, to meld with her. His resolution forged, rushing oxygen throughout his body. His blood scorched through his veins.

He gripped the back of his shirt, pulled it over his head, and dropped it to the floor.

She made a little noise. "Wow. Even sexier than the last time I saw you without a shirt."

The muscles in his chest twitched and his heart lifted.

"Turn around."

He moved in a tight circle and flattened his hand on the wall beside him. "I've never shown it to anyone, but I... Look at it." More often than he was willing to admit.

"It's exactly as I remember." Her soft breaths marked the passing seconds. "Your lyrics about the flames, the steel, and the things we talked about that night... They carried me through some lonely weeks in San Francisco."

His gut twisted. He focused on the filigree designs printed on the wallpaper, and tried not to picture her naked and shackled to Roy Oxford.

"It was as if you were singing directly to me."

"I *was* singing to you," he rasped through the dry husk of his mouth. "Your needle tapped my heart's blood that night. Every song I've written since then has been about you. For you." Even when he thought she was dead.

Her silence made him realize how creepy his confession sounded. He glanced desperately over his shoulder. Her eyes flicked up, wide and wet with unshed tears.

"Oh, Charlee." He moved to face her.

"No. Stay there." She wiped her lashes with the back of a hand. "Can I put my mouth on you?"

The request coaxed a shiver from his body and scratched his

voice. "Yeah."

She hooked her boots around his thighs and backed his ass into the *V* of her legs. Her body heat surrounded him. Her breath stroked his back and his muscles contracted. Her lips tickled his scars and shot jolts of electricity up his spine.

He pressed his hand to the wall, battled to keep it there. The other he shoved in his pocket. His fingers ached to touch her, undress her, and unravel her. He strained his neck to see her gorgeous face.

Without lifting her mouth, she tilted her eyes up at him. "Doing okay?"

"I want to touch you."

"Not yet." A soft kiss on his spine. "Now turn back around and close your eyes."

He pushed his hand hard against the cool surface, squeezed his eyes shut, and trembled in anticipation of her touch. How could something so right feel so terrifying? "Promise me when I get lost in my fucked-up head, you won't run away."

A volley of kisses fluttered across his back. "*If* you get lost, I promise."

Her shirt rustled, brushed against him and dropped to the floor. The next thing landed on his shoe. He opened his eyes. A red lace bra draped over his feet. His balls tightened.

Her bare chest pressed against his back, and her mouth, soft and wet, slid over his scars. Oh fuck, there wasn't a sensation in the world that could rival the caress of her nipples over his skin.

A rumble vibrated through his chest, her nearness like a sensual note quivering from his guitar.

"Tell me," she breathed on his skin, "what is sex like with you?"

"Wh—" He choked. "What?"

She licked along the bumps of his spine, her tongue a hot wave running over his flesh, leaving goose pimples in its wake. "Describe your most recent sexual encounters."

No fucking way. He jerked to glance at her and was met with the palm of her hand inches from his face. Was she blocking his view of her? Or of the reflection of his back in the mirror? He looked back at the door in front of him. "Why are you asking me this?"

"You know why."

Was he so messed up she needed an outline of lessons learned to navigate him? It was safer to keep his shit hidden in the dark. Still, she wanted inside, and he wanted to let her. "I don't remember most of them. I get drunk or stoned to work myself up for..."

"Physical closeness."

He nodded and dropped his head on his arm where it braced against the wall.

She peppered the valleys between his ribs with flitting kisses. "And the encounters you remember?"

Fuck, he didn't want her to stop kissing him. Deep breath. "I tie them up."

She stopped, but didn't move away. He angled his chin to see her. "I'm so sorry, Charlee. Your history—"

"Don't you dare apologize." Fire sparked in her eyes, even as she dragged her lips over his tattoo, inches from his face. "Apparently, you've forgotten I've been paying men to tie me up for three years."

His fingers curled on the wallpaper.

"Do you have unprotected sex?" She asked against his shoulder.

"Yes." He felt dirty and sick with regret, wanting so badly to be clean and deserving of her.

Her tongue darted in lazy circles over the outline of his tattoo.

He grasped for something to dig his nails into, something to reassure her with. "I tested clean at the doctor a couple days ago."

Hot breaths swept over his bicep, her mouth sucking and tasting the sensitive skin under his arm. He was going to lose her glorious mouth with his next announcement, but a swelling resignation settled around his heart. "Last night, I might've fucked—"

"I met your girlfriends. They were pretty vocal about how you *didn't* sleep with them." Her lips moved against his skin. "Though I've got to ask. Whose cum was between their legs? It couldn't have been all theirs."

The backs of his ears caught fire and saliva filled his mouth. The thoughts of his behavior with those women turned his stomach. "Charlee, I can't."

The warmth of her mouth disappeared. In its place, a strange sensation pressed down. What was she doing? He turned his head—

"Close your eyes. Please?"

Uncertainty attacked his nerves and locked up his knees. He closed his eyes.

"I'm not going anywhere. Now tell me about last night."

The firm pressure on his back distracted him. Her breasts? Her hands?

His head spun with a conflagration of images. Her red lace bra. The wind pummeling the shed. Her sensual lips. The creak of the oven door. He needed the numbing effects of blow. Sifting through his pockets, his hand came up empty. "Fuck. Fuck. Fuck."

"Maybe you did fuck them. They were covered in semen."

Her detached voice splintered the vortex of memories. Or was it his aunt's voice? *You're cold. So cold.* Why was she tormenting him?

The floor canted, and he rocked on his feet. "I don't know."

"They called themselves Charlee. I'm your only Charlee, right?"

Mildew and soot chased his rapid inhales. He smacked his hand against the rotting wood wall.

"Jay? Jay?"

Charlee called to him from outside the shed. Her lilt wasn't accusing. It was soothing and alive and breathing through him. Her lips latched on to his back, holding him to her. "I might not be able to help you, but I'll share your pain if you let me. Tell me about last night."

Something cracked inside him. The humiliation he'd tried to keep from her trickled out. "I tied them up and jerked off on their cunts." He closed his eyes. "I did it while thinking of you and shouting your name over and over until I don't remember anything else." His body sagged, and his heart rate depressed.

"Look at me, Jay."

Eyes aching with vulnerability, he turned half-way in the *V* of her thighs, stopped. Pale pink nipples filled his vision. They pointed up, one resting erotically against his bicep. He absorbed every detail from their curves and size to their velvety texture. He couldn't stop his groan nor could he stop himself from completing the turn to face her. The hands on his shoulders slid with his movement.

Oxygen vanished. Black and white flashes blotted out her face. He strained to see through it, to focus on her smile, the strength in her eyes. All the filth in his head weakened in comparison.

"My hands have been here a while." She used those hands to twist his shoulders and pull his back against her chest. "You were doing great until you saw them, so focus on me, okay?"

He dragged his gaze over his shoulder and watched her reflection in the mirror. He drank in the arch of her slender neck and the slope of her bare shoulder as she dipped her lips to the flame inked between her fingers. Fingers that massaged his scars. Fingers he hadn't noticed... Then it dawned on him. "All your questions about those girls were just a way to distract me?"

Tingling shocks zapped from her kneading hands. She gave his back an open mouth kiss. "I thought, if I could keep one of your recent memories well supplied with fuel, the older ones would stay quiet."

At that moment, he knew she hadn't just given him the pleasure of her touch. It was a challenge, a proposal of what could be, an offer of salvation. "You make me want to let all my memories surface. I want to face them."

"You will." She bit his shoulder, and her playfulness woke his dick.

The heat of her palms sliding over his shoulders, the sweep of her tongue tracing his scars, and the sweet fragrance of her hair wrapped him in a whirlwind of sensations.

"You're responding so well to my hands, I want to take advantage."

Before he could question her, she reached around and cupped him between his legs. He choked on a noisy gulp and dug his fingernails into the wallpaper. As psychologically turned on as he was, no way could he prevent the intensity of his hard-on.

She traced the curve of his erection through his leathers and smiled against his back. "Oh my God. You're ginormous."

If he didn't already know he was averagely sized, the laughter in her voice would've cued him to her teasing. His rebuff died in his throat when her other hand joined the first and her pelvis pressed against his ass.

She nuzzled his back and ground against him. "I want to see it."

A shudder skated through him. He couldn't form a coherent answer with her arms locked around his waist and her hands rubbing in synchronized motions on either side of his cock.

Sharp hot exhales followed the wet trail of her mouth down his spine. She was breathing too fast. He was breathing faster. When her fingers quickened and strengthened, he dug deep and found his voice. "I want you under me, not behind me."

"Okay." A breathy, empowering response. She was still with him.

He twisted around and captured her in his arms, pushed her back against the mirror, and devoured the heady spice of her lips. His leather pants itched and confined. Her leggings were in the way. Too many fucking clothes.

"Charlee." He drew in her tongue. She curled it with his, their lips sliding together. The kiss grew so aggressive, so fast, they were both fighting for air.

He broke away and lowered his mouth to chase her nipple, catching it between his lips, flicking it with his tongue. His excitement grew in demanding tremors. All he could think about was stripping her pants and shoving himself deep inside her.

She dropped her head against the mirror and moaned. The

sound resonated in his dick. He slid his palm over the curve of her waist to the rise of her ass and slipped his fingers beneath the waistband. His erection pulsed painfully in its cage.

He grabbed her nape and pulled her lips back to his mouth. "Charlee, take me out."

Her tongue traced his bottom lip, lapping and teasing, and she pulled back to look at him. "Has anyone ever touched you there?"

A cruel voice screamed from the recesses of his mind. He extinguished it with thoughts of Charlee, of what she was offering him. "Not in a long time."

Her gaze narrowed and softened just as quick. Fuck, he loved her eyes. They were so expressive. Authentic. Direct. Much like the hand sliding down his stomach and tugging on the button of his pants. He sucked in a breath.

The button popped free. She ensnared him with a devilish smile and lowered the zipper.

46

The warm leather of Jay's pants peeled back as Charlee eased down the zipper one metal tooth at a time. Uncovering him was as thrilling as it was terrifying. He'd said he wouldn't fuck her in a bathroom, but she teetered on the confusing edge of begging.

Would he tie her up? The idea produced a delicious quiver deep in her core, but it morphed into queasiness when she pictured the women spread out on the piano. She didn't want him to see her like that, nor did she want her intimacy with him reduced to a written contract like her Dom sessions. Problem was, she needed that brand of sexual healing.

She nudged him backward two paces and his back hit the door. She hopped off the counter and her fingers followed the strip of hair from his naval to the close-trimmed patch below the spread of his fly. The anticipation fanning in her womb exploded into a fire. "Commando." She swallowed. "Smart. No panty lines."

He groaned something thick and indistinct.

She placed a kiss on the arch of his pecs and leaned back. "I want to see you in superhero briefs."

A smile flitted across his mouth and he shook his head. Eyes locked on her hands, his thumb strolled up and down on her neck.

As tantalizing as his pants were, she wanted them off. She hadn't willingly explored a man in three years and the thought of tasting him produced a rush of wet heat between her legs.

She pulled at his waistband and yanked it down the hard lines of his thighs. Her squat forced his hands to her head as his erection sprang free. Swollen and uncut, it curved up, waiting. She licked her lips.

His legs shook beneath her hands, but he didn't drive her head forward. Rather he tried to pull her back. "Charlee, don't do this." His deep voice reverberated from her nipples to thighs.

Heat throbbed between her legs. Never had she experienced

such a demanding desire as the one pulsating between them. Could he take her to the place she sought through punishing pain, where bygones and dead endings didn't exist? Could he stretch her body and bruise her flesh until it was safe to let go?

A dark sea of thoughts stormed inside her as she curled her hand around the tip of his shaft. The Doms had coached her to focus on relinquishing control rather than making it about pain. She wanted both. She wanted to lash out with her safe word and use the pain to drown the sexual memories that always came when she released.

His erection jerked in her hand and her sick desires fissured, oiling her arousal and swelling her clit. What made it real made it shameful, and the overwhelming hunger for things she shouldn't want rose, and rose, until a fever broke out through her body.

She looked up into his heavy-lidded eyes, gripped the soft uncircumcised skin and slid it downward, slowly releasing the folds as she reached the bed of wiry hair.

Could she do painless sex? She'd experienced it with one man, but Noah's sweet nature came at a time in her life when she almost felt...healed. She would never appreciate that level of gentleness again. After his death and her second imprisonment, she was quite possibly more fucked up than the man trembling above her.

Startled out of her thoughts, she realized she was stroking him frantically, wringing her grip along his length, her other hand digging into the hard brick of his ass. His chin fell to his chest and his jaw stretched through his panting, spurring her to continue the pace.

The indentions of his muscles bunched over his torso, and veins bulged in his rigid arms. What a stunning sight. She wanted to crawl up his body and drive them both beyond their mental and tactile boundaries. Maybe she was already doing that. She *was* touching him. Was he cured? Or would he need a distraction every time she initiated touch in the future?

She laced her fingers together and hugged her palms around him. Squeezing up to collect pre-cum—slicking down, up, down—she lured ragged noises from the back of his throat. Maybe she could stroke him past the point of restraint until he wrenched her head back, bent her over the sink, and took whatever he pleased. God help her, she trembled to please him.

His chest heaved with his grunts and his hands tangled in her hair as he watched. "Charlee." A plea. "It's unreal. Your hands... On me. I can't believe how good it feels."

Nuzzling the crown with her lips and nose, she inhaled the

arousing blend of suede, musk, and man. "If the touch gives more than it takes, isn't it always good?"

He stared at her like he was on top of a new world, looking over the edge. "Yeah, Charlee. You're showing me that." He tugged the lock of hair wrapped around his finger and jerked her head back. "My turn to give."

The twinge from his tug simmered the ache between her legs. Oh, the pain he could give, it would free her. It *would*. "Harder."

His brows lowered over narrowed eyes, and he unraveled his fingers from her hair.

Shit. He'd never agree to hurt her. Her shoulders slumped. But she still had *his* climax, and it would be something to behold. She took him into her mouth, circling her tongue and raising her eyes.

His jaw opened and closed in soundless groans with each pump of her mouth. After a few minutes, he cupped her neck with both hands and halted her movements. "Come up here."

Not yet. She released him with a slippery pop. Her kisses glistened over his foreskin. "Do you tan in the nude?"

He laughed, but it strangled as she drew him back into her mouth and strengthened the suction. Gasping, he let go of her face to catch his sag toward the counter's ledge behind her. "Enough." He jerked his hips away.

She sat on her heels. "I want you to finish."

"No." In a half-crouch, he wedged his fingers under the backs of her thighs, shifted her around his hips, and sat her on the leather bench seat that hid the toilet. As he yanked up his pants to cover his gorgeous ass, rejection punched her in the gut. That was until he settled between her knees and pinned her with a scorching stare. "I want to look in your eyes and feel your gasps on my lips the first time I come in you."

A viscid, foreign feeling adhered to her heart, gluing her to him from the inside out. She closed her eyes. Their unexplainable bond took root over the three years that separated them, but in one day, they had knocked down a physical barrier, and he was weakening emotional walls she hadn't acknowledged in a long time. "This is madness, Jay."

He kissed her softly. "The comforts of madness are plenty. Enjoy them with me."

When she opened her eyes, his were regarding her with a strength of energy that pulled her mouth back to his. The air around them stirred with their breaths. His lips rolled over hers, his whiskers abraded, and the fingers along her spine emitted electric shocks. His tongue moved in a rhythmic tenor, flicking and twirling. She rocked her hips and dragged her nails over his scars before she could stop.

"I want to keep going." The scratch in his voice was at odds with the gentle stroke of his knuckle sliding over her cheek, down her neck, and circling her breastbone. "I don't know if..." He pulled his hand away and rubbed his eyebrow. "I mean, I know you've been working through some things in your...sessions." He gritted his teeth and looked away.

She touched his jaw, tried to smooth out the stiffness. "Outside of contractual sex—" His eyes squeezed shut, and she rushed on. "I honestly don't know how I'd respond. I want to try."

He interlaced his fingers with hers on his face and pressed a kiss on her palm. Then his eyes flashed open, branding her with their heat. "We are *not* too fucked up to make this work."

It was a vehement promise. Holding his face, she slid a hand across his shoulder blade and traced the first raised edge she encountered. "Your pain brought us together."

Tenderness melted his eyes. "I came to you that night to erase it, so I wouldn't have to remember." His cheeks lifted beneath her hand. "And you gave me something I never want to forget." Shaking his head, his gaze shifted to her mouth, down her neck...

Her nipples tightened, and her breasts grew heavy under his scrutiny. He moved his hands to glide them over her arms. Then he cupped them. First, one breast, then the other. The muscles in his back rippled under her caress and his breathing picked up.

He rotated his hips against the seat edge, his hands lifting and molding her. She caught sparks from each tug and twist, the sensations zipping straight to her womb.

Panting, he lowered his mouth and laved a nipple with the flat of his tongue. She arched her back. He flicked it with teasing laps. "I've wanted to do this since you first took your shirt off in your apartment."

The air whispered over her kiss-soaked skin, chilling her. "Sorry about my indecent—"

"I'm not. I've never been this attracted to anyone. No one compares to you, Charlee." He slid his torso up hers and found her lips. "This is what your three-year absence did to me." He removed her hand from his back and pressed it against his erection. Warm and bare, pushing through the unfastened zipper, it seeped moisture on her palm.

"So what you're saying is it's been a *hard* three years?" She squeezed him.

Pressing his face into the crook of her neck, he groaned a strangled chuckle. "Funny thing is—Oh Jesus, I can't tell you this."

Tracing his ear with her tongue, she worked her hand over him in long twisting strokes.

"Ah fuck, you have to stop doing that." He gripped her wrist, stopping her, and slid his mouth to her injured earlobe. The gentle kiss he placed there bathed her in tingles.

"Tell me what you were going to tell me."

He rested his forehead on her shoulder. "I used to have the damnedest time maintaining an erection. Then I met you and..." He let out a shaky breath. "I've been hard for three years."

She knew he hadn't been celibate for years. He was trying to tell her he hadn't been satisfied. Determined to fix that, she shook off his restraining hand and rotated her wrist, winding and compressing him with steady pumps.

"Unngh. Charlee, stop." The force in his voice matched the lurch of his hips as he broke away. "Keep doing that and I'm going to come so hard, I'll blow all the clouds from the sky."

She burst into laughter. "Oh my God, that's the cheesiest—"

His punishing kiss stole her capacity to think. "Ready to feel?"

The throb in her pussy ignited. "Don't be gentle."

47

Jay curled both hands around Charlee's neck and attacked her mouth. His sudden aggression sizzled every cell in her body. He tasted and teased, deepening the kiss and swallowing her gasps with each thrust of his tongue. Their breaths became one and their hips rocked, reaching to close the gap between them.

The spicy scent of his mouth and skin overpowered her senses and magnified her hunger. She wanted him to bite her. Hard. She pulled at his waistband. Wanted him closer. Trembled to pull him inside.

He consumed her lips, pushing his tongue against hers, giving her glimpses of his gorgeous smile between nips. His hands moved over her shoulders and down her arms. When they bypassed her tingling breasts, she groaned in his mouth.

A laugh rolled over his tongue, half-suppressed by his rough exhale. His hands lowered to her belly, tickling a squeal from her, and slipped beneath the elastic at her hips.

He dipped his tongue for another taste and fluttered kisses over her cheekbone to her ear. "Lift."

Body vibrating and head spinning, she arched her hips. Her leggings and panties lowered with his hands, bunching at her thighs.

"You're shivering." His naked chest pressed against hers, hot and silky with sweat.

"I'm not cold." She combed her fingers through his hair and held onto his head as his nose stroked down her neck and over her breast.

Holding her gaze, he moved down her body and ran his lips over her stomach. Then he lowered his eyes.

Inhaling deeply, he twirled a finger through the wet hair between her legs. "Christ, Charlee. The red is natural?"

She nodded, slumping back. Her nipples ached so badly, she grabbed them, wiggling them up and down with pinched fingers to release some tension.

"Aw, God." Eyes on her hands, he gripped the base of his dick and squeezed, his shoulders curling forward and his head dropping. Breathless seconds passed. Once he seemed to compose himself, he bent awkwardly in the confined space, tackled the laces on her boots, and yanked them off.

The rustling descent of her leggings and panties mingled with their heavy breaths. That done, her garments smacked the wall behind him. His hands shook as he spread her legs for his view.

A spasm hit her as suddenly as her thoughts, and she tried to close her legs. He was too close. He would see too much. Her scars. Her shame.

He scooted her ass to the edge of the seat and looked up out of hooded eyes. "You okay?" He stroked a finger over her slit as he studied her face. It slid easily through her folds and chased away some of her fear. As long as he didn't look inside. Her legs, bent over his muscular forearms, trembled with each touch. A wanton noise escaped her lips.

"Soaking wet, Charlee." His lashes lowered as he watched his caress. "So fucking ready."

If he knew what she was ready for, he wouldn't sound so awed.

He crouched further to the floor, moving her legs to his shoulders, and dragging his lips along her thigh. When he reached the apex of her thighs, he spread her open with his fingers, his inspection scalding.

She squirmed and squeezed her legs around him. "Stop looking."

He jerked his head up and his eyebrows climbed together. "Why?"

"The scars. They're disgusting." She choked back the flashes of Roy ripping and hurting, stealing everything, leaving her numb and empty.

Jay blinked, looked down, and his eyes narrowed. He eased his finger partially in, and she held her breath. He circled her entrance, stretching the skin. She wanted to feel it, tried to shed the shield that deadened her there.

He lowered his face, his breath warm on her thigh. "You should celebrate them." His gaze drifted to hers and his mouth opened. As she watched with a mixture of horror and thrall, he flicked his tongue over her clit. "They're a reminder." Slowly, delicately, he licked along her outer lips. "That you survived." His tongue passed over the scarred ridges inside her labia. "And healed."

When he covered her with his mouth, she arched her back, hands flying to his head. His lips played over her as his tongue darted in and out, flicking and stirring. He made her want to feel. Made her want to try. But it was too easy to take herself to that contaminated part of her mind, where whips and canes beat her into numbness.

He swayed his hips with the thrust of his tongue, tasting her inside and out, his fingers digging into her thighs. One hand moved up to knead her breast. The other held her open for his mouth.

Doing her best to reach climax, she ground against his face and raked his hair, twisting and pulling. She swiveled her hips, tried to find the spot. Several minutes passed, maybe an hour. Small sensations gathered, but she couldn't hang onto them.

Sexual tension clotted the room, thickening by the minute. He added a second finger and increased his effort. More pressure, more speed, and still she couldn't let go.

Without slowing his hand, he buried his face against her contracting stomach. "Come for me, Charlee."

"Harder."

A third finger joined the first two, and his thrusts increased in rhythm and strength. Not enough.

"Harder, Jay. Like you're punching me there."

"Fuck," he moaned against her damp skin. The muscles flexed in his pounding arm. He slid up her body, taking one of her legs with him, bending her in half. His knee landed on the seat beside her, and his dick ground against the back of her raised thigh. He kissed her fiercely, desperately, and his fingers drove in and out with hard hitting velocity.

She wanted to come. She wanted to hurt. What a worthless slut. His beautiful girl was so dirty and pathetic. She whimpered against his mouth and her shield quivered, threatened to collapse. No, she couldn't let it. Couldn't let her repulsive desires tumble out around him. She held it in place, stayed her orgasm, but she couldn't stop the burn ripping through her sinuses or the achy feeling in her eyes.

His mouth was relentless, moving over hers, sucking her strength, and hammering her wall. "Fucking hell, you're sexy." He spread kisses over her lips as he banged her with his hand. "And you smell incredible." He peppered a trail along her jaw. "You're gorgeous." His voice cracked, and he dragged his nose along hers. "And brave."

The storm around her heart thundered against his. She tried to blink away the wet blur as he caught her wretched wails in draining kisses.

"You're perfect. You're..." He leaned back and choked on a gasp, his eyes wide. "Crying?"

48

A tear curled into Charlee's mouth. Embarrassed, she swiped at the streak on her cheek and squared her shoulders. "I'm not crying."

Jay moved his hands to her knees and looked up, his face a white sheet. "What have I done?" he whispered.

In the next heartbeat, his arms were around her, lifting her. He took her seat, settled her sideways on his thighs, and pressed her face against his neck. "I fucked up. I'm so sorry."

What? She pushed against his chest and grabbed his face with both hands. "You did *not* fuck up. It's me. *I* fucked up."

He flinched at her touch, but before she could move her hands, he gripped her arms to hold them in place.

She drew in a ragged breath. It was awful feeling guilty when she didn't mean to upset him. Maybe it wasn't guilt at all, but remorse over her inability to make him happy. She leaned in and brushed her mouth over his in an attempt to bring back the moment they had just shared.

His lips were tight, unresponsive, and a lump swelled in her throat. Twisting her hands out of his hold, she dropped them in her lap and turned her head away, the ache in her chest threatening to well her eyes again. "I'll just get dressed."

Holding her hips to his lap, he helped her collect her clothes from the floor. As she dressed, he stared at the door behind her, his arm locked around her waist. He wouldn't let her stand even as she dragged on her pants.

"I can't decide if you're mad at me or just appalled." Her voice was so quiet, she felt it scratch more than she heard it.

He jerked his eyes to her and cocked his head, matching her volume. "What?"

She coughed. "We should go back to our seats. We're probably missing dinner." The thought of eating rippled nausea through her stomach.

"Bullshit." He glared at her. "We're going to talk about what just happened. Right here. Right now." He scrubbed a hand over his face and mumbled, "Now that you have clothes on."

Shame scalded her cheeks. Did he think she was dirty? She jumped up and he yanked her back to his lap.

She shoved at his arm. "If you find me so repulsive, let me go."

His eyes bugged. "Repulsive? Good God, Charlee. Are you crazy?" He gripped her waist and scooted her to his knee, glaring at his erection and back at her.

Oh. "You still want me?"

"Of course I still want you. I'm trying to fucking restrain myself."

"What I begged you to do. And I couldn't...come... I thought—"

"That's part of your problem." He tried to work his zipper up and couldn't stretch the fly over his dwindling arousal. "You're thinking instead of feeling." He gave up on his pants and fixed his eyes on hers. "I don't know why you feel bad about what we just did." His tone softened. "From where I'm sitting—" He shoved a hand through his hair, closed his eyes, and breathed, "It was really, *really* sexy."

Sexy? She shivered with memories of her orgasmic screams piercing the walls of Roy's stockroom. "It's not sexy. It's sick. As in Roy Oxford's favorite flavor."

He lowered his hand to hers with a delicateness that contradicted the emotions marching across his glare. "Yeah, we're going to talk about that, too. Hand me my shirt." He pointed at the floor.

Woodenly, she slid off his lap and tagged the shirt.

He rose with her, never breaking contact, his leg against hers, a hand on her hip, and leaned against her backside as he slid up his zipper. She felt him all around her, as much a part of her as her own skin. Despite the descent in his mood, his nearness comforted her in ways she was growing alarmingly addicted to.

Shifting to face him, she startled when his breath rustled her hair from behind. He brushed a wayward strand off her shoulder and replaced it with his lips. Heat radiated from his body and kicked up her pulse. With a sigh, she let her head fall back to his chest.

He walked his fingers around her waist and tugged the shirt from her hand. "Thank you." His whisper sent tingles dancing over her skin.

She turned as he raised the shirt over his head and shoved his arms through. The muscles in his shoulders and chest expanded and squeezed. A bead of sweat chased the crease between her breasts. Had the air vents stopped working?

His head emerged from the neck hole and his eyes instantly

found hers. He was so powerfully attractive, she couldn't look away. In fact, no one could. It wasn't just his fame that drew people. It was *him*.

Wrinkles grooved his forehead. "What?"

She put her hand on his chest, stopping him from lowering his shirt. "Even if you weren't famous, you'd still be the center of female attention."

The wrinkles deepened, and he shook his head.

"You're telling me that before you had a recognizable face, you didn't draw women's eyes everywhere you went?"

He sighed, watching her finger trace the dip between his pecs. Yeah, she was touching him, and he wasn't flinching. But her relief was buried under insecurity.

Could she deal with that? Constantly competing with women better looking and lower maintenance than her? "I don't have a chance in hell," she mumbled.

He snapped his head up and glowered at her. "I only want your eyes, your attention."

"Oh, you have that. Trust me. You're the sexiest man I've ever met."

He scowled and shoved his shirt down the perfectly sculpted proof, knocking her hand out of the way.

"Your sex appeal won't hold my attention forever though." She bit her lip, trammeled by the kind of hope she hadn't entertained since she was a child.

His frown fell away to blank confusion.

"This will hold me." She poked him on the chest. "You have the heart one expects to see at the center of a fire, bending and twisting like steel, but never breaking. If something happens to mine, yours would be stubborn enough to beat for both of us."

His lips parted. Then her back hit the door under the weight of his body and their lips collided in a desperate fusion. He clinched his arms around her waist and palmed her ass, crushing their hips together.

The friction of their rubbing bodies, the heat from their lips, and the harmony of their breathy noises set her body ablaze in the clutch of his arms. His fingers slipped beneath her shirt and circled her tailbone. Hers pushed through his hair. The spiral in her womb returned as if it never left, winding her heart rate higher and higher.

A fist knocked on the door, vibrated against her spine. They flung apart and stared at one another, gasping.

Another knock, followed by Nathan's muffled voice. "Charlee?"

Jay grinned, his eyes glimmering. "He's like your dad, ready to beat my ass on our first date."

"He's nothing like my dad." Her voice was sharper than it should've been.

His face fell. "Shit, I'm sorry. I shouldn't have—"

"Stop apologizing." She wiped her tingling lips with the back of her hand. "I'll tell you all about Craig Grosky. Then you'll know. Okay?"

"Craig," he mumbled to himself, rubbing his nape. A smirk slanted his mouth. He must have figured out her nicknames.

As she turned toward the door, he smacked her ass. The echo bounced through the room, the sting lingering for long delicious seconds.

His whisper caressed her ear. "We're going to talk about that, too."

She shivered, inhaled deeply, and opened the door.

Lips pinched in a line, Nathan leaned into his arm, bent on the door jamb, and scanned her face.

She gave him a reassuring smile. "Everything okay?"

He glanced over her head. She missed Jay's expression, but the muscles in Nathan's cheeks relaxed. He looked back at her. "They're holding your dinner. You should eat."

"Thank you. How long till we land?"

He glanced at his watch. "Three hours." Straightening, he clasped the latch on the door, but didn't move to leave.

"What's wrong? You seem...worried."

"Should I be?"

Her lips turned up. "Yes."

He rubbed his eyelids, volleyed another glare at Jay, and closed the door.

She locked the door and turned. Their gazes caught instantly. The physical connection was severed, but the magnetism between them pulsed, beckoning. She swayed closer. Their little vacuum crackled and heated.

Stretching to wrap her arms around his neck, she froze mid-reach. "If I touch you again, will it be like starting over?"

He took her hands in his and lowered onto the bench, guiding her knees to straddle him. "Let's find out." He jutted his chin out, the cords stretching in his neck as he stared at her, waiting.

"You put a lot of faith in me." Her fingers hovered over his throat.

"If you stay close to me, Charlee, my faith will stay close, too."

Everything inside her melted as she molded her body around his and touched a fingertip to the hollow at the base of his neck. His eyes didn't shift from hers, his muscles didn't tense, and a smile lifted one side of his mouth.

Oh, thank God. Kissing his chin, the corners of his mouth, and lingering on his lips, she wedged her hand between their chests, smoothing her palm over his breastbone and absorbing his warmth. "Good?"

"Now I am."

She went back to his mouth for a deeper kiss. He laughed against her lips and pulled back until his head bumped the wall behind him. "We need to talk."

Ugh. "Okay."

With an arm around her back, he laced their free hands together on the seat beside them. Moments passed as he watched his thumb bump over her knuckles, his eyes unfocused. Then he looked at her. "Please don't be offended by anything I say or ask. I'm making no judgments. I just want the full picture so I can try to help, okay?"

She nodded, hoping he was ready to hear the answers.

49

Charlee choked on the foreboding atmosphere, waiting for Jay to begin his questioning.

"I'm surprised and relieved that you're willing to be intimate with me after...what you survived."

She tensed against him. Where anyone else might've feared to step, he went rushing in.

He watched her closely, caution gripping his voice. "Your sessions, your openness, whatever it is you're doing, it works. I should take lessons from you."

The sudden image of him dominating her in a dungeon sent bolts of excitement through her body. "You shouldn't be surprised. I don't know what *you* survived, but I recognized the pain eating at you the night we met. I suspect your abuser wasn't so different from mine. Yet, here you are, willing to be intimate."

Without so much as a nonverbal acknowledgment, he held her through a comfortable silence. Eventually, he stirred, kissing her bottom lip. "I know it's unfair to ask you to answer my questions and not answer yours. For now, let's stay focused on you, on what happened between us, okay?"

She nodded. "For now."

"I'm trying to wrap my head around your sessions. It would make more sense if you were the one with the whip. A submissive position seems like the last thing you'd want."

His gaze turned introspective and she kept quiet to see what he'd come up with.

"I think you need the pain," he murmured.

Her throat tightened. Of course, he was right, but hearing it voiced made her want to shove him. "No. That's not—"

"No? Charlee, the harder I pounded you, the wetter you got." His timbre remained soft despite the punch of his words.

"The pain helps me focus. It's just..."

"It's nothing to be ashamed of. And as soon as we both grasp what it means, and *accept* it, we can figure out how to make it work. Help me understand. Tell me why you aren't doing the dominating to take back what Roy took from you?"

"I don't know. It's not like I have a handbook telling me what to do. I just go with what feels right for me. And it may seem like I'm yielding, but I'm not. I can stop it when I want. If I topped you—"

His eyes narrowed.

"You would have the control. You could say stop, and I would have to concede."

"Did this kind of thing appeal to you before you met Roy?"

"I wouldn't know. I was sixteen when he got me the first time."

His body turned to stone beneath her and his hands balled into fists.

"No punching the bathroom wall." She tapped his tense lips until they slacked.

"How did he get you?"

"Craig had a gambling addiction. Owed a lot of money to a lot of people. Most of his debt was owed to Roy Oxford."

"And you didn't have a mom."

"Nope."

He closed his eyes and opened them just as slowly. "You and I have lived equally lonely lives. I wish we would've had each other growing up."

A light, hazy feeling drifted through her. He would've protected her, cherished her, *loved* her when no one else did.

"What happened?"

The dreamy sensation evaporated, leaving the heavy burden of reality. "One morning, Craig woke me, told me I wasn't going to school. We were going on a trip." She looked at the door. "I had no idea I wouldn't be returning to Phoenix. Though, thinking back on it, I'm not sure Craig did either."

Jay's fingers bit into her hip.

She let her hair fall forward on her shoulders, hiding her face. She had been so gullible then. "We drove eleven hours to San Francisco. Straight to Roy's penthouse. When we arrived, he made me change clothes in the car. Gave me a short black dress to wear and led me to the sixtieth floor." And still she hadn't questioned Craig's intentions.

Jay pushed her hair from her face, and turned her chin to see her eyes. "Go on."

"There were five men gathered around a poker table in Roy's game room. Wealthy, if their suits and piles of chips were anything to go by. I knew Craig owed Roy money. I didn't know how much, but I thought he'd win back his debt." She sighed at her naivety. "I later figured out I was there as collateral in case he didn't."

"To barter you?"

"For one night. Craig was a selfish prick and an absent father, but I don't think he intended to leave me there permanently."

"I want to kill him, Charlee."

A small smile shook the corner of her mouth. "Roy beat you to it."

His eyes widened.

"Nothing worked out the way Craig planned. He certainly hadn't expected Roy's reaction to me."

Red splotched his cheeks and the torment in his eyes blistered in her chest. She tucked her chin and let her hair cover her face again.

He gathered it with one hand at her neck and used it to tilt her head back. "Stop hiding from me. I want to hear all of it."

The concern in his soft expression and his mere proximity bolstered her.

"The moment I arrived, Roy watched me in the oily way he does. Eyes sliding up and down. Smile oozing across the table. I wasn't used to that kind of attention. I was inexperienced, completely unaware of what it meant. I couldn't have guessed at the things he was thinking about doing to me. Over the course of the night, his glances grew more intense, more possessive. I should've figured it out and run."

His eyes, glassy under the fluorescent lights, cleaved straight through her heart. "You were a child, had zero power to change the outcome. You did as your father told you, trusted him the way every child trusts her parent for protection."

She nodded. "Then three women sashayed in. They were beautiful, with boobs out to here, and dressed in undergarments. They flocked around Roy, so confident in their bodies, and very acquainted with his." She blew out a breath. "Christ, I was so young. The way they touched him and kissed him, I was both mesmerized and sickened. Yet, he never took his eyes off me. He eventually waved them away and called me over to sit on his lap."

The sound of wood cracking rent the air. "Motherfucker." The cabinet handle broke off in his hand and he tossed it into the sink. After a few calming breaths, he asked, slowly, "What did he do?"

Shaking her head, she stared at a rip in the wallpaper over his shoulder. "As soon as he pulled me into his lap, I knew. Even as stupid as I was, I knew Roy had decided to keep me, to do whatever he wanted to me." He'd demonstrated it, right then and there, under the table, touching her in ways no one had before. And she had been too damn frozen in fear to fight him. She'd frozen like that for two fucking years.

Jay's body shook. "And your piece of shit father?"

"He didn't notice. He was too busy losing his card game. Within a couple hours, he'd lost our house and the car we drove there in. And still, I thought he'd win everything back. When Roy asked everyone to leave and it was just Craig and I left, he told Craig to wager me. If Craig won, he'd walk away with everything and his debt would be cleared. If he lost..."

Jay's chest heaved, his arm holding her to him.

"I understand why Roy did it. He's the big scary boss man no one wants to fuck with. He was flaunting his power over Craig. And what he wants..."

"He gets." His voice was quiet, inconsolable.

Her throat swelled. "Craig didn't even think about it. Didn't even negotiate the terms. Maybe he assumed it was one night. Maybe he thought he was going to win, and it didn't matter."

"And the stupid fucker lost everything, including his daughter and his life."

"When they walked him out, he didn't say good-bye. Didn't look at me. Probably too afraid to draw Roy's attention."

He cupped her face and kissed her lips. "It's unfathomable. You are so precious. How could anyone walk away from you?"

She rubbed a finger over the deep lines fanning out from the corners of his eyes. Roy shared Jay's sentiment, but Roy's was a sick selfish kind of obsession. "So that's it. Took me two years to escape. Met you four years after that."

"Charlee." He shook his head. "We need to talk about those two years, and whatever happened in your second kidnapping."

Full disclosure. She'd vowed not to hide from it. "Ask me then."

"You were a virgin?" The low dangerous level of his tone said he already knew the answer.

She nodded. "That night, I learned that sex didn't require my permission. He took it, regardless of how hard I fought. Anal, vaginal, oral. In that order. Most of the scars you saw were inflicted in the first few hours."

His body vibrated beneath her, rotating the air with the violence of his breath.

"It's in the past, Jay." She smoothed her hand over his jaw. "The only things he got from me were what he took from me. Even the orgasms." The last word was a whisper.

Heat reddened his face behind hard eyes. "Tell me about that." He seemed to be hanging onto his anger by a fragile tether.

"Jay, I don't think—"

"Tell me, goddammit."

A swallow scorched down her raw throat. "When I wouldn't come or feel anything when he fucked me, he hit me harder, fucked me harder." The words clawed at her throat as she forced them out. "It made him so mad when I hid inside myself. He wanted to possess me in every way and had found a way to draw me out. He used my body against me, made me feel, and forced me to orgasm when I tried to hide from his touch." Her mouth went dry. "He'd had plenty of practice over the first two years and learned how to control my body better than I could."

For a long moment, the only sound in the room was the grinding of his teeth. "And you can't come now?"

"I can. On my own, when I concentrate on remembered pain. Or in my sessions, when I have the physical pain to focus on."

"Because you've been conditioned to associate pleasure with pain."

What did he think of her? She trembled. No one would want such a damaged, ruined girl. He could do so much better. "Yeah."

"What kind of pain do you need?"

Was he considering doing this for her? "A backhand across the face. A choking restraint. Dry penetration. Those are mild forms, but they might work."

"Mild?" he croaked, shoving a hand through his hair. "Christ, Charlee." He stared at her. "Maybe when you're with me, you could try to just think about the pain like you do when you're alone."

He wanted honesty. "Do you want me thinking about Roy when you're fucking me?"

He flinched like she'd punched him, and she realized she'd just implied she had to think of another man to get off while with him.

"Jay, I didn't mean you don't turn me on, because I've never felt as good as I do with you. But when I recall pain, I instantly think of—"

"I know, Charlee. I don't like it, but I understand." He hugged her, resting his lips on her forehead. "We'll figure out another way."

In the warmth of his embrace and the stillness of the confined room, her swirling emotions abated. When she leaned back to look at him, his face was clouded in thought.

"What is it?"

His eyes cleared and found hers. "Does Roy have other women he dominates or enslaves?"

She shook her head. "He's tried with others, but he told me I was the only one it worked out with."

The emotion rolling off him was stifling. He lifted her hand to his lips, kissed her wrist, and his other hand clenched her waist. "Maybe Roy saw something in you. Something a sadist cannot resist possessing. And if I were honest, Charlee, I have an overwhelming need to possess you, too. What's that make me?"

"Someone who will hold me so close Roy will never be able to wrench me away."

He squeezed her to him. "Damn straight."

"Good. We'll figure out the rest, okay?" Her stomach growled. "We should eat." She sagged against him, finally giving into the weariness of the long day. "Then I'm going to face plant somewhere."

He kissed her nose, chuckling as he hoisted her to her feet. She noticed his hands remained on her hips, supporting her, making sure she wouldn't fall. She had a feeling he'd never let her fall.

50

Jay carried a sleeping Charlee through the spacious living room and toward his wing of the band's Los Feliz home. They had both fallen asleep on the jet after dinner, and she conked out again on the way from the airport. The fact that she didn't wake when he lifted her from the car was a testament to how long the day had been.

And what a fucking day. He woke that morning with the same ache he always had, Charlee's death at the forefront of his mind. Then there was his drug-induced meltdown after discovering her alive but in bed with another man. And the shooting. The dead man. The fans and paparazzi. And Roy. Concluding with the most intimate moment of his life while flying across the country. Through it all, he'd only used blow twice. Hadn't even crossed his mind in hours. Why would it? Everything he wanted was alive and in his arms.

"Night, lover boy." Laz's teasing voice ricocheted through the twenty-foot ceilings, followed by the squeak of leather as Rio and Wil threw themselves onto the couch.

Jay didn't slow his strides through the room. Neither did Nathan's footfalls trailing behind him.

Laz flicked the controls that sent the exterior glass doors whirring into action. The panels glided in their tracks, vanishing the wall of the *U*-shaped estate and extending the indoor space to the aqua blue of the pool, the lounging deck, and the twinkling lights of their L.A. view.

The yawning vista usually invigorated Jay with a sense of autonomy. But holding Charlee in his arms, the panorama came with susceptibility. Could someone see in from the surrounding hillsides? Were the perimeter walls high enough? Should they keep the patio doors closed and reinforce the one-way glass? "Tony, give me a security update."

She slowed her clipped pace ahead of him until he caught up. "I doubled the exterior patrol. Two men at the gates. Four more positioned throughout the property. I also contracted a third party—a company I've vetted and used before—to monitor the cameras while Colson and I sleep. The rest of the team will arrive from New York tomorrow, mid-morning."

Nathan kept the pace at his back but hadn't said a word since they entered the property. Jay knew that in his stoicism, he was scoping and analyzing.

They stopped at the double doors to Jay's suite of rooms. Tony swiped her card key and the lock clicked. As was the protocol, she walked through first, leaving him at the threshold while she swept his sitting area, bedroom, bathroom, and closets.

Jay didn't think the sweep was necessary, but since his were the only rooms that didn't have surveillance, Tony argued for the additional security search. A debate he'd given up on a long time ago.

Thank God he'd been so adamant about maintaining his privacy. After Charlee's experience with round-the-clock videoing, he doubted she'd appreciate it in their bedroom.

Their bedroom. A lazy sigh of contentment stretched through him. He turned to Nathan, who expectedly chose to stay with Charlee rather than follow Tony through her sweep.

Jay shifted her tiny frame higher up his torso. "I'll have Tony go through the employment paperwork with you tomorrow...assuming you've agreed to join our team."

Hands in his pockets, Nathan made a show of scanning the rare Macassar Ebony floors, the diagonal lines of the soaring ceilings, and the expansive open-air rooms behind him. "Depends on the pay."

"You're so full of shit. You'll guard her whether I pay you or not."

The grin Nathan flashed fell away as soon as it appeared. "To avoid a conflict of interest, you understand part of my job is protecting her from my employer."

The sweet aroma of her hair infused Jay's deep breath. "Understood." And expected.

He hugged her close. They hadn't severed physical contact since their liaison in the airplane lavatory. It wasn't her body he was clinging to as much as it was the energy orbiting her. Their attraction, their bond, was an electromagnetic force. If it lost its charge, if she turned away even for a moment, would they lose the progress they'd made? Fuck, he knew it was all in his head, this idea that some magical force field they created warded off his triggers. But something was holding him together, and the way her hand curled around the back of his neck proved, even in sleep, she clung to it, too.

The door opened, and Tony emerged. "Clear." She nodded at Charlee. "Everything she needs is already put away in your closet and bathroom. You should give Faye a raise for her quick turnaround on this assignment."

While Tony managed the security team, Faye managed the band, the household, and everything else. "I'm giving you both raises. I'll fund it personally if the guys complain."

She shifted her weight from foot to foot, her face otherwise blank.

"Thank you, Tony. For today. For everything. I mean it."

The corners of her mouth lifted up. "My pleasure." Holding the door, she pulled out her phone and tapped the screen. "I reserved a private shooting lesson at the gun range tomorrow. Seven in the morning was the only time I could rent the range exclusively."

He cringed. That was only hours away. But he'd rather do early and empty than later and crowded. He nodded.

She followed him and Nathan through the door and positioned her back at the wall near the entrance. "Nathan, your things are set up in the guest room. I'll show you the way when you're done here."

Jay strode through his sitting room and weaved through the clutter of guitars, amps, and mic stands with Nathan on his heels. He used the room as his personal studio, writing music, mixing samples, composing songs about Charlee. Their real studio was twenty feet below and stretched the length of their ranch-style estate.

At the hallway, he stopped and looked over his shoulder. "I've got her from here."

Nathan's eyebrows dipped over his narrowed glare. "I need to see where she's sleeping."

And Jay needed to clear the room of smoke, dope, blow and whatever else he had stashed, including the gear he was sure he'd left on the bathroom counter. Nathan knew about the drug use, but he didn't need to be reminded of it his first night away from Charlee. "Tony swept the room. And you know where she's sleeping. In my bed." He verbalized the last part to set boundaries and roles, and to test the reaction.

As expected, Nathan's back snapped straight, and his hands balled at his sides. He wasn't ready to leave her side.

"Just let him see." Her sleepy mumble drifted over his neck and sent a tingle down his spine. "He won't sleep well if he doesn't check it out himself."

Jay looked down into her half-lidded eyes and his heart thumped. He hated that she knew another man so well, but he reminded himself that their closeness kept her alive. "Good morning."

She squirmed to get down even as her fingers combed through the hair at his nape. "It's morning?"

He let her feet touch the floor, but didn't release her. "It's around two or three."

In the circle of his arms, she shuffled backward, pulling him along by his belt loop. "Let's see your room."

"Our room." He tried to skirt around her, his guilt over wanting to hide his drug cache squashed by his embarrassment for having it in the first place. "Hang on a second."

Ignoring him, she spun out of his arms, moving a few feet beyond his reach, beyond the circle they had spent hours joined in. A chill invaded his empty arms. Her eyes widened, locked on his. Did she feel it too?

She probably wasn't aware of her shoulders curling forward as she rubbed her biceps and scuffed her boots over the white marble floors into the bedroom. Eyes sweeping the white walls, she zigzagged around the white leather couch, the white pine furniture, and the sheet of one-way windows overlooking the pool and grounds. At the foot of the bed, she leaned against one of the massive posts and stared at the expanse of white linen.

Nathan prowled the perimeter of the room and disappeared into the bathroom. Fuck. Jay braced for the impending lecture.

"What do you have against color?" She looked around the room and eyed his black t-shirt, black pants, black Chucks.

He shrugged. "Purple leather pants are out of fashion."

A laugh rolled past her curved lips, and she collapsed on the bed. Long tresses spread out around her angelic face and blazed rivulets of fire over the white bedding. Her flawless complexion glowed under the angled lighting as she stretched. The arch of her torso, the ripple in the hollow of her belly, and the languid blink of her eyes seeped sensuality. She was so beautiful, and so unaware of it. His muscles strained with the effort to keep himself from falling over her and ravishing her like an animal.

"Oh God, this is heaven. I mean, seriously, if I were to imagine the light at the end of the tunnel, it would be as bright as this room." She twisted a finger around a lock of hair. "Pick a color. Tell me your favorite."

"Red."

She released the fiery coil around her finger like it singed her.

"Second to blue." He stared into the depths of his favorite shade and she blinked, coughed.

"Then what's up with the all-white decor?"

He turned toward the black sky beyond the windows and his reflection glowered back. The reason was simple. And haunting. "I don't like the dark."

"The shed was dark."

Hearing his toxic shit whispered in her sweet voice built a pressure behind his breastbone.

"Jay. A word?" Nathan's shout tumbled from the bathroom.

"Here we go." He flashed her a guilty look before he could stop himself. Shit. He strode across the room and through the archway to the master bath, loosening his limbs to absorb the confrontation.

Fists on his hips, Nathan scowled at the waste basket between his boots. He'd emptied the cabinets of every pill, pipe, and baggie, filling the can mid-way. "Am I missing anything?"

Yeah, he was missing the bulk of it, hidden throughout his bedroom. Jay would deal with that later when he wasn't under the watch of stabbing eyes. He shook his head.

"How problematic is this going to be?"

Jay snapped his head up. "It's not." He straightened to his full height. "Do your job. Protect Charlee. You don't need to protect her from this. I'm done with it."

Nathan glanced over Jay's shoulder, and the stiffness fell from his expression. With a sigh, Jay turned to face her.

She stared at the waste bin, chewing a nail. "Drugs are one thing I've never been exposed to. Don't have a clue what the side effects are or how hard it is to quit." Her gaze floated up and captured his. "It's not my place to tell you what to do, Jay. I'm just going to have to trust you." She inhaled deeply, and her eyes spilled over with conviction. "I do trust you." She looked at Nathan. "So drop it."

Her confidence in him scared the piss out of him, but it also got him moving. He picked up the basket and walked through the bedroom, collecting the remainder of the stash. The sock drawer, the closet shelf, under the couch cushion, the mattress, behind the painting of the Canadian Boundary Waters. "That's it." He pushed the overflowing trash can into Nathan's arms. "Boy scout's honor."

That earned him a distrusting glare. So be it. As soon as Nathan discarded his bounty, the estate would be drug-free, barring the random joint his bandmates kept.

Charlee reached around the trash can and hugged Nathan's rigid body.

Jay's pulse jumped, his jealousy rising to the surface. What did he have to offer her that Nathan wasn't already providing? He tried to scrape up some understanding, fully aware it was the first night in three years they would be sleeping apart. Yet, she clung to him like he wasn't going to be under the same fucking roof. Jay jerked toward her before he could stop himself.

Nathan set her away with a pat on her shoulder. "I'm getting you a cell phone first thing tomorrow." He bent his knees to look her in the eye. "If you need me tonight..." He glanced at Jay.

"Press star seven on the intercom." Jay stepped behind her and gently nudged her chin toward the control panel by the door. "That'll ring Nathan's room. And star one will send a broadcast to every room in the estate."

Straightening, Nathan nodded. "Okay?"

"Yep." She rubbed her hands on her thighs as if she didn't know what to do with them.

At that moment, Jay knew he could offer her something Nathan didn't. He slid his hands over her hips, laced them with hers, and wrapped their arms around her waist. An electric current coursed through them and they exhaled in unison. She leaned her back against his chest.

He slid his nose through her hair, soaking in the shampoo she'd borrowed in his shower that morning combined with her sweet natural scent. The click of the door sounded Nathan's exit, and they stood there, sharing warmth and affection, content to do nothing more but lean close together.

Together. A foreign concept, yet so recognizable when he could feel her heart beating in harmonic balance with his.

Her head turned toward the bed. "What now?"

He followed her gaze. Never had a woman lay upon his bed, beneath him, straddling him, curled around him. And the only one he ever wanted was minutes away from nuzzling into his private nest, against his very aroused body.

She slumped in his arms, reminding him how long they'd been awake.

He sighed. "Now, you sleep."

She untangled from his embrace and shuffled toward the bed, tugging at her bootlaces through hopping strides. Toed them off. Stripped her shirt. Her bra. Thrust her pants down her hips. Crawled over the mattress with her red-laced ass in the air.

Heat ignited in his belly and swept between his legs. He set his molars together to bottle his groan. "I'm just going to… I'm going to grab a shower." And rub one off. Or two. Or ten. He ducked into the bathroom without meeting her eyes, knowing they would lure him to his fantasy and his fantasy was very, very real.

51

A shower, a shave, and two self-induced orgasms later, Jay tied a towel around his hips and padded into his bedroom. As expected, Charlee's steady breathing marked her restful sleep.

He dropped the towel, paced to the bed, and stopped. He slept nude, but should he now? He wanted to crawl in there naked with her, but would she think him too eager? Well, he was. Shit. He didn't want her to think that was the only thing he thought about.

He spun back toward the closet. Did he own a pair of boxers? He dug in the back of one of the shelf drawers. Aha! Boxer briefs. He dragged the scratchy cotton over his hips and snapped the elastic band. Then he hurried back to her and eased between the sheets.

She lay on her stomach facing him, her arms cradling the pillow to her head. Her hair, full and wild, fell around the flawless lines of her back. Her auburn lashes fringed glowing cheekbones and the seam of her lips bowed up despite the relaxed muscles in her face.

He traced the hem of the sheet along the rise of her ass, shifting it lower with a careful nudge of his finger until the strip of red lace peeked out.

Blood surged to his groin. Why the hell was he torturing himself?

Soon. Very fucking soon, he would know her in every way. Even as he promised himself that, he knew he couldn't get married to it. Not with their army of demons standing in the way.

Neither of them would ever know normal, together or apart. And while he loathed labeling her, doing so rooted him in the reality of the situation. She was a masochist, whether by nature or nurture, and he was...a lot of things, but a pain-bearer wasn't one of them.

He'd tied up countless women, humiliated them, and took what he wanted. But Charlee wasn't some self-seeking fan trying to attach herself to him because he was in a rock band. Her intent seemed to be shoving, scolding, and seducing him toward happiness, no matter how fucked up he was. A token of her effort was permanently outlined on his back.

He stretched his finger beneath the scratchy lace, reveling in the velvet feel of her bottom. His obsessive impulse to take care of her muddled things. Guard her or hurt her? Maybe guard her while hurting her? What a perverse notion.

Part of him understood why she needed pain, but the other part—the part that was feeling particularly sensitive and protective, considering he'd been mourning her death only hours earlier—wanted to demand she learn a more acceptable way to be with him.

He fluttered fingertips over her back, drinking in the silky feel of her. One of her arms flopped toward his face and lay on his pillow, delicate, inviting. He twined their fingers and brought her hand to his lips. Her breath hitched and fell even again.

Could he bruise her perfect body with the force of his grip and his thrusts? Could he welt her with some cruel leather implement? Could he pleasure her for hours on the edge of orgasm, torturing her without allowing her release?

His body quaked with the need to pull her against him, to drive into her and possess her. Rolling to his back, he captured her hand against his chest and squeezed the base of his erection. His dick seemed to think he could do all those things. It also knew she lay inches from him, wearing only a tiny scrap of lace.

Beating off in the shower had done nothing to assuage this insane need. Her body, their bed, his freedom was her. If he gave her pain, would her freedom be him?

What if he couldn't bring himself to hurt her? Did that mean he loved her too much? Or maybe love meant hurting her despite his abhorrence to it.

It was the same murky feelings he often circled around when writing music. Sometimes, he would stop mid-composition and tell himself, "No. I can't do this. The rhythm is too chaotic for mainstream. The lyrics would be misunderstood." That was when he *knew* he should do it.

Was that what was happening? Did his refusal to give her pain-derived pleasure stem from some prevailing social opinion? The act of love couldn't be governed by tradition or conformity. It was an individual choice, sometimes one that was questioned and judged, perhaps abandoned in frustration, but always returned to. Just like writing music, love was a unique, hard-earned and giving experience.

Holy shit, he loved her. The revelation budded and strengthened with each thud of his heart. For three years, he'd been in love with the idea of her. It had been the sort of devotion that breathed through his songs and embraced him in his lowest hours. It was too soon to fully appreciate the woman she was, but during the course of a single day, a sweeping, chaotic sensation had taken up residence inside him. It cowered at the prospect of losing her again, but also galvanized with a sense of duty. Love wasn't a feeling. It was a mission. A driving purpose to fulfill her every desire, to give her a life worth sharing.

He tapped the switch on his bedside table and washed the room in darkness. Shifting to face her, he inhaled the sweetness of her exhales and cherished each breathy trace of her existence. She was his greatest possibility. His reason. His why. He would give whatever she needed to be whole and happy, because loving her was as essential as drawing air.

52

A faraway gasp pulled at Charlee's sleepy fog. She blinked through the dark, her eyes adjusting to the blanketing shroud. The wrinkled bedding, gray in the absence of light, was tossed back. The dip in the mattress beside her, empty.

Another distant inhale. Without moving, she squinted in the direction of the sound.

A silhouette blotted the far wall. She focused on the long, lean outline and the movement of the lower half. She needed neither light nor nearness to recognize Jay's incredible body.

She held herself still as his hands cupped his groin. No, they stroked. One up and down in long twists of his wrist, the other kneading underneath. His briefs pooled around his ankles, the back of his head resting against the wall. The sharp angle of his jaw stretched up, scissoring back and forth, and the slivers of his half-lidded eyes glinted, watching her.

A hot wave of lust descended over her and concentrated between her thighs. There was nothing more seductive than the way his smoldering gaze raked the outline of her body as he rubbed himself with furious pumps.

The speed of his strokes escalated, and his hips thrust into his rotating fist. The muffled sounds behind his closed lips skittered quivers along her thighs. Would he finish if he knew she was watching? Peeking through the narrow slits of her eyes, she held herself immobile, enthralled by the view and the man providing it.

His shoulders bunched forward, rolling the muscles in his chest. He licked his lips, panting, his neck straining, his abs crunching. And still, his eyes remained firmly locked on her.

The sight of his nude body, impeccably defined and flexing toward climax, pushed her heart beat from frenzied to dangerous. He shifted his stance, spreading his legs farther apart, and pressed his shoulders to the wall. Was he on the cusp of release? Imagining him letting go made her breath catch and her stomach take on that unnerving butterfly effect. She dug her fingernails into the pillow to keep from reaching down and massaging the pulsing ache.

The twitches cascading over his body, the heat of his gaze, and the unrestrained way he rocked into his fist were too much. So completely enraptured by his lust, she jerked her hand down and covered the triangle of lace with stiff fingers, pressing against the throb as if that could possibly sate it.

His strokes slammed to a halt, chest heaving and air hissing through clenched teeth. His lips, taut with arousal only a moment earlier, slowly slid up at the corners. "How long have you been watching me, pervert?"

Holding his penetrating stare, she sat up and scooted to the edge of the bed. The sheet pulled away, and he sucked in a sharp breath.

"Not as long as you have been watching me." She leaned back on her arms, grinning. "Pervert."

He looked at the floor, hand clamped around his cock. "This isn't—"

"What it looks like?"

His head fell against the wall with a thunk and he groaned to the ceiling. "I'm not usually this creepy." Without releasing his erection, he straightened and squinted at her. "I won't hurt you, Charlee. I promise I'll stay right here until I calm down."

Clueless man. "We're going to pretend you didn't just say that." She slid her panties down her legs and kicked them off her feet. "Any of it."

His nostrils flared, and his fist squeezed, stroking once, twice. She burned everywhere his eyes lingered. Her breasts, her mound, her legs, darting back to her face.

"Charlee." A pant. Another stroke.

Could she get him worked up enough to take her roughly? Would rough be enough to get her off? She raised her hand and drew her middle finger between her lips, out, in, out, in long sucking strokes, humming.

His free hand splayed on his thigh as his fist resumed its previous rhythm. "Fuck, Charlee." A shudder rippled over his torso. "Stop that. You're not helping."

His voice, thick with arousal, thrilled her, powered her to continue. She'd never played with a man this way, had no clue what she was doing. Each slurp of her finger and smack of her lips was answered with a strained rattle low in his throat. He leaned toward her, but his feet remained cemented to the floor.

Not enough seduction? Fine. She spread her legs, hooked her heels on the bed frame, and lowered her finger from her mouth to her clit. She looked at him, knowing her eyes conveyed an earnest request.

Dark hair clung to his forehead in a bed-ruffled mess of sexiness. He brushed it away and shoved off the wall. Given the tense lines of his muscles, she expected him to rush the distance and tackle her.

His strong, lithe legs stepped out of his briefs and moved in a deliberate, predatory stalk toward the bed. The sinews in his thighs stretched through his strides and his hand fell away from his arousal to ball at his side, his eyes intent and unblinking.

Bared in her spread position, toes curled around the bed frame and one arm wobbling to support her backward lean, she imagined him carrying a paddle, swinging the danger in waves through the room. Her desire mounted.

The way he prowled toward her with clipped breath and that made-for-sex physique, he had dangerous perfected. His dominant side vibrated at the end of some kind of noble leash. She knew it was there. Hell, she'd seen the proof of it tied to a piano. But instead of tying her down while she slept, he'd snuck across the room to jerk off at a safe distance, the polite bastard.

She circled her finger around the centermost point of her ache. "You told me on the plane that part of my problem was thinking instead of feeling. Are you taking your own advice?"

He stopped at the mattress and bowed over her, hips between her thighs, chest pumping against hers, arms braced on either side. His eyes were a rich brown in the darkened room. A thin band of moonlight glanced off his jaw, highlighting the masculine square of his chin. "Tell me exactly what you want."

The beat of her heart stumbled. "I want you to take without asking." Never would she have uttered those words to anyone else. Why him? How had he coaxed all her reckless desires to the surface so fiercely? By the softened look on his face, he understood the degree of trust and vulnerability she offered.

Their gazes clung in that stalled moment, their bodies straining toward the other, and finally, finally, he reached between her legs, nudged her hand away, and cupped her with the possessive strength she longed for.

She arched her back and sought his mouth, urgent and greedy. He drew in her tongue and pushed it back with his own. Their deep, gasping kisses energized the air and coated her body in goose bumps.

He slid his lips over her cheek to her ear and placed a gentle peck on her bandage. "Lay back. Hands above your head."

Her breath caught, and her entire body ignited with tingles. That command in his deep, husky timbre... Holy hell, what a seductive combination. She raised her arms and collapsed on the mattress.

"Good girl." One of the fingers between her legs pressed in, rotated, and slipped out with a rush of moisture.

Her impatience squeaked in her throat and she blinked in the glare of his dilated eyes.

He entered her again, fuller this time. Two fingers, maybe three. She squirmed as he stretched and stroked her walls, rippling shivers through her body.

"Stop wiggling." His eyes glimmered and his tongue slid lazily over her parted lips. He radiated heat everywhere he touched her. His breath, so close, washed over her face in a minty haze. Another swipe of his tongue and he plunged past her lips in the same curling movement as his fingers inside her.

When she bucked again, he yanked his fingers out and slapped her thigh. She sucked in a breath, his breath, breathing him in, because his mouth was there, trapping hers.

She calmed the roll of her hips and followed the lead of his nips and licks. No one had kissed her since Roy, and no one had ever kissed her in the acquiring, ravenous manner in which he controlled her mouth. It was as though he wanted to bring her inside him and consume her. It was unfamiliar and so very intimate to be enveloped and adored by man who was both intense and caring.

Fingers returned to her entrance and the invasion was deliciously forceful. At the same time, his other hand combed through her hair from root to tip with a tenderness that made her ache in a whole other way.

His assault on her pussy strengthened, quickened, and he devoured her mouth so thoroughly, she struggled to breathe. All she could think over and over was how much abandon she would find beneath the bruising strength, slamming fists, and punishing thrusts of a man she trusted. "I do trust you, Jay," she gasped against his mouth. "Please."

He broke away, panting, his body slick with sweat. "What's your safe word?"

"What?" There was only one reason he'd need—

"Safe word. I need a safe word, Charlee." He crawled over her leg and yanked open the drawer in the bedside table.

A release of tension shook from her muscles. Was it a release? Or was it an outpouring of fear? The kind of fear she longed for. "Huntress."

He froze, looked over his shoulder at her. "Huntress?" His face was tight, but a smile gleamed in his eyes.

"Yeah." She lifted a shoulder and leaned around him. "If you're looking for a condom, you don't need one. I get birth control shots. And I'm clean."

In the next breath, he fisted her hair and used it to haul her bodily up the mattress to where he knelt by the headboard. Burning stings ripped across her scalp, sparking her arousal. She moaned.

He released her, eyes wide. "Oh fuck. I hurt you."

She reached for his face, hovered her hands above the flushed skin without touching. "That's the point."

His eyes glazed over with a cloud of tortured debate. Jesus, she shouldn't have asked him for this. It was selfish and cruel and could hurt him in a way he didn't deserve to be hurt. She tugged on her hands in his clasp. "Jay, stop. This isn't right."

He shoved her to her back on the bed and knelt over her. "Stop isn't your safe word. I will ignore it. Do you understand?"

The hardened look he gave her stole her voice and swept shivering pleasure down her legs. She nodded.

He shifted to the bedside table, dug in the back of the drawer, and returned with a bundle of rope. "I've never used this in this room. In fact, other than the staff, there's never been a woman in this room. But I know how to use it safely." He rubbed his nape. "And have more times than I care to point out." He raised his eyes to hers. "Still trust me?"

She jerked her head up and down.

"I might know how to tie knots, but I'm new to this power exchange concept." He pinned her with a hard frown. "I trust you to use your safe word."

"That won't be a problem." And it wouldn't. A couple Doms had threatened to terminate her contract because she abused the power she had with the word.

She held out her hands, wrists together, and a thought came to her. "Are you tying me because you're afraid the touching trigger might come back?"

He twined the rope over her wrists in a practiced pattern. "That's part of it. We could test your hands on me like we did before, but I'm not inclined to ruin the mood if I've relapsed." The corner of his mouth popped up. "We're doing this without any hindrances. I've waited too goddamned long for you."

With a yank on the rope, he tightened the knot and used it to pull her arms over her head. A tangle of excitement and apprehension flittered through her veins.

A few minutes later, he finished with the length strapped around the mattress, under the frame to the foot of the bed, and tied it to one of her ankles. She was effectively and unnervingly restrained.

She wondered how disgusting she looked trussed up like that until he knelt between her thighs and scanned his work.

"My God." The look on his handsome face transformed. His jaw sharpened, his sensuous lips seemed to swell as they opened, and his breathing became more erratic. "I've never been so weak with want."

The affection in his eyes drained away, replaced by something primitive and stern. She could feel the change in his body, too, as he spread over her, hard-packed and heavy, and jerking in stiff, hasty movements.

She bucked uselessly against the binds as he drew the head of his erection up and down through her sopping folds. His weight pressed her body into the bed and his mouth fed on hers, one manic kiss after another. His control was slipping, his mouth moving in earnest, clumsy caresses.

Because he wanted her. Not as a possession to own. Not as a paying client. He wanted *her*. A sense of power swept through her, at odds with the vulnerability of her bound body.

He dropped his brow to hers and gripped the inside of her thigh. "I'm going to fuck you now." His words raised the hair on her neck, and he buried himself in one piercing thrust.

53

Warm. Slippery. Comforting. Better than any fantasy Jay had ever conjured. He felt every clench and pull of Charlee's narrow passage. He fucking *felt* her.

If he moved, even an inch, he'd shoot off and end it before it even started. So, he hung onto her tight little body, his hips biting into hers, hands squeezing her ass, and coached his breath.

With one ankle tied down, she wrapped the other around his back and ground against him, her inner muscles grabbing hold of his shaft, sucking him in deeper.

Tingles rippled over his glans and his balls drew up. "Stop moving," he ground out.

She continued her torturous flexing and blew out a half-sigh, half-groan.

The seductive sound and the caress of her breath threatened to flatten his control to pulp. He tweaked her nipple. "That includes no breathing."

A laugh skated past her lips, contracting her cunt, and stealing his brain cells.

He shoved a hand between them and clasped her circling hip. "I mean it, Charlee. Give me a minute."

What was she doing to him? He'd never experienced this problem. Quite the opposite, in fact. She had him so completely under her spell, he couldn't even fall asleep beside her. Instead, he had to throw himself off the bed and jack off like a blue-balling virgin.

Her fists flexed in their bonds, nails piercing her palms, knuckles blanched. She strained against him, her eyes huge and round. They begged as if uncertain he would deliver the pain she needed.

He'd spent his entire adult life seeking transitory moments of distraction, a buzz, a high, a meaningless orgasm. Now he had Charlee, and he was terrified he would make a mistake, do something stupid, and lose her.

He tilted her chin up, made her look at him. "No matter what happens, no matter where we go from here, we go together."

Damned if her pussy didn't squeeze with each word he said. Her body relaxed into the bed and a smile kissed her beautiful lips.

As charming as she was, he needed a verbal acknowledgment. "Promise me."

"I promise."

Those two words saturated the gaping hole inside him, a hole that had been empty for so fucking long. For a fleeting moment, he let it morph into a more explicit meaning. To have and to hold, for pleasure, for pain.

Eyes locked with hers, he lowered his mouth to her breast and went after her nipple. He tried to focus on what he was about to do and not the soft, wet heat sucking on his dick. He lined his teeth around the precious nub and bit. Hard.

Her neck arched, and a coppery flavor washed his tongue.

Oh God, no. There wasn't supposed to be blood. He looked into her eyes, and the smoldering arousal he found there both scared him and turned him on.

"The other one," she said softly and without a hint of misgiving.

"No! You're bleeding." Shit, that came out too gruff, and he knew his expression was a mask of horror.

Her face pinched and her head turned away. "Okay."

Well, that was one way to ward off premature ejaculation. "Look at me."

She did, her eyes glassy with shame.

"Whatever you're thinking, stop it. I'm fumbling. I know it. And this is too damn important to fuck up."

"Jay, it's okay. Listen—"

"No, you listen. I'm going to make a mess of this. It's an honest-to-fuck certainty."

"That's pessimism, not certainty." She winked.

God, she was sexy. And understanding. And maybe a little crazy. But the sexy, crazy firecracker needed limits. "No blood. Not budging on that."

He followed her lowering eyes to the tiny red bead clinging to her nipple. With a swipe of his tongue, he licked it away. This was her normal. Her benchmark for judging the value and quality of pleasure. He was an outsider, trying to get in. He'd get there. He would. In the meantime, he'd have to do things her way.

"Be patient with me." He shifted his attention to the other breast, tasted the unmarked skin. "Don't you dare feel bad when I get frustrated." He dragged his teeth over her nipple. "And I get frustrated a lot."

"I hadn't noticed."

Smart ass. He pressed forward and took her mouth. She met him with the same desperate energy, turning his thoughts to drivel. The firm slide of her kiss made him wild to deepen it, to own her mouth the way she owned him. He worked her lips over, pressing hard, biting, rubbing until they were swollen and red. He dragged his mouth over her jaw, down her throat, and sank his teeth into the rise of her breast without breaking the skin.

She blinked, bit her puffy lip.

Well, shit. The last time he bit a tit like that, the woman—*he couldn't remember her face*—screamed for ten minutes. It had killed his erection instantly.

He rotated his pelvis in slow circles. She felt like an extension of his own body wrapped around him, and looked absolutely sinful tied to his bed. It made his heart pump harder, sending more blood south. There was a good chance he was going to pass out if he didn't come soon. He needed her at his level, burning at the same fevered pitch. He pinched the uninjured nipple.

The vibration of her groan sent an electric current through his dick. It buried his balls deep. He froze long enough to keep the climax at bay.

When he thought he'd reached a safe degree of control, he reared his hand back and slapped her thigh with as much force as a hundred-pound girl could absorb.

She smiled. Fucking *smiled*.

He licked those teasing lips. "Harder?"

The turned-up corners of her mouth stretched wider.

As small as she was, he would've thought she'd be more fragile, breakable. Yet, his hands had been all over her miniature packs of muscle, and he knew her strongest spot. It could take a harder strike.

He captured her untied leg, hooked it around his waist, and used it to lift her ass away from the mattress. Target bared, he unleashed an open-handed swing.

That got him a burning palm and a twitch in her thigh. Damn, the tough little brat. He settled her on her back and rolled his hips between her legs. "I'm not anywhere close to doing it for you, am I?"

She narrowed her eyes. "I'm having sex with the only three-time winner of *People Magazine*'s Sexiest Man Alive. If that weren't enough, I'm lying in a wet spot." She wriggled her hips. "That proves you actually live up to every explicit rumor I've read about you."

Motherfuck. She followed the gossip rags. "Charlee, you can't believe the shit they write about me."

"Can't I? There are a holyfuckton of women crowing about your *unapologetic fucking*. They even named your famous positions."

Oh Jesus, she knew about that. "Don't—"

"The Limp Away From Jay Lay."

A small smile touched her lips, but he didn't miss the flatness in her tone. She was jealous. It shouldn't have, but the notion gave him a selfish little thrill.

"Then there's the Mayard Mount." She stared at his chest, eyebrows drawn.

He hated that his depravity cluttered the Internet. All she had to do was open a browser and type his name. All the shit he'd done with those women would be shoved in her face, mocking her.

"The Hands-Free Blow Me." She gave him a pitying look.

"I think I lost my hard-on." He thrust his hips to remind her where his dick was.

"Oh, and I'm currently experiencing a fan favorite, right? The Rope Burn." She twisted her wrists in the binds and glared at him.

Was she just being open with him or was she pissed? A string of ugly emotions tore through him. Leading the brigade was his regret over all the meaningless places he'd put his dick. Surely, she understood what he thought of those women?

He dropped his brow to hers. "I'm sorry, Charlee. I can give you some trite excuses about how those women meant nothing. I'd like to think you know me well enough to see that." He lifted his hips to pull out of her.

Her leg around his waist stiffened. "Fuck me like you fucked them."

Unease punched through him. He looked down into her electric, singular eyes, sparking blue with flecks of silver. *She* was singular. He'd never treat her like them. "Never."

"I know I mean something different to you. I'm not asking you to think of me the way you think of them. God, I don't think I could bear it if you did." She sighed. "I built up this really high pain threshold. I had to." Her eyes slid to the side. "And I just need you to not treat me so delicately."

Oh Charlee. She thought if he treated her like those women,

he'd be rougher with her? He scattered kisses over her eyelids, cheeks, and lips. "Don't worry about your threshold. I'll get past it." He would research, figure out how to get creative. For now, he'd have to go with blunt strength.

It would've been easier to flip her over and spank her while fucking her doggie-style. No way was he going to come in her the first time without looking into the eyes he'd dreamt about for three years.

Lowering his weight on her chest, he shoved her knee against her shoulder and rammed into her. His thrusts, harder than he'd ever attempted with anyone, filled the room with the wet sound of skin smacking skin. Fuck, she felt good.

Her body clenched against the force of each lunge, and her eyes blinked rapidly. He kept his movements measured, determined not to give her more than she could handle.

The bed scooted until it hit the wall. The headboard rocked and creaked. And Charlee's pleasure flowed out in an erotic stream of moans.

It was insane. Beautiful. Unbelievably arousing. And it was a miracle he hadn't lost his load yet. He tried not to look at the toned lines of her pinned leg beneath his fingers. The dramatic curve of her waist. The way her tits jogged with the intensity of his thrusts.

"Come for me, Charlee."

She nodded. At least he thought it was a nod. Her whole body was nodding beneath his driving hips.

"Hurry." His voice was guttural and distant beneath the roar of blood in his ears. "I'm barely hanging on."

Her arms writhed in the rope. "I want to touch you."

Christ. Fuck. Never had he considered being touched during sex, but his heart leapt at the thought of Charlee's hands on him.

It was a terrible idea. He slammed into her. "Would touching me help you come?"

She closed her eyes and breathed deeply through her nose. He didn't think so.

"Come, Charlee. Come for me." He shoved in and out, panting under the exertion, trembling against the overwhelming sensations.

She peered up through her lashes. "Okay."

"You can touch me after...I...fuck you...to unconsciousness." He punctuated the words with ram of his hips.

One of the bed posts hit the wall and dented the sheetrock. He reined in his enthusiasm.

"An after-sex cuddlier, huh?" Her voice was breathy and sexy as hell.

"Only with you." He bit her raised chin. Bucked his hips. Slapped her thigh, one strike after the other. Sweat formed on his lip. The muscles in his biceps and legs burned. And the hot, tight vise of her pussy clamped down, moments from sucking him drying. "Come. Come, now." He landed his heaviest whack high on her thigh.

Her yelp somersaulted into a long, arousing moan and blanketed his chest in hot exhales. She was so close. He vibrated with excitement.

"Look at me. I want to see you."

Her eyes flew to his, glazed and seductive. He grabbed a nipple, twisted it. Her beautiful grunt caressed his face. This was it.

The pressure between his legs rose up, spread out through his groin, reaching, reaching. "Ahhhh. God. Fuuuuck. Charlee, I'm coming. Fuck, fuck, fuck." Everything narrowed to her and him and the unbelievable rush she was giving him. Breathe. Holy fuck, he needed to breathe.

On his way down, he shivered, twitching muscles he didn't even know he had. Tingles swept over his skin and his body lay boneless on top of her. Oh shit. Too heavy. He lifted his weight and searched her face. She wouldn't meet his eyes.

"Did you come?"

She bit her lip and looked down and to the left.

Outrage restarted his triple-tempo pulse. "No? No, please don't tell me no."

She looked at him and glanced away again. "Okay."

How the hell had he misjudged that? She must've thought he was the biggest prick. He sat back on his heels where he knelt between her legs and took a few calming breaths.

Okay. He could fix this.

The best orgasm of his life collected at the entrance of her pussy and dribbled down her outer lips. He'd never tasted himself before. Couldn't be that bad. Hell, he'd never even gone down on a girl. Well, not while he was sober enough to remember it. But this was Charlee. Didn't matter what he did with her, they'd figure it out and make it work.

He slid his hands under her ass and lifted her to meet his mouth.

"What are you doing?" Panic hitched her voice.

He was going to bite the hell out of her clit. "You're going to come for me, Charlee. We're not leaving this room till you do."

She stared at him like he'd lost his mind. Then she dropped her head and said to the ceiling, "You need to shove something in my ass."

"What?"

"Quick and effective," she mumbled.

He lowered her hips, tried not to think about the things she'd experienced to fuel such a request. His mind flashed to random phallic-shaped objects in his room. The handle of her hairbrush. The Mr. T bobble head on the mantle. The glass bong under his— Wait, he threw that out.

Jesus, what was he thinking? "I'm not sticking anything in your ass." He cleared his throat. Maybe he should clarify. "Unless it's made for your ass." His dick would be a perfect fit...in an hour or so, if he could muster the stamina. "And I don't keep butt-plugs lying around."

"Let's just call it a night. It's nearly six in the morning."

He had to be at the range in an hour. "Charlee, Please—"

"Huntress." She yanked on the rope and glared at him.

His shoulders sagged. "You're going to safe word just like that? You won't give me another chance?" Christ, he'd fucked up. How could he expect her to want him if he couldn't even give her an orgasm? "I can fix this."

Stretched by the rope, she strained her arms and waited. She wouldn't repeat the safe word. And she wouldn't have to. Under the scrutiny of her eyes and with shame burning his face, he removed the rope, bundled it up, and returned it to the drawer.

Her back was to him when he crawled behind her and scooted against her until as much of her body was touching him as possible. While he was behaving like a selfish prick, he might as well take everything he wanted. And he wanted to hold her until she fell asleep.

He locked his arm around her waist. She let her hands lay limp so he could gather them and intertwine them with his against her chest. As her body sank with the weight of gravity and exhaustion, he pulled her closer, so close he could feel every twitch in her back, every beat of her heart.

"The Strong Box." Her soft voice drifted through him.

"What's the strong box?" He knew what one was, but he didn't know what *the* strong box was.

"It's a container, usually steel, in which valuables are kept safe."

She was going somewhere with this. He waited.

"It's also the name I'm giving my favorite Jay Mayard position. You know, the one where he wraps himself around his partner and makes her feel valuable and safe and a lot less broken. It's not a famous or practiced position, but it's all mine."

He melted against her back, buried his nose in her hair, and tumbled just a little bit more in love with her. Fuck that. He plunged.

"All yours, Charlee." Every. Single. Breath.

54

Disappointment rolled over Charlee when she woke the next morning. Alone in bed. A glance around confirmed an empty room. Nathan didn't often leave her to wake alone, but when it happened, dread was always the initial reaction. Not this strange dejection.

Sunlight illuminated the stark sheets and the sheen of white paint coating the walls. The white marble floors accentuated the ethereal glow. So dang bright. She raised a hand over her eyes to shade from the glare.

Not that she minded the monochromy. It was just unexpected. So was Jay.

Her gaze lingered on the wall where he had leaned in the half-light of predawn, watching her while he pleasured himself. The erotic display would forever leave a warm imprint on her desire. He confused her thoughts about what she needed in bed and evoked a reckless hope for healing at his hands.

She didn't know how to categorize him within the spectrum of her sexual history. Noah, her gentle, benevolent lover, had shown her devotion in patient touching. If her inability to orgasm had vexed him, he never expressed it.

On the other end, the violent blows from Roy had torn her down to such a weakened state, she couldn't prevent him from taking. He stole orgasm after orgasm until her broken husk was wrung unconscious.

The half dozen Doms she had contractually approved intercourse with were simply therapeutic exercises—training for the possibility of someday having a real physical and emotional relationship.

Jay was a wild and unpredictable variable on the spectrum. He swung from tender to frustrated to caring to desperate. No matter how passionate his reactions—negative or positive—his concern for her remained steadfast.

Succumbing to the lull of sleep while sheltered in his arms had been one of the most gratifying experiences in memory. And this, right after he'd seen how terribly flawed she was. How gut-wrenching he blamed himself for not bringing her to orgasm when the truth was her perversity put them in the fucked up situation.

It proved he valued her. Maybe even loved her. Her response to that was immediate rejection, but her heart tripped over itself in wanting. What if she loved him? She thought about how she felt, bound beneath his solid body, absorbing his deep thrusts, his muscles contracting around her, his fingers bruising her ass. She'd found pleasure in the way he moved, the fire behind his kisses, the feel of him inside her. What if that was enough? Could she let go of her need and conditioning for pain?

A woman with low pain tolerance and a heart tied to another would never survive Roy. Regardless of how safe Jay made her feel, she couldn't let herself forget she was one misstep away from recapture.

She flexed her sore muscles and rolled over to check the bedside clock. Just after ten. She'd only slept a few hours. Why the hell was Jay up already?

Sitting up, her hand brushed a scrap of white panties that were folded and placed on his pillow. One of the stringed sides tied around a piece of paper, which was rolled like a cigarette. Amusement tickled through her as she slipped it out and uncurled it.

Charlee,

Ain't gonna lie. You look like a wet dream stretched out in ~~my bed~~. Our bed. Leaving you this morning fucking sucks. But my errands couldn't wait.

Your clothes are in the closet. Bathroom's stocked. So is the kitchen. Explore your new home. If you need something and can't find it, hunt down Faye.

**6 on the intercom system will connect you to my cell phone. Back around 11:00.*

All yours,

J

She traced the closing words. *All yours.* It was crazy, the ache that sentiment stirred in her. Until that moment, she had never let herself want the kind of commitment he was offering.

He had his pick of the world's female population. Just thinking about him with another woman forced her nails into her palms. If she weren't careful, he'd soon have her heart. Shit. He might've already stolen it. A susceptibility that could bring far more devastation than Roy could've ever inflicted.

55

Charlee showered and readied for the day using more girly stuff than she'd seen since she was sixteen. Warming body wash. Hair products with names she couldn't pronounce. A fancy razor that looked nothing like the disposable kind she shared with Nathan.

As for all the items she didn't know what to do with—makeup, bronzers, hair clips, multi-step skin care products, curling irons in various shapes and sizes—she left those in their tidy little drawers.

The closet was even more overwhelming. Not the first time a wardrobe had been selected for her, but Roy had given her gowns and pant suits and dressy things she wasn't even allowed to look at in her second captivity.

Jay's closet was crammed with jeans, t-shirts, multi-pocket pants and big leather belts. Casual and sportive. If she had a style and preference, his shopper nailed it. The labels, though, implied price tags she would've never been able to afford.

She chose a faded pair of low-rise jeans, a white *Placebo* t-shirt, the white panties he'd left on his pillow, and a matching bra. Anxious to explore, she opted to let her hair air dry and padded barefoot down the hall. Past the sitting room and through the double doors, she paused in the diamond-shaped foyer. The door to the room next to Jay's suites opened.

Nathan stepped out, head down, phone at his ear. "We need to let this sit, Crane. He's our only eyes right now. Yeah...Yeah, she's good, but fuck, man, this news is going to kill her...No way. I don't keep shit from her, but with everything going on, I haven't had a chance to tell her about the spotter...Yeah, all right. Keep me updated."

News? Spotter? She bit her cheek. He'd tell her when he was ready.

Shutting the door, his gaze snapped up and his lips twitched. "Morning, sweetheart."

Something was different about him. He still had that stiff Marine posture going on, but he was lighter on his feet. His shoulders were looser, his eyes bluer, brighter.

"You're chipper this morning." She bumped her arm into his as they walked. "Sleep well?"

He glanced back toward the room he'd just departed and fiddled with his phone. "Uh huh." A smile fluttered through pinched lips as if he were trying to keep it from fully emerging. And why was he looking anywhere but at her?

"I didn't know the guest room was so close." Had he heard her moaning from Jay's room?

He stopped and dropped his phone into his breast pocket. Staring at the wood floor, he rubbed his jaw and propped his hands on his hips. Uh-oh. His defensive stance.

He shifted his weight. "That isn't a guest room."

A laugh burst out of her. "You move fast, playboy." She punched him in the shoulder.

"I'd take offense to that if I hadn't heard you screaming at the wee hours of the morning."

Jesus. She shouldn't have been embarrassed, considering he'd seen and heard her at her absolute worst, but she couldn't stop her cheeks from burning. "You heard?"

He grinned. "No, and thank God for that."

"Fucker." She aimed to punch him again, but he was expecting it that time and bounced out of the way.

She crossed her arms over her chest. "That's a terrible thing to joke about...considering."

A swell of sympathy curved his eyebrow and rounded his eyes. Thankfully, it wasn't pity, but he'd never been one to pity her.

He gripped her shoulders and bent his knees to meet her eyes. "If we tiptoe around our thoughts, Roy wins."

A sigh pushed past her lips. "You're right." The easiness between them was owed to their openness with one another. "You're always right."

It was so good to see his charming smile instead of the usual vigilance that tightened his expression and twisted her gut. "Look at us. We could've had our own rooms, slept diagonal in our beds and hogged the covers. Since we didn't take advantage of that, does it make us dependent creatures?"

His eyes softened. "No, it makes us lonely."

They stared at one another for a long silent moment. She knew he didn't mean it as a dig against her as a companion. He referred to the isolation that came with the lack of intimacy. She'd felt it, too, and her thoughts skipped through their years together. The constant moving. The dead ends with Roy. The persistent fear. All the sacrifices Nathan made to keep her safe.

She lifted on tiptoes and wrapped her arms around him. Apologies and gratitude weren't necessary. A place in her life was all he wanted from her. She would never be able to express to him what that meant.

He returned her embrace, his thumb stroking the spine of her back.

"Relaxed is a good look on you." She leaned back. "As are the new threads." Black button-up, crisp black pants, black leather shoes. His blond hair was longish but neatly combed away from his forehead. His familiar features, especially the grin he was donning, brought to mind another handsome face. One so like his her chest squeezed every time she looked at him. She shoved that away and lowered her voice. "Will there be any flak from fraternizing with the staff?"

"Actually, she's my boss now." His smile glowed against his flushed complexion. "We'll work it out."

"Oh." Her forehead wrinkled. Knowing he would be compensated for protecting her eased her guilt a little. "Is that what you want? To work for someone?" Since the Marine Corps, he'd been self-employed. She couldn't envision him reporting through a chain of command.

"My priority is keeping you safe. As a member of this team, I'll be able to do that more efficiently. And I happen to like my new boss."

"What about your employer? Do you like him?"

"No, but you do. That's enough."

She started walking along the wide corridor toward the main room, feeling Jay's absence like an incessant tug. "What's the plan today?"

"I'm going to get you a cell phone and meet with the security team. You are going to stay on the property until I get back."

The hall emptied into a gaping, sunlit room and with it came the aroma of sizzling bacon. The open-space kitchen on the right connected to the entertainment room on the left, which flowed seamlessly into the backyard. The *U*-shaped estate curved around the veranda and pool area, where a smattering of voices carried on the warm breeze.

The walls that would've formed the dish of the *U* were nonexistent. They rolled back somehow, but she couldn't make out where they fit into the high ceilings. And the ceilings went on forever, magnifying the vastness of the space. The leather seating, electronics and gadgets, artistic light fixtures, and a see-through fireplace at the center gave the room a lived-in feel. Even though she'd lived in luxury under Roy's roof, she'd never been able to appreciate it. After all, she'd been more a part of the furnishings than an inhabitant.

A tall, leggy blonde sashayed beyond the edge of the in-ground jacuzzi wearing only bikini bottoms, which were held precariously in place by tiny bows on her curvy hips.

Nathan's hand on her back nudged her forward past the view of sun-bronzed boobs. "Faye's in the kitchen. Go introduce yourself. I'll be back. Then we have some things to talk about." He flicked a finger over his shoulder and exited through the front door beyond the edge of the kitchen.

Who was Faye? Jay's note had mentioned her—

"You must be Charlee."

Charlee turned toward the soft voice and was met with a bright smile of a woman in her sixties. Her hair, clipped close all the way around her head, spiked in random tuffs of gray. Huge round hoops of silver adorned her ears and matched the glittering color of her eyes. She slapped a kitchen towel over her slim shoulder and held out her hand. "I'm Faye."

Charlee grasped it, surprised by the strength of her grip, given the woman's small stature. "Charlee. Nice to meet you."

Faye spun toward the long island, which separated the kitchen from the entertainment room. An eye-catching wine glass rack hung over the counter like a chandelier, tinkling as Faye glided past it.

She stopped at the stove, her Boho skirt licking at her ankles in a kaleidoscope of colors. "Are you hungry? I was just scrambling up some eggs for the pigs outside."

By pigs, did she mean Jay's bandmates? Charlee leaned against the island. "Are you the—"

"Manager extraordinaire. From band contracts to the hired help, I manage everything for these boys. But I'm not their cook."

Charlee's expression must have matched her confusion, because Faye said, "Since they have a concert tonight, I want something sticking to their ribs besides sugar and alcohol. And with the floozies distracting them out there—"

"A concert tonight?" Jay never mentioned a concert. A thrill of excitement kicked through her, but quickly evaporated. Would she have to stay at the house because of the danger Roy posed?

The topless blonde sauntered in from outside and sidled up beside her. "Faye, I need a beer."

"No, you need a shirt." Faye's eyes were piercing slivers of ice. "Get your tits off my counter and put some clothes on."

The woman huffed. "This isn't your kitchen or your house, much as you like to pretend."

Faye crossed her arms, ticking the spatula back and forth. "Yes, it is, bitch, and it certainly ain't yours. No shirt, no booze. Get out." The chill in her eyes sent a shiver down Charlee's back.

The overlarge boobs didn't bounce as the woman stomped to a bag leaning against the couch. Nor did they sag when she bent and pulled on a tight tank top. They seemed to be as hard as her eyes, glaring at Charlee. "Who are you?"

Charlee had limited experience with women, but when her tough, tattoo-seeking clientele hit her with attitude, she retaliated with kindness. She extended a hand toward the woman. "Hi. I'm Charlee."

The woman stared at her hand then jerked her gaze up. Dull as her eyes were, they were cruel in their perusal. "Well, that's convenient. Did he actually find one named Charlee?"

Charlee dropped her hand. The woman knew Jay's unnerving habit of saying her name during sex. The realization of what that meant cut her like a cane. How had he taken this woman? With the same rough passion he'd shown Charlee just a few hours earlier? A snarl of jealously seethed through her gut. Such an unfamiliar ache and her mind repulsed at the way it made her feel.

"That explains where Jay was last night." The woman smirked. "Hope you enjoyed it, because he won't need you again. He prefers blondes." She flicked her hair off her shoulder. "And it takes more than one woman to handle his brand of loving."

Charlee's teeth were gnawing so viciously she could feel the enamel grinding off. "You're being very rude."

"I'm being honest, honey. I see that starry look in your eyes. I recognize it in all the girls who come from his bed—or the couch, the pool table, and oh, right there on the rug." She flicked a manicured nail at the sheepskin in front of the fireplace. "You want him to love you, to let you touch him, to be his favorite girl. Jay Mayard is the most sought-after man on the planet, and it takes more than one woman—at the same time—to get him off."

A white-hot burn fired in Charlee's cheeks. She knew it was crawling down her neck, her discomfort a red glowing beacon against her pale skin. As much as she wanted to, and could, dispute the woman's claim, goading her would only agitate her further. And her own self-restraint was unraveling by the second.

"Go away, Felica." Faye's voice was a low vibration at Charlee's back.

"Soon's you accept that..." Felica winked. "You might be able to join the girls and me next time Jay strings us up."

The front door slammed.

"Shut your fucking face, Felica." Jay stormed through the room, black bags swinging from his fists, and a portrait of pissed-off twisting his expression. "Get out of my sight."

Felica's jaw dropped. "Jay? Baby? We had a date with a hot tub, remember?"

"Out!"

The wine glasses rattled overhead.

"Felica?" Laz walked in from the pool area, his arms spread open, bare-chested, his trunks hanging low on his hips. "Where's my beer, babe?" He looked at Charlee. "Oh hey, Charlee. Go get your suit on. Join us."

The band could call on the most beautiful women in L.A., and the estate's floor plan was designed for entertaining. It was easy to imagine all the sex-charged parties that went on day and night. Behind him, half-naked women lounged and giggled on the veranda, soaking the California sun into their golden skin. Charlee was a scrawny pale comparison to their beauty. How many of those women had Jay fucked?

She looked at Laz, shook her head.

Felica returned from the fridge with an armful of beer bottles and flashed Charlee a Hollywood smile filled with too-white teeth. Why wasn't Jay asking her to leave the property? Probably because he couldn't chase away all the women he'd slept with. The thought was sobering. And unproductive. She straightened her spine and swallowed past the mass of crap in her throat.

He set the bags on the counter and approached her. Dark circles outlined his eyes, his handsome face haggard beneath his scowl. "Charlee."

"It's okay." She reached to cup his jaw and remembered she couldn't. Her fingers curled back. "You need to eat and get some sleep. I didn't know you had a show tonight." She stepped back. "I'm just going to...uh, walk the property. I haven't explored yet."

All yours. Had the superstar whispered that to other women while he was fucking them? Damn her sappy wanton heart, but she believed him when he'd said it to her. Still did, and she didn't want to scare him away with the surf of jealous emotions burning the backs of her eyes.

56

Charlee made a beeline past Jay and slipped out the front door. Definitely not the way he planned to reunite with her after missing her so goddamned much all morning.

Fucking Felica. He strode out to the veranda and found Felica straddling Laz on a lounge chair, pouring beer on his nipples and lapping it up.

"Stay away from Charlee." His voice was low, pulsing with anger.

"Who? The redhead?" She rounded her I'll-fuck-anything eyes and shoved her tongue through the hoop on Laz's nipple, watching Jay as she pulled the string free on her bikini bottoms.

Had he really stuck his dick in that? Dozens of times. An itchy wave of disgust spread over him. He needed a fucking shower.

Five other women lay around the pool in various stages of undress. Quick glimpses of their faces—and some of their tramp stamps—confirmed he'd fucked all of them. No wonder Charlee had high-tailed it away from him.

He returned his attention to Felica. "You will not talk to Charlee or look at her again. In fact, everyone out. Pool's closed."

A chorus of disapproving moans rumbled back.

Rio tossed the packet of Fun-Dip he was licking and jumped up from his lounger. "Let's go inside and have a little chat." He bumped his barrel chest into Jay's, bullying him into the house with the sheer size of his body, careful to keep his hands up and out.

Jay wasn't about to throw down with his drummer. For the first time, he questioned the wisdom of all them living together. Too many egos under the same roof. But if they could endure sixteen weeks crammed in a tour bus, they could share a thirteen-thousand-square-foot mansion.

"Is this about your little red snatch?"

So much for not throwing down. Jay swung his arm, put his

whole body into it, and hit the brick wall of Rio's chest. The man looked down at Jay's fist dropping uselessly away and grinned.

"Call her that again and I won't be above breaking your fingers while you're passed out." Jay spun toward the front door and shook out the throb in his hand.

Rio beat him there. "My life is a haven of tight cunts and tighter drumbeats. You cannot and will not change the way we live just because your little Huntress can't handle it. Look at me." Rio rarely showed anger, but when he did, it boomed. "Nor can you change your past." He lowered his voice. "Does she know what you gave up after you met her? No sex. No drugs or alcohol. You lived like a fucking monk."

"I'm drug-free now."

One brown brow climbed toward Rio's bald head. "Good for you." His tone was dry, disbelieving.

"Fuck you."

"Straighten out your fucking head, Jay. Feel me?"

Rio's voice rattled louder than the door slamming between them. Jay followed the path around the estate and through the manicured front lawn. Palm trees fringed the property, but they were aesthetically placed. The true barrier was the eight-foot privacy fence behind them.

Straighten out his head? Fuck if he could. Charlee had it spinning around so damned fast, he didn't know which way was straight.

Yeah, he did. It was whichever way she was headed.

Shouts hurtled from the edge of the garden. Following the voices, he found her shoving Nathan in the chest. The man's stiff posture didn't ripple beneath her hands.

"I'm going."

"No. You're not." Nathan propped his fists on his hips and stared down at her.

She circled him, hands balled at her sides, and shoved his back. "I am. You can't stop me."

Jay froze. She wanted to go? She'd only just arrived. Seeing her so fired up to leave roiled his stomach, keeping his feet rooted and his presence silent.

Nathan sighed. "Charlee, beating on me won't change my mind."

She punched him low in his back, and he chuckled. "Now you're just behaving like a bratty teenager."

"Arrgh." She flopped down on one of the stone benches. "Maybe because I never got to be a teenager."

Nathan rubbed his eyes. "I'm not falling for that one again."

She pressed her forehead to her knees and held up her middle finger. Nathan stepped toward her toe-to-toe and twined his finger with the one she held up. Jay swallowed back his jealousy and forced himself to watch.

"Why do you *have* to go so badly?" Nathan squatted before her.

"Because, all the—" She stomped a foot, her head bobbing on her knee. "You wouldn't understand. Just go away." Despite her slumped posture, her tone was fierce.

Nathan released her hand and shoved her head up with the press of his fingertips on her brow. Much the way a guy might handle a bothersome little sister. Jay's shoulders relaxed.

"What wouldn't I understand?"

She looked up, blinked those huge blue eyes. "There will be women everywhere tonight. Women he's fucked." She glanced away, blinked again. "They'll be pawing him, and he doesn't do well in those situations. I want to be there to protect him, to support him. I want to hear him sing."

Oh, Christ. She didn't want to leave. She wanted to go to the concert. Jay's heart raced, as did his feet. Around the hedges and along the path to the corner where they huddled. He skidded to a stop behind Nathan. "Let me talk to her."

Nathan stood, dug in his pocket. "Be my guest." He pulled out a phone and handed it to Jay. "This is hers. Tony had a spare. I've programmed the numbers of the protective team and the household staff. Will you look over them, make sure I'm not missing anything?"

Jay nodded and pocketed the phone.

With a tap on Charlee's head, Nathan said, "When you're done here, I need to talk to you. I'll be up at the house."

When Jay could no longer see Nathan beyond the privacy of the garden, he joined her on the bench. She cast a worried look at him then focused on her fingers twisting on her lap.

He settled a hand over hers and stilled the movement. "For a minute there, I thought you were begging Nathan to take you away from here. Away from me."

She jerked her head up, the depths of her eyes gleaming an unfathomable turquoise hue in the sunlight. "Oh no, that's... No, I don't want to leave."

The skin between her fingers was as soft and soothing as a classical guitar riff. He wanted her velvet touch gliding effortlessly over his body. Probably not an appropriate time to want such a thing, but it didn't stop him from imagining it. "Going to the concert is a bad idea,

Charlee."

Her face crumpled, but she still managed to clench that stubborn jaw. "When do you leave for your next tour?"

Motherfucker. He hadn't even thought about that. "In two weeks."

"Two weeks." She stared across the garden. "And what? I stay here and wait for your return? For how long?"

No fucking way. "It's a sixteen-week tour."

She nodded, swallowed, and maintained her faraway stare. "That's a long time."

Too long. "You're going with me."

A little noise squeaked in her throat. She looked at him with so much longing, her eyes burned with it. So did his. She didn't ask him to repeat what he said. Hell, he wasn't sure he could. Taking her on tour with him was dangerous and selfish, and Nathan would stab him before he allowed it. And the groupies...Christ, the groupies would eat her alive. How the fuck could he protect her on the road?

With an army of highly-trained bodyguards, that was how. He sure as hell couldn't guard her with sixteen weeks and hundreds of miles between them. "I'll deal with Nathan."

That earned him a smile that made him want to make more rash promises.

"I'd like to make an amendment to the Charlee Constitution."

He arched his eyebrow, waited.

"The amendment states that I go with you tonight. You know, as a practice run, see how the team guards both of us."

Anything. Anything at all to keep her smiling like that. "I'm finding it very hard to say no to you." He dropped to his knees and wedged his body between her legs, gripping her hips. "Amendment approved."

She searched his face, her eyes a soft stroke everywhere they rested. "Let me touch you." Two fingers hovered over his mouth, waiting.

The need for her touch was as a strong as his fear of the things it might rouse. Fuck it. He nodded.

Keeping her fingers at a teasing distance, she leaned in and kissed his cheek. "If the bad stuff creeps in, sing to me, okay? I'll hear you."

57

The flutter of fingers tickled Jay's mouth. Charlee's lips joined the sensation. Then her breath. The flutter moved over his cheeks and down his throat. His pulse picked up and the edges of his mind curled away, taking the sunlit garden with it.

He focused on the heat of her lips, the fragrance of her skin, but there was a flame at his back and it burned. Oh God, it burned.

"Sing to me."

A lulling voice in the dark. Where was he? Not the shed. Not with the fingers trailing all too gently down his arm. Not with the sweet voice humming from the mouth pressed against his.

He blinked, tried to displace the darkness, couldn't. So he sang. He could smell charred skin. He sang louder, let it pour out from deep within him.

Lay still. Stop sniveling, boy. He wanted to put his clothes back on. Aunt El wouldn't leave if he fought her. He pressed his face in the musty mattress, tried to suppress the tears she hated, tensing as the bed springs shook beneath her weight.

A light, graceful peal shattered the dark. Someone laughing. He reached for it, sang along with the blissful sound. More laughter. He followed it out of the shed and into the blinding sun. She was there, inches away. Oceanic eyes, pale smooth skin of a pearl, cheeks rosy with the glow of amusement.

He held himself still, wishing he'd never have to leave the center of her dancing gaze. "Something funny?"

Her hands slid up his chest and rested on either side of his throat. She shook her head at him, smiling, still laughing. "I'm your oyster?"

The remnants of his nightmares rippled off him as he pulled her from the bench to straddle his lap. Her hands went to his back, circling over his scars.

"Tell me I wasn't singing the oyster song." He tucked her head under his chin.

"You're mine oyster, which I...with tongue will open...and suck out your juices." She half-giggled, half-sang the lyrics he'd drunkenly written one night while fantasizing about her. "Who did you write that for?"

"You're my muse, Charlee. All of my songs are inspired by you." His bandmates might've been annoyed with his three-year infatuation, but *The Burn* didn't hit the charts until he started embedding her into their music.

Her fingers moved up his spine, flirting with the hair at his neck. "I don't know what to say to that except... How exactly do I inspire oysters?"

"You're shaped like one." Bottling the laugh blooming in his chest, he couldn't see her face tucked below his chin and forced himself to wait for her reaction. When she didn't say anything, didn't even pull his hair where her fingers toyed, he said, "You're smelly, too. And you definitely don't have any feelings."

She yanked his head back by the hairs on his nape and shoved his chest until his back hit the grass. As she followed him down, his horizon filled with her beautiful smile, his body tightening beneath her.

"And here I thought it had something to do with my hidden pearl." Her voice was smoky, pure seduction. She licked her lips.

Eyes locked on the glide of her tongue, he swallowed. "That, too. I also like Shakespeare's analogy. *The world's mine oyster, Which I with sword will open*. The oyster is wealth. Opportunity. Possibility. You're my oyster."

With her bent over him, her face so close, he could make out the pale dust of freckles on the arches of her cheekbones.

She traced his eyebrows, the curve of his nose, his lips. "And your tongue is the weapon in which you acquire the opportunity. Not just in the obvious sense. Your tongue, through music, acquires the oyster, doesn't it?" Her lashes fluttered downward. "It had this oyster three years ago when *Huntress* replayed over and over in Roy's penthouse."

He lifted his head, used that weapon to part her mouth and delve inside. She welcomed every lick and nip with matching intensity. Their legs twined together, and their thighs rubbed, her toes sliding down his jean-clad calf and digging into the leg opening. She clung to his shoulders and his fingers bit into her hips.

He cracked his eyes and hers were squeezed tight in

concentration. She could kiss him with a passion that arched his back and wrenched him from his memories with the mere sound of her laughter.

It was a known fact that every great song slipped in a riff where the chords went to a unique, unexpected place. She was that song, those non-scale chords. Fuck, did he love this girl.

Too soon, she broke the kiss and pushed up on her elbows where they perched on his chest. "I triggered your memories, huh?"

He tucked a fiery lock of hair behind her ear, the soft ends slipping over his fingers. "*I* triggered them. *You* shut them off."

She stroked the stubble on his chin, studied his face. Then her gaze turned inward, and her nose scrunched.

"What are you thinking?"

She shook her head, eyes flicking away.

He curled up to a sitting position, adjusting her legs around him, groin to groin, chest to chest. "If you don't tell me, I'll just throw you over my knees and spank it out of you."

She straightened her back, eyes wide. "I think I just creamed those pretty white panties you picked out for me."

It was his turn to squeeze his eyes shut. "Jesus, Charlee." Could he take her right there? Lay her out between the hedges and slide between her legs? Who was manning the cameras? Could he block their view? He glared at her. "You're distracting me. Tell me what had your face all scrunched up."

An irritated hum vibrated in her throat and her little bounce in his lap didn't help his swelling erection.

"Oh fine. I was wondering how many women it takes to get you off on a normal night. Maybe I just lucked out last night. Maybe you were thinking about orgies with big-boobied blondes while you fucked me." She blew out a breath. "There it is. I said it."

An onslaught of vertigo slammed into him. His cologne suddenly smelled pungent rather than exotic. His jeans cut into his groin, vulgar in their tightness. She wasn't suggesting he was shallow and repulsive, but the feeling hit him with dizzying regret.

He searched for the right thing to say and couldn't grasp it. An apology was just words. His anger with Felica would distress her. Action would prove his devotion, but that took time.

Gathering her against him, he nuzzled his face into her neck, breathed her in, memorized the soft curvy feel of her. There was one thing he could clear up. "You were blonde when I met you." He let that sink in, felt her lift her hand and move it over her scalp, probably imagining the shorn blonde hair she wore that night in her tattoo shop.

"Oh."

Not enough. He raised his head. When her eyes idled on his, he said, "I didn't want intimacy with them. More than one..." *Just say it, fuckhead.* "More than one woman at one time guaranteed no intimacy. It's a disgusting reason, but it's the truth."

As if in slow motion, a swallow bobbed in her throat, weighting the delay in her response. "I want intimacy."

A surge of relief washed away some of his unsteadiness. "Me too. Only with you."

She nodded, and it seemed to be more for her sake than his.

"Okay." She jumped up, offered him a hand. "Nathan has something to tell me about Roy. It won't be good. Will you join me?"

His head was still spinning around her last declaration. He reached for her hand, but stayed where he was. "Those women are vicious. Almost as bad as the tabloids. Stay away from all of it, Charlee, and I'll protect you from it as much as I can."

Her eyes turned to frozen lakes. "I assure you, I've endured worse. I'll deal with those women. You don't need to protect me from everything."

He rose and used his height to punctuate his stance on this. "I do, and I will."

A muffled titter floated up. He angled his head and glimpsed a twitch in her lips. The little brat was chuckling. He reared his hand back to swat her ass, and she darted. In a flash of red hair, she disappeared around the wall of bushes. Fuck, she was fast. He chased her, his own lips pulling away from his teeth.

Up the path and through the front yard, he couldn't tear his eyes from the sway of her ass through her strides. He tripped over the curb of the sidewalk. Righting himself through a forward lurch, he picked up his pace and caught her at the front door.

She was frozen, muscles tense beneath his grip. He followed her gaze to the entertainment room, where Roy Oxford's face stretched across the sixty-inch widescreen.

Nathan stood before it, a hand on his hip, the other pointing the remote, adjusting the volume.

"Your sources are accurate, Meredith." Roy's smile oozed from the screen and crawled over Jay's skin. "Negotiations began this morning. Oxford Industries will acquire Windsor Records."

58

"Dickless psychopath."

Charlee realized she'd spoken her thoughts out loud when Jay and Nathan swung their heads toward her. Their faces held the same shock that had arrested her at the front door. Roy's retaliation was expected, but beginning acquisitions of *The Burn*'s label in less than a day? That was one hell of a quick play.

The clatter of silverware pulled her attention over her shoulder. Faye slid a plate of eggs, sausage, and cantaloupe across the island to Tony. The aroma of fried pork seasoned with red pepper hung over the counter in a cloud of lip-smacking spiciness. A reminder she hadn't eaten since the flight the prior night.

Seated around Tony, Jay's bandmates shoveled through their own plates of breakfast grease. All eyes were on the TV as Nathan rewound the clip and started it again.

Charlee's situation with Roy affected the entire household. A heavy weight of guilt made her want to crawl in the corner and disappear, but that kind of weakness wouldn't help anyone.

"Go eat." She pushed Jay toward the island.

He glanced at her hands where they rested on his arm and gave her a small smile. She'd touched him without thinking, and he wasn't having a meltdown. At least, they had that.

Without moving her hands, she faced Nathan. "When did this air?"

"Twenty minutes ago." He paused the image of Roy's face pinched in concentration and stared at it as if it held some hidden solution to all their problems.

"He's in his home office." She gestured at the leather wallpaper and rich wood shelves in the background. Had there been a slave between his legs, sucking him off while leashed to a chain? Dread rolled over her in shuddering waves.

"We had him tailed after we left your apartment yesterday," Tony said around a mouthful of melon. "We assumed he went back to San Francisco, but we couldn't confirm his arrival. This is good news. We know where he's at."

They knew where he was twenty minutes ago. Charlee wasn't sure what her expression held but Jay set his half-filled plate on the island and tugged her under the mantle of his arm. "San Fran is a six-hour drive from here. An hour and a half by plane."

He was telling her she had a couple hours before she needed to worry about Roy circling the property in person. She nodded.

When she turned back to Nathan, she noticed the vacant veranda behind him. Where were all the girls?

"We sent the visitors home," he said, perceptive as always. Worry lines creased the corners of his eyes. Something else was going on.

Her head throbbed. "Nathan, how'd you know about the record company acquisition before it was publicly announced?"

"I didn't." He powered off the TV. "This isn't the news I received this morning. Sit down, Charlee." He pointed to a deep cushioned chair in the living room.

Her hands shook as she dragged her bare feet over the wood floors. Was Roy already blackmailing the band? Had they decided to turn her over to him? A violent surge of fear choked her breath. Worse, was the alarming pressure behind her eyes at the thought of being separated from Jay.

Jay stayed at her side, carrying a plate piled with bacon and buttered toast. Lowering into the chair, he pulled her with him into his lap. "Half of this is yours." He held the plate under her nose.

Dishes rattled in the kitchen and multiple footsteps shuffled in around her. Faye perched on the armrest of a love seat. Rio, Laz and Wil spread out on the couches, unusually quiet as their eyes lingered on her longer than she was comfortable with.

Nathan must have gestured them over. Why was everyone staring at her as if they'd never seen her before? Her insides knotted, and she tried not to fidget under their scrutiny. Their expressions were heated, not with the anger she expected, but with a rawness that turned her stomach.

She jerked her gaze to Nathan. "You told them." How much had he told them? Did they know every sickening detail of her time with Roy?

Tony paced into her periphery and stood beside Nathan. "We both did. They needed to understand—"

"It's fine, Tony." Jay set the plate on the end table and shifted Charlee in his lap to face him. "I was going to tell them regardless. The band and everyone we employ will be impacted by your presence here, whether it's adding more guards, upping the safety precautions... changing record labels." His eyes were soft, gentle.

Guilt stabbed her anew. In a way, it was a relief to not have to live in subterfuge and filter everything that came out of her mouth, but she didn't want those luxuries at the expense of Jay's friends and their careers.

She swiveled in his lap to meet their eyes, the effort in her movements slogging with shame. "I knew this would reach beyond me, and I came here heedless of the trouble it would cause. I'm sorry." She held the eyes of each musician. "Did they tell you everything?"

Laz shrugged and leaned back in the couch. "We got the cliff notes. I already knew some of it, what you told me in the limo in New York. They filled in the rest. Imprisoned twice by this Oxford prick. He did things to you. Bad things. To his guards. Killed your boyfriend, too." His expression was soft in the way that made her neck sink into her shoulders. He knew exactly what those *things* were.

He sat forward, elbows on his knees. "Then there's the arms-trafficking. Blackmailing. Bullying acquisitions. And now he's on a mission to destroy our band." He shrugged. "To rip us apart from the top down. That about sum it up?"

She nodded, numb. He hated her. As he should. She looked at Wil, who fiddled with the drawstring of his trunks. His eyes rolled up and snagged hers. "I just want to know when you're going to tattoo Laz's dick."

A ripple of chuckles relieved some of the tension in the room. *Well played, Wil.* But the muscled legs beneath her turned to stone.

Jay moved to the edge of the chair, taking her with him. "Are you mentally handicapped? She's not going anywhere near Laz's dick."

Wil flicked a blond coil out of his eyes. "A bet's a bet."

"A bet I didn't make. Someone else can do the tat."

Nathan rubbed his temples. "Can we focus on the point of this meeting?"

"You're touching him." Rio's deep bass jerked every head in Charlee's direction. "Fucking hands all over his fucking body." His dark eyes were the size of cymbals and wrinkles formed on his bald head.

Charlee's palm stilled on Jay's bicep beneath his shirt sleeve. The other pressed against the sinews straining in his neck.

"No one touches Jay," Rio rose. "No one ever touches Jay."

Laz dropped his jaw. “You’re a fucking miracle.” He pointed to guys, grinning. “She’s cured him!”

In the next breath, Rio’s massive body plowed into them, knocking the chair backward and sprawling the three of them across the floor. Charlee rolled free of the grappling limbs.

Rio pinned Jay to the floor, straddling his hips, and arms hooked around him in a bear hug. She crawled toward Jay’s head to make sure he wasn’t lost in his memories.

His eyes were shut, his arms crossed over the other man’s back, and a smile tugged one side of his mouth. It was a pose that might’ve made a straight man blush. A man outside the intimate circle of the band, anyway.

Nathan hadn’t moved from his spot near the TV. Hands in his pockets, eyes on Tony’s stiff stance a few feet away. He seemed to be taking advantage of the diverted moment. He looked so content, Charlee hoped he had a lot more of those moments in his future.

Charlee climbed to her feet to watch the strange display of affection from afar. Laz and Wil jumped on Rio’s back, pulled him off and took his place. Wil grabbed Jay’s hands. Jay widened his eyes just as Laz’s fist caught him in the stomach.

Gasping, she jumped up to intervene, but Jay caught her gaze and shook his head. His smile convinced her to back off.

Rio pulled away from the twisting pile of bodies and approached her. “How’d you do it?”

The touching? She shouldn’t have been surprised by how affected they were by it—or lack of it. “He’s doing it. He’s fighting it.”

Without warning, Rio’s arms came around her, pinning her hands at her sides and lifting her from the floor. Oh shit. His lips landed on hers, slobbery and aggressive.

“Riooooo.”

At the sound of Jay’s distressed bellow, Rio released her and bent over, clutching his knees and roaring with laughter. “Dude, I kept my tongue to myself.” He stepped away, hands in the air, eyes twinkling. “Next time, I won’t be such a prude.”

Laz used the distraction to slap Jay’s face. His hand stayed there, holding his jaw. “I’ve wanted to do that for so damn long. And this…” He shoved Jay’s face away, rolled him over with Wil’s help, all three grunting with the effort to out-wrestle each other.

“Hold him.” Laz fought Jay’s arms while Wil put a knee in his back, pressing him to the floor.

What were they going to do? She looked at Rio in a silent plea to stop them, but he only stretched an arm in front of her to block her. Poor Jay was on his own.

Laz reached under Jay's waistband and yanked his briefs.

Jay's yelp accompanied the rip of cotton. "Sonofabitch. The one day I wear underwear—"

"That's payback for giving me a wedgie in front of Cindy Hollis in ninth grade." Laz grinned at Charlee as if her witnessing the performance was the true punishment.

Jay flopped to his back in a fit of uncontrollable laughter. All these years, they could never hit him, hug him, or seek childhood restitution. She could see now the barrier his triggers had put between him and his friends. Yet, they had somehow maintained a bond that ignored limitations.

"Jesus." Nathan paced beside the wrestling match. "Can we have the touchy-feely reunion another time?"

But they were too caught up. Jay was still laughing as the three of them rolled through the room, red-faced, throwing legs, ripping t-shirts, and slamming each other into the wall.

Charlee stood back, her fingers curled against her lips, her heart right there with them.

A high-pitched whistle pierced through the grunting and fist smacking. Faye stood on the leather ottoman, fingers between her teeth.

The guys broke apart and stared up at her, panting. She'd done this before.

"As much as I don't want to disrupt a *happy* fight for a change, Nathan's been trying to get your attention. Sit your asses down and give it to him."

After a few skull smacks and playful shoves, everyone returned to the couches. Charlee righted the chair, climbed back onto Jay's lap, and handed him his breakfast. Hair mussed and face flushed, he gave her a brilliant smile.

59

Charlee's earlier anxiety returned as Nathan approached her. Seeing his tense expression and hands on his hips took her back through their years on the run. He was worried.

"We have a spotter at Roy's penthouse."

"Another one?" Adrenaline heated her blood, energized her. This was great news. Nathan had been the one and only spy they knew of. Given the manner in which she escaped, it was safe to assume Roy wouldn't be so trusting with new employees.

A twitch rippled over his jaw. "He works for Henry Munt."

"The same Henry Munt who funded your undercover assignment?" After losing his family-owned company to Roy, Henry was determined in his revenge. And Nathan fucked that up by blowing his cover when he rescued her.

"Same Henry. His spotter has been embedded within Roy's ranks since before I was there. I remember him. He's good. I never suspected he was anything other than one of Roy's corrupt guards."

"Why did Henry hire you if he already had a spy in position?"

Nathan shrugged. "To cover his bases. In hopes one of us succeeded."

Holy hell. That meant the spotter had been working undercover for over three years. She filed through all the possibilities. "He should've found a way to collect video footage by now. Of me. Or maybe of some of the behind-the-door conversations of Roy's dealings."

Nathan sighed. "Impossible, Charlee. Roy's business is defense technology and information security. His shit is locked down. Videos feed to unknown locations. All data transmissions are encrypted. And with alerts on his equipment, he knows the moment someone tampers with it."

Of course. Her excitement fizzled. "Then what has Henry's spy been doing all this time?"

"Reporting Roy's activities to Henry, who is waiting for...hell, I don't know. A slip-up, I guess." He rubbed his forehead, leaving red streaks from the pressure of his fingers. "Henry contacted me yesterday to tell me about the spotter. Seeing your whereabouts in the news prompted him to loop me in. He doesn't know you, but he knows about you. He wants to do what he can to keep you safe from Roy."

As part of Roy's security team, Henry's spotter would've seen her on the cameras. She swallowed and asked the question she'd feared the answer to since the day she escaped. "Has Henry's guy reported other women? Other slaves?"

He pinched the bridge of his nose and stared at his shoes. "That was the call I received this morning." He squatted before her. "Roy picked up a girl on the way home from the airfield last night. First girl he'd brought back to the penthouse since you left. We don't know who she was."

Was. The temperature in the room soared. Saliva pooled in her mouth. She remembered the look on Roy's face when they drove away from her apartment. Returning to San Francisco empty-handed, his fury would've known no bounds.

A warm pair of hands gripped hers. Not Nathan's hands. Jay's. He was a silent, comforting presence against her back.

Distress radiated from Nathan's eyes as he looked at her. "He bludgeoned her to death in his stockroom."

Blood drained from her face and limbs, chilling her. Images of the devices hanging on the stockroom wall flickered through her mind. The aluminum side-handle baton. The old police nightstick. The rattan cane. Charlee had felt the cuts and bruises from all of them. "It should've been me."

"Bullshit." Jay jumped from the chair, lifting her with him, knocking Nathan out of the way.

Cradled against his chest, she watched the walls blur by. Was he spinning? Or was the room spinning? Nausea bubbled up. "I'm going to be sick."

More spinning and a trashcan was shoved under her chin. Holding the can, Faye blinked glassy eyes at her.

Too much coddling. Too much protection. She was inconveniencing these people's lives. And she definitely didn't deserve their sympathy. She wriggled in the cradle of Jay's arms. "Put me down."

He let her legs drop, but didn't let up on his squeezing embrace around her waist. She gripped the edges of the can and dry-heaved. A few noisy gags and nothing came out.

"You don't have anything in your fucking stomach." His voice strummed with anger. "Fine fucking job I'm doing taking care of you."

She handed the can back to Faye and nodded her thanks. Then she turned to Jay and cupped his jaw. "Don't do that. You've done nothing wrong."

The muscles beneath her fingers flexed and his attention zeroed in on Nathan. "She's going with me tonight."

"No fucking way."

Jay grabbed her wrists and pulled her arms around his hips, tucking her close. "She doesn't leave my sight. If she stays here, I stay here. End. Of."

The rest of the band crowded close, their faces stretched in shock and helplessness.

Laz shook his head at the floor. "Since you sing from the outfield, she could be riding your cock and fingering your ass, and no one would be the wiser." He looked at Jay. "We can't perform the show without you, man. I say she goes."

Wil nodded. "I agree. She goes where we go." Rio echoed him.

"No, no, no." Nathan threw up his hands and paced a tight circle. "This isn't a fucking democracy."

Tony touched Nathan's arm and gave him a look. Charlee didn't know what that look meant, but Nathan dropped his head back and said to the ceiling, "Christ in heaven. Call a fucking meeting with the protective team. We've got a lot of preparation to do."

As everyone parted ways, Charlee stared at the TV's blank screen. As much as she wanted to go to the concert, her wants now felt so fucking petty.

Jay hadn't left her side, and she could feel him watching her. A few voices mumbled in the kitchen, but they were otherwise alone.

Her thumb made a swipe over his hip bone beneath his shirt and his trigger remained dormant. "What are you thinking with regard to Roy and your label?"

"I'm not. In fact, it's the furthest thing from my mind." His timbre was low, drifting over her.

"Oh." She followed the indention between his hip and the bricks of his abs. Goose bumps cropped up around the path of her thumb. "And the closest thing to your mind?"

"The 9mm I bought and practiced with this morning. Thinking about how I'd use it without hesitation to protect you."

His early morning errand was indirectly for her. If she weren't so grateful, she'd be ashamed he gave up his sleep for her.

"And those black bags on the counter." He pointed at kitchen. "Thinking about how I'll use their contents to bring you to orgasm."

Holy shit, he'd been busy. A sex shop before eleven in the morning? A hum charged her body. It electrified as he wrapped his himself around her, around something inside her that desperately needed him, something she didn't even know was there.

"The biggest thing on my mind"—his lips brushed the shell of her ear—"is how very, very serious I am when I say you will not leave my sight. There's a pair of handcuffs in one of those bags."

Oh God. The past twenty minutes blurred away with the rumble of his words, his breath on her neck, and his hands stretching over her ass.

"Yeah, you're hearing me. I'm going to be so far up in your business, you're going to get sick of looking at my ass. You may very well feel like you've lost your freedom again."

She climbed up his chest and hugged his hips with her thighs. She was lucky enough to find her way into his life. Twice. She had to find the courage to keep him. "I'd rather be imprisoned by you than by him. In truth, I'm looking forward to it." She scattered kisses over his jaw. "And I'll never get sick of looking at your ass." She covered his mouth with hers and let him feel the trust behind her words.

60

Filtered light bled through the black canvas behind the main stage. The din of twenty thousand people in the indoor arena energized the atmosphere and hiked up Jay's blood pressure. Kicking off the tour with a concert in their hometown would reap millions of dollars.

And he could give a shit. He'd rather be at home writing music or in bed with Charlee.

She hadn't let go of his hand since they exited the SUV and hurried through the backdoor entrance. Her eyes were wide and glittery in the bated light as she took in the racks of guitars and the mayhem of speaker cabinets, amp heads, and sound boards.

They stood in the crossover space, concealed from the view of the audience by the drapery. The crew of roadies, technicians, and sound engineers swung in a fast pace around them, carting and testing equipment. Thankfully, the journalists were sequestered by the arena's security staff in the backroom, waiting with their slew of intrusive questions. The guys could deal with that.

Charlee passed a thumb over his knuckles. "Don't you need to be in the dressing room, getting ready, or doing whatever it is you do before a show?"

He needed to warm up his voice, but he wasn't taking her anywhere near the dressing room. His bandmates would raise hell if he tried to kick the groupies out. No doubt Felica would be there, along with the many other women he used in the past to take the edge off before and after his shows.

She twisted her fingers in her hair and wobbled on her heels. Was the dissonant sound of thousands in wait making her nervous? Or maybe she was worried Roy lurked among them.

A shiver skittered from his neck to his toes. His nerves were common in this setting, made worse by Charlee's situation. He didn't want her sharing that fear. He brushed his lips over hers, tried to take it away. "Don't be nervous."

Her head jerked back, lips in a heart-shaped pout. "I'm not nervous. It's just..." She glanced down at her tight tank top, denim mini skirt, and sexy black heels with strappy things that wrapped around her ankles.

Hot damn for the hundredth time that night. He definitely owed Faye a raise for picking out an outfit that bared her gorgeous legs.

"It feels suspiciously like we're in the one place your groupies aren't."

Perceptive brat. "Do you know how beautiful you are?"

"Do you know how avoiding-ful you are?"

A laugh exploded from his chest. "Avoiding-ful?"

She released the hair around her finger and tugged at the hem of her skirt. She didn't look comfortable. Maybe he shouldn't have been so pushy about her wearing something that gave him such a stunning view of her legs. But Christ, they went on and on and on—

She touched his jaw and pushed it closed. "You've looked at my legs a lot since we left the house and every time feels like the first time you've seen them. That alone gives me the confidence to stare down some bitches." She lifted a knee and hooked an ankle around him.

Fuck, she was perfect. Compassionate, but she didn't put up with people's shit. Mature, yet she glowed with youthful energy. Her inner beauty alone outshone every single woman. His hand flew to the back of her thigh, her skin like velvet under his fingertips. How the hell did she keep her legs so soft? He couldn't stop from stroking along the toned lines and reaching under the skirt.

Over her shoulder, Nathan tossed him a glare that raised his hackles and brought the cockblockalypse down upon him. They needed a secluded corner, pronto. That spot right there between the double-stack of Anvil cases and the wall—

"Jay! You're needed in the media room," Faye shouted from the stage wing. "Meet and greet time. Get a move on."

His heart pounded, and the hustle of people around him closed in, smothering. Damned pre-show signings. How would he manage without his usual distractions of drugs and mindless lays? Not that he wanted the latter, but the tightness in his throat made him desperate for anything that would spare him the looming panic attack.

Charlee dropped her leg and stepped back, swinging their hands between them. "You going to be okay?"

Jesus, she must have thought he was the biggest pussy. "Yeah. Great. Let's do this."

He led her through the storage of sets, past the technician work area, down a fluorescent-lit corridor, and backstage—the *back-of-house*. Scrutinizing every face, every shifty hand of the passing crew members, his alertness spiked. Roy's goons could be anywhere.

Following the clamor of voices, he stopped outside the media dining room. Sweat beaded on his brow and his stomach ached.

A hand slipped over his groin and squeezed. A surge of arousal rushed to her grip. Hello, distraction. He groaned as she dug in her fingers. Fuck.

She blinked up at him with eyes that haunted his dreams. "What can I do?"

Rub harder. Don't stop. "Stop. Or else I'll scare off the fans with a massive boner."

Her hand fell away, and a mischievous smile curled her lips. "I think I've got a rubber band in here somewhere." She opened the bag strapped across her chest.

God help him, she was adorable. "No rubber bands. I'd like to go in there with at least some of my dignity left."

A glance behind him confirmed Nathan was on their heels. Jay reluctantly handed her over to her bodyguard. "She stays in my sight." Girding his spine, he walked through the door.

61

The room erupted in high-pitched screeches, flapping papers, and flashbulbs. The rest of the band stood behind stanchions and velvet rope, signing posters and CD jackets. The rope wouldn't stop an enthusiastic fan, but it served as a reminder that the dozen security staff provided by the arena would remove a line-jumper without hesitation.

Numbness tingled through Jay's fingers and toes as he approached the energetic mob of fifty or more. Arms reached over the line, fingers wiggling and band paraphernalia waving.

He reminded himself the adorers appreciated his music and that very moment might be the most memorable in their lives. Idolatry and all of that. He got it. He would've been the first in line had Jimi Hendrix risen from the grave.

Faye appeared at his side and handed him a black marker. Having his own pen helped him maintain minimal contact with the fans.

Nathan guided Charlee to the back wall, his eyes alert and posture rigid. Good.

A probe through the room would've probably revealed his ten-man protective team, but Jay's attention was ripped away by the doe-eyed girl before him.

"I love you so much, Jay." She shoved a portrait of his airbrushed face at him.

"Thank you." He never knew what to say to them. Reciprocated love certainly didn't make the list of automatic responses. Did that make him a dick?

"I love you, too." Rio smiled at a girl down the line, pinching her nose and wiggling it. She bounced up and down, squealing.

Across the room, a small smile turned up the corner of Charlee's mouth. At least she was enjoying this.

Forty-five minutes later, Jay autographed the last photo, grabbed Charlee's hand, and pulled her out of the overheated room.

"Fifteen minutes till show time," Faye shouted after him.

He flicked a finger over his shoulder and strode down the hall. He didn't have to look behind him to know Nathan and Tony were on his trail. Two more of his bodyguards, Colson and Vanderschoot, swept past, blending into the stream of crew members in their jeans and t-shirts.

Hyper-aware of his security team, Jay strummed with an intense feeling of dread. Tony was usually his only shadow backstage. The extra personnel should've comforted him. Instead, it was a reminder of the threat against the precious woman at his side.

He scanned the halls and rooms they passed, straining to see something or someone out of place. Protecting Charlee gave him a sudden appreciation for how hard Tony's job was.

Did Roy have access to these tightly secured areas? Of course he did. He owned their record company, which owned their production company. Jay's dread magnified.

A man in suit pants and a collared shirt loitered outside a storage room. Who the fuck was that? An access pass hung from a lanyard around his neck.

Jay pulled Charlee close to his side and kept them moving toward the stage area.

The squeak of sneakers echoed around the bend. A wiry guy with dreadlocks skidded into view, balancing lighting equipment. Where was his badge? Was he a legitimate member of the lighting crew?

"I need to pee. Do I have time?" Charlee pointed at the restroom a few feet ahead.

Nathan moved around them and disappeared behind the door marked *Women*.

"Jay Mayard?"

A male voice, one startling similar to the fucker Jay heard on TV that morning. His pulse spiked as he spun and shoved the man against the wall.

An armful of CDs tumbled to the floor and a pimple-faced kid in his twenties stared up at him out of wide eyes. His overlong hair tangled around the kind of headset worn by the band's stage crew.

Fucking hell. He'd lost his ever-loving mind. Jay jumped back, releasing the kid and crunching plastic cases underfoot. The threat of Roy, the usual pre-show jitters, and his anxious need to keep Charlee pinned to his side created a fog of dizziness that shook his knees. He searched his pockets and remembered the overflowing trash can Nathan had carried out of his room the prior night. Fuck, fuck, fuck.

Tony stepped in front of him. Jay couldn't see her face, but the kid cowered.

"I...uh... My little sister loves *The Burn*. I'm... I work on the backline crew and was wondering if Mr. Mayard would sign my sister's CDs?"

"Bathroom's clear." Nathan held the door open for Charlee.

She slipped out of reach, eyes narrowed at Jay under lowered lashes. Was that disapproval?

Jay's heart rate escalated, his nerves fraying. "I'll go in with you, Charlee."

She looked away and slipped into the restroom. Dammit to hell. His face fevered.

"Sign your albums," Nathan said from the doorway. "I've got this."

The door shut and rattled the walls. Fuck Nathan. Jay lurched forward, fists clenched and ready. He tripped.

The kid grunted from the floor where he gathered the CDs. He shook out his fingers.

Great. Not only had Jay shoved him, he'd stepped on his hand. Feeling like an ass, he dropped to a knee and picked up the cracked cases. "What's your name?"

"Kevin." He lowered his voice and flicked his gaze at Tony's back. "Brady told me to give you this." He tugged a tiny zip-locked baggie out of his pocket and stretched his arm toward Jay. "Said if I did, you'd sign this stuff for me."

Brady. His longest-standing roadie and hook-up for all things drug-related.

Jay dragged his eyes away from the mix of yellow and white pills. Oxycontin with a Phenergan prep for nausea. He knew it well. "No. Not interested." His finger twitched.

Lips as red as the poor kid's pimples curved downward, as did his bony shoulders.

"Tell you what, Kevin. Give Faye your contact information, and I'll ship you a signed copy of every album we've produced. Okay?" He held out the broken CDs he'd collected.

The baggie dangled from Kevin's trembling fingers, waiting.

Just beyond the bathroom door, Charlee was peeing under Nathan's watchful gaze. Motherfuck, he wanted to punch something. If he hadn't lost his shit, he would've been in there with her instead of her donkey-fucking hero.

In a few short minutes, Jay would be singing to thousands. So much pressure. So many people. So many notes to fuck up. And he hadn't slept since the nap on the plane the prior day. What if he glanced at his fingers on the fret too long and Charlee disappeared from view? He was strung so tight, he wouldn't make it through the first song without breaking down.

Forty migs of Oxycontin would give him a little lift. Buzzy enough to smooth his edginess, but not too potent to steal his vigilance over her.

With a peek at Tony's back, he slipped the bag from Kevin's fingers as he dumped the CDs into his hands. "Find Faye, our manager. And I'm sorry about the shove. And stepping on your fingers."

Kevin jumped up. "No worries. Thanks so much, Mr. Mayard."

No worries. Good one. Pacing in front of the bathroom door, Jay checked the number stamps on the pills. Nice thing about Oxycontin was there were no real side effects as long as he managed his use. He wasn't an addict so there was no harm in this one pill. Charlee didn't even need to know about it.

A twinge of guilt lodged in his throat. He swallowed it back and chased it with a yellow forty and white twenty-five.

In twenty minutes, he would be ready to rockatize the arena.

62

The bounce and sway of twenty thousand concert-goers electrified the air, sparking off Charlee's body and lifting her skin with goose pimples. The sea of waving arms and camera phones flickered through the stands as far as she could see. They probably would've fought each other for her seat. Guaranteed the owners of the dozen or so eyes burning into her back would have.

She wouldn't let the groupies barricaded in the wing ruin the moment. It wasn't her fault they weren't allowed on the stage. Jay told her where to sit, she sat, and no one questioned him.

She perched on a bass cabinet on the stage deck. If the fans in the front row squinted at the shaded edge, they might've seen her. And despite their chanting pleas, Jay refused to emerge from the shadowed recess beside her.

The panorama of the boys on stage, glistening with sweat and jamming in tune with a house of energetic people, sent a tingling rush through her body. Experiencing the most popular bands of her time perform feet away would stay with her forever.

Through the first two songs, Jay sang while facing her, hands in the pockets of his leather pants. The rhythmic flow of his voice penetrated her chest, deepened by the fix of his gaze. His timbre reverberated through the sound system to thousands of idolizers, yet the arousing way he moved his lips behind his headset microphone, never looking away from her, it felt as though she were his only audience.

He ended the second song on a series of erotic exhales and she felt those breaths low in her core and warm in her cheeks. He must have sensed her reaction because he winked. Lord have mercy, he was a sexy man with a killer vocal range, and if she weren't mistaken, he was enjoying himself. A startling contrast from the hot-tempered barbarian twenty minutes earlier.

As the band transitioned into the third song, a roadie waved to

Jay from downstage and held out a guitar. Jay ignored him and took advantage of the reprieve in vocals by stepping between her legs.

Movement on the stage glinted light across his brown eyes. He reached out and trailed his fingers down her arm, around her hip, made the short trip over her skirt, and under the hem.

What the hell was he doing? The arena thundered with Rio's percussional lead and the spunky pluck of Wil's bass. The roadie with the guitar frantically waved his arm at Jay.

"What are you doing?" she mouthed.

He pushed his fingers between her legs, separating her thighs and curling them inside the crotch of her panties. His eyes looked... Off. Out of focus maybe. Was it nerves? Arousal?

Two fingers breached her opening, sliding in, to the knuckles. Her breath caught, and her knees fell open as far as the skirt would allow. Desire pulsed where he stretched her, lubricating his entry. She buried her mouth in her shoulder, unsure if her moan would be picked up by his mic.

One thrust. Two. Three. His hand disappeared, leaving her empty and panting. He stepped toward the panicking roadie, working those leather pants simply by walking backward, smoothly and confidently. He wiggled his fingers at her and she desperately wanted them back.

She wiped the sheen of perspiration from her cleavage with the heel of her hand. Holy hell, it was hot in here.

Screams piped from the women leaning over the gate at the front of the stage. They must have glimpsed *The Burn*'s reclusive singer. Heads bobbed and swerved as if trying to score the best view. When the squeals threatened to drown out the instruments, she *knew* they had seen him.

Accepting his guitar and strapping it over his body, Jay still hadn't released her gaze. An odd smile quirked his lips. Then he stepped from the shadows and into the edge of the stage lights.

The crowd exploded in hopping bodies and piercing shrieks. His stage appearance excited Charlee as much as the fans, but what had prompted him to cross that barrier? Was he showing off for her? Doing it because she wanted him to? Perhaps his new freedom from triggers gave him the confidence? Her fingernails bit into the cabinet beneath her as she waited to see what he would do next.

The guys must have doubled or tripled the length of the instrumental intro because they were still playing, following Jay's lead. The guitar solo waned, and Laz arched a brow at his vocalist.

Jay missed it, his eyes on her. Raising his two wet fingers, he pumped them in and out of his mouth. The crowd shrilled, seemingly unconcerned that his head was turned sideways, eyes focused offstage.

"Good Evening, Los Angeles."

A stunned hush fell over the arena. Jay's greeting made Rio jerk, missing a drumbeat. Laz and Wil slowed their strumming and straightened their stances.

The quiet erupted into the ragged screams of thousands. From videos of the band's live performances, she knew he sometimes addressed the crowd, but never from a visible position on stage. What in the world had gotten in to him? Devil-may-care, she surged with pride.

Watching her over his shoulder, Jay ambled further upstage, sucking on his fingers. "Nothing flavors rock-n-roll like the sweetly pleasing taste of pussy. Ain't that right, Los Angeles?" He flicked those fingers in a peace sign and pivoted his body toward her.

The house went wild, as did her emotions. Who was this guy and what had he done with the man who loathed mobs and attention? She wasn't offended by his declaration about pussy. In fact, she hungered for the confident musician strutting toward her, tapping the body of the guitar, even as something about his behavior slithered under her skin and raised the hairs on her nape.

A woman in the front row yelled, "Try my pussy, Jay."

Holding Charlee's gaze, he lurched back toward the crowd until his body was once again bathed in spotlights. "I found my huntress." His eyes seared into hers. "My Charlee. Let me be very clear."

For the first time since the show began, he looked away from her and toward the audience. "No one fucks with my girl." He squinted into the lights, sweeping a pointed finger over the endless landscape of faces. "No one."

Huntress. *Charlee*. The titles of their biggest hit songs. Before she could ponder what the crowd must be thinking, his eyes swung to hers and he belted the first verse of the first song she'd ever heard by them. "Huntress of the room in my head. Fearless and knowing." The fluctuation of his beautiful voice was as haunting as the muddy notes humming from his amp.

The roadie pointed at an *X* taped on the stage in front of the drum kit. Jay walked past the designated spot, whipping the power cord so that it dragged behind him unhindered. He didn't see the roadie stomp a foot and point at the *X* again.

She covered her mouth to muffle a laugh. Must have been a new guy. Surely the seasoned ones were used to Jay's rebellion.

For the remainder of the set, Jay's stage presence remained in the shadows. His charisma radiated an energy that rooted inside her, transforming her. He sang his heart out, hitting octaves that vibrated her bones.

She latched onto the passion behind his words, let it weave through her soul. The aroma of his musk-laced sweat rode on her inhales, fueling her body and rendering her paralyzed. She couldn't avert her eyes from his smoldering ones as he performed song after song written for her.

On the fringe of her periphery, Laz and Wil jumped around center stage, their heads nodding to the beat of their instruments, in sync with the verve heaving from the crowd. The fog of pungent smoke—which could only be produced from the greenery passing through the crowd—was thick enough to drown out the perfume-weighted estrogen fuming behind her.

When the last note of the encore buzzed from Jay's amp and drifted through the house, he yanked out the power jack. Holding the guitar out to the side, he didn't look at the roadie who grabbed it. His eyes were on her, and they were hungry.

Applause thundered behind him as he inched closer. Arousal mounted on his face and pressed against his fly. Shit. Was he going to fuck her right there?

He reached for his belt buckle, released it. Unzipped his pants. The head of his erection pushed through the open flaps. He rolled back his shoulders.

Oh God. This was what he did after his shows. He didn't have to leave the stage. His choice of lays would've been waiting in the wing. She squared her shoulders. He didn't need them anymore.

But was that what she wanted? To go at it right there in view of the crew breaking down the equipment?

Her pussy throbbed. Exhibitionism defined the whole of her sexual history with Roy. Every interaction recorded and observed. It should've deterred her from wanting that with Jay, but like all her sexual desires, she craved it in spite of her initiation to it.

Nathan and Tony stood near the stage curtain. Charlee caught Nathan's gaze, reached for the hem of her skirt, and sent him a silent plea to look the other way.

He tapered his eyes, clenched his jaw, and put his mouth at Tony's ear. A few words passed between them, and he moved toward the wing, turning his back. Tony's vigil returned to Charlee and Jay and everyone around them.

"Charlee." Jay's gaze made an explorative journey over her body, pooling heat everywhere it idled. He went back to her face, his tongue rolling over his bottom lip.

She gathered the skirt and bunched it up her hips until her thighs were bare. Biting down on a fingernail, she spread her legs.

63

The click-clack of multiple heels stampeded over Charlee's shoulder. The groupies must have been released from their cage.

She straightened her spine, but in the next breath, she forgot why. Jay was on her. His hands bit into her thighs. Moved to her hips. Ripped the strings on her panties. The ruined lace dropped somewhere behind him. His tongue pushed past her lips, slashing with hers. She raised her pelvis, meeting his groin, grinding, unbidden and impatient.

A long-lost sensation uncoiled and heated where he thrust against her. The tease of penetration. The aggression. The onlookers. The threat of Roy in this public place. Her adrenaline spiked. Heaven help her. If he fucked her, she might come.

"Charlee, fuck. Tell me I'm not dreaming. You're my here, my now, and God, if I'm lucky, my hereafter."

The force behind his words illuminated their darkened recess. She sighed into his mouth and wrapped her fingers around his length. "If you throw me down and fuck me, I'll be your hereunder."

A shadow fell over them. Felica curled her pleathered body against his side, one hard nipple poking out of her low neckline.

Jay leaned in and sealed his mouth over Charlee's, breathless and demanding. Did he not notice Felica rubbing up against him? Maybe he didn't care.

Bristling at his disregard for her feelings, Charlee released his dick and tried to punch Felica in the stomach, but she hopped out of reach. Maybe she'd take the hint.

Charlee had an overwhelming urge to beg him to take her somewhere else, somewhere intimate. But that would've been running from this thing she knew she needed to confront. He'd told her he only wanted her. Had he lied? As much as her heart rejected the idea, she needed to see how far he'd let this go.

He sank his teeth into the spot below her injured ear, shooting a warming pang through her body. The pressure from his bite intensified, and he lined up his erection at her entrance, his groan vibrating down her back.

Dammit, the audacious woman pressed against him again, hands at her sides, eyes on his mouth where he nuzzled Charlee's neck.

"Jay, wait." Why wouldn't he push her away? Tell her to fuck off? Charlee's arousal fizzled by the second. "Get that woman—"

He thrust, buried in one long stroke. His neck arched, and he shouted something indiscernible to the rafters.

Stars flashed through her vision and heat exploded between her legs. "Ahhh, Jeeeeesus."

Hips pumping, he gripped her thighs and lifted her lower body to meet him. The new position dropped her on her back, head hanging off the edge of the half-stack, the plastic casing digging into her shoulders. He followed her down, flexing his hips. The pain was so arousing, everything else fell away.

"My turn."

The feminine voice crawled over Charlee's skin. She snapped her head up and met Felica's frosty blue eyes. A violence of emotions ripped through her and she reared back to punch whatever pleathered body part she could reach.

He twisted his neck and glared at Felica. "Don't you dare touch me. Go away." His voice dipped, low and commanding.

"Come on now. Why does *she* get to touch you?" Felica pointed at Charlee's hands where they gripped his shoulders.

She had a point. His triggers weren't tripping.

"Because *she* is Charlee. This is the last time I'll tell you. Go. Away." He swatted a hand behind him, missing Felica by a ridiculous margin.

The woman rolled her lips between her teeth, turned on her heels, and strutted away. He looked at Charlee out of glazed eyes. Was he having a hard time centering?

She shoved his shoulder. "What's wrong with you?"

His eyebrows pulled together and snapped back. A smile skittered across his swollen lips. "I'm buried seven-inches in, baby. Ain't a goddamned thing wrong." He powered into her. The strength of his thrust spiraled through her womb. It burned so good, but something was off.

Clumsy. Overly confident. Unfocused eyes. Oh God, he was high. Her muscles tensed to fight him off.

His eyes dilated, and he pinned her hands to her chest, stroking her womb with his lunges. She should tell him *No*. She should shout it through the arena.

But that would bring the wrath of Nathan with fists flying as he dragged her from L.A. Her molars slammed together. She could deal with this.

His mouth fell over hers, and she head butted him. Undaunted, he fucked her with the potency of his strength and the weight of his body. It might've felt orgasmic if he weren't fucking high.

Self-loathing trembled off her in waves. She wasn't behaving any different than his countless meaningless lays. She brushed the miserable feeling away and wrenched a hand free of his restraint at her chest. "Jay, stop."

He drove harder, faster.

Stunned, she gasped. No air. The weight pounding into her smothered her reasoning. Roy's heavy-bodied arms pinned her down. Fragments of shuffling down the long corridor with the chain on her ankle burrowed in her throat, strangling.

He rotated his hips and shoved a hand in her hair. Brown eyes met hers, Jay's eyes, soothing her, until his face twisted in ecstasy.

No more. She grabbed his chin to stay his disoriented gaze. "Huntress."

His jaw moved with his smile, twitching beneath her hand. "I wrote that song for you." His thrusts caught a hiccupping pace and he crashed to a halt, buried deep inside her, eyes rolled back in his head. "Unngh. Fuuuuck!"

The power of her safe word faded with his orgasm. She shoved his head away. He swung it back, looking down at her, lips wet and slack. "Best. Fuck. Ever. How about you?"

She slapped him. "Not even close. Get the fuck off me."

He jumped up and back, hand covering his cheek where she hit him. He narrowed his eyes. "What the fuck, Charlee?"

Her lip quivered. *Don't give into it. Get up, dammit.*

She rose, teetered on her heels, and adjusted her clothes with trembling fingers. Her panties lay on the stage. Ruined. Just like her pride. Fucking bastard.

But the shame gripping her body was no one's fault but her own. She'd allowed Jay to use her, trusted his sobriety, and depended on him to honor her safe word. So naïve. "Do not follow me out."

She turned slowly, deliberately, and schooled her gait as she walked away. The lump in her throat could stay where it was. She was *not* going to let it burst into a wet mess of emotion.

"Charlee." A question lay beneath the sternness of Jay's tone. "Don't run."

So he was coherent enough to know he'd given her a reason to run. Deep breath. She stopped, looked over her shoulder. "I'm not hanging around so you can fuck me again while you're high."

He looked down at his dick hanging exposed and partially erect. A choke ripped from his throat, and he stumbled back, shoving himself in his pants and zipping up with more force than was needed. "Oh fuck. Oh Jesus." He raked his hands through his hair, pulled at the messy strands, and jerked his gaze to Charlee. "No. No, no, no. This isn't... I'm not... Charlee, wait."

The hitch and wheeze in his voice threatened to melt her backbone. For a flickering moment, the man she thought she knew looked at her, actually saw her. The sag in his eyes and the twist of his face chased her heart to her throat.

She turned away and strode toward the corridor behind the main stage toward Nathan's back. Passing him, she tapped his hand without slowing her steady stride. "Time to go."

As if floating out of her body, her feet carried her past the control booth and down the hall.

He was so lit. Did he even know who he was fucking? He'd said her name while he was *seven-inches in*. Oh, but he called all his girls Charlee. Tears welled in her eyes.

Jesus, hold it together. He hadn't let Felica touch him. It would've killed her had he interacted with her. And the horror warping his expression when he finally realized what he'd done was somewhat assuring.

Whatever. The fact that the asshat ignored her safe word was an unforgivable snap of a whip through the heart.

"What happened?" Nathan's hand settled on her lower back.

"Jay fucked up. Let me deal with it, okay?" She followed the bend in the hall, veering around techs juggling equipment.

"Does this change—"

"Nothing changes. I'll have it fixed by morning." And she would. Jay owed her an orgasm, and dammit, he would give her one. A half-baked plan sprouted, soothing her. He wasn't going to like it, but fuck him.

The protective team's familiar faces popped up at every corner, bend, and open doorway as she weaved through the flow of roadies with Nathan's hand a bolster at her back. They formed a comforting perimeter around her, adjusting their formations to maintain a circle of protection as they moved through the back-of-house.

The exit came into view, and a man in a suit flashed through the bustle of crew members rolling crates through the door. The suit and dark hair were familiar. Too familiar.

She skidded to a halt, her pulse thick and distant in her ears.

Nathan stopped with her, hand pressing against her spine. "Charlee?"

The man in the suit looked up, complexion dark beneath a thick mustache. Not Roy. Relief settled through her shoulders. Until he narrowed his eyes on her.

"That man is looking at me." Did he know her? What the hell did he want? Oh God, he was walking their way.

Nathan pushed her behind him and held up his hand. "Identify yourself and don't take another step."

"Alan Patera. Executive Assistant to the CEO of Oxford Industries."

She locked her knees and gripped the back of Nathan's shirt.

"What do you want, Mr. Patera?" Nathan's clipped tone did not invite idle conversation.

A technician in baggy jeans pushed a cart past her, its wheels screeching with each rotation.

Patera extended a thin hand, holding a crisp white envelope. "Mr. Oxford sends his regards."

Shooting an arm toward him, Nathan grabbed the envelope, but Patera hung onto it.

Patera narrowed his eyes. "A response is expected." He released it.

Shifting back with an envelope in hand, Nathan grabbed her wrist and led her around the smiling Craig.

"What was that about?" Her heart pounded an impatient tattoo as she glanced over her shoulder. The Craig was gone.

Outside, Colson opened the door to a waiting SUV.

Nathan's attention swept left to right as he stuffed the envelope into his breast pocket. "Message from Roy."

A throb erupted behind her eyes. He wrote her a letter? Was he out there, watching her? In one of the hundreds of cars in the lot? Standing behind one of the windows veneering the building? Waiting for an opportunity, for the millisecond of time when all of her guards might be looking the other way?

"Please, get in the car, Miss Grosky." Colson waited, eyes on the exit behind her, hand on the door of the car.

She shivered and bolted in, sliding across the bench and bumping into Vanderschoot with a screech. “Oh, hi. Sorry.” Damn her out of control pulse.

The seat bounced with Nathan’s weight beside her. He reached for the door handle and pulled.

A hand shot through the crack of door, gripping it and preventing it from closing.

She gasped, frozen to the seat, as Nathan wrestled to close the door. His free hand stretched for the gun at his hip.

The knuckles around the door frame were grooved with callouses. Callouses from guitar strings.

She clamped down on Nathan’s hand over his holster. “It’s Jay.”

Nathan squinted at the door and let go of the handle.

Jay’s drawn face lowered into view. His gaze moved through the car and stopped on her. A tornado of emotions whipped across his weary expression. His Adam’s apple bobbed, and he ducked his head, wedging into the third row behind her. The leather seats creaked as he scooted in, Tony following.

Colson steered them into the concert traffic, and Charlee decided to be the first to break the tense silence. “I said not to follow me.” Sandwiched between Vanderschoot and Nathan, she kept her eyes on the windshield.

“And I said you were not to leave my sight.” His deep, dominating tone caressed her back, the bastard.

“Are you still high?” Good grief, she sounded petulant. Maybe she was. She shifted to look at him.

“I’m coming down.” He studied her face, his own pinched in pain. “I’m so sorry.” A whisper.

She would find out shortly how sorry he was. She turned back and looked into Nathan’s soft blue eyes. Looked at the envelope in his breast pocket.

His fingers were hesitant as he pulled it out and handed it to her. “It’ll be obtuse, you know. Anything in writing will be worded in a way that won’t implicate him for what he’s done or plans to do.”

Flipping the white envelope over in her hands, she nodded. “I know.” She couldn’t stop the resignation from dulling her voice. “I’m expecting a legal-team-approved death threat.”

64

The god-awful regret constricting Jay's voice snapped when he heard the bleak acceptance in Charlee's. "What death threat?"

Bile flooded the back of his throat. She'd already endured so much misery. His after-show performance settled around him like a miasma. Shame constricted his heart and darkened the very fiber that made her soul shine. He did this. He was no better than Roy.

Her fingers flicked over the controls on the roof until dim light illuminated the envelope in her hand.

"What is that?" He didn't like the way she held the corners, not opening it, as if there were a bomb inside. "Is that from Roy?"

Her shoulders twitched, and she hunched slightly to the right, toward Nathan.

Nathan touched her hand. "Want me to read it?"

She shook her head. "I'll do it."

So Jay was the only asshole she was ignoring. He earned it, but he didn't have to fucking like it.

She held up the nondescript envelope to the light. White. Standard size. No writing or logos. Was it a correspondence from Roy? A swarm of hostility took over his muscles, tensing him from neck to feet. "Did you see Roy? Was he here?"

She picked at the sealed flap, shoulders bunched to her ears.

His hands clenched with the urgency to be closer, to hold her pain for her. "Vanderschoot. Switch with me."

The guard swiveled his balding head, looking around the tight seating arrangement, probably wondering how he would maneuver a switch while the vehicle was in motion. "Right now, Mr. Mayard?"

Charlee let her head fall back and glared at the roof. "Jay, would you please just sit there—" she let out a ragged, drawn out exhale "—and shut the fuck up."

His face caught fire, his shame reigniting. If he were perfect, she'd be too good for him. He was far from perfect. "I deserve your anger, your hate, and anything else you want to throw at me." None of that mattered while her life was in danger. He needed to be very clear, make her understand. He couldn't face losing her again. "My fuck up does not change your need for protection." He shifted to the edge of the seat and the force of his breath ruffled the crimson river of hair flowing over her seat back. "I employ your protective team, so I need to know what the fuck is going on."

He snapped his fingers at Vanderschoot. "Switch."

The lean man folded his body and crawled to the back beside Jay.

"Thanks." With a lot less grace and an unnecessary hand on Charlee's shoulder, Jay tumbled into the second row.

Gorgeous blue eyes narrowed on him, stealing his breath. Her lashes fluttered closed through a deep breath. "I'm pissed. Hurt. Ashamed...Frustrated." She glanced out the windshield and whispered, "Blue ovaries frustrated."

Jesus, she couldn't have hit him any harder. He'd left her unsated. Again. While one of his weakest decisions fogged his head as *he* climaxed. He buried his face in his hands, wanting so badly to take it all away. Too damn late. The ugliest, dirtiest side of himself had sauntered out of its hole and spread its legs in her face.

She didn't run. Instead, she seemed willing to talk about it. He raised his head. "You want to do this right now? We can. My protective team knows all about my indiscretions. They've carried my unconscious ass out of more concerts than not. And maybe Nathan should hear what kind of a fuckwad he's working for."

Nathan drummed his fingers on his knee and stared out his window. "I'm already well-informed."

"Be nice, Nathan." She massaged her temple. "And Jay, please don't insult yourself. It's not helpful."

Jay blew out a breath and leaned back. "The kid I shoved in the hallway slipped me forty migs of Oxycontin."

She snapped her head toward him. The flash of passing headlights glanced off her rounded eyes.

"I wanted a light buzz, a dose of energy. Oxycontin gives me that without the appearance of being high."

"So does Red Bull. And Starbucks." She was back to staring out the windshield, the envelope twitching in her hand.

"Touché." He bent his elbows on his knees. "I also needed a panic attack suppressant. I thought what I took was Oxycontin. Maybe I got the dose wrong. Maybe it was mislabeled. Because the high has...had a delusional effect. Like heroin."

It had been only him and Charlee in that arena. No crowd. No groupies. Everything had peeled away, leaving an erotic euphoria with her at its center.

Narcotics had a way of driving him through the worst of his anxiety. A numbing appeal. But he would lose her if he didn't take the wheel and confront his weakness head-on and sober.

"Are you delusional now?"

The single pitch in her voice vented her suspicion. He knew she was thinking if she couldn't recognize the side effects, how would she ever know when he was high? Worse, he'd annihilated any trust he might've earned. "I'm clear-headed enough to know I made the second worst decision of my life tonight."

She looked away from what he knew was desperation burning in his eyes.

"I'll give up the tour, the shows. The band. Anything to make this right." Yeah, he was choking with desperation. He hadn't lied. He'd give it all up.

"Drama queen." She flipped the envelope over and over through a weighted moment. Then she tucked her chin to her chest and asked, "What was your worst decision?"

The memory of the night he met her coiled around him, suffocating and intoxicating all at once. "St. Louis. Three years ago. Letting you walk away. If I'd delayed you, took you for coffee, kidnapped you myself..."

She cupped her mouth and closed her eyes.

Christ, he'd reminded her of Noah's death. "Charlee—"

"It's okay." She dropped her hand, eyes resting on her lap. "Walking away was my worst decision, too."

His heart flipped over. Sure, if she had joined him for coffee, Noah would've survived, but he told himself she was thinking of the three years she might've had with Jay.

"Roy's assistant delivered this." She shoved a finger under the seal and tore it open. Chest heaving, she unfolded the letter and held it under the dome light at an angle the three of them could read silently.

Miss Charlee Grosky
27124 Los Hermosos Way
Los Angeles, CA 90027

Dear Miss Grosky,

Oxford Security is pleased to offer you a position as Resident Artist for our organization. We are excited about the talent you would bring to our company.

Should you accept the offer, you will be working in the San Francisco penthouse, where our security teams reside. You will report directly to the CEO of Oxford Industries. Your initial task will be to sketch a portrait for one of our high-ranking security officers. The commissioned work will be presented to the officer's niece as a gift for her nineteenth birthday.

You will be classified as an executive-level employee. Your initial compensation package includes full medical and dental coverage, and fringe benefits. In addition, Oxford Security will loan you an amount equal to all of your expenses incurred by The Burn. *Should you remain with Oxford Security at least three years, the loan will be forgiven in its entirety.*

We look forward to your arrival at our company and are confident your skills will play a key role in the morale of our personnel. Please sign this letter and return it to me at your earliest convenience as a written acceptance of the offer. Let me know if you have any questions or if I can do anything to make your arrival easier.

Sincerely,
Alan Patera
Executive Assistant to Roy Oxford
Oxford Industries

Jay's stomach turned and bucked. "What the almighty fuck? He's offering you a job?"

"The threat is here." She traced a trembling finger over the paragraph about the nineteen-year-old niece and looked at Nathan, her voice dropping to a whisper. "I'm not seeing it. What am I missing?"

Nathan leaned close and slid the letter from her hand. His eyes flickered over the words as his free hand gripped hers.

Jay wasn't sure which felt worse, his jealousy or his exclusion from their history together. He knew their shared torment was what connected the two of them in the most intimate of ways. He stuffed that to the back of his mind and focused on the letter.

She was right. Roy wouldn't offer her a job. He'd blackmail her. "Nathan, how well did you know the high-ranking officers? Who has nieces this age?" He flicked a finger at the letter.

"I don't know." Nathan rubbed his brow, his tone low and deadly. "We didn't discuss our personal lives."

Then why would Roy mention anything about an employee's family if Charlee and Nathan didn't know them? "What about the undercover guy? Do you know—"

"Fuck." Nathan pulled his phone out of his pocket, swiped the screen, and held it to his ear. "Mr. Munt...Yes. Sorry to call so late. I need to know if your contact has a nineteen-year-old niece...That's right. If he does, he's been compromised...I'd rather discuss it over a more secure line...Understood." He returned the phone to his pocket and met Jay's eyes. "He doesn't know the spotter's identity. He hired him through a private company. Personal details best kept personal for obvious reasons. He'll find out and call me back."

Jay reread the letter in Nathan's outstretched hand. "What about the expenses incurred by *The Burn*? What is he threatening with this?"

"He's saying that if I return to him willingly for three years, he'll *forgive* you by leaving your band alone."

The buzz of Nathan's phone cracked the tension, and everyone seemed to hold their breath as Nathan answered it.

"Mr. Munt." Silence. "Keep me updated." He lowered the phone, lips taut, jaw squared. "The spotter isn't answering his phone, but this isn't unusual given his position at the penthouse. Munt put a call into the private company that employs him to get a warning to his family. He'll call back."

She frowned. "See what Crane and the rest of your guys can make of the letter." Laying her head back, she touched Jay's knee, lingered there for a moment, and returned her hand to her lap.

Was she testing his trigger? Touching him for comfort? Did it matter? Her caress left behind a tingle that swept through his bloodstream and invigorated him with purpose. He had a lot of self-improvement to do.

65

The SUV passed through the gate of the band's estate and parked in the garage. Jay glued himself to Charlee's side and stumbled when she veered in the opposite direction of the interior door.

He wanted to reach out and grab her, but opted for patience. "Where are you going?"

As the guards moved inside, the click of her heels followed her to the back wall where the utility boxes and carpentry tools lined shelves and cabinets. She rooted through the drawers until she found a palm sander.

"Charlee, talk to me."

She handed him the sander and a sheet of sandpaper and moved to the workbench.

He turned it in his hands, unease trickling through him. "What am I supposed to do with this?"

"You'll see." She opened a metal box. "Oh! This is perfect."

A bundle of rubber-insulated wire flew toward him.

He caught it, surprised by the heavy weight. "Electrical cable?" Did she plan to hook his dick to a generator and fry it off?

She scanned the garage, chewing on a nail, lifting up and down on the balls of her feet. Given the horrible events of the night, she seemed a little too excited about whatever was going through that gorgeous head of hers.

Realization sucked the blood from his face. She wasn't looking for tools to torture him with. They were for her. A sickening amount of panic gripped his gut. "You want me to hurt you." His certainty was thick and strangled.

She yanked something from a bin of gardening tools, turned toward him, and held out a bamboo plant pole. "Yes."

They stared at one another with that menacing pole raised between them. She didn't tell him he owed her this. It flared from her stony unblinking eyes.

His heart pummeled against his ribs. She didn't want to scream at him or kick his ass. She didn't want to walk out and never see him again. She wanted him to man the fuck up and be her Dom.

Big breath. Another. He nodded. A jerky movement. "Okay."

She lowered the pole. "Okay?"

"I'll give you whatever you need." He held out the sander and cable. "But electric shock, Charlee? I'll fucking kill you."

She let out a soft huff and shook her head slowly, lips twitching. "Percussion play. Electric shock won't be necessary."

"Percussion?" The image of her strapped over Rio's drum kit inappropriately tumbled into his head.

She breezed past him in the direction of the interior door, twirling the garden pole like a baton. "Impact. Flogs. Whips. Percussion."

Jesus. "Charlee. Wait. Just...stop a second and talk to me."

Her hand was on the doorknob, but she didn't turn it. Nor did she turn to face him.

"Look at me."

Her chin moved, perched on her shoulder and she glared at him. It was a defiant glare, coloring her cheeks and brightening her eyes. And fuck him, but it looked good on her.

"This is what you want?" He raised the devices that guaranteed nightmares in his near future.

Her stubborn chin tipped up and down.

"I know how this works. Limits are set on both sides, right?"

The muscles in her cheeks flexed.

He set the sander on the nearest cabinet. "Power tools are one of my limits." He held up the sheet of sandpaper to show her he still had it.

She looked at the sandpaper, at the sander, back at the sandpaper. "You better know how to use that."

He nodded. He didn't have a fucking clue.

66

Charlee sent Jay to his room with an emasculative point of her finger. Apparently, she didn't appreciate him groaning over her shoulder as she dug through the kitchen drawers.

Tooth picks, chopsticks and saran wrap? He would've given her points for creativity, but she'd already maxed out her quota in the garage. He tried not to imagine what room she might've been rummaging through at the moment.

She behaved as if she held the power over what was about to happen. A perception he would soon rectify.

In his closet, he shed everything but the leather pants, leaving the top button. Rolling back his shoulders, he lengthened his neck and spine and cycled through several deep breaths. Bringing to mind everything he'd learned in his BDSM research on the Internet, he gave himself a pep talk.

He could do this. He would do anything for Charlee. He definitely could... Holy motherfuck. He couldn't wuss out now. For the next however many hours, the right mindset would be the key to unlocking her.

Control. Roy abused her with it in a slave role she never agreed to. Consensual control in the bedroom was another matter. To administer the pain she desired, Jay needed to take her in hand. And no more cringing at percussion tools like a bitchboy.

He lifted the thickest leather belt from his rack, folded it, and whacked his thigh. His quadriceps jerked through the sting. Might not compare to the crack of an electrical cable, but he needed to start off with something a little more conventional.

Striding through the bedroom, he opened the desk drawer and collected four metal finger picks for an old banjo he sometimes messed around with. He slid one on the tip of his index finger and scratched it down his arm. A smile pulled at his lips.

He grabbed the three black bags by the door and dumped the contents on the bed. The exclusive sex shop owner had been overly helpful that morning. Her flirting was as ineffective as her perfume, but she was a well-known masochist in L.A. and her advice lifted some of the veil from Charlee's sexual mystique.

Not only did it lift it, her explanations made sense of it, normalized it. Charlee was no different than so many others. Pain simply unlocked the core of her desire.

Which brought him back to the importance of mindset. The focus was her pleasure. He could probably just beat the ever-loving shit out of her, and she'd find release through her twisted conditioning. He'd rather massage away the taint Roy left on her primal core by giving her pain through devotion and respect.

The fact that Jay would have this privilege was ludicrous after the shit he put her through that night. All the more reason he needed to assume the role and prove to her he could be the man who was valuable enough to dominate and worship her.

From the pile of purchases, he separated a butt plug, lube, nipple clamps and a Hitachi wand. The rest went back in the bags and into the closet.

The door to the bedroom clicked open behind him, and his heart thumped wildly. Go time.

He pivoted toward her, slowly and methodically, relaxing his shoulders, issuing his breath from his diaphragm, and holding his head high. "Go to the bathroom and clean your pussy. You have five minutes."

Eyes wide as saucers, she lowered her arms and clutched her loot to her stomach. One of Rio's drumsticks, a bucket of ice, an ice pick, a cheese grater, and some root thing that looked like she'd just dug up from the backyard filled her hands.

Holding his neck straight and relaxing his eyelids, he waited.

She didn't waste words asking him if he was sure. Maybe she saw the certainty in his eyes.

She scampered toward the bed and dropped her findings next to the sandpaper, cable, and bamboo pole. A glimpse at the things he'd collected made her lips flicker up. Then she scurried to the bathroom.

He let out a breath. Washing her cunt wasn't necessary. He liked knowing traces of his come were between her legs, even if his behavior would forever mar that memory. But he needed to set the tone and give her something to do while he prepared.

In short order, the household pervertables were lined up on the desk, and his rope was tied to the bedframe. He wrapped the sandpaper around the end of the belt strap and used the ice pick to punch holes in the scratchy paper where the belt holes lay beneath. With guitar string from his desk, he knitted the paper to the belt through the holes and secured it together.

The water tap shut off followed by soft footfalls. She appeared in the archway of the bathroom, and he settled into a tremble that tightened his body. He breathed through it and let it ripple away.

Gloriously naked, she stood with her head down and her hands at her sides. Flawless white skin, outrageous dips in her waist, the flare of her hips, and the auburn tuft between her legs.

Good night, she was formed perfectly. His knees wobbled. He locked them and used his most commanding voice. “Raise your head.”

She did, instantly, but it took longer for her eyes to follow. Her gaze inspected the floor in front of him, tarried over the space beside his hip. Finally, she met his eyes.

“Don’t ever lower your eyes. Hold your head high, Charlee. We clear?”

“Yes, Sir.”

Was that what she wanted? To address him as some superior asshole while they played? He wasn’t a sexed-up Sir or Master, and he most definitely wasn’t Roy. But he’d read up on all the lingo and knew the designation was part of the atmosphere.

Her eyes dropped and flew back up. Good girl.

“One more thing. What’s your safe word?” He knew what it was, needed her to say it so they were both clear.

“Huntress. Not that it matters.” An angry fire lit up her eyes.

“What’s that supposed to mean?”

“Seeing how you ignored it last time, not sure why we’re even discussing it.”

Last time... Last time, when did he ignore—? His equilibrium abandoned him, and he grabbed the edge of the desk. “Oh no, oh God. Please, tell me I—”

“Didn’t shoot your doped-up come inside me after I used my safe word?”

His stomach dropped, and he scrambled for the right words. He couldn’t find any, because they didn’t exist.

“Forget it.” She pushed back her shoulders and thrust out her tits. Facing the world’s biggest douche-bag while nude would’ve made a common person cringe. Not this amazing woman.

“You were high, and while it’s a sad excuse, here I am.” She waved a hand at the rope stretched over the mattress. “I either trust you with this on some subconscious level or I'm recklessly vindictive."

"You're not vindictive or reckless."

"Really? Because I know you don't want to do this, and, for whatever fucked-up reason, that just turns me on more. Even if it's just a two-second moment of escape, I want my damn orgasm. Don't make me regret it."

There it was. An opportunity he didn't deserve and one muddied with all kinds of bitterness. But he'd take it. "I'll earn back your trust, Charlee."

He loosened out his arms, legs, and chest, spreading out to fill the space he occupied. Face muscles slack. Steady gaze. Deep breath all the way down to his balls. "Get on the bed."

67

Long, toned limbs stretched in an *X* on Jay's bed, his most perverted fantasy come to life. Even face down, Charlee made a picture that inspired men to fight, live, and write music. And he was about to mark it up. His mind revolted against the idea, but his cock throbbed in readiness.

Metal guitar picks tipped his fingers. Dragging his eyes away from the mouth-watering apex of her legs, he crawled up her legs and straddled her hips. Leaning over her back, he dug the tapered ends into her shoulder.

She arched as much as the rope allowed and released a soundless gasp. He raked the points down her back, not breaking skin but hard enough to leave four grooved trails. Over and over, he etched red lines on her back and sides.

When she wiggled her ass, his dick jerked. He frustrated them both and skipped over her bottom, knelt beside her, and scratched her thighs and calves.

Once her lower half was as drawn up as her back, he sat on his heels and admired his work. Blistered lines crisscrossed her body from neck to feet, leaving the globes of her ass as white as the sheets. Perspiration dotted her arms and spine. Fiery hair cascaded in shiny waves from her profile, her mouth open but silent.

"Fucking beautiful."

She closed her eyes and her mouth, and smiled. Rosy lips and glowing cheeks, her contentment was blinding.

He climbed up her body, pushed his metal-tipped fingers through her thick mane, and dug them into her scalp. "I see your light." He brushed his lips over the healing gash in her earlobe. "Let it burn bright, Charlee."

"Mmm." Her eyes cracked open. "Tease."

"Complaining already?

Another smile. Hell yeah, his kinky girl liked it. He fastened his mouth over the welts on her shoulder, sucking and flicking with his tongue. Then he moved to the other scratches, giving them the same attention.

"Ah God, that feels good." She lifted her torso and pressed it against his mouth.

He grabbed her ass with the metal claws and squeezed. Her gasp had voice that time. A breathy grunt.

The creases around her eyes were peaceful not distressed. Good. Time to move on. He jumped off the bed.

Ginger root. That was what she'd carted in. With one end shaved down into the shape of a fat finger, there was no question about its purpose.

"I bought a butt plug this morning." He ripped open the package and set the plug beside her hip. "We don't need to improvise."

"The ginger is for figging. It's better." She twisted her neck, blinking up at him, and must have read the disbelief in his expression. "Burns like a sonabitch."

He cringed, even as he forced a bored look on his face.

"Use both. Double penetration."

A formidable rock landed in his stomach. He refused to grip his gut like a squeamish chump, so he mentally chanted. *I am relaxed. I am in control. It's all for her.* He rolled the affirmation over and over in his head until the rock disintegrated, and his fingers hung loosely at his sides.

He tagged the lube from the desk.

"Don't need that." She looked over her shoulder at him and raised her ass. "Just shove her home, Jay."

Tempting. *Not*. Anal penetration might've been uncharted territory for him, but he knew that *shoving* anything in there was not safe. "Charlee, would you please just lay there—" he blew out a dramatic breath and tossed the lube over his shoulder "—and shut the fuck up."

She threw back her head and let out belly-deep laugh. It was the sound of fucking music, and he couldn't stop himself from launching onto the bed, grabbing her face, and turning her head to stare into her eyes.

How could she look at him, let alone laugh with him? He'd used drugs when he told her he wouldn't. He fucked her shamefully in public. Add to that the threat of Roy, who was out there planning her next enslavement. Through all of that, she didn't castrate Jay or throw a spectacular fit. She didn't cower in a fetal position. Instead, she confronted him with balls of steel and laughed while tied and exposed on his bed.

Laying on his side next to her, faces inches apart, his heart brimmed to bursting. "I fucking love you. I don't deserve to love you, but I will spend the rest of my life earning that right. You are my music, do you understand?"

Her eyes blinked furiously in the frame of his hands. "Okay."

"Okay." He dipped his head and kissed her. His mouth moving over hers and their tongues coiling and whipping, he fed her his breath, his love, his promise to make her happy.

When they broke apart, her lips were swollen and wet, her eyes half-lidded.

"So damn beautiful."

She grinned. "So you've said."

Perched on his elbow, stretched alongside her body, he'd say it again and again until she tired of hearing it. He wanted to wrap around her and bury his face in her hair. "You're beautiful."

"Uh huh."

"So fucking bea—"

"All right, Casanova. Enough."

He could feel himself sinking into the mattress. The longer he lay there, the heavier his limbs became. He rubbed his eyes. He hadn't slept in over twenty-four hours. Focus. He still owed her an orgasm, and he wouldn't face plant until she had it.

68

Charlee missed the heat of Jay's body the second he left the bed. Boy, he was full of surprises.

He loved her. It was one thing to suspect, but to hear it vocalized with such vehemence made her insides soften into squishy, girly goo. Didn't mean she wasn't still furious—

Crack.

Her ass cheek smarted under a sensational burn. She twisted, looked over her shoulder.

A metal buckle wrapped around his hand as he reared back the modified belt. Not what she had in mind for the sandpaper, but damn brilliant.

Crack.

"Unngh. Jesus." The other cheek pulsed in time with the first. Liquid heat gushed to her pussy. "Again."

The belt clattered to the floor, and she buried her face in the mattress. "You suck."

"As you wish." His hands slid over her inflamed cheeks, spread them, and his mouth sealed over her folds, sucking and licking.

The bedding bunched in her curling fingers where her arms were stretched, tied down near the headboard. He went after her clit with probing fingers as his tongue delved in and out and along her labium. Her insecurity over her scars drifted away under his affection.

The wet slurp of his saliva and her arousal layered the air. After his metal fingered foreplay, the lingering burn on her ass, and his demanding tongue, the climb toward orgasm dangled, a distant promise, but a promise nonetheless.

His mouth disappeared, and hard rubber pressed against the pucker of her ass. "How long has it been, Charlee?" He nudged it against her, not inserting, just a pressing threat.

She arched her hips, tried to push against it. Ugh, she wanted to propel past this without examining the reasons why.

"How long?"

Damn him. "Three years." It had been one of the few limits she set in her contractual negotiations with the Doms. She carried most of her scars there, but the memories cut much deeper.

The rubber tip moved away, and he lowered his body over her back. The heavy weight of him pressed her into the bed, suffocating and wonderfully comforting.

His breath was warm and steady at her ear. "I'm not going to hurt you there like he did, even if you think that's what you need. No figging—"

She bucked, wanting the burn from the ginger. Needing it.

"Now hang on a minute. I've never done this, and you're obviously trying to speed past a painful barrier. That's not the right approach, Charlee."

Acid turned through her gut. It would tear and bleed, but she wanted proof that nothing could hurt her anymore. "I don't want to talk about this."

He stroked the hair from her face, his fingers lingering on her jaw. "Shh. I know. We'll ease into it."

Those gentle fingers were influential things. They fluttered over her cheek, lulling, mastering the strain of her muscles until her face was slack with gravity.

The mattress bounced, and his weight lifted. The rub of leather rustled through his movements around the bed. His palm slipped under her belly, lifting. Soft plastic, a rubber ball by the feel of it, pressed against her clit. In the next breath, it filled the room with a loud buzz and shot a jolt of vibration through her pussy.

"Hitachi wand. Best clit stimulator from what I'm told."

No fucking shit. She pulled her hips up to escape it. His hand caught her waist and pressed her back down.

Oh God, it was so overwhelming, everything below her waist was beginning to numb. Which might've explained why she didn't notice the plug easing into her ass until he popped it past the ring of muscle.

Ahhhh. No pain. Only a heavenly tingle and a dominating sense of fullness. Never had pleasure accompanied anything penetrating her ass. Was this what it was supposed to feel like?

The buzz of the wand increased that pleasure, winding her tighter and tighter. Her arousal concentrated, contracting, building. "Jay. Fuck. Oh God."

His hands caressed her ass, her back, and paused to knead her shoulders. His lips followed the same path until they veered off and met hers. He licked her gaping mouth, circled his tongue inside. "Come, Charlee. Come, now."

It was there, teetering, ready to spill. She rocked against the powerful whir of the wand and clenched the muscles in her ass, reaching, straining—

Whack.

Pain zapped across the back of her thigh and all the air rushed from her lungs in a surge of body-stunned pleasure. An immense feeling of elation swam through her, ripping away everything except the trembling bliss taking over her body and the man consuming her mouth. It arched her back, emptied her thoughts, and weighted her limbs. So fucking good. Better than any before it. The best sensation she'd ever experienced. She floated through it, fevered and sated.

The vibrator clicked off, and he rose on his knees. "Ready for another?"

Jesus. She panted, lost to the residual tremors tickling through her body.

The ties at her ankles loosened, released. His arms came around her torso, flipping her, the rope crossing above her head.

"So you liked the garden pole? Should've started with that, hmm?" He smiled down at her looking pretty damned pleased with himself. As he should've been. He'd rocked her. Hard.

"The pole pushed me over— I can't believe your aim was that good considering you were kissing me when you swung."

His smile widened. "The pole has a nice reach."

"Well done, but the sensual build-up was what got me there. You...uh...really know how to make a high-maintenance girl feel loved."

The gold in his brown eyes sparked. "Only you, Charlee. And you're not high-maintenance. In fact, now that I've gone through orientation, I'm about to show you how easy it is to service you." He reached a hand between her legs and put pressure on the plug.

She dropped her legs open, gasping.

"Yeah, you're ready for round two."

Round two rolled into three, and four, and hell, she lost count. Her anger with him had deserted her with the first orgasm, giving way to adoration. He trussed her up in various positions, nipple clamps dangling, ice pellets melting in her pussy. She begged him to stop, to keep going, harder, slower. Mostly, she begged him to fuck her. He ignored her pleas with a snap of the drumstick on her breast or the wave of the cheese grater. Like that was a threat.

As each orgasm faded, she swore she couldn't reach another. He pushed her until she lay slumped over the hard ridges of his body, both of them smothered in sweat and exhaustion.

Free of the binds, she stretched a hand between them and gripped his erection through his pants. For two hours, she'd watched it stretch his fly, waiting for it to rip a hole through the leather. "Your turn."

He grabbed her wrist and removed her hand. "No. This is my penance."

The break in his voice undid her. "Jay, please. You don't need—"

"Let it be, Charlee." He pulled her further up his chest and cupped her head against his throat.

The blend of pain and pleasure he'd gifted her exceeded her expectations, but that wasn't what freed the things that had been tightening her chest for so damn long. He'd given her something that wasn't easy for him to give and he'd done so without taking.

Yeah, her anger with him was long gone. In its place was a soaring, unsuspecting love.

As she settled into the steady rise and fall of his chest, a startling realization tumbled over her. He whipped her and stretched her ass and commanded her every move. And not once, had *Huntress* whispered through her head.

69

The bedside clock read ten, and the sun beating through the glass doors agreed. Yet, Jay lay like a dead man beneath Charlee. No, not dead. His chest emitted warmth and vibrancy. With his head lolled on the pillow, his heartbeat pulsed against the arch of his throat.

She shouldn't wake him. Lord knew he needed sleep, but his penance for the prior night was over. She eased off him, tugged down the sheet, past his waist, to his feet, and revealed a golden landscape of dipping and cresting muscles.

He'd lost his pants sometime in the night. No surprise there. She couldn't understand how he wore leather, let alone slept in it. But damn, it cupped him in all the right places. Her mouth watered.

Arms bent above his head, lips slack, legs spread, he was vulnerable and masculine and unconsciously begging.

Kneeling between the strength of his thighs, she lowered her mouth, hovered over his half-erect penis. A lick around the glans, and she drew him in.

His eyes flew open, and his hands floundered until they found purchase on the rungs of the headboard.

She slid her lips to the tip and kissed the crown. "Good morning."

"Hell of a way to wake up." His voice was groggy and sexy as fuck.

Gripping him in hand, she waited. No flinching. No meltdowns. She smiled and worked him back into her mouth. His shaft had doubled in length in a matter of seconds, his balls tighter, higher. She pumped the suction of her lips, circling and flicking her tongue.

The tendons in his neck strained, and his chin jerked toward the ceiling. "Ahhhh, fuck, Charlee." He panted and grabbed the back of her hair to halt her movements. "Up here. Now."

Holding him between the careful bite of her teeth, she walked her fingers over the bumps of his abs and up his chest. Watching him do his daily crunches was as arousing as feeling the results beneath her fingertips.

He followed her hands with hooded eyes. No tripped triggers. Had he defeated it? His reaction to touch was unpredictable and the underlying source of it remained locked away, but at that moment, the feeling of sweet victory rushed through her.

He grabbed her wrists, dislodging his dick from her mouth, and pulled her up his body until she straddled his hips. "Ride me."

A warm wet trickle accompanied the throb between her legs. She curled greedy fingers around him, centered him at her sex. Rocking down his length, she threw her head back and groaned through the riot of stimulation. When her clit bumped the trimmed thicket of his hair, she reached down and traced where her folds wrapped around him.

The corners of his mouth stretched, forming a pinned line, his eyes glued to her hand. "I don't deserve you."

Did she forgive him for the drugs? Did she trust him with her safe word? She checked her heart, and it hid behind an even thump, the unhelpful thing.

She didn't need trust or forgiveness for this. She pinched his nipple, twisted it between her fingers. "Shut up."

The buck of his pelvis spurred her into motion. Up and down, she rotated her hips around his cock, pulling grunts from low in his throat. His hands shook where they clenched her waist and his thighs flexed beneath her.

"Jesus. Gonna make me come, Charlee. Slow down."

How sublime it must be to climb to the precipice so easily. She was still circling the bottom of the steep, trying to find a way up. That was okay. This was for him. She gathered her hair on her head and held it there. Pulling in her stomach muscles, she rolled her hips, flowing over him in a liquid movement.

"Beautiful."

The gruffness in his voice aroused the hairs on her nape. She kept her mop pinned on her head and rocked faster, closing her eyes and memorizing every stroke along her inner walls.

"Feels so good. I can't...I can't—" He bent at the waist, arm around her back, and flipped her. Following her down, he thrust his hips and filled her again.

His mouth fell over hers, open and sweeping, parting her lips and tongue nudging inside. His licked lazily, but the exploration consumed her. He tasted clean and human and something else she couldn't name, but it attached to her recognition of him. A flavor that didn't belong to anything or anyone. It was wholly Jay.

He drew in and out of her pussy, setting a plateauing pace. Neither building nor slowing. His hands roamed her body with the same deliberation. He seemed to be simply enjoying. Legs entwined, they moved as one. Their bodies rose and fell together, breaths giving and receiving.

Her thoughts flickered to the prior night, the nylon cinctures, the heat of the pole, and the stretch of the plug. She caressed the muscles playing over her, envisioned how much pain they could bear if he chose to unleash his strength. A needy shudder unfurled through her limbs.

She raised her chin and found him watching her from inches away. His hips ground into her, harder and less-controlled with each rotation. Lips parted, eyes dilated, his inhales deepened. "Come with me."

If only. She let that hope disintegrate before it could grip her.

His hand shot up and squeezed her throat, not hurting, but digging in enough to paralyze her breath and cut her voice. His gaze bore into hers, his expression unreadable, but there were no signs of teasing. The pressure on her jugular was serious. Did he know what he was doing? If he pressed too hard, too long, he could choke her.

A different kind of pressure coiled through her pussy and exploded without warning. Full-body shocks rippled off her, loosening every last knot. The stroke of his cock bumped the pulsating spot inside her, over and over, drawing out her release. Her muscles seemed to melt into the bed, her exhales vibrated with her moans, and the heated look in his penetrating eyes carried her away.

Twitches skated along her body, and her breathing calmed, even as his hips continued to flex and his fingers pressed against her throat. His rhythm sputtered, and his muscles went taut.

Buried inside her, his body rigid and eyelids pinched, he groaned through a gaping mouth. If he thought she was beautiful, he should look in the mirror while he came. Suffocating under the clamp of his hand, she could die this way, watching him. What a way to go.

"Breathe, Charlee."

She couldn't. His fingers were still pressing against her throat. She yanked on his arm, and it wouldn't budge. A dizzying cloud weighted her movements.

"Focus on how loose my fingers are and take a breath." His eyebrows slammed together. "Now."

Why wouldn't he release her? Lungs burning, she sucked in a

gulp of air. Another and another. The fog in her head thinned and scattered. She moved her hands up his arm, felt his fingers locked around her neck. No pain. Just a heady feeling of restraint. "You're not hurting me." Holy shit. How did he do that? He fucked her, brought to orgasm, but where was the pain? Her chest swelled with adoration. "It doesn't hurt."

"No. And I never constricted you harder than this." His grip fell away and the sudden loss of it shriveled her with insecurity, no longer protected under the detainment of his hand.

Before she could dwell on how fucked up that logic was, he rolled them, flattening her body over his with a hand sliding down her spine. "You okay?"

She dropped her cheek on his chest and let the strong beat of his heart fortify her. "I don't know. How did you do that? There was no pain...and I came...and why couldn't I breathe?"

He stroked her hair and spread the layers across her back. "You were breathing just fine right up until you climaxed. Then you locked up." He tapped her temple.

Did he think it was all in her head? He'd tricked her, dammit. How had she not perceived what was real and not real? Heart hammering, she let her hair slide forward and curtain her face.

"Charlee, look at me."

She did, and he stared back from beneath dark brows. "I don't think it's the pain that gets you off. It's the anticipation. The fear of it."

Her rebuttal scrambled to the tip of her tongue and hung there. Wasn't that how she found release during masturbation? She would think about depraved acts, anticipate them, and yes, fear them. "And you learned this in one night?"

"It was a long night." He held her chin in the brace of his hands and kissed her, far-reaching and persistent and full of teeth. With a nip to her nose, he pulled back. "Let me show you something."

She followed him to the bathroom, his unfinished tattoo waving at her through the flex of his shoulders. The outline of flames and curling skin and riveted steel beneath made her fingers itch to complete it. "I need to finish your back."

He threw a glowing smile over his shoulder that sent her heart tumbling. "Soon."

In front of the vanity, he turned her back to the mirror and hooked his arms around her waist. His cock jerked against her thigh, and she looked up with an arched eyebrow.

"Ignore it. Look behind you. What do you see?"

Twisting to peer beyond her shoulder, she flinched at how the artificial light glared off her white skin. "A pasty girl in desperate need of some sun." She caught his glare in the mirror.

A muscle ticked in his cheek. "Don't you dare tan that pretty hide." The corners of his mouth kicked up. "That's *my* job."

"Har har. What am I looking at?"

"Bruises. Discoloration. Blemishes. Any of the usual post-pain leftovers."

She squinted at her reflection. A couple of pink lines marked her shoulder. Otherwise, her skin was flawless. "I don't understand. The implements you struck me with should've left marks."

"I *think* after the first hit of the pole, your mind stayed in the zone without your body needing further punishment. You tensed before each strike and that's when you seemed to be the most turned on. As long as I kept you guessing, I could feint a lot of the follow-through."

"Like the choking." She turned that over in her head. The collar of his hand hadn't strangled her. She'd held her breath, imagined danger associated with it. "Wow. I'm a head case."

He pinched her chin, angling it until her body followed so he could look her directly in the eyes. "No, Charlee. You're a survivor, packing all kinds of hidden weapons. But I'll be honest." His hand moved to the back of her head and his forehead lowered to hers. "Hurting you is a very difficult thing for me to do. I'll do it. Whatever you need, even as I hope like hell I'm right about this."

She sank against his long frame and traced the indention between his hip and thigh. Pleasure without the soreness? Orgasms without planning? Never mind all that. The hopeful look in his eyes made her want it more than anything. "Me, too."

70

The spray of the shower head wasn't what spiraled heat over Jay's body. It was Charlee's hands as they lathered soap across the ruined skin on his back.

He'd never showered with another. Had never even removed his shirt in front of someone other than his doctor, and that had been a very long time ago. "I love your hands on me."

"How are you really doing with all the touching?" Her tone was soft, careful.

He braced his arms on the tile and let his head drop between them. Suds collected between their feet, hers so small beside his. "The fear is still there. Touch never *guaranteed* a breakdown, but knowing that it *could*, I've always restricted it." Like a big pussy. The expectation of panic was worse than the reality. He *knew* that, just couldn't move past it.

Her hands lowered to his ass, fingering soap into the cleft. The little devil wasn't going to leave a single cranny unwashed.

"You told me in New York that talking about your demons was a trigger." She squatted behind him and raked her nails over the backs of his thighs. "Can we test that?"

Fuck no. He couldn't talk about the shed or the horror within its thin walls. She had enough nightmares of her own. She didn't need his.

She wiggled around him, her beautiful face hovering below his and blinking against the deluge of water.

The muffle of slapping guitar beats sifted through the bathroom. She cocked her head. "Why do I hear the song *Punk Rock Girl*?"

He leaned down and captured her lips with a shower-wet smack. "Because I set your ringtone. Like?"

"Love." She grinned, and her lips curved down just as quick. "It has to be Nathan. Maybe he has news about the letter." She slipped out of the stall before he could catch her.

Damn Nathan, the hater. Interrupting his shower time.

He followed the trail of wet footprints out of the bathroom and found her bent over the desk, dripping water on the phone in her hand and tapping on the screen. She held it up, wide-eyed and gorgeous. "How do you work this thing?" Then she returned to her frantic swiping. "I haven't owned a phone in years."

Probably not since Noah. Who was she going to call? A twinge pulled his chest. He closed the distance and held out his hand. "Give it here."

When she stretched it toward him, he grabbed her elbow. "Go dry off properly. Water on marble inspired Bon Jovi to compile *Slippery When Wet*."

Her eyebrows climbed then dropped over narrowed eyes. "You're so full of shit."

He pinched her ass. "Walk back to the bathroom like I'm not."

The pound on the door sent him lurching into the closet. He dropped the phone and fought a t-shirt from its hanger. Yeah, so he still didn't want anyone looking at his back. Motherfucking knee-jerk reaction. He yanked on a pair of workout shorts and didn't belittle himself too much for it until he skidded out and found her answering the door stark fucking naked. "Charlee!"

She startled and dropped her jaw as if she had no clue why his face was on fire.

Nathan strode around her, and the fucker was lucky he didn't lower his eyes below her chin.

"Charlee, go put on some clothes." His voice rattled the glass doors. Fuck it. He spun into the closet and wrestled another t-shirt off the rack.

Back in the bedroom, neither of them had moved. Both stared at him with identical sets to their jaws, likely for different reasons. He tossed her the shirt.

She turned it over in her hands, locating the head hole not near fast enough. "Calm down, Jay. He's seen—"

"He doesn't need to see it again."

The shirt hit him in the face and fell to the floor. Okay, maybe his tone was a little too coarse.

She propped her fists on her hips. "You might remember that next time you fuck me onstage."

His balls curled up as if they'd been punched, but the real pain throbbed behind his ribs. He scooped up the shirt and pulled it over her head, stretching it over her little fists and down to her thighs.

His memory of the show was muddy, but he realized she'd enjoyed the exhibitionism before the groupies showed up. That realization set his nerves on fire. Jesus. Clear-headed, he never would've put her on display. Was that what she wanted? Would this be another sticky point in her closet of kinks? "We'll talk about this later."

She pushed her arms through the holes and turned toward Nathan, who was watching their interaction with a blatant scowl. "Nathan? Is this about the letter?"

He nodded, facing her, and shoved a hand through his hair. Not good.

"Dennis, the spotter's alias, isn't answering his phone. Munt tracked down his family." He dropped his hand. "He has a nineteen-year-old niece who went missing two nights ago."

The night they flew back from New York. The odds sucked.

Her hand shot behind her, reaching for a bed that was too far away. Jay wrapped an arm around her waist and walked her backward until she sat on the edge. He perched beside her, heart racing.

"The message about the girl killed in Roy's stockroom came from Dennis' phone. Text. Not voice."

A chill swept through him. They were being played. "You don't think Dennis sent that message?"

Nathan shook his head. "Two bodies were found early this morning in an abandoned warehouse on the Wharf. Middle-aged man. Teenage girl. Suspected murder-suicide. An anonymous caller reported them."

A tear streaked down her cheek. "Roy discovered Dennis. Probably knew about him for some time and waited for the right moment." Her voice cracked. "He killed the niece. Killed Dennis. Staged the murder-suicide. An easy trick with the assistance of San Fran's law enforcement. The letter makes more sense now."

Jay jumped to his feet, shaking out his fists when he so badly wanted to swing them. "Why would he do that? What was the point of threatening you with it?"

She stared out of shadowed eyes at the wall behind him. "It wasn't a threat." Her voice sounded dusty. Dead. "It was my punishment."

71

The next three days drudged by. The bodies in the warehouse were identified, confirming their suspicions about the spotter and his niece, and Jay watched Charlee slip further inside herself. If helplessness had a taste, it would've been the rancid decay curdling in the back of his throat. He fed her, protected her, and loved her. But he couldn't heal the hurt dulling her eyes.

Since Roy had proven himself unpredictable, Jay kept Charlee within the guarded walls of the estate, always in his eyeshot.

During daily band practices, she perched on the basement stairs, watching and sketching. Sometimes a smile bent her lips when the guys teased one another, but it never lingered. He doubted anyone noticed her silent grief, but he glimpsed it in the languor of her gestures and felt it when her gaze flitted from his.

Each morning, Tony brought in a martial arts practitioner to teach him basics of self-defense. Charlee watched and often participated in the drills. His flashbacks surfaced once during a weapon disarming technique under the strike of her hand. She'd coaxed him back to the present by singing a *Pixies* song. Her endearing, off-key rendition of *Where Is My Mind* shooed away the nightmare, but it cast a lasting pall over her eyes.

He knew she carried a hefty load of guilt regarding Roy's potential threat to the band, but their lack of offensive strategy seemed to plague her most. Hell, restlessness vented from the pores of every member of the household. The estate bristled with it. The band and the staff argued over canceling the tour, how many guards to hire if they went, and how best to protect Charlee. During one of the debates in the basement studio, Faye jumped from her laptop and announced that the seventy-show tour was officially sold out.

"Maybe the Oxford prick won't fuck with the tour now." Laz adjusted a tuning peg on his guitar and plucked the string. "Think of the millions his new acquisition would lose if he did."

Impatience bunched Jay's shoulders. The tour babble had grown old an hour earlier. He had what Roy wanted, and she was right freaking there, stretched on the couch and studying the ceiling tiles. Jay wanted nothing more than to protect her, tour be damned. Trouble was, the decision affected his best friends and hundreds of thousands of fans. "Roy can't cancel the tour. Technically, he owns our record company not our production company. He can pull our CDs from the stores and prevent radio stations from playing our songs. He can't tamper with our performances."

"Windsor Records owns our production company," Laz said around the pick between his teeth, angling his head near the fingerboard of his guitar. "All of the subsidiary labels and corporations report to the same damn head."

"And that head got away with murder." Her voice floated from the couch, hushed and distant. She rolled to her side, pillowing her face with the bend of her arm, and looked at Jay. "He has a weakness. Use it against him."

The challenge in her eyes boiled his blood. What the fuck was she suggesting? Use her as bait? He would never use her for anything related to Roy. The set jaws and hard faces around him indicated his friends wouldn't have either.

That night, another band meeting sprung from an impromptu argument in the kitchen. The fifth one in three days. When it fizzled to a close with no resolution, Charlee rose to her feet and slammed her hands on the island. "Keep the tour dates, and double the protective team. Because you know what? Roy can't do much while you're standing in the limelight. If you cancel, you might as well break up the band and sell your home. Gonna let him win that easy?"

Silence. The kind of silence in which ideas were formed and fashioned together. His girl had her fire back, and it burned in a fierce glow on her face. He wasn't sure if her decision was a sound one, but his stance had been clear. No matter the consensus, she would not leave his sight.

A collective breath released through the room and disintegrated the animosity from moments earlier. Rio kissed her first. A peck on the check. Wil and Laz followed in turn, and Jay surprised himself by smiling as he watched the reciprocal effect. They didn't want to cancel the tour, but each man's kiss confirmed they would've given it up to keep her safe.

Grins radiated from them as they reminisced about their debauchery on their last tour together.

Nathan stormed from the kitchen, his ears blood red. His job had just become impossibly more challenging. For the first time since Jay met him, a feeling of sympathy swelled for the poor guy.

Since the news of the murders, Nathan had pulled in every law enforcement and private security connection he had to pin the crime on Roy. Three days into the effort, Jay didn't have to see the defeat in Nathan's eyes to know the case wasn't reopening.

The next day, Colson lumbered through the front door, balancing five boxes.

Expecting the delivery, Jay bounded from the kitchen island and abandoned the repairs he'd been making to his guitar's bridge pickup. "Thanks, Colson." He accepted the packages and strode to the couch, his nerves alight with anticipation.

Charlee sat cross-legged at one end, angled over a sketchbook. Multicolored arcs leapt off the page she was shading with art pencils.

Rainbows? What, was she twelve? He bit back the impulse to tease her, unsure if the illustrations had emotional meaning. "Charlee?"

She looked up and blew a rampant lock away from her eye. It drifted back and clung to her long lashes.

"Are you freaking kidding me?" Wil pounded the buttons of a controller, ass hovering over the other couch, eyes fastened on the zombies shuffling across the TV screen. "Come on!" More pounding. "Aw yeah. You got owned, beyotch."

She shook her head, a smile gracing her beautiful face.

Privacy would've been preferred for this, but Wil's energy seemed to return some vividness to her face. Jay stacked the boxes on the coffee table and perched on the edge, facing her.

She reached up and skimmed a tentative finger over his lips. He held still, lost in the blues animating her eyes.

She poked his dimple, rose from the couch, and stretched over his shoulder to look at the packages. "Whatcha got there?"

The press of her tits against his chest and the sweet scent of her hair tickling his nose were hell on his focus. He was there to give her something, and it wasn't the pest jerking in his jeans.

Despite her somberness, their bed hadn't grown cold. Whenever she'd led him there, he followed, feeling his way through her mood. Since the morning he'd feinted choking her, she refused pain or any semblance of it. Knowing how that impacted her, he wanted to refuse her. But she'd pull him close and he'd sink into her, his intentions scuttling.

So for four days, he'd had orgasms and she had no-gasms. She claimed the comfort he gave her was all she wanted, but it rubbed at the back of his mind, a persistent and consuming thing.

"These are for you." He reached behind him and offered her the largest box. "But I'll reap the benefits, so I'm pretty fucking excited about them."

Her eyes blurred as she sat back. She blinked at the package, once, twice, and tore it open. Bubble wrap and box discarded, she balanced three tattoo machines on her thighs. One hand pressed against her mouth. Fingers of the other fluttered over every detail.

Flames engraved the steel frames. In his e-mail to the artist, he'd tried to convey the design Charlee had outlined on his back. Given her shining smile as she stared at him in amazement, he figured he'd succeeded.

"The black steel is the liner machine." He picked it up and tested the one-pound weight. "The red one is the shader. Blue is the cut-back shader. Each has been tuned, tweaked, and set-up to do what it's supposed to."

She turned the cut-back shader over. "I've always used one machine. Had to jack with the tension in the rear spring to adjust the gaping from front coil to arm bar. You know, to switch between outlining and shading? Could never get the precision right. It was a poor man's way to do it, but three irons? This is...How'd you even know what I'd need? And custom crafted so quickly?"

Money and fame had its benefits. "The artist was very accommodating."

She lifted the liner machine from his hand. "All handcrafted, and the engravings match your tat. My God, Jay, they must have cost... I don't even want to know." She glanced up, eyes clear and bright. "I don't know what to say."

The wonder in her voice filled him with pride. He stole a kiss from her curved lips. "Say 'thank you'."

She set the machines on the cushion beside her and stared at them, lashes fluttering rapidly. In the next thump of his heart, she tackled him, hands in his hair, mouth crushing his. She smothered kisses over his face, sparking every happy receptor in his body, and rested her forehead against his. "Thank you."

"It's full on double rainbow time." Wil reached into one of the boxes behind Jay and pulled out several bottles of ink.

The boxes should've held every color available, along with needles, tubes, stencil stuff, and anything else the supplier thought she might or might not want.

Wil dropped the bottles in the box and scooped up her sketchbook. "Hell yeah. We're so doing this tattoodle."

His bassist might've been hippie, but a rainbow tattoo? "Seriously?"

She grabbed the book. "It's not for Wil. Since inking Laz's dick is a sensitive subject—"

"It's not a subject, because it's not happening."

"—Wil settled on an alternative tat." She tapped the cartoon rainbow.

Jay cocked one eyebrow and glared at Wil. "The issue isn't the design. It's the placement."

"Lose the bitchbrow, man." Wil returned one of his own. "Laz is getting a tramp stamp."

Nice. Jay could live with that, though he wasn't sure Laz could.

Wil cupped his hands around his mouth and angled toward the patio. "Laz! Get in here!"

Two hours later, Jay forced himself to recline in the chair across the room in a guise of cool collection. His jealousy would've shattered the morale Charlee had so effectively lifted.

Laz lay face down on the couch, arms bent above his head, expression a picture of tranquility. She knelt beside him, hands low on his bare back, tattoo machine vibrating the air.

His bandmates and some of the security staff had gathered to watch, and a heady buzz bounced around them. Even Nathan hovered, a smile floating on his face.

As Laz's rainbow-shaped embarrassment arced from the rise of one ass cheek to the other, the tiny movements of her machine held the room captivated. Humming her out-of-tune melodies, she brushed the needle over the cartoon of colors with a vivacity that put everyone in a lively mood.

His shoulder blades tingled. He wished it was him on the stabbing end, but when she'd snagged his gaze before she began, the silent question arching her brow, he shook his head. He hadn't wanted to quash the excitement whirring between his friends. And when the time came to complete his tattoo, it would be an intimate session. Momentous. Just like the night he met her.

A groan drifted from the couch.

Jay's graciousness slipped, his face heating. "Laz, if you're trapping a hard-on under there, so help me God, I will break it off. With a sledgehammer."

He groaned again. Louder. "Cool story, bro."

"Wow. I missed this. I haven't inked in a week." She winked at Jay. "It's been a very long week."

Her wink spiraled through his chest and stole his breath. There she was. His girl was back with light flickering in her eyes. As relief settled over him, he relaxed in the chair and watched her work. Her scrunched nose, brow pinched in concentration, and the tune drifting from her throat hurtled him back to Kilroy Tattoo. He'd changed his life that night to earn a future with her. It was time to confront the past so he could hold onto that future.

A shiver passed through him. It had been his lot to suffer an abusive childhood, but he would make damn sure her lot didn't include another second in chains. He'd accept a death penalty if that was what it took to eliminate Roy.

He wanted her safe and happy. More than he wanted freedom, or music, or breath.

72

Charlee focused on the tattoo equipment in her hands, scrubbing the shiny steel until it shone and tucking it into a box. If she glanced up, she knew she'd be ensnared once again by the heat of Jay's gaze. She was also certain that one more shared look and her devotion to equipment care would be deserted for sex.

Hard, rough, painful sex. The promise radiated from his stiff posture. Oh, he had one leg draped over the arm of the chair, the other stretched out in front of him to accommodate a full-body slouch.

He wasn't fooling her. Aggressive arousal emanated from him in the unmoving way he watched her, the slack of his parted lips, the minute press of his fingertips in the armrest, and the tell-tale stretch of his fly. Her fingers itched to slip out that top button and free him.

Boisterous laughter stumbled in from the patio. Everyone had congregated outside with beer and chips, their spirited mood wafting into the night sky.

"You have a magical way of bringing people back to life, Charlee." His timbre was husky, his gaze burning her skin.

Too bad she couldn't bring nineteen-year-old girls back to life. She gave herself a mental slap. Hadn't she beaten herself up enough? "Nothing's more magical than a six-inch double rainbow over your ass." She packed up the last machine and bent to close up the box. "All done."

Fingers curled around her hip and she jumped. Sneaky bastard. She turned to face him with a spurt of mischief pumping through her veins. Stretching her jaw, she let out a dramatic yawn and snapped it closed. "Race you to the bedroom."

She spun. Through the living room, down the hall, around the bend, she pushed off the wall and threw open the double doors to his suite.

The slap of bare feet closed in behind her, kicking up her pulse. He slammed the doors and caught her in his sitting room. Arms around her waist, he doubled her over the back of the loveseat. She clawed at the leather, tried to plunge headfirst into the cushions, laughter tearing from her lungs. Ass in the air—

Ow, fuck. He bit her. His teeth clenched through her jeans and pinched the crease between her thigh and cheek. His hand followed with a smack that shimmied a twinge from her hip to her feet. Wowza, he meant business. Desire curled in her pussy and pulsated with a force that stole her breath.

His weight bore down on her, chest pressing against her back and lips fluttering over her ear. "Go to the bedroom. Remove your clothes. Face the foot post on my side of the bed, feet spread and arms above your head. You have two minutes."

She nodded, voice strangled, a fever blooming over her skin.

One minute later, she stood in the commanded position, her yearning wet and clinging to her inner thigh. She shuddered, the footfalls behind her magnifying the tremors.

Soft fabric touched her cheek, and the room disappeared. He secured a blindfold around the back of her head with a knot.

"Too tight?"

"No, Sir." Damn, she sounded breathy.

He chuckled and gripped her wrists where they stretched along the post above her head.

The click-click-click of felt-lined handcuffs filled her ears and restrained her hands.

She tried to lower them, and they didn't budge. "There's a hook in the bedpost?" Had it always been there? Why?

"Had an eye bolt installed yesterday." He slapped her ass.

The smack was lighter this time, but the sting lingered without the protection of denim. Her clit awoke, pulsing. "Harder."

His breath came out in heavy gusts, tangling in her hair and winding down her body. He ran his hands along her stretched arms and circled her breasts, lifting them.

Was he naked back there? Was his erection straining to reach her? "Move closer. I want to feel you."

He shifted, and the disappointment of denim brushed the backs of her legs. But, oh God, the heat pouring off his bare chest mingled with hers and plastered her flesh. He slid down her body until his breath brushed the apex of her legs. The throb there was met with the warm stroke of his tongue.

He covered her pussy with his mouth, his licks deep and urgent. She raised herself toward him and ground against his face. His groan vibrated inside and out as his hands heated every inch of skin he could reach.

His warmth disappeared, replaced with the chill of the A/C vent somewhere above her. She remained still, tried to follow the rustling sound of his jeans.

Whack.

Pain fired over her ass. Holy fuck. Didn't he say he didn't need to hit her—

Crack. Crack.

Both thighs. Low and sharp. Damn it hurt good.

The hollow sound of wood clattered to the floor. The bamboo pole? The scratch of his zipper lowering produced a clench between her legs. The velvety head of his cock rubbed against her folds, and she pressed her ass against him, needy and impatient.

Leaning against her back, his body engulfing her from head to toe, he must have caught his weight with a hand on the bedpost. His lips skid over her shoulder, his breath hot and rushed, his free hand squeezing her breasts and lowering over her belly, between her thighs, and guiding him to her center. Right there. Oh God.

He pushed in, and the sure-fire stroke shot ripples through her womb.

"Aw fuck. Your pussy just lets me right in." His hips moved into a pounding rhythm. In and out in driving circles, his pelvis slammed into her backside and her mound rubbed against the unforgiving wood post. "Jesus, you feel good."

The absence of sight intensified the scratch in his voice and the burn of his lips on her neck. He kicked her feet farther apart and his hands were everywhere, yanking her hips against him, squeezing her breasts, tugging on her clit. His torso, taut and smooth, glided over her back, flexing against her, controlling her movements.

He pinched her clit, and she sucked in a breath. His teeth sunk into her shoulder, and he pinched harder. The pressure was overpowering, demanding, pulling her in until nothing existed but the mounting stimulation.

She clenched her inner walls, tried to hold back the orgasm, to suspend the sensation, to savor the moment.

His tongue flicked across her skin between the brace of his teeth and his thrusts rolled and bucked. When his breath caught, she lost her self-control, her release pouring over her in powerful waves. "Ahhh, Jesus. Oh fuck." Her body tingled, slumping in the clutch of his.

He rocked once, twice, and rammed to the hilt, grinding as he moaned a delicious cacophony of noises.

Hands slid over hers, and the shackles released. The blindfold followed, and she squinted against the brightness of the room. He scooped her up, arms behind her back and thighs, and tumbled them into bed. He positioned her on her side, tucked her chest into his, her head under his chin, and caressed a palm up and down her back. "Okay?"

"Mmm. More than." She angled her head back and fell into his heavy-lidded eyes. "You used the pole to keep me guessing, didn't you?"

His smile softened the strong lines of his gorgeous face. "If the threat isn't there, if I never *hurt* you, you won't anticipate."

Hurt. The way he whispered that word reminded her of what it cost him. "Thank you." She stretched her neck and covered his mouth with hers.

He parted his lips and rolled his tongue with hers. Tilting her head, he deepened the kiss, shifting her to her back and blanketing her with his body. His hands raked her hair, jaw working and tongue stoking a low burning fire.

When he slowed to a gentle slide of lips, she touched his cheek, smiled. "Good lord, you know how to kiss." His head jerked back, and his eyebrows crawled together. She guessed he'd never tried to please a woman before, never needed to. But, holy shit, he was good at it. "What's wrong?"

He rolled them to their sides, face to face, and smoothed a lock of hair behind her ear. "When I kissed you in my room in New York—" he smiled, traced the shell of her ear "—that was my first kiss."

Her heart gave a thump. He had intimacy issues, but surely he'd kissed someone at some point. "Ever?"

He shifted close, so close their noses touched. "Ever."

73

Charlee emerged slowly from a content sleep. The bedside lamp shed a soft glow through the bedroom. She was alone in bed, but not alone. Jay's silhouette reclined in a lounger on the veranda, the back of his head a smudgy shadow against the winking lights of the L.A. skyline.

The waning moon drifted beyond the open doors. She must have dozed off in his arms an hour or so earlier. She snagged one of his t-shirts from the closet in case of a chill in the evening air, shrugged into it, and swiped her cell phone from the desk on her way out.

A puff of smoke billowed above him. With his back to her, he seemed lost to a million thoughts, or perhaps just memorized by the view of the distant lights. He lowered a cigarette and scattered the ash to the breeze.

The smell of tobacco permeated, kicking in the urge to share it with him. "You smoke?"

He flinched, facing her, and fumbled for the ashtray, cigarette aimed to be squashed.

"No, no. Don't put it out. Here." She curled her fingers back and forth. "It smells delicious."

He held it out, reluctance in his wide eyes. "You smoke?"

"I asked you first." She plucked it from his fingers and climbed between his spread legs, back to his chest. Cigarette poised between two fingers, she swiped through the screens on her phone. *Lebanese Blonde* by *Thievery Corporation*. Perfect. She set it to play on a low volume and placed the phone on the side table.

With a hand on her tummy, he pulled her close and leaned them back in the lounger. "No. I don't smoke." His tone was deep and teasing.

She pulled a drag through her lungs and exhaled. "Me neither, but over the past couple years, I'd get this lofty feeling of nostalgia and buy a pack." She took another pull and passed it to him. "Ask me why."

He accepted it, fingers lingering over hers. "Why?"

"You stayed after I inked your outline, smoking your cigarette, waiting for me. I didn't give it much thought then." There was so much on her mind that night. Marrying Noah. Running from Roy. She fought a shiver and caressed the denim-clad thighs bracing her, reveling in the strength of the man and his heart. "You liked me, and you weren't ready to let me go. I figured that out months later. So I'd smoke and try to touch that moment in time. I'd imagine myself waiting with you. Waiting *for* you."

The cigarette butt skipped over the concrete patio. He flipped her, chest on chest, and stared into her eyes, his expression stripped bare. "I love you."

"Mm. I can't relate love to writing music or personal experience, but I have this terrifying and wonderful sensation flowing through me." Making decisions for her, consuming her. "It's more powerful than any label I could give it, but if I had to name it, I would call it love."

He pulled her up his chest and buried his face in her neck. A comfortable silence whispered over them.

"I quit that night."

Quit? Quit what? His chest rose and fell steadily beneath her. She waited.

"I quit smoking. Drugs. Booze. Sex. I wanted to be clean and worthy of you."

Her heart soared. Drug free and celibate? For her? Oh, what a soothing balm for her jealousy.

"I was a reformed man for two months. Then I flew to St. Louis to see you."

And she was in the penthouse, grieving Noah and clawing at her chain.

"I only made it two weeks after that. Two weeks." His tone was low and thick with regret.

"You thought I was dead. And never mind that. You owed me nothing. I was just a girl in a one-hour blip on your way to a successful life."

"No, Charlee. I was just a boy who was too low to find success. And too high to care. One hour with you showed me how to succeed."

The rumble of faraway planes passed above. Water splashed in the pool around the corner. She snuggled into him, no longer needing the nostalgia of tobacco, no longer waiting. She suddenly wanted to wash away the nicotine lingering in her mouth. "I'm going to go get something to drink." She lifted off him and moved toward the corner where the pool deck lay beyond. "Want anything?"

"Not dressed like that, you're not."

His t-shirt reached her thighs. Seriously?

"I'll go." He rose and stretched that fine muscular frame. "Share a bottle of Merlot with me?"

"Mmm. Yes, please."

He scanned the pitch-black acreage, probing the perimeter hidden by the night. There must've been half a dozen guards out there, strolling the grounds. If she couldn't be left alone in his supermax fortress, she couldn't be alone anywhere.

His gaze strolled over the roof's edge, pausing above the door, the windows, and the corners of the wing. Cameras. Probably dozens of them.

The corner of his mouth curved in a half-smile. Shaking his head, he disappeared around the corner, his black shirt and jeans reflecting a silver glow in the moonlight.

"I love you." She marveled at how good that felt on her lips and wished she would've said it before he left.

In the next breath, he was there, hands on her face, kissing her until it was just him and her and the relief of her words. He laid a wet one on her lips, his smile somersaulting through her. "I love you, too. Be right back."

She settled into the lounger, grinning like a girl. She sighed. A girl floating in a dream.

Punk Rock Girl blared from her phone. The vibration bounced it on the side table, startling her.

Unknown Caller. Weird. She tapped *Decline* and stared at it.

The guitar beats kicked off again. *Unknown Caller.* Jay? Maybe it was a celebrity thing to block the number. The obsessive fool never called her because he never left her side. Of course, he was calling her now. She pressed *Accept*. "Hello?"

"Ignore my call again and you won't like the outcome."

His voice stripped away the deterring fence line, the patrolling guards, and the security of surveillance cameras. *Yes, Sir* shot to her throat and stuck there, along with a barrage of violent objections.

"Walk to the northeast corner of the veranda where I can see you better."

A chill snaked through her body. Was he nearby? Had he planted cameras? Darkness strangled her heart, raising goose pimples down her spine.

Fuck him. He couldn't hurt her. She was safe here.

"Don't make me wait, beautiful girl."

Where was northeast? The urgency to find Jay powered her to stand. She moved toward the corner of the wing, remaining in the line of shadows and placing the pool area in view. The surface of the water was still, the patio vacant of life. The living room and kitchen beyond were equally empty. Jay must've gone to the wine cellar. Where was Nathan? Her stomach rolled. He didn't guard her when she was in Jay's wing.

"Very good. Now remove that hideous shirt."

Fuck. Shit. Shit. How was he seeing her in the dark? No way was she going to run across the well-lit pool area. She spun back toward Jay's room, slamming her knee into a chair, slipped through the door, and locked it behind her. "How'd you get this number?"

The desire to hang up was overwhelming, but somehow hearing his voice gave her a sense of traction, as if keeping him with her prevented him from sneaking up on her.

She ran to the bedside table and hit buttons on the console until the curtains hummed, covering the windows and doors. A relieved breath slipped past her lips.

"That was a mistake, Charlee. You'll be punished severely for it."

The curtains shifted, reopened. She flinched and recovered by hitting the buttons. Nothing. The damn thing wasn't working.

Vulnerability crept into her bones. She backed toward the interior door. "I hate you for everything you've done to me. Most of all, I hate you for taking all those lives." Heart punching against her ribs, she bolted out of the bedroom and raced down the hall. "How many have you killed? My father, your guard, his niece... Noah."

"I haven't killed anyone."

Fucking liar. He excelled at distortion, built an enterprise with his forked tongue.

She burst through the double doors and into the corridor. Where was everyone? Oh God. What if he was there? What if the Craigs—

"Ah, there you are. Take off that shirt. Now."

She glanced down. *The Burn* emblazoned in red flames across her chest. Her pulse raced.

If Roy were on the property, he wouldn't have been on the phone. She turned in a circle, followed the angles of the soaring ceiling. There. A corner-mounted camera.

"Yes, Charlee. I have eyes everywhere. Come home."

Her knees buckled. She turned back toward Tony's door, the nearest room, tried the handle. Locked. She pounded her fist.

"Mr. Winslow and Ms. Tony are in the control room trying to recover the faulty security system."

The security system was down? Chills ran through her, and sweat beaded on her face. She pressed her back against the wall, cringing at the storage room door and the shadows in the bends and nooks of the suddenly too-long corridor. "If you cared about me at all, you'd let me live my life." *Keep him talking. Find Jay, Nathan, someone.*

"I'm so very disappointed you're fucking him, Charlee. You belong to me. I don't like what I saw outside his bedroom. You will be punished for that, as will he."

A crash barreled through the phone. Oh God. She hoped he was alone. His fury never missed its mark when there was a living punching bag nearby.

She crept along the wall toward the basement doorway which would take her to the wine cellar and the control room. She reached it just before the living room and a black hole yawned from below. Where was the light switch? She fumbled along the wall, searching, and brushed her hand over it. Nothing. She flicked it again and again. The darkness below held still.

The living room lights blinked out. The kitchen and hallway followed, plunging her into blackness. She gripped the phone and tried to slow her breathing. Goddamned fucking Nathan. Why had she let him take her gun? "Where are you?"

"Right here, beautiful girl. I can see your lovely tits heaving. I'm still waiting for that shirt to be removed. Every act of disobedience is a strike against your friends."

Her eyes darted over the ceiling and locked on a solid red light.

"That's right. Lucky for us, the cameras have infrared illuminators."

Lucky for her, that confirmed he wasn't in the house. Unless he was fucking with her. She eased into the stairway. Were there cameras there? Fuck, she should've paid attention. This was the price she paid for letting her guard down.

The estate was so damn automated. The lighting, communications, and surveillance controls must've been tied together. "How are you controlling the automation system?"

"RAT. Remote Administration Tool. A nasty, covert piece of software delivered by way of a spear phish. Someone there ignorantly clicked on an e-mail attachment and let my tool drop in. That overpaid security team can look for it, but they'll be chasing ghosts. It would take electronic forensics to find the barest remnant of it, but I'm not holding my breath." He chuckled. "Though it appears you are. Breathe, Charlee."

How long had he been watching them? Her heartbeat roared in

her ears and her fingers followed the wall as she tapped one foot in front of the other down the stairs.

"You asked the wrong question." The sick purr in his voice must've meant they'd come to point of his game.

She reached the bend in the stairs. Halfway there. What was the question? She'd asked how he was doing it. "*Why* are you doing this?"

"Good girl. To demonstrate that you're not beyond my reach. Your punishments can be delivered anywhere, anytime. Accept my job offer immediately and a certain amount of leniency will be considered."

If he could break through their security, something was keeping him from just coming in and taking her. Maybe the band's spotlight really was protecting her. If Roy kidnapped her again, Nathan and the band could hold a press conference, expose him, demand he open up the penthouse for inspection. Their fame alone could wrap him up in allegations, hurt his business, and sever his business connections. Would Roy chance that?

Yeah. He could shut down the gossip with a flick of one of his innovative switches.

"I'm waiting, Charlee, and my patience… Well, you understand the limits of my patience. Intimately."

The last word slithered over her like cold fingers in the dark. She brushed it off. He was boasting his almighty power and attempting to control her with fear. "Fuck you."

Silence. On the phone. In the endless black suffocating her. She inched forward, straining her eyes uselessly and waving a hand in front of her.

Her fingers bumped a shirt, a solid chest beneath. She screeched.

"Charlee?"

The lights flashed on, blinding and confusing, accompanied by the blare of a bazillion alarms.

Jay stared down at her, the skin around his eyes tight and tinged pink. His arms came around her, and the tension bunching her muscles released in shuddering waves.

His mouth moved, but she couldn't hear him over the alarms. She slumped against him and looked down at her phone. No live calls. The call log showed on the screen, and the last call was listed eight hours earlier from Nathan's phone. No unknown callers. *Chasing ghosts.*

The sirens silenced, but the ring lingered in her ears.

"Are you okay?" His hands moved over her, his gaze searching her face. "I was in the wine cellar. The door locked. I couldn't get out."

Automated door locks. She had a sudden dislike for all things electronic. She handed him her phone, anxious to be rid of it. “Roy called.” Her voice quivered, choked. “He’s hacked your automation system.”

74

Five days later, Charlee rested her head against the window, the glass cool against her brow. The activity swarming around the tour buses filled her view from the rear of Vanderschoot's warehouse loft. The bodyguard had moved the entire household—the band, her, Nathan, Faye, and the ten-man security team—into his two-thousand-square-foot building the night Roy hacked into the estate.

Locating Roy's RAT proved unsuccessful, so the home automation system had to be dropped offline. Every piece of software and some hardware would need to be replaced. This included HVAC, lighting, shading, security, intercoms, and all personal devices such as laptops, tablets, iPods, and cell phones. Anything with a Wi-Fi connection to the internal network was at risk of infection.

Charlee knew she wore her guilt in dark rings around her eyes, but she tried not to let it dampen her mood and that of the others. On a bright note, the days confined in the warehouse with the band and their personnel had brought her further into their fold. They slept on cots, shared a single bathroom, and no one complained. Jay reminded her they would be living in tighter quarters for the next sixteen weeks.

Nathan and Tony utilized the time surveying tour routes, coordinating watch schedules, and interviewing bodyguards. Once they hit the road, every member of the band would have two personal guards shadowing his every move outside the bus. The interview process was specific and time-consuming, leveraging all of their references to avoid new hires planted by Roy.

The band spent the days practicing their set list. Charlee inked several tats for Rio and Wil and some of the men on the security team. At night, they played a lot of cards. She hoped the easy camaraderie carried over when they climbed aboard the buses.

"Never thought I'd say this." Nathan braced his forearms on the window sill beside her. "I'm ready to board that bus."

Apparently after five days in a one-room warehouse, he didn't share her team spirit.

Outside, roadies and security staff flurried around two sleeper buses. Four Suburbans parked at angles in the rear lot, shoring the buses and creating a barricade against traffic.

At the edge of the perimeter, armed guards held back a crowd of onlookers. Through the duration of the tour, the protective team of twenty would stagger their sleep schedules, utilizing bunks on the second bus with the roadies and Faye, and escort the buses with a moving formation of Suburbans.

What a cavalry they would make. That was the point. Roy wouldn't risk a physical attack while they were in the blinding spotlight of public attention.

"So you're ready to get the show on the road?" She bumped her shoulder into his. "Because sixteen weeks on a bus will be better than five days in a warehouse?"

He smirked. "There are curtains on the bunks."

Ah. He missed his private Tony time. The notion filled her head with images of Jay moving over her in a tiny bunk. A thrill squirmed through her. "Curtains?"

He smiled, huge and full of teeth, prompting them both into a spontaneous burst of laughter. She jabbed him in the ribs.

Across the parking lot, Jay leaned against one of the buses, arms crossed, and head nodding as a tall, lean woman jabbered with animated expressions and hand gestures. A breeze caught wisps of her waist-length blond hair, lifting it around her. She blew it out of her face and looked up at Jay, smiling.

"Who is that?" Wow, she sounded bitchy. *Get a grip*.

"Ella Naas. Tour manager." He tossed Charlee a knowing look. "Better make friends. She'll be sharing our bus."

Yay. Why did she have to be so pretty and smiley?

Standing a few feet behind Jay, Tony raised a hand, palm out, and gestured with her index finger toward the window at Nathan.

He straightened. "Ready for this?"

Charlee nodded and followed him out, snaking around the hustle of crew and security.

Jay stood at the rear of the bus, his back to her, his attention on Ella. Charlee gnashed her molars together and turned her head away.

The door folded open, and she climbed stairs into the hushed cabin. No one had boarded yet.

Nathan relieved the guard posted at the door and took his place.

"Your things are already on board, Charlee. Get situated. We're rolling out in thirty minutes."

"'kay." She moved to the center of the bus.

Her breath swept out. Wow. Longer and more spacious than it appeared from the outside, there was so much to look at. Brown leather couches curved around both sides. Dark wood glossed the cabinets and enriched the moldings. Sliding doors covered every cranny. Strips of lighting chased the aisle and roof and reflected off the black marble floor. Stereos, gaming consoles and flat screens mounted four corners.

It was a monstrous, eight-wheeled symbol of luxury and arrogance. She curled her toes in her Doc Martens to refrain from bouncing with excitement.

The door swooshed behind her, followed by the steady gait she'd memorized over the past two weeks.

"Let me show you our bunk."

His deep voice caressed her ear and the heat of his body enveloped her. Would he always have that effect on her?

Hands on her waist, he nudged her down the aisle, past the sitting area. The galley nestled in a corner cabinet on the left. On the right, a bench for four wrapped a fold-out table.

"Keep going." His fingers tapped her hip bones.

The door behind the galley opened to a toilet and a miniature vanity and shower.

"The band has one rule on the road."

She twisted her neck and met his twinkling eyes. Oh, this should be good. "Only one?"

"We made a second rule that required Laz to wear clothes in the front lounge, but it backfired. He wore banana hammocks the entire tour, claiming they were clothes by definition."

She turned, pressing her mouth against his chest, and muffled a half-moan, half-laugh. "Do I dare ask what the one rule is?"

"No shitting on the bus."

"What?" Looking up into his face, she was sure hers was an expression of horror.

He grinned, gorgeous and taunting, his hand clutching the door frame above her.

"Oh my God. I thought you were serious."

"I am." He was still grinning. "I mean, there's a grinder to... You know, grind shit, but I promise you don't want any of those guys taking a dump in here. Small space. No airflow. Dining table and kitchen a foot away. You get the idea. We make regular bathroom stops."

It was going to be a long sixteen weeks. She pushed a drape aside and entered a narrow corridor. Yikes. Tight squeeze. A glance behind her confirmed his shoulders fit, but they brushed the wood panels on both sides.

Eight bunks enclosed her. Four on either side, stacked two high. "Crammed in like—"

"Rockstars?" He cocked his head, lips twitching, and pointed. "That one's ours."

She rolled into the last bunk on the bottom driver's side and stretched out. A few inches remained above her head and below her feet, but a tall guy like Jay would have to bend. "How the hell are we going to share this?"

He crossed his arms. "How the hell would we not?"

Their bus would sleep the four performers, Tony, Nathan, the tour manager, and her. Eight bunks, eight bodies. There were enough beds, but he didn't want to sleep without her. Damned if that didn't make her insides melt into warm squishiness.

She leaned out of the bunk. The aisle ended with a door. "Who gets the bedroom?"

"We don't rent the coaches with a bedroom suite. We'd just fight over it." He squatted to her level. "There's a second lounge back there. Gives us another place to hang out or get away so we're not all stuck up front." He climbed in the bunk and lay atop her, his thighs, hips, and chest flattening her into the memory foam, his mouth hovering a kiss away. "The spare bunk will be our junk bunk. Trust me, every bus needs one."

The weight of him combined with her accelerating heartbeat made her breath ragged and noisy. She wanted to dig her fingers into his tight ass and hold him against her. She gripped the sheets instead.

His regret over leaving her on his veranda that night had darkened his temperament for days. She wasn't sure if his brooding was the catalyst, but his trigger had become more sensitive. After several breakdowns in the warehouse from the casual brush of her fingers, she was hesitant to touch him at all.

"Is this how we'll sleep then?" She looked up to catch him watching her. "If so, you might have to massage the blood back into my limbs in the morning."

His laughter wrapped around her as he shifted them. A few bumps into the wood paneled wall and he had them positioned on their sides with his hips cupping her ass. "How's this?"

Heaven. "Pull the curtain and wake me when we get there."

His hand slid up her thigh and patted her butt. "I want to show you a couple things before everyone piles in." He crawled over her and pulled her by her hand into the aisle. Reaching under the frame of the bed, he turned a crank she hadn't noticed. A couple rotations raised the closest edge of the mattress and angled it toward the cubby's roof.

Oh, wow. Extra storage space. Daylight streamed from the compartment below. He gripped the wood frame and hopped in the hole. "I had this modified hatch added so we could access the storage area from inside or outside." He ducked, closing the exterior door on the concrete landscape beyond.

"I thought you rented this bus?"

Standing, he rested his forearms on the top edge of the compartment. "True. After what happened at the estate, I called the bus owner and sold him on the benefits of emergency exits and flashed the almighty green dollar."

"*Pimp My Ride,* rock star style."

He grinned.

Did his need for an escape hatch have anything to do with his burns? "What's the real reason you need a secret hide away?"

He reached behind him and removed a handgun from his waistband. "Gun laws for civilians vary by state. Some states require the piece to be separate from the ammo and stored under the bus. I don't want any trouble with the law, and I don't want the gun out of reach." He twisted, bending, and tucked the gun in a pocket on the compartment wall.

"I had a Bodyguard 380." Used it to kill a Craig. Bile hit the back of her throat. "But Nathan confiscated it." The bastard.

He jumped out. "You know where mine is if you need it, but don't shoot at the door or windows. I had everything replaced with bulletproof glass." He rotated the crank, returning the mattress to its seated position. "Sit down. I want to show you one more thing."

She lay down on the bunk, and he knelt in the aisle beside her. Lifting a folder from the pocket on the wall at her feet, he opened it on her tummy and raised it so she could see the first page.

Her eyebrows clenched as she skimmed the headers.

Oxycontin. Recreational Uses. Side effects. Street names. Pictures.

She flipped the pages to the next tabbed section. *Heroin*. Same list of headers. Next tab. *Cocaine*. Same headers. A numbness settled around her heart, and she wasn't sure if it was relief or worry.

He lifted her chin and rubbed his thumb over the skin around her mouth. "I can't ask you to trust me. I have a long way to go to earn that back, but I hope having this information will take some of the constant out of constantly wondering. If you know what to look for, I won't be able to hide any of these addictions from you."

The rawness in his expression tightened her chest. She pinned her lips between her teeth to hold back soothing words she might not mean. She didn't know if she trusted him to stay clean, which probably meant she didn't.

He leaned in and pointed to two stars hand-drawn beside *Cocaine*. "I double starred my old favorites. A single star denotes I've used it at least once. And there's information on today's most common street drugs, narcotics I've never tried, but could easily acquire."

"Do you...? Are there side effects from coming *off* drugs?"

"Some." He swallowed. "I didn't cling to any one chemical, so I don't feel the usual withdrawals. Cocaine bugs was the worst, but I haven't experienced the crawling feeling this time around."

"You did before? When you quit three years ago?"

"Yeah."

She caught his deep brown eyes before he kissed her cheek and sat back on his heels.

"I'm sorry you have to worry about this on top of everything else." He stared, unfocused, at a hole on the inner thigh of his jeans, picking at the scraggly edges. Then he seemed to gather strength from his thoughts, rolled his shoulders back, and seized her with a penetrating gaze. "I won't let you down. For what it's worth, I'm so fucking happy you're here with me. You make facing the crowds and the press and the long nights something to look forward to."

"I want to be where you are, Jay." She loved him enough to tackle the reason he turned to drugs in the first place. "I appreciate your openness about the drugs. It helps." And it did. He wouldn't intentionally hide it from her. If he slipped again, it would be in an impulsive moment of weakness. Didn't comfort the throb behind her eyes. She needed more from him. *For* him.

"But?"

She took a deep breath and let it out slowly. "You're not open with me. I know nothing about your past, how you got your scars, or where you go when your memories surface. If you want me to trust you, open up."

His face closed off and his eyes darted away.

"I'm no doctor, Jay, but it doesn't take one to know your drugs, isolation, and rejection to touch and intimacy are harmful ways to self-medicate. I won't give you my trust, or the touch of my hands, until you talk to me."

75

Dare to be vulnerable with me.

The beautiful woman blinking up at Jay was anything but vulnerable, yet she'd spoken those words to him the day they'd reunited. She'd put up with his issues for two weeks, never pushing him beyond his limits, never demanding he open his past.

The message was there now, but her tone was softened with concern and love. She wouldn't judge him, not even if he cried while he walked her through that year of his life. The challenge would be recalling the things that happened to that six-year-old boy. Those memories were flashbulbs. Could he piece them together and shed light on the dark gaps between?

"I want your trust, Charlee. And Christ, you haven't touched me for two days." He scrubbed a hand over his face. "But that's not why I'm going to tell you what happened. You're right. I'm self-medicating, and it's hurting us both." If he talked about it, maybe it would... What? Cure him? Fuck, he was terrified to confront the issues of his past and who he was.

The bus wobbled with the clamor of boarding bodies. Voices drifted from beyond the drape that separated the bunks from the front lounge.

"I'm here when you're ready." She propped up on an elbow. "Just don't take too long."

His lips burned to kiss her. She wouldn't touch him, but that didn't stop him from cupping her face and sealing his mouth over hers. He buried his tongue past her lips, and she met him thrust for thrust, relaxing beneath his lean as he pushed her into the mattress.

"Hey, there." Ella's southern twang tumbled through the cabin. He broke the kiss and kept his eyes fastened on Charlee. Ella was nice enough, but tour managers, in general, crawled under his skin. "Well, shut my mouth. Sorry for interrupting. I... I thought you said no touching." Ella tossed a bag on the bunk facing his.

Charlee's eyes widened, and he blew out a breath. "Charlee, this is Ella. Our tour manager." He bent a knee and propped an elbow on it. "Ella, this is my girlfriend, Charlee. The only person that can touch me."

Charlee rose from the bunk and held out a hand. "I'm not the only person. I mean, I'm not some psycho who doesn't let people touch her boyfriend. But let's not test it, all right?" She grasped Ella's hand, the threat punctuated in her none-too-gentle grip.

Fuck, he loved her jealousy. It stirred a feverish storm in his chest, vibrating like a loudly strummed minor chord on his Les Paul electric. It also made him hard as a rock. He adjusted himself as he climbed to his feet.

Ella smiled. "That's cool. Don't you worry about me. I'm just here to keep things organized." She flicked her eyes to him. "Schedule's posted on the microwave. Check it every day to find out when and where you need to be. Y'all pick out your bunks?"

Charlee chewed a nail, watching her with a blank expression. "Uh, yeah. We've got this one." She raised a boot behind her and tapped the toe against the mattress frame.

"Man, oh man, I'm in high cotton. Touring with *The Burn?* And first stop... San Dieeee-ego!" Her voice was high-pitched and way too fucking eager.

He twined his fingers with Charlee's. "Let's head up front."

Past the drape and out of Ella's earshot, Charlee whispered, "Is she new?"

"New tour. New tour manager." He kissed her head. "We have to reeducate them every time."

An hour later, Charlee nestled into the crook of his arm and stretched her legs along the couch in the front lounge. They cruised down the Five just south of San Clemente. The ocean view on the right sparkled in a luster of blues, yet not half as captivating as Charlee's eyes as she took it all in.

Black Suburbans shadowed the views out the windshield and on the left. Unwanted but necessary reminders of what was out there, waiting for them.

Wil and Laz sprawled on opposite ends of the couch on the other side, hypnotized by whatever video game was sucking their brain cells. The slamming of the fridge and microwave doors meant Rio was eating. Again. Tony, Nathan, and Ella moved to the back to go over the schedule for that night's show in San Diego.

"I've never swum in the ocean." Charlee circled a finger on the glass, eyes on the coastline. "First thing I'd do is pull down my pants and stick my butt cheeks in the sand."

A laugh burst out of him. "I better be there when that happens. I'll help you clean the grit out of those hard to reach places."

He pulled her in, crushing her back against his chest. They would be pushing out of San Diego immediately after the set was broken down, and the remainder of the trip was inland. He kissed the crook between her neck and shoulder. There would be plenty of downtime after the tour to take her to every ocean in the world.

Swift footfalls that could only belong to Tony whispered through the cabin. Phone to her ear, she grabbed the remote and switched off the guys' video game.

"What the fuck, Tony?" Laz held the controller in the air, his mouth agape.

"Got it. Thanks, Faye." She pocketed her phone and flipped through the channels, stopping on a news station. "Alan Patera, assistant to—"

"We know who he is." Adrenaline heated Jay's cheeks and spiked his pulse.

Charlee straightened, her twisting fingers echoing his unease. He clutched her hands.

Tony shifted to unblock Charlee's view of the TV. "He called to warn us of a news report coming— Here it is." She dialed up the volume, and the camera panned to a middle-aged anchorwoman with botoxed lips.

"Recently retired CEO of Windsor Records, Maxim Windsor, announced today that Jay Mayard, vocalist and guitarist of the popular rock band, *The Burn*, has been having sexual relations with his daughter, Sylvia Windsor. It is unknown if these relations began before Sylvia's eighteenth birthday last month. If accused, Jay Mayard could be facing statutory rape charges in the state of California."

Dread constricted his airflow, and Charlee's fingers tugged uselessly in his flexing fist.

"What the fuck kind of fucking bullshit is this?" Laz hurled the controller, and it smashed somewhere in the galley.

"Shh." Tony slashed a hand in Laz's direction.

"...Oxford Industries' acquisition of Windsor Records, Mr. Windsor stepped down from his position as CEO of the label; however, he contends that *The Burn's* popularity is owed to Jay Mayard's relationship with his daughter. Jay Mayard has declined to comment on these allegations, and Sylvia Windsor could not be reached for comment.

"Jay Mayard is not new to lawless behavior. His career has been plagued with drug use. In 2011, he was carried off the stage at Madison Square Garden due to a supposed overdose of speedball."

"Turn that shit off." Jay jumped up, shoved his hands in his hair, pulling, twisting, his heart tearing through his chest.

"That is so not cool." Wil reached for the remote and clicked off the screen. "Jay has never OD'd."

"Jay. Sit down." Charlee's tone was soft, too soft.

No way would she believe him after everything he'd done. He didn't want to face her, didn't want to see any more pain straining her face.

"Sit." Stronger that time, but not angry.

He sat, dragged his eyes, burning as they were, to meet hers.

"Have you slept with her?"

The ache in his eyes clouded his vision. His teeth sawed at his cheek. An eighteen-year-old? Never. He was twenty-seven, for Christ's sake, but why would she believe him?

She raised a hand to touch his cheek and withdrew it before she made contact. His heart sank.

"No, you haven't slept with her." Her eyes brightened. "Have you met her? In public or otherwise?"

Wait. What? She just looked at him and saw the truth? He gathered her to his chest and squeezed her harder than he should have. He didn't care what the press said about him. Only Charlee's opinion of him mattered.

He pressed his lips against the top of her head and cupped her face, lifting it to look into her perceptive eyes. "I met her once. A promotional event *after* we signed with Windsor. She..." He stroked her cheeks with his thumbs. "She propositioned me."

"For sex?"

His stomach rolled. "I turned her down." His response was coarse and tasted like acid. He remembered the girl's determination, her attempts to touch him. He hadn't let her down easy.

"A woman scorned." She sat back, eyes rimmed red, and his hands slipped from her face. "She made Roy's favorite score too easy."

"Favorite score?"

"Slander. I've witnessed him rip families apart with false scandals, destroying reputations to get what he wants." Her lip quivered, and she bit down on it, inhaled deeply. "I'm so sorry, Jay."

"Don't. This is *not* your fault. And it's not the end of the world. There's no evidence to charge me. Faye will take care of it from the legal side."

She looked up out of glossy eyes. "Faye?"

"She's a lawyer." Laz leaned forward, elbows on knees. "And a badass one. She'll handle it."

"The damage is done." She rubbed a palm on her thigh. "How will this affect the tour? It's defamation of your image. And why did they say you declined to comment?"

Jay placed a hand over her restless one. He'd say or do anything to take that look off her face. "The tour's sold out. And we'll make a public statement. It'll be fine." The fans would be outraged, and records sales would decline. Fucking woohoo. He didn't give shit. They weren't playing for the money.

Laz stood and moved toward the bunks. "The record company handles our publicity, our *image*, and interacts with the press on our behalf. Roy Oxford graciously declined to comment for Jay." He held the drape aside, gaze falling on Charlee. "Don't worry about the band. That asshole put us in headline news. Totally fuels our rockognition." He grinned and dropped the drape behind him.

Creases fanned from the corners of her eyes. "Rockognition?"

"Recognition of a rock star." Wil smiled, powered up his video game, and slouched into the couch. "Really, Charlee. We could give a fuck what people think of us. We just want to play music."

Jay rolled back his shoulders and let his tension slip away. Roy's slander might hurt his other targets, but he'd sorely misjudged what mattered to this band.

76

San Diego, Tucson, Albuquerque, and Denver whisked by. Four concerts in four days and Jay was straining through the simplest activities, even struggling to lift himself into their bunk. Sixty-six shows to go.

The sway of the privacy curtain brushed his arm, and the mattress vibrated with the propulsion of their metal home. He lifted his wrist from Charlee's waist and angled it above his face. The tritium dials on his watch glowed through the darkness. Three in the morning. Mountain time? Central time? Whatever time, it was late, and his eyes burned, refusing to close. Funny how fatigue did not equate to sleepiness. Especially when his mind wasn't ready to shut down.

He flattened his palm against her lace-covered mound and pulled her ass into the bend of his hips. Tracing the thin material down her center, he followed the seam of her lips beneath. Christ, even in sleep, she was damp. He was too tired to stop his fingers. Maybe even too tired to take it further, considering the week they'd had.

Despite the sold-out tour, the stands had been thinner at the first three shows than what they were accustomed to. This was made worse by the sudden halt on the distribution of their albums to retail channels. The label stopped production on the basis of some bullshit legality related to the charges against him. Thank you, Sylvia Windsor, for alleging that he didn't just fuck her, but he'd done so before her eighteenth birthday. He shivered.

Faye hadn't wasted time sharpening her teeth with a legal defense. He'd given his statement to the D.A. following the accusation, and Faye assured him the charges would disintegrate without litigation.

Roy wasn't after a trial. The fucker wanted to torpedo Jay's character. Jay guessed the true motivation was to drive a wedge between him and Charlee.

True to form, Faye held a news conference in Albuquerque the previous day without the consent of Windsor Records. Jay had attended but left the talking to Faye. Her press statement highlighted convincing truths about his one face-to-face meeting with Sylvia and cited the reports she'd collected from witnesses of that meeting.

The communication soothed disgruntled fans if the ovation at their Denver show that night was any indication. Every seat in the canyon amphitheater held a bouncing, cheerful body.

Charlee, on the other hand, wasn't so easily soothed. Her self-reproach for his bruised reputation and the cease in CD distribution put an ever-present slump in her shoulders. He and the guys tried to convince her it wouldn't hurt their pockets, but her regret over all things Roy knew no bounds.

She wiggled her hips against his.

"You awake?" His whisper broke through the hum of tires on pavement.

"No." A groggy croak.

With his arm trapped beneath her waist, he kept his hand pressed against her pussy. His other found the soft curve of her shoulder, traced her arm around the elbow, and twined their fingers.

She'd remained steadfast in her ultimatum, refusing him the caress of her touch. Still, her hand had become a permanent fixture in his. In every town, on every stage, steering through mobs and paparazzi, she never left his side. Reaching for her hand and lacing their fingers had become as reflexive and certain as his love for her.

He circled her wrist with his thumb. "Why aren't you asleep?"

"There's something hard jabbing my ass," she whispered, though they both knew their bunk mates wore ear buds to bed.

He rocked his hips. "Can't help it. You're a wiggler."

"And you're a freak. Who sleeps in a t-shirt and no underpants?"

He missed sleeping nude with her. On the road, she slept in panties and nothing else while he wore a shirt at all times to hide the scars from their bus load of roommates.

He shifted their entwined hands into the valley of her tits, and she stretched her fingers to roll them over her nipple.

Christ, he was desperate for her touch. "Please. Put your hands on me." He ground himself against her to emphasize the area that needed the most attention.

"Tell me about the shed."

He flinched. Damn her stubbornness to hell. "We have a break in the schedule tomorrow night. We'll talk then. I promise."

"All right."

"So you'll touch me?"

"Yes. Tomorrow."

"Fuck, Charlee." He let a hard edge dominate his voice, even as excitement skipped through his bloodstream. Hopefully, his iron tone would provoke the twinge of anticipation she needed to climax.

He shifted, rolling her beneath him, and settled between her legs. His fingers met the moist crotch of her panties, and he tugged it to the side. He lined up his erection and bit his lip. Slowly, torturously, he pushed in. Her heat encased him.

"Ahhhh, yeah. Ah, God, feels so good." The bellow in his heart exploded with the thrust of his hips. He couldn't see her eyes through the dark, hated he wouldn't be able to read her expression.

He pushed two fingers past her teeth, curled them, and put pressure on her jaw. Leveraging the grip, he turned her head toward him and strengthened his fingers to hold her in place. It was a perception of dominance rather than pain. He hoped the acceleration in her breathing was testament it was working for her.

He pressed kisses across her open mouth, licking over and around his fingers as he stroked and rotated his hips. So fucking warm and wet, the sensation of her spread through his groin and enveloped his body. Good God, he wanted to come. He picked up his pace and pulled harder on her jaw.

Her sharp, heavy pants unraveled the reign on his release. He pushed the surging sensations back, pounded into her, his free hand flexing beside her face. Her hips met him punch for punch. Was she close? Getting closer?

She bit down on his fingers, arched her back, and the hot walls of her cunt contracted around him. Oh, thank fuck.

He yanked his hand from her mouth, balls curling up. "Unngh, I'm gonna come. Oh, Jesus. I'm coming."

"Mmm." She bucked with him. "Come in me. God, I want to feel you come."

Amplified by her throaty whisper, the spasm of bliss shot through his dick and tingled over his body. He collapsed onto his elbows, braced on her pillow.

Laughter tumbled from the bunk above. "Who needs groupies when I can listen to you two every night? Can you pass me a sock or something? I just spewed down my leg."

Fucking Laz.

77

The next night, Charlee padded through the bathroom of their suite in the City of Fountains. Who knew Kansas City boasted over two hundred outdoor water-jetting displays?

Extra tubes, needles, ink, and green soap scattered the marble vanity. The remainder of the tattoo equipment waited with Jay in the bedroom, machines prepped and ready.

The old leather sketchbook she'd carried for three years lay open to the illustration she'd just transferred to stencil paper. She knew the drawing intimately, had doodled it so many times through the years, it was sketched it into her memory.

She washed her hands in the sink. No need for gloves. The body fluids they shared daily were much more intimate than blood and sweat.

Hands dried, she held up the stencil by the corners, her nerves aflutter. Hadn't every day since the day she'd met him led to this?

Whatever you gave him made him look at things differently, made him want to get better.

Laz's words came back to her from the night they fled the Cuban restaurant. Jay had worn his partial outline for three years. How did he envision the finished design? He didn't know about the sketchbook, unless he'd snooped in her messenger bag while she slept. What if it disappointed him? Or worse, what if the completion didn't give him the catharsis she knew he anticipated?

Deep breath. The forge of fire and steel was destined to exist on his back. She just needed to go slow, not screw it up. They had twenty-four hours until the Kansas City show. Plenty of time to help him uncover what he'd hid for so long.

Another lungful of air. She lowered the stencil behind her and walked to the bedroom, her gait jittery, her heart more so.

He sat on the edge of the bed, palms flat on his thighs. "It's time." He addressed Nathan and Tony, who stood in the sitting area outside the bedroom, but his gaze was on her.

The bedroom door clicked closed followed by another click of the outer exit.

Jay had demanded total privacy for the remainder of the night. Because their suite was a fraction of the size of the one in New York, it made it easier to convince the protective team to guard from the hallway. In reality, they were only one room away.

She placed the stencil on the desk and moved toward him until her knees brushed his bent ones. "Ready?"

"For three years." He removed his shirt, tossed it behind him, eyes on her, overflowing with emotion. Was he as anxious as her? Was he having second thoughts?

Her need to touch him, to connect to him, roiled inside her and spread to her fingertips. Her equilibrium wobbled. "We'll go slowly. Stop me when you need to. If you change your mind, if the memories come—"

"Charlee." He rose a breath away and rested his hands on her waist. "I want this." Dipping his head, he opened his mouth and swept his tongue over hers. Pushing past her parted lips, he licked and nipped, sensuously, lovingly, restoring her balance.

She pulled back, breathless. My, how their roles had flipped. The last time she aimed a needle at him, she'd taken the lead, controlled the outcome. "Do you want to see the stencil before I start?" Nervousness cramped her gut.

He turned, lay across the foot of the bed, face down, one arm hanging over the end. "I want you to stop deliberating and finish what you started." Impatience sharpened his tone, but the gold in his eyes glimmered with amusement.

"Good. I don't need a stencil anyway since I'm just doing a big ol' sheet of black." She diluted a paper towel with Dettol antiseptic and swiped long strokes from shoulder to shoulder.

"Since you inked the first outline freehand, I'm confident you could make even a black square look like art. Can't wait to see what you do with a stencil." He turned his head away, and the muscles in his back loosened under the rub of the towel.

It had been a huge risk inking him without a stencil the night she met him, but she'd had little choice in her sneaky offense to defy his wishes.

She squirted a dollop of stencil gel at the top of his spine. "Here come my hands." She waited for his deep breath and eventually let out her own when his tension never came.

With hesitant fingertips, she spread the gel over the nearest cluster of scars. His back rose and fell with steady breaths, his trigger quiet.

She worked the gel lower, and his skin took on a tougher, more wrinkled texture across a horizontal line from armpit to armpit. Was his back curved and chest tucked in when the burns were inflicted? The bubbles weren't raised enough to be noticeable, but the discoloration made them impossible to miss. A motley of reds blended into browns and pinks. The damage covered his upper back from just below his neck to under his armpits.

Once the gel covered the areas to be inked, she positioned the stencil on his back and adjusted the ohms on the machine. "You know, I don't know your full name."

He twisted his neck to face her, cheek resting on the mattress, eyelids heavy. "James Kristopher Mayard."

"James? Really?" She removed the stencil and blew on his back.

The arm he dangled off the bed shifted, and his hand curled around the back of her bare calf. "I changed it to Jay when I started *The Burn*."

She tested the machine with a few pulses of the needle. Jay. Laz. Rio. Wil. "All your proportioned names would make charming tattoos. You could wear each other's names in a matching design." A smile tugged her lips as she touched the machine to his skin and began the first stroke.

He chuckled. "I love those guys, but not that much."

She followed the stenciled lines, dwelling on three-lettered names. One in particular tried to scorch her mood. She would not allow Roy to taint this moment. "What are their real names?"

"Lazarus Bromwell." One dark eyebrow arched.

"Of course." She moved to the most disfigured section, where a nickel-sized patch of skin had twisted as it melted. Watching his face for distress, she inked a line over it. "And the others?"

"Richard." A gentle fondness intoned his voice.

"Rio? Richard Ketch?" She laughed. "Catchy. And Wil must be William."

He shook his head, creasing his smile against the bedding. "Bruce Sima."

The machine went still as she tried to pair that name with Wil's young, surfer-boy face. "No way."

"It's probably no surprise it was his idea to change our names. I guess Bruce the bassist didn't have the right ring."

His scars blazed red beneath the stab of her needle, prompting her next question. “The band’s name was your idea?”

He nodded. “You’re the only one who knows what led to the name.”

Hopefully, sometime soon, she would know what led to the burns. Lulled by the buzz of the machine, she drifted into a *Fugazi* song, humming the in-your-face chords with abandon.

“*Waiting Room*.” He sighed. “You’re subtle.”

She snorted. “It’s a good song.”

“Especially in your adorable tonality.” His eyes danced.

“Hey.” She held the needle away and pinched the tender skin under his arm. “You’re not paying me to sing well.”

He jerked back from the sting of her pinch, lips crooked up. “I’m not paying you at all.”

She wiped Vaseline over a finished flame and shifted to outline the next one. “Laz paid me twenty grand for a rainbow.”

“Laz got ripped off.” His voice broke with laughter.

“So true.”

They fell quiet for a time, sharing glances and smiles as she worked. Her mind raced to the final design, mentally shading between the bold lines, trying to predict his reaction. It would be primarily black. Red and brown ink would be used sparingly to blend the drawn scars into the existing ones.

She took her time, following the outline with a steady hand. Working over the scar tissue, she must have hit a sensitive area because his body shuddered. “Sorry. You okay?”

“Wasn’t you, Charlee.” A ragged exhale. “I was thinking about my parents’ death, of the burns that occurred over the year that followed.”

78

The machine jumped in Charlee's hand. She held it midair, hovering, her heart thundering.

"Keep going." Jay's palm rubbed up and down her leg. "I need the distraction."

She swallowed and brushed out another rivet in the steel plate beneath the outline of charred skin.

"We lived in Canada, a rural area near the Boundary Waters, and the land is only accessible by plane. They were on one of their supply runs when their plane went down."

"How'd it happen?"

"A malfunction. My father was a pilot, owned an old plane. I usually joined them on those errands—so I've been told—but they'd left me with the closest neighbor that day. Some family that lived a few miles away." A pause. "I was an only child."

He'd carried his loneliness his entire life. Her chest ached, and her stomach tumbled as the machine vibrated in her hand. "Abandoned and alone."

"You, more than anyone, can sympathize with that. Makes this next part easier to talk about."

Brown eyes scrutinized the wall behind her with more interest than it warranted. "My father inherited the land and a great deal of money before I was born. His sister didn't receive a crumb."

"Aunt El?" Her brain scrambled to put the pieces together. Bitter aunt. Traumatic childhood. Acid seethed through her gut.

"I've said her name?" His face tightened with wide eyes. "When I...flashback?"

"Yeah." She kissed his shoulder beyond the reach of the ink.

He relaxed beneath her lips. "Elena Mayard. Something was wrong with her. I always thought of it as unexamined viciousness. She was manic, I think. I don't know. Before my parents died, she'd kept herself isolated from the family, so much so my grandparents cut her out of their will."

"Did she...? Is that who raised you when you lost your parents?"

He nodded. "My parents didn't have the foresight to prepare a trust. I was left with my only blood relation. She got me, the money, the house, and the land." He glanced away, eyes hard. "She moved in for one year."

Why just a year? What had gone wrong? She was terrified to push. "Is she...?"

"Dead." The brawn in his back flexed beneath the needle. "Died in prison."

Prison? A fury of nausea flooded her. What had the woman done? Was she responsible for his scars?

Charlee circled fingers around the damage, mesmerized by the strength of the man beneath. Unwilling to drown him with the questions piling up in her throat, she pressed her lips together and finalized the last curve of the outline.

Finished, she disassembled the liner machine, plugged in the shader, and mixed a thimble of black ink with distilled water for blending. She added two more thimbles of red and brown.

For the next hour, the buzz of the machine overlaid the quiet between them. Sketched shreds of skin emerged from the real scars, curling away, and giving the image a three-dimensional effect. She kept her mind on the design, unable to justify the urge to ply him to talk. If she pushed him, he might shut down completely.

Midway through the shadowing on the final steel plate, he raised his head. "Take a break."

In a jumble of anxiousness, she swiped the freshly inked area with Vaseline, clicked off the power supply, and set the machine aside. Then she looked at him expectantly.

His gaze, exposed and patient, burned through her, singeing away any lust she'd built up while touching the defined muscles on his back.

"Please put your hands on me."

Whatever was pouring from his expression welled up from deep inside him and had nothing to do with her. She climbed over him, straddled one of his legs, and ran her hands over his middle back, careful to avoid the fresh ink.

"I don't remember my parents. My earliest memory begins with Aunt El in a shed. It was an old ramshackle building behind the main house. One room, one window, one door. I think it had held my father's tools at one time, but after he died, everything was cleared out." He propped his chin on his joined hands and stared across the room. "Everything was gone except an old mattress and a Bolo oven."

Saliva pooled in her mouth and blood surged through her veins. Were his burns connected to the oven? He'd whispered *Bolo* a few times during the worst of his nightmares. Had he crawled in it? Maybe he fell asleep and someone turned it on? She gripped her stomach.

"Please don't take your touch away."

Her hand flew to his bicep, caressed the sinews of muscle. Her other traced his lower back along the waistband. She leaned to the side, put his strong profile in view.

He closed his eyes, a tic bouncing in his jaw. "That first time, I'd done something my aunt disapproved of. I don't know. The memories are just snapshots. Feelings are clearer. I remember her anger. It warped her face when she locked me in the shed."

Biting back the comforting words that sprang forward, she massaged his arms and shoulders and pressed kisses through the short strands of hair behind his ear. She knew he wanted her to listen and touch. Not blather on with useless reassurances.

"The film over the window blocked the light and the darkness seemed to freeze time in there. In the beginning, I think the punishments were just short stays. The feelings that remain with me though, the endless hunger and the cold... I was probably in there through the night. Maybe several nights. Toward the end, I wasn't allowed out at all." His throat worked, and a quiver twitched along his back. "That's where they found me."

Grief and fury swelled in her throat and seared her sinuses. "How old were you?" Her voice broke.

"Six."

The image of a six-year-old Jay, locked in a shed in freezing nowhere Canada threatened to shatter her outward composure. Why was his tone so indifferent when she was seconds from exploding?

Climbing off his leg, she crawled to a better position to examine his expression. Stretched alongside him, her chest to his side, her hand on his arm, she lay her cheek on the mattress.

Face-to-face, he watched her watching him. "I've tried to make sense of my memories, to fit them into the reports the detectives filed...after." He raised his arm and hooked it around her back, pulling her close.

"Watch your ink. Don't roll over—"

"She put me in the oven."

His words echoed between them. Horror numbed her limbs. Her heart pounded. The constriction in her lungs spread through her body. "How...how could...?" She couldn't say it, couldn't ask how a little boy could fit in an oven. Or the question that wouldn't have an answer. Why?

"It was an enlarged modification of a vintage single-door Bolo used for roasting flanks of wild game, deer, moose, whatever my father hunted. I was nineteen when I returned. It was still there." His nostrils flared. "It was barely visible amongst the charred debris when I burned down the shed." His gaze turned inward, cloudy. "She forced me to squat on a pillow inside, warned me not to touch the walls. The thermostat must have been set to warm. I remember the...burn, but I don't think it was hot enough to singe my skin."

The scars on his back rebuked that. Her veins boiled with the lethal hammer of her pulse and her eyes ached, blurring her vision.

"I must have grown taller over that year," he said softly. "I couldn't keep my back from touching the wall anymore."

"The burns accumulated over time." Layer upon layer over his young skin. She choked back bile.

He jerked his chin, up, down. "The scars might not have been so terrible if she'd cleaned them, treated them. Infection set in. I got sick. I guess she phoned a doctor, asked questions, made him suspicious." His chest heaved and his hand fisted, digging into her spine.

"And the doctor reported it? That's how they found you?"

He squeezed her tight, trapping the air in her lungs. "She was taken away in handcuffs. Never saw her again. I spent the next thirteen years in foster care, and the land became mine when I was nineteen. Because she died from a heart condition. Everything went to me."

"She'd have to own a heart to have a heart condition. How could anyone put a little boy in a...?" She choked, fought the tears from her voice. He'd said she was manic. Fuck, manic didn't touch that kind of sickness. Unexamined viciousness? Pure evil was the only explanation.

"She put me in the oven because she said I was cold when she..." His body shook in violent waves around her. He jerked away and shoved off the bed. His fists flexed, his eyes on fire.

She scooted off the bed and followed him at a distance, dread weighting her feet.

He paced to the bathroom, picking up speed, hands in his hair, ripping at the short ends. The sheen of Vaseline accentuated the tension rippling his back.

At the vanity, he splashed water on his face and stared at the drain. "I hated the darkness, the loneliness smothering that shed. More than that, I hated when she visited me, when she made me lay on the mattress." His knuckles blanched across his grip on the counter.

No. Oh God, no. She recognized that hate. It spawned from the terror of imminent visitations. She wedged in front of him and cupped his face. "You don't have to tell me the rest."

"Charlee. I do. I need—" His jaw clamped, and his eyes pinched shut beneath his rubbing fingers. "I hated that I *liked* how she made me feel. I don't remember what she did to me, what she made me do, but I know that I liked it."

His whisper crushed her heart. She blinked back tears, but they escaped anyway. Pulling his face into her neck, she stroked his hair and kissed the side of his head. "Maybe she didn't—"

"I remember the dread, the embarrassment, the *anticipation*." He pushed away, glaring at her, his gorgeous face twisted in anguish. "Those feelings are as unchangeable as the fucking dark. I feared her. I hated her. But I fucking liked her touching me!" His roar cleaved through the room, slamming into her and tightening her tear-drenched face.

He bent away, launching at the toilet, and retched violently through incoherent shouts.

Her heart vaulted to her throat as she battled her own nausea and squatted behind him. With his hips between her thighs, she wrapped her arms around his torso and held him as he purged his grief. She stroked the strained muscles in his chest and biceps, and restricted her pain to silent sobs.

When his stomach was empty, and his head hung, she handed him a towel and flushed the toilet.

Stone-faced and mute, he moved to the sink and brushed his teeth with mechanical movements, the silence thick between them.

Perched on the counter's edge, she gathered her words, her desperate emotions based on her own experiences. "You didn't like it. It was rape, Jay."

He froze, glared at the toothpaste foaming in the sink, and resumed brushing.

"Your body betrayed you." She touched his arm, his muscles pressing against skin, tense and restrained. "It wasn't your fault." With Roy, her orgasms were forced. Her body had writhed in pleasure, treacherous and unwanted as it was.

He looked up, eyes tapered as if penetrating her thoughts. He dropped his toothbrush and pulled her against his chest. "I love you. Fuck, I love you so much. You and me... This—" He crushed her body against his. "This is why we'll win."

His declaration electrified her, much like his grip on her soul. “We’ve already won. We escaped with our hearts intact. This—” she returned his unyielding embrace “—proves it.”

He clutched her hips, pivoted her toward the vanity, and met her eyes in the mirror. “I want you, Charlee. No games. No Roy. Just you and me.”

She nodded rapidly, pulse sprinting, and yanked her shirt over her head.

The strings on her hips dug in as he gripped the back of her thong and ripped it off. His belt buckle rattled. The sound of the zipper followed. His smoldering eyes reflected in the mirror and the nudge of his cock between her legs stole her breath. A few strokes through her folds moistened his entry. He pushed, working in and out, delaying the fullness.

She pushed her hips back, chasing his length. He sprawled a hand over her heart, the other crossed her belly and wrapped around her hip. Seizing her eyes in the mirror, he crashed his hips into her, fully buried.

The reflection of his parted lips and soundless gasp mimicked hers. They inhaled as one, absorbing the stimulation of their union.

“Best feeling in the world,” he breathed, stroking his length, hands enveloping her breasts. “You *are* my world.”

He pulled out, scooped her up, and laid her face up on the floor. She didn’t have time to question him. In the next breath, he was on her, in her, and kissing her with ferocity.

She responded with equaled ardor, bucking her hips and deepening the kiss. His hands burned over her thighs, squeezed her ass and caressed her clit with talented fingers.

Dragging her nails up his arms, mindful to avoid his back, she raked her hands through his hair. With an upward flex of her hips, she clenched her inner muscles and watched with happiness as his head fell back and the tendons in his throat strained.

Her flesh tingled, her nerve endings alive with arousal. His legs rubbed and twined with hers as he pumped in and out.

She raised her hips, meeting his thrusts, the urgency building with each heady stroke. Her cunt stretched, swollen, primed, ready.

“Charlee. Charlee, baby. Oh God, I’m—”

“Don’t stop. Shit, shit, I’m coming,” she screamed, and the sound surprised her, the pleasure spiraling through her body.

His shout followed on the heels of hers, and he ground to a halting collapse of limbs. He released a ragged breath and rolled to her side, half-draping her, his thigh between hers. "You came? Just like that?"

She cupped his jaw and padded her thumb over his lips. "Guess my liberation was waiting for yours."

Their bodies entwined, and his face inches from hers, there was something missing from his unblinking eyes as he regarded her. They were clear and focused, the flecks of the gold in the brown brighter.

Uncertainty. That was what was missing. His chin lifted a little higher. His shoulders sat farther back. The fingers on her waist were pliant and still. The afterglow of sex? She didn't think so.

"What now?" She arched up and kissed his swollen bottom lip.

He moaned, smiled. "Now, you finish my tattoo."

She did, naked and humming. Six hours later, her back ached, her hand was numb, but her heart was light and purring with eagerness.

She led him back to the bathroom and turned his back to the mirror. Chewing a nail, she calmed under his gaze. There were no more mountains between them. Exposed, vulnerable, and fearless with one another, they couldn't have been any closer. "Okay. Take a look."

"I leveled the house in Canada." He pulled her hand from her mouth and traced the skin between her fingers. "Burned down the shed and rebuilt on the land. I want to live there again. I could hunt like my father. The cabin has a studio. I could write music there." He entwined their fingers. "Live there with me. The landscapes and wildlife are some of the most picturesque countryside in the world. You could sketch the terrain from the back porch. Or I could hire a pilot to take you town where you could tattoo—"

"I would love to." She raised their hands and kissed his knuckles. For the first time in nine years, she let herself imagine a future without Roy. Dreamy as it was, it gave her power. Jay deserved that future, and she would do anything to make sure he got it.

His gorgeous smile filled his face, and he held up the mirror. Long moments passed. His smile faltered, his gaze fixed on the reflection in his hand.

The black flames danced over his back, reaching for his shoulders and giving an illusion of melting skin in its path. The skin, a blend of real and drawn scars, shriveled away, exposing peeks of riveted steel beneath.

Pride buzzed through her bloodstream. If he didn't tell her he loved it, she'd…she'd give him a stiff knee to the happy sacks.

He lowered the mirror and set it on the counter. Slowly, irritatingly, his gaze climbed to meet hers. Expression unreadable, he stared at her for a few breathless seconds.

She opened her mouth to demand a response, and his arms came around her, lips falling over hers. His tongue stroked, his kiss tender and giving. It spiraled through her and curled her toes.

Pulling her close, he caressed her with the slide of lips, the nuzzle of his nose. His cheek burned over her face as he trailed kisses over her jaw. Returning to her mouth, he fed her his appreciation, nourishing her, loving her.

Fuck words. Actions were louder. She melted in his arms and decided it was the safest place she could ever be.

79

Bands of natural light leaked through the privacy curtain of Jay's bunk. A murmur of voices whispered in from the front lounge. He rubbed his eyes and pressed a kiss into the mass of red hair tangled over his pillow. He thought his lips met Charlee's cheekbone. Maybe her jaw. Hard to tell under that thick, gorgeous mane.

Careful not to wake her, he tugged on a pair of shorts and crawled out. Joints creaking, he tumbled into the aisle. The skin was tight around his two-day old tat. He loved that feeling, a reminder of her gift and the permanence of its hold.

He hadn't paid her for her work, but he didn't need to. What she didn't know was he'd made her co-owner on all his accounts, and she was now the sole beneficiary in his will. His parents' mistake wouldn't be repeated, and Charlee would never be without money again.

He took a piss, brushed his teeth, and strode through the lounge, giving Tony and Nathan a chin lift. When Ella looked up from her laptop and smiled, he reluctantly smiled back.

"Mornin', Jay! Don't you forget to check that schedule now," she called after him as he jumped down the stairs to the exit.

She greeted him every day with the same prompting. He refused to remind her a third time that one of the few things he liked about touring was stumbling off the bus when he woke, comatose and foggy, not knowing where they were or what time it was. Unawareness had a calming effect.

His bare feet hit the rocky ground, and he stretched his arms to the mist-laden sky. Four waiting guards flanked him as he crossed the lot to the guardrail. High above the terrain, the rolling landscape extended for miles in every direction.

Lush green hills emerged from wisps of ground-hovering clouds. The humid air plastered to his skin, the aroma mossy and alive. The single building of bathrooms and rows of parking spaces stood out in the otherwise undeveloped scenic overlook. That and the parade of buses and Suburbans.

The surreal vista swayed in waves of silver green, rich with life and energy. Not unlike his state of mind. His thoughts were light, his heart lighter. His triggers seemed to have surrendered with his memories. It was as though he'd scaled a mountain and had roosted at the top.

Footsteps crunched on the gravel, approaching from behind. "We're in Northern Arkansas. Pretty, ain't it?" Ella asked.

His shoulders shot to his ears. So much for the calming effect. He kept his gaze fixed on the view.

She stepped around him and offered a mug of coffee. "You don't like me, do ya?"

Accepting the cup, he raised it to his mouth. It was the Hawaiian blend he kept in the back of the cabinet. Dark roast and black, the way he liked it. No surprise she'd been paying attention. "I don't like anyone. Ask around." He didn't like any of his tour managers. They were too often intrusive and demanding, assigning rigorous schedules and nagging endlessly about itineraries and travel expenses.

"I see." Her face crumpled.

For fuck's sake. "You're a nice girl. Don't take it personally. Just do your job *quietly*, and we'll get along fine."

She nodded, molding a smile in her creased expression. "We're fixin' to roll out in a few minutes. Gotta be in Little Rock in a couple hours. After the sound check, we need to check into the hotel suites—" Her gaze flicked over his shoulder, and her smile wavered.

Hands ambled around his waist, and a tight little body pressed against his lower back. He handed his mug to Ella and twisted in the circle of arms.

Darts of silver shimmered in the blue eyes smiling up at him. Heaven help him. "You're so fucking beautiful."

Her rosy lips bowed up. "Still not tired of hearing that."

With one hand framing her face, he cupped the back of her thigh and lifted her to straddle his hips. She crossed her ankles over his ass and drew his bottom lip between hers.

He'd never get enough of this woman. He spread kisses over her mouth. "Mmm. Morning."

"It's four in the afternoon," Ella huffed.

Charlee pushed her hands through his hair. "Mmm. Coffee. It tastes like morning on your lips."

"Ella." He nibbled and licked at Charlee's mouth. "Some

privacy?" Another nip. "We'll be along shortly."

"Sure thing."

80

Three hours later, Charlee cruised the dining room in the rear of the Little Rock arena, one hand in Jay's, the other gripping her growling stomach.

"You should've eaten on the bus." He narrowed his eyes at her as he led her along the tables.

Brisket, sourdough rolls, coleslaw, potato salad, and a dozen other catered dishes scattered the surfaces. The hearty fragrance of liquid smoke and seasonings produced another rumble in her belly.

"Let's see. Microwave burrito on the bus? Or catered meal? Hmm..." She slammed to a halt. "Oh, wow. Is that—"

She released his hand and lurched toward a small bowl filled with a smooth yellow mixture specked with green and orange chunks. She fumbled for a spoon and dug through it. Chopped eggs, pickles, oranges. She thought her favorite dish was her own secret concoction. Apparently, it was a catered side in Arkansas.

"What the hell is that?" He scrunched his nose.

"This is the way to my heart, Jay. Pay attention. Egg salad. Mandarin oranges. Chopped gherkins." She cradled the bowl to her chest and shoveled in the first bite. The tangy sweet ambrosia launched her taste buds into a writhing orgasm. "Oh, God. I'm so not sharing this."

His lips rolled, working to contain his laughter. "I don't think you'll be fighting anyone off."

He was right about that. An hour later, she plodded after him to the edge of the stage, the entire bowl of egg salad pitching violently in her stomach. She perched on an Anvil case and wrapped her arms around her waist.

The din of screaming fans thundered from the stands, inciting a rip-roaring headache. She moaned.

"Charlee?" Brown eyes hovered as he squatted before her. His hand prodded her brow, cheek, and neck. "Fuck, she's burning up."

Another hand followed the same path, less gentle. "I'm going to take her to the hotel." Nathan raised her chin and lifted one of her eyelids.

"Stop." She swatted at his hand and a burn hit low in her belly, doubling her over.

"One minute till show time." Faye skidded next to Jay, swiping a finger over her phone screen, with Ella on her heels. Faye glanced up. "Oh honey, you don't look so good."

"I'm fine." Nausea twisted her insides. A chill chased the sweat on her spine. Ugh, she'd eaten too much.

The guitar intro tiptoed in, hushing the roar of the crowd. Jay remained in a crouch between her legs, worry wrinkling the skin around his eyes.

She spread clammy fingers over his cheek and attempted a smile. Her hand fell away, limp and trembling. Dammit. "Your fans are waiting. Go do your thing and blow them away."

His jaw set, and his fists flexed on his thighs. He jerked his chin at Nathan. "Take all the guards with you except Tony." Eyes boring into her, he rose, mouthed, "Love you." Shifting into the shadowed corner beside her, he clicked a button on his headset and rolled into the first verse of *Running Up That Hill*, a Kate Bush cover song.

For a moment, the pain dimmed as she absorbed the calming tones of his timbre. He sang the song like *Placebo*, eerie and dark, a soul-deep vibration.

Another pang slammed into her. She cupped her mouth and swung her head, catching Nathan's eyes.

He half-carried, half-ran her to the nearest bathroom. Standing over her, he gathered her hair as she heaved bile and eggs. After a few more violent projections, she gasped, spit, and slumped to the tile floor.

"I don't know what's worse." He muffled his mouth in his arm as he kicked the flusher. "The smell or the fact that I recognize ninety-nine percent of what came up. Eggs? Did you even chew them?"

A shiver battered through her and her mouth teemed with saliva. "I don't feel good."

"I know, sweetheart." He lifted her in the cradle of his arms, set her on the vanity, and wet a paper towel under the tap. "Can you make it to the hotel before you toss any more eggs?"

"Funny guy." She yanked the towel from his hand and wiped her face and mouth. She didn't want to go and abandon Jay with only one guard, but it would've been an argument she didn't have the strength for. "Better scrounge up a trash bag or it might be a really long ten-minute drive."

81

Charlee emerged from oblivion with a throbbing head and a sandpaper tongue. She patted the bed through the dark. Cold and empty. She was in the suite she shared with Jay, but where was he? "Jay? Nathan?"

The dim light beyond the bedroom door caught flickers of a pacing silhouette. She shuffled through the room and stopped at the threshold.

Phone to his ear, Nathan's expression was severe, cheeks crimson. He looked up. "She's awake. Call you right back."

She toyed with wet strands of her hair. Must not have been asleep that long. "What's wrong?"

"How do you feel?" He approached her, rested a palm on her forehead. "Fever's broke."

"Who were you talking to? Was that Jay? Is the show over?" Why wasn't he there? She shook off the paranoia creeping over her.

He dropped his hand. "Anymore nausea? Diarrhea?"

She sunk into her shoulders. He'd officially seen it all. At least she'd had enough coherency to wipe her own ass and administer her shower in privacy. "No. I think it's passed. No more egg salad. Ever."

That didn't produce that smile she was expecting. The nausea returned. "Is it Jay? Where is he?"

He studied the black screen on his phone. "Charlee... He... Fuck!" He spun and paced through the room. "The show ended two hours ago. He's...he's in the hotel."

Some of the tension unclenched in her stomach. "So he's safe? Roy doesn't—"

"No, Roy doesn't fucking have him. He's safe for the moment."

For the moment? "Did he do something to piss you off? What are you not telling me?"

His pacing made helter-skelter zigzags through the sitting room, his hands on his hips, eyes on the floor.

Head spinning, she reeled into the bedroom, flicking on lights and shoving on a clean pair of jeans. "He's in the hotel? Where?" she shouted as she tagged the water bottle from the table and gulped it down. Turning, she slammed into Nathan. "Take me to him."

He scrubbed a hand over his face and stared at her out of hard eyes. "Tony's with him. It's in her employment contract. Fuck, it's my contract not to interfere." He pressed a fist against his thinned lips, his eyes flicking through the room, divulging nothing.

Her heart galloped a furious tempo. Was Jay drunk? Oh, God, was it drugs? *Please don't let it be drugs.* "What's. Not. In the contract?"

Lifting his phone, he tapped the screen and held it to his ear. "We're on our way...Yes, *We*."

Without meeting her eyes, he treaded to the door and stepped into the hallway. He spoke in low tones to the dozen or so guards lining the corridor. Something about formations and doorways. She didn't pay attention, her mind whirling through a binge of scenarios. Jay passed out in the lobby. Jay swimming in his own puke in the hotel pool. Jay spread out beneath a mob of naked groupies. Her stomach bucked.

She trailed Nathan's stiff stride down the hall. Maybe hers was just as stiff. She couldn't feel her legs amidst the confusion of emotions gripping her body. Rather than turning toward the banks of elevators, he continued toward the opposite wing. As with most hotels, the band leased the entire top floor. He was in another room? With one of the guys maybe?

Tony's rigid profile appeared ahead. As Charlee drew near, she didn't detect anything different about the guard's stance, but the look in Tony's eyes flooded her with dread. She knew that look, saw it in the faces of Jay's friends when they'd learned about her past.

Standing in front of Tony, she squared her shoulders and met the Marine's gaze. "Whose room is this?"

"Ella's."

Her shield surfaced, an internal reaction, one she hadn't experienced in years. It spread over her body and shrouded her heart. Beside her, barely-restrained rage fumed from Nathan. She'd deal with him in a moment. "Is he high?"

Tony didn't blink. "Yes, ma'am."

The shield wavered with the cracking twinge in her chest. Disappointment rocked her body. She dug the heel of her bare foot into the carpet, a subtle thing, but it rooted her. "Do you know who gave him the drugs or when he took them?"

"No. I watch his surroundings. It's not my job to notice a sleight of hand between friends."

Maybe one of the roadies, then. Forget it. The how or who wouldn't undo the damage. She just hoped... What? That it was a mistake? That there was another explanation? That he hadn't shit on the trust she'd given him. Again. What a fool she was.

The door to Ella's room glared at her. She knew she was stalling. She had to go in there, but it might destroy her.

Tony shifted her weight. "It's against my contract to dictate where he goes. I can only advise."

"But you called Nathan so I would know."

Her face softened. "It's the best I could do. I'm sorry, Charlee."

"Me too." She stood taller and faced Nathan. "I'm going in there alone. No punching on Jay, unless it's defensive."

He gave her a reluctant nod, his chest puffed out, muscles seemingly ready to ignore her.

"I mean it. No drama, okay?" Fuck, was she strong enough? How would she survive this? A clog of heartache choked her voice.

Tony swiped a card key and turned the handle.

Charlee wasn't sure how long she stared at the crack in the door. Her armor quivered around her, her blood seemed to have drained from her body. Tingling and numb, she walked through the door.

82

The scene that greeted Charlee locked her limbs and stole her breath.

Jay lay nude on his back, his erection glistening with the saliva stringing from Ella's mouth. She glanced up, naked and straddling his legs, then leaned down, lips parted to resume her ministrations.

"Get off of him. Now." Charlee's calm tone was at odds with the turmoil shaking her body. Oh God, oh God. Keep it together. This was not happening. He was not allowing this.

Ella licked her lips. "Now darlin', that's up to him." She gestured at the man between her legs.

He stared at the ceiling, moaning and bucking his hips.

The urge to run from the room and give into the tears burning the back of her eyes was overwhelming. She straightened her back and moved toward the bed. "Get the fuck off of him."

The bitch dropped her head and wrapped her mouth around his dick.

Charlee swung, and the back of her hand crunched into the bridge of Ella's nose.

Screaming, Ella fell off the bed, cupping her face. "He begged me to fuck him, you jealous cunt."

Jay clutched the bed sheets, eyes closed, hips thrusting the air.

Her words hurt. Hurt so fucking much as they splintered inside her, shredding her to a million useless pieces. "Did he call you Charlee?" Her reedy voice echoed in her ears.

Ella dropped her hands and climbed to her feet. "Yes." She smirked. "I hear he calls us all Charlee."

It was a punch in the gut, one that stole the last of her composure. She unleashed her fist and caught Ella's nose in the same place.

Blood spurted over her wailing mouth. She wiped at the mess uselessly, panic flaring her eyes.

Charlee stretched her fingers and curled them again at the sight of blood staining her knuckles. “Get out before I start punching on your underdeveloped tits.”

A sharp inhale interrupted the woman’s sobs. She gathered her clothes, tugging them on as she ran to the door.

She balled her fist and turned toward the bed.

Eyes squeezed shut, his hand wrapped around his erection, hips pumping manically. A groan rumbled low in his throat.

Her stomach turned, and her feet carried lead weights as she trudged toward him, fighting back tears. “Jay.”

His eyes flashed open, roamed over the ceiling, and his hand fell to his side. “Charlee?”

She closed the final few feet and sat on the mattress beside his hip, placing his erection outside of her periphery. “What did you take?” She waded through what she’d read in the file he’d given her. What drugs increased libido? “Was it ecstasy? Meth?” Neither of those had been starred in his list.

Could Roy have orchestrated this? Drugged him somehow? Jay only drank bottled water during his shows. And Roy’s drugs would’ve knocked him unconscious, not sent him into mindless arousal. She knew the effects of Roy’s concoctions too well.

Besides, Jay had proven he could slip back into drug use under the right circumstances. She couldn’t trust him.

His eyebrows pulled together, and his gaze bobbed over her face, unfocused. “I didn’t take anything.”

Anger burned through her cheeks. “Okay, then you were sober while you fucked Ella’s mouth. That makes it all better.”

He curled to a sitting position, awkward and sluggish, and his eyes landed on his erection as if seeing it for the first time. He gripped it, stroked. “Ah, God, Charlee. I need... I need to fuck you. Come here, baby.” He reached for her.

Heart sprinting, she jumped from the bed and backed toward the door. His betrayal was unlike anything she’d ever felt. It was a riptide, slamming into her over and over, pulling her under. Her knees buckled, and a sob crawled through her throat.

She gripped a cabinet and swallowed helplessly, unable to gather enough air. “I trusted you. I loved you so goddamned much. I... I—” She slapped a hand over her mouth, gulped harsh breaths, her voice reaching high-pitched hysterics.

He stared at her, but she was certain he wasn’t hearing, wasn’t seeing. He fell upon his back and resumed his self-pleasure.

"You broke my heart," she whispered from the emptiness inside her. Opening the door with measured and determined movements, she stepped into the hall.

83

Charlee clicked the door behind her, the pain wrenching her chest, cutting off her air. Just a few more minutes and she could finally break down.

"Will you call Laz?" She stared at the button on Tony's shirt, not wanting to see the pity sagging those steel gray eyes. "He'll know how to deal with whatever drug is in his system. Make sure he doesn't…overdose." She cleared her throat. "Get him back to his room safely. I won't be joining him."

"Of course."

Nathan gripped Charlee's chin, raised it. His eyes were fierce and imposing. He wouldn't ask her if she was okay. Not if he was reading her face. "I had our things packed. Our bags are downstairs. Was that…? Is that what you want?"

Bless him for his foresight and saving her that dreadful task. "Thank you." She moved toward the cluster of guards, knowing what would come next. Jay's actions didn't just impact her. They hurt Nathan, too.

Nathan wrapped his arms around Tony's waist and leaned his forehead against hers. They spoke softly, Tony nodding, her face drawn and her lip sucked in.

Maybe Charlee could convince him to come back before they left Little Rock. What could she say to make him stay with Tony? The throb in her head magnified with the pain stabbing her heart.

He cupped Tony's face, kissed her deeply, passionately. Charlee turned away and swatted at the tracks of tears burning her cheeks.

A moment later, his hand slid over her limp one. "Let's go."

As Nathan led her to the elevators, she plodded beside him, borrowing his strength to move her legs, to leave behind the guards and their semblance of safety. The further they walked, the more brittle her spine felt.

Should she have handled it differently with Jay? Maybe waited until morning to talk to him when he was sober? What if she misinterpreted what happened? Betrayal gripped her insides. There was no way to misunderstand Ella's mouth wrapped around his more-than-willing erection. She choked, muffled it behind trembling lips.

Bags in hand, Nathan led her to a waiting cab, his eyes scanning the street and windows of nearby buildings. Following her in, he barked an address at the driver. They made it a block before her grief exploded, trembling her body, clogging her sinuses, and soaking her face. She let it go, let him hold her as she wept the broken pieces.

By the time they pulled into an underground garage of some swanky hotel, her eyes were dry, and her breathing had returned to normal. Emptiness set in, deadening her. In a shocked haze, she followed Nathan out and froze.

Edison, one of *The Burn*'s bodyguards, waited behind the wheel of a nondescript subcompact car.

She backed up. "No, I'm not going—"

"He's driving us somewhere." Nathan shoved her face first into the backseat, tossed their bags on the floorboard, and crawled over her, his weight pressing her down.

The car moved, but he didn't. "We were probably followed. This should throw him off."

Right. Of course. Roy was always watching. Numb and drained from crying, she concentrated on loosening her trembling muscles.

The car stopped. Another underground parking lot. With a nod at Edison, she trailed Nathan up the stairwell and through a tiny hotel lobby.

The mechanics of check-in and bedtime preparation went by in a blur, and she lay on one of the double beds in their shared room, blinking through the dark. Her body, exhausted and weak, would not shut down.

"You want to talk about it?" His bed creaked with his movements.

"I want you to stay with Tony." Silence. Her chest squeezed. She pushed on. "Do you love her?"

"Yes."

"I'm going to move forward on my own, Nathan. I have to." Her heartbeat sputtered in terror. "I have twenty grand. I'll hire a lawyer and a bodyguard until I can build a case against Roy."

His sigh tumbled through the darkness. "If it were that easy, we would've done that three years ago. If you don't want to talk about what happened with Jay, go to sleep. We'll discuss everything else in the morning with clear heads."

Shifting to her side, her back to Nathan, she buried her stinging eyes in the pillow. The horrible feeling clawing inside her had been preventable. She didn't have to fall in love with a drug addict. She'd let him in, fully aware of the risks. Hell, he'd given her a manual bulleting all the fucking dangers. Yet, looking back, would she have changed anything? A tear skipped down her cheek. She loved him. She would always love him.

"For what it's worth..." He shifted, rustling the bedding. "Jay's behavior tonight was unexpected. It doesn't feel right. He loves you, Charlee. I don't think he'd ever intentionally hurt you. I don't... I just don't understand why he did it."

A blast of jealous anger broke through the heartache. Image after image of his dick in Ella's mouth, his hips thrusting, and his mouth parted in ecstasy. She wanted to flush out the acidic hate eating through her gut, and she knew how.

She'd make the phone call in the morning. There were Doms in every city, and she knew enough of them. Someone would be able to give her a referral in Little Rock, Arkansas. Tomorrow, she would replace the internal ache with physical pain, and regain some fucking control.

One decision made, she embraced it, narrowed all her thoughts on it. Her muscles loosened, and her head sunk into the pillow.

"Thank you for seeing me on such short notice." Charlee sat on the edge of the chair in Master Conrad's home office in downtown Little Rock.

The wood boards creaked outside the door under Nathan's angry back-and-forth circuit. She detested that he came but couldn't muster the energy to fight with him.

The middle-aged man behind the desk leaned back, his shoulders stretching beyond the chair back. His huge frame dominated the room, his deportment more so. Clipped black hair shaped his olive complexion. The sharp lines of his square jaw reminded her of a battle-hardened Marine, but he'd disclosed his day job was in real estate.

"When was your last BDSM scene?" He stared at her, unmoving in his perusal, a characteristic common to every Dom she'd met.

Duke in New York had been her last contract. "Two months ago."

"Master Duke e-mailed your contract. With your permission, of course."

Of course. Duke had referred her to Conrad that morning.

"Why are you here?"

The question startled her. Did revenge pour from her eyes? Was her hatred bleeding from her pores? If she told him the truth, he'd send her on her way. "I need help moving past an emotional barrier."

He studied her for a long moment with apathetic eyes. "Very good." With two fingers, he twirled the paperwork on this desk to face her and pushed it across the mahogany surface. "Look over the contract. Cross off anything you want to exclude from our scene. Write in anything you want to include."

Leaning forward, she accepted the pen and scanned the document, pausing on the punishments clause.

Punishment of the sub is subject to certain rules designed to protect the sub from intentional abuse or permanent bodily harm.

Punishment must not incur permanent bodily harm, or the following forms of abuse:

Death

Damage that involves loss of mobility

Permanent marks on the skin, including scars, burns, piercing or tattoos

Breaking of the sub's bones

Dismemberment

Burning of the sub's body

Drawing blood

Dramatic loss of circulation

Internal bleeding

Loss of consciousness

Cutting or pulling out the sub's hair

Her pulse hurtled through her veins as she thought, not for the first time, that she should mail a copy of this contract to Roy.

Satisfied with the definition of punishment, she skimmed until she reached the hard limits.

No scat or fecal play

No public nudity

No verbal humiliation

No unprotected intercourse

No anal

Restricted physical humiliation: No licking shoes, eating dirt, simulating dog/cat such as eating from the floor and crawling on all fours, etc.

"If you don't have any changes to the limits, initial here." He tapped the box on the contract.

She scrawled her initials and moved the sub's role, lingering on the section she'd anticipated.

The sub shall keep her body available for the use of her Dom at all times. This includes and is not limited to sexual intercourse: vaginal and oral. The sub acknowledges that her Dom may use her body or mind in any manner He wishes within the parameters of safety and any limitations in this Contract. He may hurt her without reason to please Himself.

He rested his forearms on the desk, his presence filling the distance between them, shrinking her. "Sexual intercourse was included in your contract with Master Duke. It's not a common practice in my dungeon, but I will honor it should you choose to include it. Condoms will be used, but I require a second form of birth control. Write your birth control in the space provided or cross out the clause to exclude it. Then initial in the box provided."

A heavy weight pushed down on her chest. If she had sex with the Dom, would she be doing it to balance the hurt Jay had inflicted on her? Would she feel vindicated after? The thought of going back to clinical, negotiated fucking festered in her gut.

Conrad watched her steadily, his face smooth and slack. His nose was slightly bent, his lips a bit too thin, and his hair was too short, too dark. Jesus, he wasn't Jay, but she didn't feel even a twitch of attraction. Still, wasn't intercourse the reason she was there? To flush out the jealousy by lowering herself to the same level? It was wrong. She was so fucked up, yet she continued to mull over it. Eventually, she made the required adjustments, finished the read-through, and signed by the *X*.

"Before we proceed," Conrad said, eyes on her. "Explain the man pacing outside."

"He's my bodyguard, but he won't interfere."

Not a wrinkled movement in his face. Not even narrowed eyes. He stood. "Follow the hall to the end. Remove your clothes at the door. Inside, assume the submissive position by the St. Andrew's Cross. Once you enter the dungeon, you are my sub. Your body belongs to me."

"Yes, Sir." She rose on wobbly legs, a cluster of fear, uncertainty, and excitement battling through her.

Nathan's gaze bore into her back as she walked down the hall and stripped her clothing. Naked, she stepped inside and drew in a shuddering breath.

85

"I didn't take any fucking drugs!" Jay's pulse thundered in his ears. He swung his head, meeting the glares of his so-called friends, as he marched through the suite, trying his damnedest not to hurl nearby lamps and vases. "Tell me! Where the fuck is she?"

Tony stood by the window, holding onto her stubborn reticence.

He whirled on her, finger trembling as he aimed it at her face. "You know where she is. Tell me, goddammit!"

"I promised Nathan. I will *not* betray him."

Betray. There it was. The accusation by the one person who witnessed his blackout from beginning to end. Even then, she didn't believe him. How could he defend himself when he didn't remember a damned thing since the end of the show?

He woke thirty minutes ago with Laz slapping his face and screaming at him about how Charlee caught Ella sucking his dick. What the fucking hell? His anger leaked from his muscles, and he collapsed on the couch, face in his hands and stomach rolling.

He deserved this. His past mistakes clung to his back, as eternal as his tattoo. "I was drugged." What did he drink at the arena? Bottled water. Nothing else. Was the cap sealed? "Who delivered our water? Where did it come from?"

"The production company provides it." Faye sat beside him and straightened nonexistent wrinkles in her skirt. "Ella passed out the bottles last night."

His hammering pulse returned with vengeance and his fingers curled into fists. "Call her. Get her in here right now."

Faye nodded and scurried from room.

He jumped up and stepped into Tony's unwavering posture. "If you're not going to tell me where she is, at least send the protective team to her."

"We're supposed to be on the road, Mr. Mayard. The buses are waiting."

"She's all alone out there." His voice was harsh even to his own ears. "Goddammit, Tony." He spun away, hands curled in a helpless clench.

"The next two shows are smaller venues." Wil rested his hands on Jay's shoulders, his touch hesitant, his eyes less so. "We'll cancel them. Refund the money. This is important, Jay. We're all in agreement. Make sure your girl is safe."

Desperate for the support Wil was offering, Jay dragged him into an embrace, one he'd never shared with the man. His pounding heart pulverized his chest, threatened to bring him to his knees. "Thanks." His voice broke, and he stepped back. "I didn't do it. I was set up. I was—" Drugged. Poisoned. He jerked his head around the room, met the stark faces of Rio, Laz, Tony, and six or so bodyguards. "Did any one eat the egg salad yesterday?"

"No one touched that nasty shit." Rio rubbed his bald head. "We would've had to pry it from Charlee's hands anyway."

A chill sped down Jay's spine. "She got sick at the show last night. The egg salad..." Oh God. Oh fucking no. "This goddamned nightmare has Roy written all over it. Poisoning Charlee forces her to leave my side. Drugging my water gives Ella the opportunity to drag me to her room." His blood boiled, exploded. His fist flew and crashed into the sheetrock, spraying dust into the air.

"Calm down, man." Laz sidled between him and the crumbling wall. "We'll figure this out."

The door opened, and Faye hauled in a blank-faced Ella by the arm.

Ella wrestled away. "I get it, okay? I'm fired. I was just leaving."

Jay's muscles contracted with revulsion. "What the fuck happened to your southern accent?"

She shrugged, her gaze trained somewhere over his shoulder.

"Sit down." He thrust a finger at the couch.

Her sashay carried her across the room, but there was a wobble in her step as she neared. When she sat, he leaned over her and let her feel the rage pouring off him. "What did you put in Charlee's lunch?"

Her entire body flinched, and her wide eyes landed on his for the first time. "I don't know anything about that."

He glanced at Tony, knew if she could be convinced of his innocence, she'd take him to Charlee. Her taut jaw gave nothing away.

"What did you put in my water?" His tone was powered with lethal anger. "Speak carefully. Administering narcotics to another is

Assault in the Second Degree. I can make this go very, very bad for you."

She pinned her lips.

Rio's knee appeared beside her hip, and he lowered his bald head inches from her face, his big body vibrating with unleashed fury.

Perfect. Jay could use Rio's intimidation to his advantage. He leaned in. "Listen up, little girl. Rio doesn't give a fuck about assault in any degree." He grabbed her hand and pulled it toward Rio. "He'll start with your fingers and move up your arms, breaking every weak, pathetic bone until you tell us what you know."

Rio uncurled her index finger and slowly bent it backward.

She gasped and covered her mouth with her free hand, fingers shaking. "No. You can't do that."

Rio bent it further, and the intent look in his eye made Jay wonder if he'd really do it.

A wail tore for her throat, and she jerked her arm uselessly in Jay's clutch. "I...I don't know. I was given a vial. He told me to dilute it in your water. He...he..."

They released her, and she crumpled into her shoulders, hands pressed to her tear-drenched lips.

Rising to his full height, he closed his eyes, inhaled deeply, and pierced her with unleashed hatred. "Roy Oxford."

Her quivering chin jerked up and down. "He approached me at the restaurant where I waited tables, offered me a lot of money." She whispered, "He's scary."

"Did the scary man tell you to rape me?" *Rape* sat like acid on his tongue. It had damaged so many years. His. Charlee's. He would *not* allow it to take anymore.

Her wailing escalated into howling sobs. "I...I di...didn't know." More yowling. "He said...said you'd fuck me...and...and he'd handle any repercussion."

Tony's hushed voice murmured over the wailing. On the phone, head down, she relayed the information. After a second of silence, she glanced up and met his eyes. The surprise widening hers knocked his knees. Then her face smoothed. "Thanks, Nathan. We're on our way."

"Is she okay?" He chased her swift pace to the door.

"Yes. Only a few blocks down the road."

Relief cascaded over his tense muscles, and his shoulders rolled back. "Faye, will you deal with that?" He thrust his chin at the weeping bitch on the couch.

"I just reported it. Police are on their way."

He nodded and sprinted out the door to find Charlee.

86

The idleness during the five-minute drive allowed Jay's hangover to surface in a pulsating headache. At least he'd had the presence of mind to shower and brush his teeth before he'd walked into the nightmare waiting for him outside his room, the suite that had been vacant of Charlee. His heart ached.

The Suburbans rolled to a stop in front of a multi-level condominium in downtown Little Rock. He angled his neck, strained to see out the windows. Residential buildings fringed both sides of the road. His head swam. "What is this? She's not in a hotel?"

Bodyguards filed out of the three SUVs, spreading over the sidewalk and around the building.

Tony opened the door. "I advise we discuss it inside, Mr. Mayard." She stepped out, alert and irritating in her formality.

In other words, she expected him to make a scene, one she wanted to manage. Dread mounted on his already tight shoulders.

Inside, Nathan answered a door on the ground floor. Jay pushed past him, sweeping through a living room decorated with modern furnishings. By whatever stroke of luck, Roy hadn't snatched Charlee the previous night. Perhaps he was waiting until she left town. Maybe he was still playing games. If the fuckwad had a pulse on this apartment, he wouldn't be able to access it now. Not with the twenty bodyguards posted at every exit, entrance, and hidey hole.

"Where's Charlee?" He ferreted around a corner and into an empty kitchen. "Where is she?"

"She's here." Nathan tailed him, curling a fold of papers in his hands. "She's..." He held out the unraveling documents. "Here. This is her copy of the contract. I don't know what she's told you, but this will explain her *therapy*. This is why she's here."

Accepting the pages with numb fingers, Jay didn't need to read them. He knew her what her *therapy* entailed. Intimately. Every muscle in his body readied in preparation to kill a motherfucking Dom. "Which room?" He twisted around Nathan.

His back hit the wall, pinned beneath Nathan's weight.

"She thinks you betrayed her." Nathan shoved his forearm against Jay's jugular, applying enough pressure to prick a burn behind his eyes. "I've watched her endure an ungodly amount of suffering over the years. She's hurting. This is the only way she knows how to deal with it. Look..." Nathan released him and yanked the contract from his hand, opening it to the second page. "See? She excluded all sexual activity from the scene. She's here for the pain."

Jay read the paragraph twice. Flipping to the beginning, he read the entire contract, each section shedding more light on her therapy.

Stepping back, Nathan rubbed his eyes. "I know why she does this, but I hate it. Makes me sick. She needs treatment, Jay. Conventional treatment. She's broken inside."

The hairs on Jay's nape bristled, and a fevered vehemence swelled through him. "*Nothing* about her is broken. She's the strongest fucking person you will ever have the privilege of knowing. Say that shit again and you'll be eating through a straw for the rest of your miserable life. Got me?"

Nathan's brows shot up his forehead, and his mouth hung open. Then his cheeks twitched, and his gaping mouth spread into a toothy grin. "Last door at the end of the hall."

Purpose surged through Jay's blood as he weaved through the crowd of bodyguards, past the living room and down the hall. He could break down the door, raise ten kinds of fist-swinging hell, and distress her more than he already had. Or he could knock, ask to observe, and maybe gain more insight into how he could give her what she needed.

He raised his fist and tapped on the door. After a painfully long moment and one...two...three lock clicks, the door cracked to the length of a short chain.

Two narrowed eyes peered out, widened. "Well, I'll be damned. Jay Mayard from *The Burn* is standing in my hallway."

"Fucking hell." Charlee's adorable mutter floated through the crack and nuzzled his heart.

The eyes behind the door vanished as the man turned his back. "Is *he* the emotional barrier?"

"The worst kind." Venom tightened her voice.

Jay choked. Worse than Roy? He couldn't condemn her anger, but fuck, that didn't make it any easier to swallow. "I'm the boyfriend. I get that she hates me. I just need one minute to change her mind about that."

"Go away, Jay." A muffled stomp accompanied her shout.

One kick. One fucking kick would snap the chain on the door, and he'd be in the path of her gorgeous—albeit furious—glare. Big breath. "Charlee, please don't make me do this from the hallway. I'm only asking for one minute."

The silence was so stifling he thought he might pass out from the anxiety of it.

"Sixty seconds," she said. "Then Master Conrad has permission to toss your deceitful, cheating ass to the curb."

Ouch. That was vicious, but if she'd been indifferent and numb he would've been more worried. He could deal with her ire.

The door snapped shut and reopened all the way. Only one end of the room was visible. She was hidden around the corner. *Master* Conrad stepped aside and locked them in.

As Jay sized him up, he knew the other man was doing the same. Alpha male? Yep. Wielding weapons? Nope, unless Jay counted the guy's fifty extra pounds of muscle. That settled, he moved around the bend and froze.

Sweet Mother of God. Bent at the waist with legs spread, Charlee's ass arched up and out in a trussed offering. Her wrists and elbows were bound together behind her back. A long rope connected her wrists to a point on the ceiling, raising them at a horizontal position in relation to her torso, forcing her to double over. His mouth went dry.

Her hair hung in sheets from her inverted head, reaching for the floor. A metal rod connected one ankle to the other, forcing her feet to stand wider than her shoulders.

Every inch of her flawless skin was on display, but he couldn't drag his eyes from the visual feast between her legs. Her folds were swollen and glistening. The tiny pucker of her ass peeked between her spread cheeks.

His face heated, and his cock engorged. She was his, and he shook with the primal impulse to prove it.

He rolled his shoulders and reminded himself that she was probably mortified having him see her like this, considering the gut-wrenching position he was in the last time she saw him. He was there to soothe her and help her.

Moving toward her, he remembered he wasn't alone. Another fucking man shared his glorious view. A sideways glance confirmed Conrad didn't have a hard-on, and his eyes weren't directed below Charlee's waist. That saved the man from an automatic beat down.

"Forty-five seconds," she ground out.

Fuck. Shoving his hands into his pockets to dissuade himself from touching her, he shifted to squat beneath her bowed head.

Rancor burned in her eyes. "Like what you see? Where's Ella to take care of that problem in your pants?"

Christ, her hurt was palpable, a hiss singeing his skin. He coaxed his lips to smile. "I love what I see, which is why I'd never cheat on you."

Pain flashed through her glare. "Thirty seconds."

"I think Roy paid someone to poison your egg salad to separate us for the night."

Her eyebrows crawled together, her face red from the stooped position.

"Did he know you liked those little oranges in your salad?"

"Yes." A whisper. "He knows everything about me."

Not everything. The sick fuck didn't know how to make her happy. He drew in a lungful of air. "Ella confessed she was hired by Roy to drug my water and...seduce me. No doubt he expected you to catch me in the act and flee." He scooted closer, placed his fingers over the rapid pulse on her throat. "I don't remember any of it, Charlee. I don't even remember singing the encore at the show."

Her lashes dropped, fringing her cheeks. "You were hard as a rock, thrusting your dick at her, spurring her on. Drugged or not, that shit is seared into my eyes. How do I know your accusation against Ella isn't a trick to get me back on the bus?"

Bile simmered through his chest, and his fingers flexed against her neck. "I've got a metric fuckton of faults, Charlee, but I've never lied to you."

Her breath hitched, and she held it, bottom lip trembling as she searched his face.

Boots appeared beside his sneakers. "She's been in the strappado long enough. I need to let her down."

Jay nodded and climbed to his feet. This time, he didn't stop his hands from roaming her spread thighs, the horizontal line of her spine, and the silky tresses of her hair. She didn't cringe, so he continued his exploration as Conrad removed the spreader bar and untied the knots.

Conrad worked meticulously without an unwarranted touch or lustful glance. When her hands were free, Conrad cupped her wrists and offered them to him. "Massage the bound area to assist the blood flow."

Jay raised her arms, rubbing and kissing the circle of pink around her wrists.

She wiggled free from his grasp and touched a finger to his

dimple, his chin, and his lips. He held himself immobile, not breathing, waiting.

A glassy sheen slid over her hypnotic eyes and a tear escaped, glancing off her cheek. "Am I...? Are we safe here? If Roy orchestrated our separation, could he have followed me here?"

Yes. Roy was probably waiting for the right moment, trying to avoid a scene like the one at her apartment in New York. "There are twenty bodyguards surrounding this building. We're as safe here as we are on the bus."

A smile trembled on her lips and fell away. "I'm sorry I doubted you." She pulled her hand back and curled it against her belly.

He cupped her face and rested his forehead against hers. "I'm sorry I ever gave you a reason to doubt me."

She nodded, released a tattered breath, and threw her arms around his neck.

Spinning on the edge of giddiness, he kissed her face and her lips and dreamed of all the ways he wanted to make her glow. Her flesh warmed under his palms as he ran his hands down her spine and over the taut globes of her ass. "Just like heaven."

"You look like you've been through hell." She mussed his hair with one hand, the other clinging to his waist. "Have you eaten?"

He stretched his fingers around the back of her thigh and curled them between her legs. "I want to eat *you*."

"Put her on the bed and you can." Conrad appeared behind her, the rope wound over his shoulder. "That is, if you plan on sticking around for the remainder of the scene."

87

"What do you mean, the remainder of the scene?" Jay swung his head, scanning the room for Charlee's clothes. Where did she leave them?

She uncurled from his embrace and lowered to her knees, head bowed. His mind scrambled to make excuses for the change, even as he knew what the pose meant.

Conrad watched him from beneath dark brows. "The look on your face tells me you've never witnessed a scene before."

Did internet videos count? He'd also perused fetish sites while she slept, trying to glean safe techniques to use on her. "We've...played."

"How's that working for you? Both of you?" Conrad hung the rope on a hook on the wall. "Are you comfortable in your role?"

No. Not if his role meant hurting her. Jay bent, brushed the hair from her face. "Charlee, is this what you want?"

Hands folded behind her stick-straight back, she stared at the floor beneath her spread knees.

"Address me. Not her." Conrad walked to a tall cabinet. "This is *my* dungeon. *My* scene. She entered this room because *that* is what she wants."

Jay's dignity insisted she choose between him and Conrad right that goddamned minute, but he knew it would've been an ignorant thing to force on her. He was there to learn from the man, not battle him in a dick-measuring contest.

Rifling through a drawer, Conrad pulled out a form and handed it to him. "Half of my clientele are couples. Often, I'm helping one learn how to dominate or submit to the other. Sign this waiver, and we'll proceed."

Her subservient posture rooted Jay in realization. It wasn't *just* the fear that got her off. It was the submission to it. His visceral response was to drag her far away from this lifestyle, but his devotion and attachment to her had him reaching for a pen and signing the form.

Conrad returned the paper to the cabinet. "You didn't read it."

"Doesn't matter." Resolve pulsed deep in his chest.

"If I break your famous fingers, you can't sue me for ruining your career." Not a wrinkle of a grin on Conrad's face.

Great. Said fingers curled into his palms.

Conrad lowered his gaze to Charlee. "In this room, who is your Master?"

"You are, Sir."

Jay's spine snapped straight.

"Who is your other Master?" Conrad moved to the wall and retrieved a whip.

"Jay." The twitch in her cheek matched the smile in her voice. "Sir."

"Master Jay is your Master, and I am his Master."

Jay was certain the macho-egotist stated that for his benefit, but he put his own ego aside and bit back his *Go eat a dick* retort.

"Remove your clothes." Conrad leveled his gaze on him. "Place them on the chair by the door."

Her head shot up, crimson locks tangling in her blinking eyes. "Sir? He—"

"I've got this, Charlee." Jay toed off his sneakers, removed his socks, and shoved down his pants sans briefs. His cock pointed to the floor, dispirited by the chafing conversation. "The shirt is staying on."

Turning his back on Conrad's scowl, he placed his jeans beside hers on the chair and sorted through the questions storming his thoughts. "She can come without pain if she's anticipating it. If I stop hurting her, she'll stop anticipating it. Can I get her there without ever hurting her?"

"You sure you're hurting her?" Conrad unraveled the whip.

Reflections of a sandpaper belt, bamboo pole, clamps, and spankings flickered through his mind, ushered by a throb in his head. "Yeah."

He padded to her side and wondered if she was entertaining a private chuckle about his attire. He tugged on the collar of the t-shirt, the only thing he wore, and smiled. Yep. She was definitely laughing at him.

"The hurt she experiences is relative." Conrad aimed the whip at the empty side of the room and snapped it through the air.

The crack shot Jay's shoulders to his ears. Beside him, Charlee didn't flinch.

"I spoke at length with her Dom in New York. She's a masochist." Seriousness smoothed Conrad's expression. "This means she processes pain differently than we do. She feeds from it, eroticizes it." He closed the distance and stared down at her. "She may not have an ache for it every time, but if she's struggling with something, if she's having a bad day, she'll need it. If you're open with each other, she'll tell you when and how severe to make the discipline."

Were they open? Jay considered the days following the San Francisco murders and the grief she carried over the death of the nineteen-year-old girl. She'd erected a wall and refused pain during sex. Dammit, he should've prodded and recognized what she'd needed.

"BDSM is a trade of power. Many are driven to the lifestyle because of unhealthy power dynamics in past relationships." Conrad thinned his lips and scrutinized the top of Charlee's head. "Submitting to a Dom in a safe and *consensual* environment can help her prevent bad dynamics in her current relationships. It trains her how to control her responses to power, and she can find a great deal of freedom and triumph in that."

He had to give the guy credit. Conrad illustrated a logical perspective on kinksters. In fact, shit was a whole lot clearer. Since the power in BDSM play was consensual, it made it superior to the systems of power experienced in everyday life. Anyone working a job under the rules of a boss was forced into a position of nonconsensual power. Hell, the regime at Windsor Records dictated how he smiled and what songs to write. Discriminations on social castes, gender, sexual preferences, and race were other forms of power. All nonconsensual.

Jay placed a hand on her head, sifting fingers through her satiny hair. Abuse and rape, the most potent case of nonconsensual power, was why she was there. Time to find out if he could give her the control she sought, in an authentic dungeon, under the watchful eyes of a professional.

No pressure. He steadied his breath, relaxed his limbs, and sat on the edge of the low mattress. "Charlee. Come here. On your knees."

She crawled the distance to Jay, her eyes locked on his rising cock. As if her stare had cast a hardening spell, he swelled to full length.

He skimmed a finger over her bottom lip. "What's your safe word?"

"Huntress."

"Suck me." Imparting those words pumped determination through his veins and a throb to his groin.

Kneeling between his legs and flattening her back, she circled her lips around him, flicking her tongue and sliding up and down in a slow rhythm. A tremor raced over his thighs and his breath caught. Fuck.

Focus. He met Conrad's eyes.

Conrad shook out the whip, and the tail skated across the wood floor. "First lesson, Jay Mayard, is understanding the difference between good hurt and bad hurt."

Jay lay back on the mattress and gathered her hands on his chest, restraining them there. He understood bad hurt, knew it deeply, but he would listen and watch intently. He needed to give her the required pain without *harming* her. When Conrad finished his verbal instruction on how *not* to use a whip, he reared back his arm.

Crack.

Her gasp swathed his dick. He tilted his head and glimpsed a pink line blooming on the rise of her ass. *The hurt she experiences is relative.*

Crack. Crack.

Her mouth glided over and under him, her breath steady, eyes closed. Fucking hell, she was magnificent. The cracks of the whip continued a steady pace as did the suction of her lips. A dozen or so strikes later and his orgasm was simmering, too fast, too soon.

"Straddle me." Jay sat forward, coughing to clear the thickness in his voice.

She unfolded in a smooth rise and stood before him, gaze resting on his. Pushing her hands through his hair, she climbed onto his lap. Her face dipped, closer, closer, and he arched his neck to meet her lips.

She parted her mouth and rolled her tongue with his. It wasn't one of her blistering, fuck-me kisses that stole his breath and tightened his balls. Instead, her lips moved over his with apology and gratitude, so yielding and peaceful, his throat tightened, and the backs of his eyes ached.

When the kiss ended, he pulled her to his chest and they sat in silence, bodies molded together, neither of them making a move to loosen the embrace. Call him a man, but it was a treasured closeness, with his erection trapped between their bellies, her swollen nipples rubbing through his shirt.

After a few shared breaths, he gripped her waist and raised her, working his fingers inside her. So fucking wet. He replaced his hand with the head of his cock and entered her, gazes fused in a helpless lock. Slowly, effortlessly, he slid her down to the hilt and her groan rivaled his.

Arms hooked around her hips and ass, he held her immobile. "Master Conrad, can you strike her back in this position?"

"Yes." Conrad tagged a short rope from the wall. "If her hands are bound with yours behind you."

With a few practiced knots, Conrad shackled her wrists with Jay's and secured them at the middle of his back.

Jay sucked in a breath as Conrad's hands moved over his wrists. No shed. No oven. Nothing but Charlee's muscles sheathing his dick and the energy shifting between their joined bodies. He shuddered. The urge to thrust sent his molars crashing together. He was a pussy-clench away from ejaculating. "Hold still."

She closed her eyes and twisted her hands against his back until their fingers half-laced together. Her face glowed in the natural light of the room.

"I love your eyelashes." He smothered them with kisses. "So red. Why didn't I notice that when you were blonde in St. Louis?"

"Mascara." Her lips twitched, and her eyes remained closed.

Whack.

Her eyes flew open, and she rose up on his cock. The tiny movement teased electric shocks down his legs. Over her shoulder, Conrad reared back a leather flogger.

Whack. Whack. Whack.

Jay moaned with her as her cunt contracted. He thrust again and again, bucking and grinding, their fingers clenching together and their mouths colliding. With each hit of the flogger, he moved faster, harder. Her breath sharpened, and her tongue slashed urgently with his.

"Jay. Jaaaaay." Her head fell back, and her body shuddered.

The quake of her release stroked him into a mindless world of sensations, tearing his climax from him in violent waves. "Unnngh, fuck. Oh, fuck. I'm coming."

Floating down with noisy gasps for air, he dropped his head on her shoulder and savored the sweet aroma of her skin.

She squeezed his fingers and pressed her lips to his ear. "Huntress."

He felt her message deep inside him. She'd gained what she sought without abusing her safe word. His happiness demanded he kiss her. So he did, thoroughly.

Conrad knelt behind him and unlaced the rope. "We're scheduled for another hour. I can show you some things to take on the road."

"Thanks, yeah, let's do it." Jay didn't try to mute his post-coital grin. "But don't expect me to remember your name in the morning."

Charlee's laugh burst through him, split open his heart, and filled it with light.

88

Charlee huddled against Jay in the crowded corridor of Conrad's apartment building. Eight or nine bodyguards cocooned them, blocking her ability to see the front door and the street beyond. She caught Nathan's vigilant gaze where he stood beside her and offered him a smile.

He returned it. "The buses have been making laps around the city for the last hour, waiting for you to emerge. They'll be here any second."

Her cheeks heated. She'd been so wrapped up in Jay, so eager to watch him take charge in the dungeon, she hadn't considered the dozens of people waiting for them.

Jay raised her chin with a knuckle. "Don't worry about them. They have a fucktillion ways to entertain themselves. Rockstars, remember?"

"What about your schedule?"

"What schedule? We don't have a tour manager anymore."

Ugh. Thank fuck for that. She wasn't sure what her expression held, but his blazed with his smile. "Faye will manage all that. For now, we have the next couple days off."

Behind him, Tony dropped her hand from her ear and hovered it above his arm. The morning after the tattoo, he'd given her leave to touch him, but she still practiced caution. When he nodded, she gripped his elbow and stepped into his side. "Buses just rolled up. Perimeter's clear. Ready?"

He patted his left shoulder with his right hand, his visual cue.

"Principals are Oscar Mike," Tony said into the mic on her headset.

With a collective heave, the entire hallway filed through the door and spread into formations over the front lawn. Suit-clad shoulders crowded Charlee's view, but the rumble of the buses and Jay's arm around her waist guided her.

Yellowed grass and brick sidewalks blurred beneath her Doc Martens, the humid air abuzz with the distant chatter of onlookers.

"Jay! Jay Mayard! Over here. I want an autograph." The voices carried from the street. From behind the buses maybe?

The entourage and motorcade must have drawn the crowd, but how had they glimpsed Jay buried in the fold of the security team? Or was Roy behind this?

Her boots hit the curb and she followed Nathan onto the bus. Colson smiled from the driver's seat. "Welcome back, Miss Grosky."

"Thanks, Colson." Her heart calmed to a normal pace as she left Nathan at the front and turned into the aisle.

The guys reclined on the couches in various positions and stages of undress. The black hair of a woman's head bobbed between Rio's legs. Another woman ate at his mouth. Beside him, two blondes sandwiched Laz in a naked, writhing tango.

On the opposite couch, Wil tossed a pair of briefs over his naked lap and tipped back a beer in a long draw. "Hey, Charlee. Did Jay grovel enough?"

She smiled. "No groveling needed."

The bathroom door opened, and a brunette swayed out, nude and smiling. Her gaze shifted from Charlee to beyond Charlee's shoulder, and her smile widened. "Oh. My. God. It's Jay Mount-Me Mayard!" She bounced up and down, as did her tits.

Charlee shook her head, lips curving up, and moved down the aisle toward the galley. Jay pressed against her back, arms hooked around her belly, breath hot on her neck.

Poor guy was probably terrified one of the girls might touch him, and not for the reasons he'd once had. He didn't need to worry. The fact that he'd tracked her down and accepted her sexuality in the dungeon was a comfort no one had ever shown her. His commitment and loyalty had restored her trust in him.

She twisted her neck and kissed his pinched lips. "Fucktillion ways to entertain themselves? I'm just now getting the meaning of that." Wasn't the first time groupies came aboard the bus, but the orgies were usually contained to the hotel rooms. She kissed him again until his lips relaxed and parted. "See anyone you know?" She didn't want the answer to that, but the question tumbled out unbidden.

His eyes widened, and he croaked, "No, Charlee. God, I'm not..."

"Jay Mount-Me Mayard? I've got two hours in a dungeon that proves the mounting."

The engine purred, and the bus rolled into traffic. Nathan exchanged a few words with Colson and stood at the center of the lounge, hands on his hips. "All right, ladies. The fuckateria is closed for the night. We're dropping you back at the hotel. You can catch cabs from there."

Moans volleyed back. A pair of fuchsia panties landed on his chest and dropped to the aisle.

Chuckling, Charlee rifled through the fridge and removed lunchmeat and condiments. "Hard salami sandwich, baby?"

A smile pulled the tightness from his lips. "You don't need to wait on me." Jay uncurled his body from hers and tugged the wrap of meat from her hands. By the time he devoured his second sandwich, the bus was pulling away from the hotel, leaving behind the smiling, sated groupies.

Sitting at the foldout table in the galley, he inhaled the last bite and rubbed his stomach, exposing a band of golden skin in the process. Her fingers itched to feel the muscle beneath. She crawled over the seat beside him, ducked her head, and bit him above the belt buckle.

His hands flew to her head and his abs rippled against her lips. "Keep doing that, and I'm going to take you right here on the table."

Footsteps approached behind her, and Jay covered his eyes, groaning. She glanced over her shoulder and exploded in laughter.

Laz bent at the waist and dug through the galley cabinet, clad in a too-tight gold thong.

"Jesus, man." Jay's forehead hit the table top. "We talked about this. No grape-smugglers."

Unscrewing a jar of peanut butter, Laz looked over his shoulder and tugged the gold strip from the clench of his ass. "What's wrong with the rockstrap?"

"Rockstrap?" Charlee's amusement shriveled as he reached his thong-tugging hand toward the open jar of peanut butter. *Don't do it. Don't do it.* He plunged his fingers inside. "Put your name on that jar. It's all yours."

He narrowed his eyes at his snack and shrugged. "I don't know how Jay rocks with his cock on the loose. The rockstrap—" he snapped the string on his hip "—keeps the twig and giggles from bobbing and chafing on stage."

Jay raised his head. "Did your parents have any children that lived?"

Lifting a glob of peanut butter to his mouth, Laz swirled his tongue over his fingers in a disturbingly erotic fashion. "You know, Jay, I was so miserable without you on the bus today, it was almost like having you here."

And so the barbs continued for the rest of the day and however many miles through Louisiana and Mississippi. Laz modeled his collection of rockstraps, Wil and Rio played video games, and Nathan and Tony drifted into the back lounge.

Jay led her to their cozy bunk where he described the beaches he would take her to and the cabin in the Canadian Boundary Waters that he would transform to accommodate a BDSM dungeon.

For the duration of the tour, however, their quad-axle home was her icon of security. There were no untrustworthy staff members. No automation systems to hack. No concealed corners where Craigs could hide in wait.

But as the next venue grew closer, anxiety built in her belly. Nathan and Faye worked a legal offense against Roy, using Ella as fuel, and what they found was an all too common story. Ella met Roy once while he dined at the restaurant she worked at. Her payment was delivered in cash by a third party. Nothing connected her to Roy. Her word against his.

A dead-end prosecution was the lawful approach. Follow the legal system, let justice take him down.

Justice. What an anemic concept. Charlee could do better than that.

Death was a sure way to end it. Just put her close enough. She wouldn't hesitate to shoot next time. No question, she would welcome her own death before she let Roy drag her back to San Francisco. The thought both eased and terrified her.

Rocking with the sway of the bus in the protection of Jay's embrace, she drifted to the places he'd talked about, but the destination didn't matter. *He* was where she wanted to be. "Do you think your triggers are gone for good?"

Lying beneath her, his chest rose and fell through a sigh. "I don't know, but for the first time in memory, I *want* people to touch me." His eyes softened. "You gave me that. Thank you."

Her heart soared. She was so damned proud of him. "Thank you for today. I know the scene isn't your thing. You gave me that, and wow, Jay. You make a sexy dungeon Dom."

Arching up, his lips found hers. He kissed her sensuously, his tongue licking and swirling inside her mouth. It tingled over her face, down her spine, and curled her toes.

She pulled up and smiled. "You've never had a massage, have

you?"

"No, baby."

"Roll over and take off your shirt."

A pause. "Can you do it with the shirt on? In case someone pokes their head in?"

She pushed down the impatience bubbling up inside her and bit his lip playfully. "One of these days, Jay Mayard, you will wear those scars with pride."

Starting on his pecs, she kneaded over the bumps and valleys, working her way to the sinews connecting his neck and shoulders. He grinned and moaned and dug his fingers into her ass. As she ground her knuckles, the weight of the day pressed down, and her body slumped closer and closer toward his. She stared into his golden-brown eyes until his eyelids drooped and hers soon followed.

89

A hollow reverberation woke Charlee. She jerked upright and banged her head on the bunk's ceiling. "Ow, shit. What was that?"

Jay untangled their limbs, rolled off her and thudded into the aisle.

Feet pounded through the bus accompanied by Tony's shout. "Delta team's transport is down."

What? One of the Suburbans? Charlee's muscles locked up.

Pop. Pop.

"Alpha and Bravo down," Tony barked. "I repeat. Three Suburbans are disabled." Multiple footfalls filled the front and rear of the cabin.

Terror gripped Charlee's insides and a shiver chased her spine. "Jay?" She jumped into the aisle. "Jay, was that a gun?"

Pop.

"Echo team down. We're on our own."

"Charlee!" Jay shoved the drape aside, his expression tight. "Charlee, get on the floor. Cover your head." The white of his eyes glowed in the dim light.

She dropped to her knees and choked, "You better get down here with me."

Pop.

The brakes squealed, and the force of the stop threw him into the front of the bus, beyond the fall of the drape. Her head slammed into the frame of the bunk. She rubbed at the throb and climbed to her feet only to drop again with an onslaught of dizziness.

".50 cal shots. Engine blocks targeted." Tony's shout ripped through the sudden hush. "Colson, are we hit?"

"Affirmative. Engine block."

"Fuck, fuck, fuck." Tony's tone pitched. "Set up the perimeter. We need to get off this goddamn bus."

Charlee's heart hammered, and her pulse screamed through her veins. Get off the bus? She knew they were sitting ducks, but how many Craigs would be waiting for them to pile onto the road? Was there traffic? Maybe someone could help them.

"Faye has 911 on the phone," Nathan said from somewhere up front. "Where are the shooters?"

"A thousand meters. Could be more. That ridge, maybe," Tony said through a rushed breath.

Thank fuck for their headsets. Charlee put all her faith in the communication and organization of the protective team.

A strong fiery smell tickled her nose. She moved toward the drape as Jay shot through it, grabbed her wrist, and pulled her into a wall of smoke.

She coughed, blinked through the haze. "Fire?" How would his triggers react? He seemed calm enough, in control.

"Engine's smoking. I don't know." He pushed forward along the aisle, and the white cloud enveloped him. He was only an arm's length away, and she couldn't fucking see him.

"Jay! The gun. We need the gun."

"I've got it." His voice was hoarse, breathless. No oxygen. Too much smoke. "Pull your shirt—" He hacked, wheezed. "Over your mouth. Eyes closed."

Wetness blurred and stung her eyes. The burn from the smoke forced so much saliva into her mouth she had to spit it out. She yanked the collar of her shirt up to her eyes, buried her face in the thin material, and let him guide her.

"Charlee!"

Nathan. Somewhere ahead. She tried to respond, but her voice choked. She clung to Jay's hand and waved the other in front of her. She cracked an eye and regretted it instantly. Tears flooded down her face in a hot surge.

"The smoke doesn't smell right." Nathan's rasp was muffled and too far away. Where was everyone else? No other voices hopefully meant they'd fled the bus.

Jay stumbled, kicked something out of the way. The clutter made their progress painfully slow, and the smoke weakened her lungs and weighted her movements.

"Almost there." Jay squeezed her hand, slick with sweat.

Her boot caught the edge of a large open case. It flipped into her leg and knocked her off balance. She tottered, lurched, and a sharp prick seared through her bicep. Ouch. What the hell was that?

Jay's hand tightened in hers as he turned. "Charlee?"

His voice echoed in her head. Numbness chilled her limbs and spread through her core. The cabin fell quiet, the smoke grew thinner, and something wrapped around her throat, pulled from behind.

"There's something..." Her voice slurred. Wheezing. Dizzy. There was something back there. Something there. Then, there was nothing.

90

Charlee's hand ripped from Jay's grasp, and the panic he'd tried so hard to stifle tore from his throat. "Charlee!" He gulped, toxic air scorching his insides. "Charlee!"

No answer. Christ, did she fall? Hit her head? He fell upon his knees and shoved aside guitar cases and electronics. "Charlee? Charlee, where are you?" He raced over the floor on hands and knees, sweeping the couches, under the dining table, the seats around it.

The heat smothered him. The smoke. So much smoke. His body locked up, and the walls closed in. The oven. Oh God, he was too big. He curled into himself, didn't want to touch the scorching walls.

His lungs burned, his eyes scratched and watered, and he couldn't see his hand in front of his face through all the goddamned smoke. No. Not the oven. He was on a bus... A bus... A bus. With Charlee. He shot to his feet and stretched his arms. Fuck. "Charlee, please. Answer me."

"Jay?" A deep baritone.

"Colson?" He spun toward the voice.

"Yes, sir. You need to get off the bus. It's going to blow."

Blow? His heart rate spiked, and his shoulders stiffened. "I can't find Charlee. She was right here. She must've tripped. I don't know. I can't fucking find her." His hands swung over the floor, slamming into furniture and bouncing off the luggage and can goods strewn over the aisle.

"Okay," Colson said from behind him. "I'll search the front. You take the back."

She couldn't be anywhere but right fucking there. Tears mixed with smoke and poured down his face. His lungs wheezed and labored. He crawled over the floor, dread rising with every lift of his legs. "Charlee! Charlee!" His voice shredded his raw throat. Fuck, where was she?

"I've got her. I've got her," Colson shouted from the front of the cabin. "I'm getting her off the bus. Hurry."

"You have Charlee? You've got her?" Jay scrambled to his feet and plowed through the shit in his way.

"Yes, sir. I'm taking her to safety." Colson's voice floated in from outside the door.

His blood pumped faster with the urgency of his strides. He crashed into the front dash and stumbled down the stairs. The billow of smoke followed him as he pitched across the asphalt, staggering to stay upright, coughing and blinking through stinging eyes. "Charlee? Colson?"

He swung around, the landscape obscured by the pitch-black sky. No streetlights. No headlights. The road appeared deserted except for their motorcade. The Suburbans and buses angled haphazardly around him, submersed in plumes of smoke and swarmed by the silhouettes of his protective team. Charlee was nowhere amongst the mayhem.

The door behind him swooshed closed, and the engine turned over.

Blood drained from his face. No, no, no, no. He spun, drew his gun from his waistband. The bus rolled forward, accelerated.

He ran, raised the gun, fired at the door. The glass cracked. Just the surface. Fucking bulletproof. His heart thrashed in his chest, and his legs burned from the exertion of his sprint. Pain exploded through his jaw from the force of his clench.

The smokescreen within held its thickness. How the fuck could the driver see?

The bus picked up speed, moving faster than Jay could run. He shot a tire. Another and another. They continued to spin. Too many tires. Too far away. The gun clicked. Out of ammo.

Nausea tore through his stomach and boiled through his chest. He didn't slow his strides. He couldn't. Couldn't let the taillights out of his sight. "Tony! Nathan!"

The taunting red lights faded, vanished, swallowed by the night. His heart fractured, releasing unbearable agony. He clutched his chest, his eyes swelling, his throat constricting. No, he wouldn't give into it, wouldn't let his grief take the wheel and drive.

He pulled out his phone and dialed 911, hoping the police could track a tour bus in the middle of goddamned nowhere, fucking praying they weren't on Roy Oxford's payroll.

91

Charlee's eyes flew open and collided with Roy's. His face hovered inches away. The pungency of his cologne set off her gag reflex, and her heart banged against her ribs.

She jerked her arms where they stretched above her head, her hands imprisoned by rope. The leather couch creaked beneath her. Still on the bus, the only remnant of smoke was the burn lingering in her lungs.

The strips of lights on the ceiling cast a muted glow, highlighting the creases in his pale face. He raked a hand through his black mass of hair with an uncharacteristic yank and inhaled deeply, nostrils flaring. "You're awake." He released his breath. "I was worried. Propofol is... *Tricky*."

"Propofol?" Her head spun, not with a post-drug fog, but with the will to overpower, to control how this would end.

A hush enveloped the bus, but she refused to let her thoughts leap to the cruelest explanation for Jay and Nathan's absence. Outside the windows, metal walls surrounded them. She'd been transported somewhere, hidden in a building.

He brushed her hair behind her ear, sparking shivers where he touched. "The injection was Propofol. The milk of amnesia. How do you feel?"

How did she feel? Seriously? She gave him her coldest glare. "Like you care."

He hung his head, and his hand crept over her belly. "I care, Charlee. I've always cared. Perhaps a bit too much." His fingers whispered over the waistband of her jeans, slipped the button free, and lowered the zipper.

Everything inside her bucked, but she wouldn't give him the satisfaction of a reaction. "Where are we?"

"Mississippi."

Helpful. Not. "Are we in a shed?"

"A hangar." His eyes followed his fingers as they slipped inside her pants.

She recoiled uselessly into the cushion.

"Our plane will be ready shortly." He spread the fly open, lowered his head, and pressed his lips against her silk-covered mound.

A violent tremble invaded her body. She could tell him Jay's semen still coated her pussy, but the backlash might be more forceful than her bones and skin could withstand. His lips delivered light kisses over her belly button, and she tensed up, magnifying the tremors. She sucked in a breath. "There are cameras on all the vehicles that feed live footage to a remote location. They have evidence of you boarding the bus and driving it away."

"Oh, Charlee. So many blanks in the puzzle. What would you give me for the answers?"

What could she stomach? "A kiss?" He'd kiss her regardless. Could she kiss him back?

His tongue burrowed inside the opening of her pants and found her clit through the barrier of her panties. "A real kiss."

That was too easy. "Yes, Sir."

"Your bodyguard planted a hack in the recording software for me, disabled the GPS, and *he* drove the bus away."

Her stomach twisted, and saliva rushed through her mouth. "Who?"

His exhale blew a sick heat over her groin. "Colson was easily bought. Three kids in private universities and an ex-wife who continues to drag him to court for more money. He couldn't turn down the paid tuition and the quieted ex."

"But how?" Her head throbbed to make sense of it. "The bus was on fire, the engine destroyed."

"My shooters tapped the engine blocks on all the vehicles but this one." He raised his head and propped an elbow on the cushion between her bound legs. "Colson laid the smokescreen with a phosphorus grenade and chased your friends off the bus with a warning of explosion. The distraction allowed him to pop the needle in your arm and hide you in the bathroom."

She closed her eyes until she could wrestle down her heart rate. "How did he drive with all the smoke?"

"Thermal imaging goggles and a gas mask." He gestured at the head gear tossed on the galley counter.

"That's a far-fetched story. The protective team wouldn't have evacuated without me." Jay had been an arm's length away. He wouldn't have let her go unless something happened to him. Dread squeezed a fist around her throat, crushing her ability to breath.

His lips twitched, and her stomach dropped. "Don't look so sad, Charlee. Nathan Winslow and Maryanna Tony didn't abandon you. Colson told them he'd hidden you safely in the nearby woods." A tic jumped in his cheek. "They might still be searching for you there if Mr. Mayard hadn't created such a disturbance."

The blood in her veins turned to ice. "Where is he?"

"An hour away. Soon, he'll be an ocean away. How does Italy sound, my beautiful girl?"

Panic shook her body. Her blood pressure elevated with every breath. "You will *not* kill him."

"No." He traced a line from her pubis to her bra, dragging her shirt up with his invasion. "I've made mistakes in the past. Some unforgivable." He stroked her flesh, rising goose bumps across her belly.

Her molars scraped, grinding in her ears. "Oh, you mean Noah, my father, the guard, and his niece? Did you rape her?"

The skin around his mouth tightened, and his eyes flicked down and back up. The air congealed around him. Dense and oily, it crept the distance between them and trickled over her skin, chilling her from head to toe.

His hand moved from her chest to her face, cupping her jaw. The movement was deliberate as though he were forcing himself to do it slowly. He bent above her, his face lowering, his eyes glazing over. "I'll collect that kiss now."

Her pulse beat a ringing drum in her head. She held herself immobile as his mouth covered hers, his tongue piercing through her lips and his fingers digging into her cheek. She tongue lay limp, her stomach rolling.

The grip on her face controlled her jaw. He was ruthless in the way he kissed her. His teeth sliced her lips. His tongue whipped and slashed.

When a sharp, pained cry escaped her throat, he sat back, lifted his hand, and smacked her. "Kiss me like you kiss Jay Mayard, and I won't harm him, his band, or their careers."

The heat from his strike rippled over her cheek, but the prick of his words was worse. How many times had Roy watched her kiss Jay through the hacked cameras at the estate? The violation was too much. No more. This ended now.

The clamor in her head narrowed, concentrated into a plan.

Intent pumped through her blood and strengthened her limbs. "Promise his safety." The promise wasn't needed, but it was an expected thing to ask.

He studied her face with his uncanny ability to see everything, and his eyebrows lowered over hard eyes. "Not just one kiss, Charlee. Every kiss from now on. As long as you continue to give me that, I promise his safety."

Resolution settled around her heart. She nodded, knowing it would only be one kiss, because she would *not* be walking off that bus.

Leaning forward, he sought her mouth, and she gave him what he wanted, a kiss she'd never given him before, one that would knock him off balance long enough to execute her plan. She drew in his bottom lip and nursed it tenderly. Licking and nibbling, her tongue pliable but demanding, she stroked deep into his mouth, tried to touch the innermost part of him.

Rather than kissing Noah's murderer, she told herself he was just a man. A normal man made of flesh and muscle and stable mind. His hands tangled in her hair and swept down her neck. It was both revolting and heart-wrenching the way he welcomed her gentleness, hungry for affection, moving his mouth to follow hers as if she were his oxygen.

He broke the kiss, his cheek rubbing against hers, breath heavy and content. "I'll do better," he whispered. "I won't hurt you anymore."

Wow, real convincing, Roy. It'd been a whole two minutes since he'd raised his hand against her. "I believe you." Because he'd never have the opportunity to do it again.

His hands clenched on her shoulders, his gaze boring into hers. "I won't live another day without you. Do you understand, Charlee? If something happens to you, if I lose you again, I will not go on."

Knew that. Counted on it. She blinked, expression blank.

"Mr. Oxford." The Craig's voice carried up from the bottom of the steps. "The jet is ready."

"Thank you, Salvador." His eyes never drifted from hers. "It's important you believe me," he said, softly. "I want you to *want* to be with me."

What fueled his change of heart? Watching her with Jay on the cameras at the estate? Seeing her plastered all over the Internet and in magazines, always on Jay's arm, smiling and happy?

Delusional, self-important prickadonna. He had a rather high opinion of himself to think she could ever have that with him.

He reached for the knots at her ankles and worked them loose. "My armed guards are just outside the door. I'm taking the first step in our new relationship." He released the ties on her wrists. That done, he rose and stared down at her, a smile bending his vile mouth.

Holding out his hand to her, he must have thought he was making colossal progress letting her walk with him without restraints. In about thirty seconds, it would be one of the chief regrets in his life.

She closed up her pants, grasped his hand, and tried to ignore the escalating beat of her heart. With each step to the stairs, her breathing quickened and her palms grew slicker with sweat.

As he stepped into the stairway, she glanced at the ignition switch. No key. She grabbed the railing with her free hand and moved to follow him, slowing her pace, letting the distance stretch between them.

The hand he held slipped as her arm went taut with the extension of his pull. She yanked it back, gripped the other handrail. Bracing her upper body with the rails on either side, she hauled up her boots and kicked the middle of his back.

He propelled forward, missed the bottom step and rolled over the concrete. She spun and slammed her hand into the manual crank. The doors crashed closed as he launched for them, the seal catching his fingers.

His hand recoiled, and a red tide washed over his face. "Charlee." A restrained growl. He slammed his palm against the door, tried to pry it open. "Salvador! The key!"

Shit, shit, shit. The electric door mechanism could be unlocked from the outside, but what about that time Rio locked out Laz when they were arguing over a video game? He'd engaged a manual override somewhere. She fumbled over the crank, up and down the handle. There. She flipped the lever and turned toward the door, hands shaking.

Two bullet holes splintered the outside surface of the glass. Frightening images infiltrated her mind of her friends in a gun fight while she slept in oblivion on the bus.

The Craig worked the key until Roy shoved him away and tried it himself. "Charlee, open the door." His low, cool tone vibrated with an edge of agitation.

His persistence guaranteed he'd find a way in. She raced down the aisle, through the drape, and scrambled over her bunk. Nathan had given her a new phone at the start of the tour. She'd never used it, wasn't sure if it would be charged. She dug through the pocket beside the plate of outlets and device ports. Following a white cord from the dock to the pocket, she found the phone still plugged in.

A gale of air escaped her lungs as she swiped through the contact list. Nathan. Tony. Jay. She tapped his name and held it to her ear.

The call connected, and Jay's deep timbre barked through the phone. "Who is this?"

"It's me." Her heart leapt to her throat. "I don't have much time."

A rustle whispered over the line. "You're on speaker. Where are you?" His breath was heavy with exertion, panic.

"On the bus inside a hangar. A private airport, maybe. An hour from where he took me." If Roy hadn't lied about those details.

"Are there any signs, anything indicating the location?" Nathan asked.

Gun shots fired outside the bus, the echo rattling her bones.

"Was that gun fire?" Jay's voice thrummed with fury. "Where's Roy?"

She crept to the rear lounge, bent low to the ground, phone clutched to her ear. "I locked him outside the bus. Will the lock hold?"

"The key can't override it," Tony said. "But he can find a way in with a few tools and a little time."

Peering over the nearest window, she scanned the interior of the hangar. "No signs on the walls. Doors are closed. No windows. Just the bus, the plane, and... Four guards." The sight of Colson among them curled her nails into her palm. "If this doesn't work out, Roy said Italy was the destination."

"We're working on it." Tony sighed. "There are five airports within a hundred-mile radius of our location. We don't know which direction Colson went after he passed the nearest town. The cops..."

"Were paid off." Wouldn't be Roy's game unless he'd cheated, lied, and corrupted. She flinched as bullets plinked off both sides of the bus. "Would the tail number on the plane help?"

"It's doubtful he registered it." Tony's soft tone mimicked her doubt. "Read it off."

"November Charlie 276 Alpha. NC276A. Are there guns or anything on the bus that I might be able to use?"

"No, and you will not engage him," Jay said. "Hide in the hatch. There's a crank inside the compartment to close it. Don't try to leave the bus. Wait there until we arrive. We're coming." His command lost its intensity toward the end, drifting into thready, pleading territory.

"Jay, take me off of speaker." She moved to the aisle, past the bunks, and rummaged through the cabinet beneath the sink, pulling out a fire extinguisher, lighter fluid, and grill lighter. Lucky for her, the guys liked to grill out.

"Just me on the line. Are you in the compartment yet?"

The report of multiple guns popped around her. Splintered dots multiplied on the windows and windshield. None of them pierced all the way through.

"Aim high, you piece of shit," Roy screamed from somewhere near the door. "I'll kill you myself if you hit her."

"Listen to me," she breathed into the phone. "I know how to beat him." Her memories hurled her back to the night Roy choked her, the look in his eyes when he realized he was killing her. *Would you survive my death?* Her heart pounded with resolve. "I need that steel core of yours, now more than ever. Don't give up, Jay. Do you hear me? If you do, he wins."

"What are you talking about?" His voice was thick and strained. "I will *never* give up. We're on our way. Tony's weeding through the law enforcement. We'll get them to every airport. Did you find the hatch crank?"

His idea was so fucking tempting. Sweat beaded on her hairline, dripped into her eyes. If they found a clean cop in the area, the raid wouldn't ensue soon enough. Hiding in the storage space only delayed the inevitable. Roy knew she was on the bus. He'd locate her before anyone arrived.

"Are you hidden yet?" Jay's concerned voice spiraled through her, fortifying her. "Answer me, Charlee."

"Remember when I said your heart is stubborn enough to beat for both of us?"

"Yeah, Charlee. Right now it's trying to tear through my ribs."

"I'm depending on that. Keep it beating for me, Jay." The heartache over the hell she was preparing to put him through swelled in her throat. Roy wouldn't survive it, but Jay was made of steel. He had a lifetime experience in surviving.

Her eyes stung, and her voice clogged with unshed tears. "My heart, my life, and my love are yours. I give you those things, because I love you."

She lowered the phone and pressed *End*. A stab passed through her chest, and her lungs burned with gulping breaths. Her lips curled back through the surge of grief.

The phone buzzed. She powered it down, wedged it into her pocket, and pressed a fist against her breast bone, over the ache that weakened her knees.

The boom of gun shots thinned, and silence settled over the hangar. She grabbed the lighter fluid and lighter, gathered a bundle of blankets and pillows, and sprinted over the cluttered aisle.

A blast of adrenaline accelerated her movements. Her vision was clearer, her mind more so. She dropped the grill supplies on the driver's seat and flung the bedding into the stairwell.

Roy leaned against the door, forearm braced above his head. The gun in his hand thudded slowly against the spider-webbed glass. He stared at her out of red-rimmed eyes. "I wanted this to go peacefully. I wanted..." Stepping back, he pressed the butt of the gun against his head, grinding it into his scalp. "I didn't want to punish you." He dropped his hand. "You've left me no choice."

The Craig appeared at the door with a pry bar. Shoving the flat end in the crack of the doors, he worked it back and forth, bending and screeching the metal.

She tagged the lighter fluid, flipped the cap, and submersed the blankets. Twisting, she snatched the lighter and squatted on the top stair.

"She's up to something, Mr. Oxford." The Craig removed the bar.

Roy slammed his body against the door, eyes wild. "What are you doing?"

Holding his gaze, her insides knotting with the horror of her plan, she sparked the lighter. "Would you survive my death?"

He threw his shoulder against the door, over and over. "No! No, don't do this!" Hands in his hair, gun rubbing along his head, he screamed, "Get that fucking door open."

The Craig shoved the bar through the crack, and she touched the flame to the blankets. The fire flashed in a brilliant yellow flame and curled into a roaring blaze, consuming the stairs and door.

"Noooooo, no, no, no." Roy bellowed, and the bus rocked under the bang of something against the side. Presumably his body.

The smoldering air chased her into the lounge, burning down the back of her throat and scorching her lungs. She knelt on the couch and pressed a hand against the window. "Put that gun in your mouth," she shouted.

He ran to the window, eyes up and blinking with helplessness. "There's an extinguisher. Find it. Check the galley." His hand clenched on the collar of his dress shirt.

"You did this." She coughed, her voice rattling with phlegm. "You killed me."

Squeezing the lighter fluid, she sprayed it over the aisle, couches and walls. Smoke blanketed the cabin, and Roy vanished behind the thick screen of smog.

Nose buried in her arm, she danced around the flames, scooped up the fire extinguisher, the gas mask and goggles. The heat scalded her skin, her clothes drenched in sweat.

Outside the bus, his wails roared over the whoosh of devoured air and the crackling and crashing of things falling down around her. She strained to hear that final gun shot, knowing it wouldn't come. He would scour the charred remains for her body. If he couldn't identify her, he would watch Jay, analyze his behavior. His thoroughness rivaled his persistence. He wouldn't turn the gun on himself until he had the evidence, until he saw her death in Jay's eyes.

Her lungs burned from lack of oxygen and dizziness swept over her. She wrestled with the head gear, wondering why she'd want to watch the inferno consume her. Hands trembling, heart racing, her earlier resolve seeped away with her strength. Panic flooded in. Too late for that.

The fire rushed toward her. She backed toward the bunks, awaiting her death, comforted by the howl of Roy's sobs.

92

Jay lay in a bed, in a room, unsure of when or how he arrived, his mind still entombed within the smoldering skeleton of the bus. He was simply a cell in his body, breathing, existing, nothing more.

A shadow had stretched over him, blocking light to his thoughts, picking at old scars, and softening the steel beneath. Outside the shadow, hours passed. Days maybe. But time held still in the darkness.

He gathered a pillow to his chest, wishing it was one of Charlee's shirts, her messenger bag, her sketchbook, something of hers to hold. He had nothing. Everything that signified her had burned. Gone. She was gone.

An aching void crawled from his gut, hollowed out his chest, and swelled in his throat. It wouldn't relent. No matter how many tears or how deep the pain, it wouldn't be satisfied until it swallowed him whole.

Every release of every breath, he battled the overwhelming pull to follow her into death. So he clung to the news of Roy's incarceration and the consummation that could bring.

Apparently, Roy hadn't had enough time to buy off every local cop. When they hauled him from the crime scene, he was in a sobbing state of hysteria. He was so panic-stricken his own thugs hadn't been able to pull him away before the cops showed up. Not that Jay had reacted differently when he arrived at the hangar. The stench of soot and the grit of ash on his skin replaced his old nightmares with new ones.

He buried his face in the pillow as the torment exploded in his skull and erected a stabbing pressure behind his eyes. He choked, gasping for air.

The door creaked open, flinging a stripe of light over the bed. He mustered the strength to clench his jaw and abandon his sniveling.

Footsteps approached. The mattress shifted. "You haven't left this room in a week, Jay." Laz leaned over and shook the empty water bottle on the side table. "At least you're hydrating."

A paper bag rustled, and the aroma of fried food invaded his nose and turned his stomach.

"Not hungry." His voice grated from disuse.

"Not asking." Laz reached for the lamp and light flooded the room, searing Jay's eyes. "Nathan called. If you're going to identify..." His voice croaked, cleared. "You have to identify the remains by the end of the day."

The room tilted, and the simmer in his gut burst through his chest. He bolted from the bed, lurched across the room and to the toilet. His heaving expelled wet air, his stomach empty. He was empty.

Laz pressed a glass of water into his hand and rubbed his back. "I'm so sorry, man. I..." He looked away, lips blanched. "I miss her, too. We all do."

Jay wiped his face on his sleeve and moved to the bed, numb. Pulling the blanket to his chin, he curled up beneath it, the shroud of the darkness guiding him in. "I can't do it."

Blinking dully, Laz's eyes were bloodshot, his spiky hair unwashed. "You don't have to. Nathan already did it. He just thought...thought you'd need that."

What he needed was to step through the fucking shadow sagging over him. It wasn't bringing her back, wasn't cleansing the pain of her death. Same thing he told himself the last time he retched the nothingness inside him. And the time before that. He could hear her in his head, screaming at him to get the fuck up.

"There's something else." Laz wandered to the window and drew back the curtain. "Roy Oxford has been cooperating with the questioning, but he's got one hell of a legal team. There's not enough to keep him detained." He turned, lowered his voice. "They let him fly back to San Francisco this morning. He's under court order to stay put until the investigation concludes."

A fire ruptured from Jay's chest and burned through his muscles. He tore off the blanket and shot to his feet. Fists clenching, he marched a circuit around the bed. What was he going to do? Fly to San Francisco and murder him? Then what? Go to prison?

He slammed a fist into the mattress. She didn't surrender her life for him to serve the remainder of his behind bars. He pounded the bed again, over and over, until his fist slowed, his lungs whistled, and his heart broke all over again. What would she say if she were there, witnessing him crack so spectacularly?

She'd call him a big baby and tell him to buck up. He drew in a serrated breath, rubbing his eyes, missing her so damn much.

Desperate for something of hers he could touch, he paced to the bathroom, stripped his shirt, and turned his back to the mirror. Reaching over his shoulder, he rubbed his fingers over the ink, anchoring himself to the fire and steel, to the woman who bestowed it, to the life she gave him.

A gasp drew his attention to the doorway. A look of wonder rounded Laz's face, the paper-wrapped hamburger forgotten in his lowering hand. "Wow."

"Pretty great, isn't it?"

"Better than great. And way better than double rainbows. The scars..."

"My aunt gave me the scars. Charlee gave me the reason to display them."

Laz set the burger on the counter and reached a tentative hand over the ink. With Jay's nod, he brushed fingers over the rippled skin, the air around his caress thrumming with electricity.

The sweet wretchedness of the touch splintered through Jay. A reminder he would never feel her hands again. He leaned into Laz's fingers and pressed his fist against his mouth, thwarting the grief trying to break free.

Arms came around him and Laz pulled him close, holding him as the loneliness poured out.

When the last tear dripped from his chin, he leaned back, wiped his face and blew out a mirthless laugh. "Sorry you had to witness that."

Laz shook his head, his eyes downcast. "You're not the only one hurting."

A miserable silence stretched between them. Jay's own misery pummeled through his slumped body. "What do I do? How do I move through this?"

"Leave Mississippi. Either we finish the tour or we go home."

Leaving meant leaving without Charlee. His heart hurt so badly he didn't know how it continued to function at all.

Laz rocked from foot to foot, hands in his pockets, eyes on the floor. "Play the show tomorrow night." His tone was soft, cautious. "The guys are ready if you are."

The mounting ache in his eyes spread to his throat. He swallowed the mess of snot and despair, only to lodge it in his chest.

"Tomorrow's show is in St. Louis."

He choked, wobbled, and leaned against the edge of the counter. "St. Louis." Where he met her. Where he lost her the first time.

Don't give up, Jay. Do you hear me? If you do, he wins.

"Yeah." Laz looked up, the skin around his eyes creased and tired. "I know what that town means to you and—"

"I'll do the show." He would stand on that stage and prove she wasn't wrong about him. Then, he would come out the other side and take down Roy Oxford.

As he forced down the cold hamburger and packed up his things, he felt the shadow changing over him, shedding its suffocation, and clearing the way.

93

The stadium roared, filling Jay with the energy of thousands. He rolled his neck and bounced in place off-stage, secure in his purpose and driven by an overpowering commitment. No more dark corners. No more triggers. His curl-up-and-cry button was broken.

Charlee's medicinal nudging had been light-years ahead of modern-day PTSD therapies. She would continue to be his cure, his solace. The memory of her huge blue eyes and brilliant smile soared through him, taking the edge off his persistent ache.

"Hey, man." A roadie stepped beside him and dropped his voice. "Need a hookup? I can get you anything you want."

Jay closed his eyes and sucked in a long breath. Not even a whisper of a craving for what the man offered. Instead, his blood boiled at the thought of using drugs. It would've been like spitting on her grave. He looked over his shoulder and caught Tony's eyes.

She pushed away from her post and closed the distance. "Problem, Mr. Mayard?"

"Have this man searched for drugs and escorted out of the arena." He glared at the roadie. "I emailed our drug policy to every member of the crew yesterday. Apparently, you didn't read the memo."

The man gritted his teeth. "I thought it was just a procedural thing."

Jay turned his back, leaving him in Tony's capable hands.

"Good evening, St. Louuuuey." Laz's shout rocked the speakers and rumbled through the stadium. "Boy, do we have a surprise for you tonight."

The crowd erupted in shrills, and the lights dimmed. Jay reached up, grabbed the collar at his nape, and yanked off his shirt, tossing it somewhere behind him. Readjusting his headset, he accepted his guitar from a wide-eyed crew member and strode across the stage, past his grinning friends, not stopping until he reached upstage center.

Hands whipped and slapped at the edge of the stage, bodies doubling over the metal gates with straining eyes, gaping mouths, and blaring tonsils. The throb in his chest reminded him why he was there, shirtless and exposed. She was dead, but she could never die. His heart beat for both of them.

An overhead spotlight blinked on, illuminating a circle around his feet. He plucked out the beginning chords. The melody penetrated him, and he felt her in the tune, her musical laughter sifting through him. He felt her.

The heat of thousands of eyes rested on his bare skin, the vibration of his soul chanted her name, and the ghost of her touch tingled over his tattoo. He felt her everywhere.

He squared his shoulders and switched on his mic. "This is called *You Weren't Just a Girl*."

Laz approached his side, a small smile pulling his lips as he strummed, blending with Jay's notes through the eerie riffs. Jay phased out his guitar chords, and the instruments dropped off. A hush fell over the stadium.

"When I walk into your eyes, I see forever." Jay straightened his back as the burden of her absence tried to curl him forward. "I see you sleeping next to me. I see you holding me." He bit down on his trembling lip. "I see you loving me."

His voice was breathy as he huffed through the speakers. "You weren't just a girl." His heart swelled, strengthened with the refrain. "You were a vision. And with that vision, I will endure."

Wil joined his other side, his shoulder touching Jay's as he slapped and plucked the bass strings in a creeping rhythm. As the guitars reentered, Rio accelerated the tempo.

Jay climbed the fret, the energy of the crowd powering him through the finger slides. "I know something about pain. I have enough to liberate. I'm letting it go." His vocals rose. "But I will never let you go."

His skin pulsed beneath the tattoo. With the reinforcement of his friends' sidelong glances and their approving smiles, he sang the chorus with the steadiness of steel. "You weren't just a girl. You were a vision. And with that vision, I choose to live."

I envisioned you on stage in a crowded arena proudly baring your tattoo. The tattoo I hoped you'd grow to appreciate. The one I hope to finish.

His heart thumped to fulfill her wish. A heavy inhale drew intent deep into his chest. He turned toward Rio and bared his back to the stands.

The crowd exploded, their fanatical screams saturating the instrumental progression. The widescreens above him displayed his scars, panning in on the exquisite detail in her work.

The instruments fell quiet as he hummed into the revised lyrics of the next verse, feeling the words deep inside him. "In my vision you see steel. You see me."

The lights went out. Applause and whistles ensued.

One of these days, Jay Mayard, you will wear those scars with pride.

He stood in place, numb to the squeals of the fans, shrouded by the ever-lasting darkness. His body shook from the shock of his reveal, from the disbelief of her absence. As the next song bounced in with Laz's pithy chords, Jay swelled with pride in the life she gave him, even as he silently wept for the life she'd lost.

Jamming alongside his bandmates, he held her around his heart, her strength moving his fingers over the strings. Beneath the heat of the lights, he slapped hands with the fans in the front row, the first time he'd willingly touched them. The interactions shifted something inside him, warming him. She would've been proud.

He remained upstage until the final song, then drifted into the shadowed corner and sat on an Anvil case. From the perch she would've been sharing with him, he plucked the notes, leading into the song named after her, and sang the lyrics he'd written in those lonely months after he met her.

Many people told me what love is
No I'd never experienced it
I know a world who thinks love is lust
The first time I recognized your pain
I realized it was much like mine
I'm scared of this thing inside of me
I can't bear to see you fade from me
My world is collapsing inside of yours
And I want more...of you
Your world is filled with such regret
I hate that you were part of it
I see your eyes staring back at me
I can't look away

94

Two days later, Jay sat in the backseat of the SUV, anxiety tying his stomach in knots as Vanderschoot parked outside of the San Francisco penthouse. The mirrored windows of the tower reflected the orange glow of the sun setting over the bay, a contradiction to the darkness lurking within its walls.

Beside him, Tony fiddled with his phone and angled the screen toward him. "The app is running in the background, undetected. It's recording now, sending live audio to the entire team." She grabbed her phone from her lap and checked the display. "I'm receiving it. We'll be listening to every word, ready to move in if necessary."

He sucked in a breath and zipped up his leather jacket, slipping the phone in his pocket. Faye had made progress in their prosecution against Roy, but they were missing the irrefutable evidence that would trample his powerful legal team.

"You shouldn't go in there alone." Her eyes softened. "You look..."

Broken? Lost? He rubbed at the creases around his swollen eyes. "Yeah, and the way I *look* isn't changing anytime soon. I'm doing this." He had to.

"The risk outweighs the reward. The man is a murderer. You pay me for my advice. Allow me to go with you. Or Nathan could—"

"Nathan's not here." He'd vanished the night Charlee died. Jay didn't hold it against him. Everyone grieved in his own way, and Tony would look after her lover. "I'm going in alone. I need Roy to feel comfortable enough to talk."

Her jaw tightened. "Even if you got a confession out of him, it could get thrown out of court."

"Then we'll distribute it over the Internet and let the court of public opinion destroy him." He reached for the door handle.

"You know Roy would squash that before it reached public

attention. He's outmaneuvered every attempt we've made to go to the press."

He let his breath out. Fuck Roy Oxford and his pristine public image. The reminder only made Jay's attempt to secure a confession more imperative.

"Nathan's connections, all the local detectives he trusts, are waiting nearby." Tony's eyes bore into his. "If anything feels off, if you need to abort, say the words *Tick Tock*. We'll be there in seconds."

He nodded, heart thumping against his chest. What would Roy do? Beat him with a baseball bat?

"You have to leave the gun. His guards will pat you down at the turnstiles."

He pointed at the seat pocket in front of him. "It's there. If I took it in, I'd blow his fucking head off." There would've been an extraordinary amount of satisfaction in that, but spending the rest of his life in jail wasn't what Charlee wanted for him.

He swung open the door and jumped onto the sidewalk. As he strode toward the front doors, he wondered if Charlee's boots had ever touched down where his did, if she'd walked into her prison either time or if she was carried in through a lower level. The thought incensed him, heating his muscles, and fortifying his backbone.

Inside, a glass wall blocked the corridor to the elevator and a security guard rose from the desk at the center. "May I help you?"

"I'm here to see Roy Oxford."

"Do you have an appointment?"

"Tell him Jay Mayard is here." He let his resolution ripple through him, bracing his feet, raising his chin.

The guard picked up the phone, pressed a button. "Mr. Oxford...Yes, sir. I'll send him up." He swiped a badge on the nearest turnstile. After a pat down and a few passes with a handheld metal detector, he waved Jay through.

Another guard met him on a waiting elevator, swiped a key card, and punched the button for the sixtieth floor. It lurched up, as did Jay's stomach. He rolled back his shoulders, determined and clear of mind.

The elevator doors opened, and a familiar face waited on the other side. The dark-haired, dark-eyed gunman from New York. Jay smirked. "I see the earlobe still hasn't grown back."

The man bared his yellow teeth. "Follow me."

Through a formal living room and down a long corridor, Jay's escort halted at the second door to the last on the right and opened it.

"Leave us, Salvador." The voice from inside was cool, soft, and way too fucking calm.

Jay's escalating heart rate heated his blood. His muscles went taut. He stretched his fingers at his sides, breathed deeply through his nose, and walked through the door.

Brown leather wallpaper veneered the walls. Mahogany bookshelves wrapped the huge slab of a desk. Behind it, Roy Oxford sat straight and still. "Have a seat."

"I'd rather stand." An unnecessary rebellion, but he preferred to look down at Charlee's abuser.

His black hair was neatly coiffed, smoothed away from his pale face. His shirt buttoned to the collar and pinched with a red tie. Despite his put-together appearance, there was something identifiable in his expression, creasing his eyes and drooping his lips. Seeing his own pain mirrored on Roy's face would be something to reflect on and savor later.

Roy brushed a nonexistent hair from his face and returned his hand to his lap. "I saw your concert in St. Louis."

A cringe twitched his shoulders. "You were there?"

"You're a loyal employee, Mr. Mayard, out there making me money rather than petitioning Human Resources for a bereavement leave."

Jay forced back the emotion simmering through his chest.

"Your tattoo was a nice touch. Windsor Records has seen a thirty-five percent increase in revenues since the show. I made a shrewd call reinitiating production on your albums." He tapped a finger on the desk. "She limned that design in her little sketchbook. You must've been the musician she was penciling it for."

She'd drawn it while with Roy? His heart hurtled into his throat, and his hands shook from the ache of it. He shoved them in his jeans pockets. *Keep him talking. Get the fucking confession.* "I met her the night you killed Noah Winslow. The night you kidnapped her in St. Louis."

A dim haze passed over Roy's eyes, and his fingers circled over a thick bundle of papers on his desk. "You don't fool me, Mr. Mayard."

Ice raced down his spine. He blanked his face and cocked his head.

"You walk in here with your shoulders back and purpose in your step, but in truth, you're crawling on your belly, wallowing in your delusions of purpose. It's only a matter of time before all the what-ifs and should've-beens lure you in and smother you." Roy's gaze turned inward, and his hand stroked the papers, back and forth.

A burn tunneled through his sinuses. Why hadn't he snuck the damn gun in? Fuck the confession. He could've ended this with a trigger pull. He steeled his legs, his words powered with impatience. "You enslaved her twice. Raped her repeatedly. Your third attempt killed her."

Roy hardened his glare. "As long as we live, she will haunt us with her burning eyes." A tremble rippled through his fingers. He yanked them to his lap, looked up. "I considered the prospect that she'd escaped the fire, impossible as it was, and anticipated you falsifying her death." He thinned his lips. "I see the romanticism in that now. Your eyes are weighted with reality."

A buzz ignited in Jay's head. He'd shared that hope, but it had crumbled when her remains were excavated. He slapped those thoughts away before they suffocated him, replaced them with the reason he was there. "You might as well have set that fire yourself. You killed her."

Roy straightened his back and leveled his gaze. "Mr. Mayard, I am a very wealthy man. I own the largest enterprise in the world, homes on every continent, private jets, and more money than you could aspire to earn in multiple lifetimes. As you are aware, since I invested in your band's label, I do not back losing schemes. It is unfortunate my most important asset—one you had temporary possession of—was lost in that fire." He opened a desk drawer and placed a revolver beside the papers, barrel aimed at the chair Jay stood behind. "Have a seat."

Resolution descended over him, pulling him toward the imminent outcome. Charlee was gone. Looking down the barrel of Roy's gun would be numbing. If the hammer came down, the audio recording would capture Jay's death. He moved around the chair and sat, chin raised and spine braced.

With one hand stroking the gun's grip, Roy collected two glasses from the side cabinet and set them on the desk. He poured a finger of amber liquid in each and scooted one to Jay. "I nurtured her, pleasured her, and made her what she was. Tell me. What could you have possibly offered her?"

Lifting the liquor to his lips, Jay emptied the glass in a burning swallow that wasn't close to rivaling the fire in his chest. "Happiness."

Roy shifted his thumb over the gun's hammer, cocking it with an empty expression. "Happiness is fleeting. An unquantifiable nonentity. Her *real* needs were met by *my* hand. She simply couldn't live without me."

Enough of the fucking mind games. "Is that why you kidnapped and tortured her?" *Admit it or pull the trigger, motherfucker.*

Silent seconds lapsed. Roy's finger traced the trigger guard. "If your eyes weren't convincing enough, your impudence despite your position—" He glanced at the gun, back at Jay "—is evidence that she isn't waiting for you. It is done." He lifted the stack of paperwork and flipped it to face Jay. "A copy of my will. For the inconvenience caused to you and Nathan Winslow by the loss of Noah Winslow and Charlee Grosky, you are both coheirs to my empire. However..." He tossed back the scotch and set the empty glass to the side. "She will always be *my* beautiful girl, and I *will* possess her again in the afterlife." He raised a revolver.

Jay flinched, and his heart stopped, ready, waiting.

A cackle tumbled from Roy's chest. "Relax, Mr. Mayard. I will acquire her on the other side before you get the chance." He shoved the barrel in his mouth and squeezed the trigger.

The bang reverberated in Jay's ears and shuddered down his spine. Brain matter spurted on the bookshelves behind Roy's slumped body.

Footsteps stomped around him, voices shouted, alarms rent the dense air. A red light blinked in the ceiling. The recordings captured a suicide instead of a confession. It was over.

It should've loosened the fist squeezing Jay's heart. He stood, moved to the wall, and braced an arm against it, anticipating the retribution to wash over him, to fill the vacuum with... What? Nothing would replace her loss. Not Roy's billions or his death.

He pulled out his phone and said with a voice thick with spit, "Charter a jet, Tony. I'm going home. To Canada." To scrape up what was left and rebuild. For what purpose? The hollowness inside him expanded, crushing his organs, consuming every dream.

Charlee ended her life knowing it would stop Roy from fucking with his. Had she considered how meaningless it would all be without her? He would've gladly spent a lifetime running and fighting if it kept her at his side, her hand in his.

As he strode from the room, his heart battled between grief and anger, his arms burning to hold her, his hands itching to paddle her ass. But he wouldn't be able to do either. Never again.

95

They say the only thing certain in life is death. As Jay leaned his head against the window of the seven-passenger Beaver floatplane, he felt that certainty like a tumor in his chest. It rooted its stems through his heart and coiled branches around his lungs, constricting, strangling. Her death had no intention of letting go.

They also say death gets easier. He was much less certain about that. The plan was to spend the next few months oscillating between being pissed off at her and unproductively depressed. Maybe he would write a few angst-filled songs to express the utter helplessness of his mind.

Tony sat in the front, beside the contracted pilot, her hands folded in her lap. As the plane nosed down for descent, the vivid blues and greens of Birch Lake filled the horizon. The humidity in the air lay in a thin mist over the glassy water. Across the cove, his four-thousand-square-foot lodge stretched along the shoreline, interrupting the tundra of wild shrubs, sedges and pines.

Isolated and pristine, his corner of the thirty-five-mile lake was only accessible by plane or boat. He'd ventured there twice since demolishing the original structures, but his last visit had been before he met Charlee.

The caretaker had moved into the guesthouse the year the construction completed. Thomas lived there year-round, the only person who had resided on the property since Jay was six years old.

Dipping in for the landing, the floats skidded over the water's surface, dispersing a flock of ring-necked ducks into the curling fog. When the plane drifted to a stop at the edge of his dock, he grabbed his duffle bag and guitar case and climbed out. Tony's soft footfalls lagged behind.

The mustiness of dark rich soil mingled with nearby mint and the floral of woodland laurel, bathing his lungs. Charlee would've loved the authenticity of the land, and for a moment, he let himself imagine her walking along the dock with him, smiling as the scenery saturated her brilliant eyes.

Did her soul exist in an eternal place? He'd hoped so right up until Roy Oxford uttered his despicable final words. But could Jay cope with the alternative? The thought of her dwindling into an airy nothing was more than he could bear.

Cradled by the low-lying forest, he followed the rocky path to the cabin and stopped.

Two silhouettes darkened the floor-to-ceiling windows that plated the length of the cabin. He expected Thomas, but his curiosity about the other person prodded his boots into motion, drawing him toward the house.

The overcast sky muddled the details of the profiles moving past the windows to the backdoor. As he neared, the floatplane's single engine sounded its departure and gravel crunched behind him.

He slowed his pace. "Tony, who's here?"

Jogging to catch up, she adjusted a large tote on her shoulder. "Nathan."

Though Jay had told her not to come, he wasn't surprised she did and was even less surprised she'd want her lover there, too. Neither he nor Tony had seen Nathan in two weeks.

The backdoor swung open, and Nathan ran out, tugged her bag to the ground, and pulled her to his chest in an adoring kiss.

A storm of hunger and loneliness twisted brutally inside Jay. No way would he be able to share the house with the two of them. He swallowed thickly and forced his feet to move.

"Jay." Nathan joined his side, his tone hushed with pity. "I'm sorry. That was...insensitive. Listen. We need to talk." He put a hand on Jay's arm, staring at it as if the world might come crashing down.

There wouldn't be any detonations. The triggers were gone, and Jay was already standing on ground zero. "Can this wait, Nathan? It's been a long trip."

"No. It's—"

The drone of a familiar two-stroke engine rumbled in the distance, growing rapidly louder, closer.

Jay set down his bag and guitar and moved to the side of the house in the direction of the sputtering. "Who's on my dirt bike?"

The caretaker was in the house, so it wasn't him. Jay glanced over his shoulder and caught Nathan's thinned lips before they relaxed. Tony's eyebrows pinched together, her eyes narrowed on Nathan.

What the hell was going on? The croak of the engine labored under whoever was racing it through the forest. The two-stroke was his most reliable bike. He'd had it shipped the twenty-two hundred miles from L.A. the night Roy swallowed the bullet. Three long days ago. "Who's here, Nathan?"

The *put-put-put* of the exhaust popped over the hill, snapping Jay's head toward it. The orange fender flashed through the woods on the zigzag trail. The rider swung the bike right to left, narrowly missing trees and shrubs, the foliage giving glimpses of a small frame, blue jeans, red hair...Red hair...Oh God, Oh god... Red hair.

He stopped breathing. A stinging sensation numbed his skin. He clutched his chest, strained his eyes, and realized he was lurching along the path through trees, sprinting toward the bike.

The rider rocketed around the bend ahead, the wind whipping the tangle of red hair behind huge blue eyes. She skidded to a stop, sliding the bike sideways along the trail.

"Oh my God. What the fuck is this?" His lungs burned with his whisper, and his tongue felt heavy, numbly expressing his confusion. "Are you real?"

She let the bike fall as she scrambled off it and launched at his chest. He stumbled back, breathless, dazed, arms around her too-thin waist, and tripped over a branch. His back hit the ground, her body draped over him.

Then her lips fell upon his, moving desperately, urgently, wet and salty with tears. She scattered kisses across his face, his cheeks frozen in shock. "I didn't expect you until tonight." She kissed the corners of his mouth, his chin, his nose. "I'm so sorry, Jay. I'm sorry. I missed you so much."

He traced the smatter of freckles on her cheekbone, the satiny skin warm with life. "I don't understand. How is this real?" He slid his hand through the hair draping her face and watched it fall through his splayed fingers, mesmerized.

She sat upright, straddling him, her jeans hanging from her bony hips. "Let's go inside." Climbing to her feet, she bent over the bike.

"Leave it." He missed her weight instantly, slight as it was, and desperately needed it pressing against him to validate his sanity.

As they walked back to the cabin, he intertwined their fingers, staring at her, unable to look away for fear she would disappear. "You haven't answered me."

A smile lifted the edges of her mouth. "Colson didn't know about the custom hatch in the bus?"

He tripped over something beneath his feet, his eyes locked on hers. "No one knew." It was a hiding place for his gun, and no one outside of the security team carried one. "You hid in the storage compartment?"

"I escaped through it with a gas mask, thermal imaging goggles, and a fire extinguisher." She held up her arms, his hand still laced with hers. "Didn't even get a burn." She smiled, lowered her arms. "Though I wouldn't have minded matching scars." She brushed her ear where the bullet had grazed her. Then she reached for the backdoor and held it open. "I worried if Colson knew about the hatch, Roy would figure it out."

He followed her inside, the tingling in his body residing, though he was far from lucid. "The remains... They removed a body."

"Wasn't the first time I framed her death." Nathan stepped out of the kitchen and walked through the living room, approaching Jay slowly with his hands in his pockets. "Borrowing a charred cadaver was one of the easier tasks, especially since it didn't need to be placed at the crime scene. Its existence was for you and Roy only. Though I may never be able to repay all favors I owe from this little venture." He shrugged.

Jay's emotions rocked from confusion to elation, landing in a blood-boiling rage. His teeth snapped together, and his muscles quaked. "You knew? You fucking knew all this time?"

She slipped between them and held up her hands. "Jay, calm down. This was my idea. It was the only way to end it."

A red haze swarmed his vision. "Am I the only asshole who was excluded from this brilliant plan?"

"No." She stepped into him and settled her hands on this chest. "Nathan was the only one who knew, and I didn't call him until I made it out." Her lashes fluttered over her hollow cheeks. "You couldn't know. Roy would've seen right through you."

Fuck Roy. His heart pounded as he sifted through all the risks she took, all the ways it could've gone so horribly wrong. He wanted to wrap his arms around her and never let go. And he would, after he sorted out all the hurt battling through him. "Go to the bedroom. I'll deal with you in minute."

She huffed and balled her hands on her hips.

"Now!" He thrust a finger at the hallway.

Charlee's shoulders shot to her ears, and she took off in the desired direction.

He dropped his hand, flexing it at his side, and glared at Nathan. "You've lied to me about her death not once, but twice. Never. Again."

The skin around Nathan's eyes tightened. "There won't be an *again*."

"No, there fucking won't be." He nodded to Tony, who lingered in the kitchen doorway. "Call that pilot, ask him to come back. You and Nathan have the next three months off. A paid vacation. Go on a trip, practice drills, fuck each other's brains out, do whatever it is bodyguards do."

He pushed past Nathan and followed Charlee's sweet scent down the hall. Two weeks of pain lifted little by little with each step. He breathed clearer. His feet moved steadier. It was funny how a passing of time could rip you apart, and all it took was one freeing moment to solder the pieces back together.

Closing and locking the bedroom door, he turned to face the incarnation of his universe. She was a goddess in a way, wielding the power to destroy and rebuild him at will. His blood pumped with appreciation, respect, longing. It also thrummed with the need to balance that power. "Take off your clothes."

A flicker lit her eyes, and she scrambled to follow his order. When her shirt, boots, jeans, and undergarments thudded to the carpet, she straightened her back and raised her gaze.

He circled her, his fingers trembling over her collarbone, down her spine, and around the dip of her waist. "Why have you lost weight?"

"I couldn't eat." She cleared her throat and whispered, "I missed you."

His heart flipped. "You have two weeks to put the weight back on. If you don't, you'll be spending a lot of time eating off the end of my fork."

She nodded, smiled.

He continued his circuit around her, trying like hell to maintain some semblance of composure. She was alive. Right there, beneath his hand. "How did you escape the hatch unseen?"

"The smoke hid me when I slipped from the compartment on the driver's side and out the back door of the hangar. I found an unlocked shed a few rows down and waited there. Roy didn't leave the passenger door, and luckily, his guards stayed with him."

The blazing innards of the bus would forever be burned into his mind. She'd been right down the road while he'd crumbled apart in that hangar. "*Luckily*. That's exactly right." He stopped before her, glared down into her wide eyes. "I'm infuriated over the risks you took with your life. *Our* lives. Did you consider what your death would do to me?"

"You're so strong." She dropped her eyes to the floor. "I watched the concert on the Internet. You were amazing." She looked up, didn't flinch from his hard glare. "There were a lot of flaws in my plan, but your resilience was *never* a doubt." Her chin trembled. "Still, I deeply regret putting you through that."

The conviction in her words settled over him. His heart skipped through his chest, thumping to the beat of effortless chord changes. *G. D. E...D.*

Christ, he loved her. He moved to the bed, sat on the edge, and pointed to his bent knees. "Come here."

She sank her teeth into her lip and closed the distance.

Gripping her wrist and thigh, he bent her face down over his lap. Her legs and arms dangled on either side of his knees, and her gorgeous ass rose up, filling his view and rushing a pulse of heat to his groin. "You will never put your life at risk like that again." He let his palm fly, sending a smack through the room as it landed on one cheek.

When she wiggled, he leaned in and bit the flush his palm left behind.

What had the forums said about domestic discipline? Be mindful of the depth of her emotions and pain threshold, monitor her arousal, and make her count it out. He curled his fingers between her legs, and they slid smoothly between her wet folds. His dick jerked. "That was the first of twenty. Count them out."

"One," she breathed, and fuck if her voice didn't send him hurtling toward a quick finish in his pants. Nineteen more. Good God.

As he pommeled her ass, each breathy count tested his restraint. When the last slap rippled over her perfect pink bottom, he spun her, tossing her face up on the bed, and climbed between her legs. The mattress groaned as he thrust against her mindlessly, eating at her mouth, hands tangling in her hair.

She laughed against his lips. "Jay, your jeans?"

Fuck. He launched off the bed and shoved his pants past his ass, not bothering with the boots. With his ankles shackled by the jeans, he crawled over her, gripping his dick, and buried himself inside her wet warmth.

"Fuck, fuck. Oh, God, Charlee." The sensations waved through his body, heating him from head to toe. He flexed his hips, panted against her mouth. "I'm going to last about two point two seconds."

She flung her arms around his neck and rocked against him. "Me too."

Her lips slid over his, and her fingers dug into his nape. He pulled her in, as close as they could be, and spread his legs to open her wider.

He sank into her over and over, grinding against her, speeding up and slowing down.

Energy crackled between their slick bodies, and her pussy clenched around him. Eyes locked on his, she arched her back and found her release. The bedding wadded in his fists as her climax crashed over him, gripping him with quaking shocks.

His thrusts increased in rhythm and intensity, and an inexpressible emotion exploded inside him, a desperate feeling that had nothing to do with his building orgasm. He wanted to crawl inside her so violently, he crushed her body to his. He wanted to meld her to every cell of his being. He fucked her harder, slamming his hips between her thighs. He was buried in his universe, and still, he wanted more of her, wanted her so entangled with him, they could never be unraveled.

The drum of his heart thumped in time with his lunges. Ecstasy frenzied through his mind and body. He powered in and out of her until his release tore from him with a ragged shout.

At length, he lifted his weight from her chest and kissed her deeply, running a hand over her heated face. There was nothing he could say, no words he could utter, to voice the immense relief washing over him. Loathing the idea of separating their joined bodies, he stayed put, softening inside her, relishing the intimacy. "Have you been here the entire two weeks?"

She nodded, her lips curving. "Thomas has been very accommodating." She whispered, "I don't think he gets any visitors."

God, he missed that smile. "Guess I need to talk to Thomas about the hazards of letting strangers move in. How did you know I'd come here?"

She shrugged. "We'd decided our future would be here, and I knew you wouldn't give up on that."

Hadn't he? He must've been frowning, because she poked her index and middle fingers in the corners his lips and shoved them upward.

She grinned. "Maybe you didn't consciously acknowledge the reason, but you boarded that plane and came to me, nonetheless." She shoved his shoulder. "Now feed me. I'm withering away here."

He kissed her lips, rolled to his back, and decided *they*—whoever *they* were—didn't know what they were talking about. The only thing certain in life was Charlee.

96

Six months later...

"Thanks, Fredrick. See you next week." Charlee waved to the pilot and raced up the dock, the bitter chill in the air biting her nose and stinging her eyes. After a twelve-hour day at her tattoo shop in the only town on the other side of the lake, bent over back-to-back customers, she should've been exhausted.

But vigor danced through her limbs. The absence of Roy's shadow was so fucking liberating, the need to look over her shoulder dwindled with the Canadian temperature.

Breathing in the crisp air, she wrapped her coat tightly around her, bounded to the ice-covered shore, up the path, and burst through the backdoor. "Jay?"

The muffled vibration of his electric guitar floated from the basement. She tossed her coat on the couch and swung into the stairway, heart pounding, her hands slick with sweat.

He'd asked her to marry him. Woke her that morning with his mouth between her legs, his teeth pinching her clit, and said, "Marry me."

She told him to buy her a ring and brush up on his charm, but neither of those excuses were the reasons for her non-answer. She'd anticipated his proposal for weeks and needed the day in town to accomplish the response she'd planned out.

At the bottom of the stairs, she tugged off her boots and slipped into the music studio.

He squatted on a stool at the center of the room, his shirtless back to her, and a guitar in his lap. "Roll it again. Pick it up from the third verse."

The rest of the band flickered across the widescreen on the wall, moving in and out of camera shot. The angle showed the L.A. estate's basement studio, the drum set, and the couch where she'd spent numerous hours watching them practice.

Laz rose from the couch and shuffled to his amp, clicking it off. "We've got this. Let's call it a night."

Wil fidgeted with the tuners on his bass and rubbed his furrowed forehead. Behind him, Rio scooted away from the drums, twirling a stick in his hand, grinning at whatever Laz was doing off camera.

"Let's take a break, then we'll roll through it a couple more times." Jay seated his Les Paul in the guitar stand beside him and straightened his back, flexing his shoulders and thrusting his elbows behind him in an upper-body stretch. "You're consistently a half beat late into the segue between the chorus and the second stanza."

His leather pants sagged an inch or more below his narrow hips, exposing a tantalizing panorama of sculpted lines over his lower back and the ridges of his ass. She licked her lips, her nostrils flaring to accommodate her heavy breath.

He bowed forward, forearms on his spread knees. The ambient lighting accentuated his sexiest muscles, the contour of his *V*-shaped torso beneath the animation of black, red, and brown ink.

The pads of her fingers tickled to worship him. She covered the few feet between them and rested her palms over his scars.

The tightness in his back melted away beneath her hands and he leaned back until he was looking at her upside down. "Mmm. Practice is over, guys."

The faces on the screen glanced up and a chorus of '*Hi Charlee*'s' bounced back. She gave them a chin lift. "Hey. You taking good care of Nathan?"

Rio shook his head. "That's Tony's job. Besides, we rarely see them. They don't leave the bedroom."

She pressed her lips against the soft vertical grooves between Jay's eyes, giddy and content that Nathan had found happiness. "He is, after all, a very rich man. He can do whatever the hell he wants."

Sure, Roy's money was tainted, the means by which he accumulated it questionable. When Jay refused to touch his share of the inheritance, she reminded him the fucker stole nine years of her life and was responsible for putting Jay through her death. Twice.

Point made, they spent the money indulgently, donated to charity, and gave an ample sum to the family of the murdered guard and his niece. It also funded the elaborate dungeon in the room next door. The irony of that was bitter sweet.

Wil stepped so close to the camera, she could count the follicles of his eyelashes. He fluttered his eyes, his cheeks puffing up. "We'll see you in a couple weeks? And you'll give me the tat I emailed to you?"

The mermaid with a skeletal face and huge tits? What a goofball. Damn, she missed those guys. "Yep. Two weeks." They would spend the rest of the winter in L.A. while *The Burn* recorded their new album.

"Good deal." Wil's arms reached up, and the image on the screen shook as he wiggled something on the camera. "Signing off."

The screen blinked to black.

Jay reached back, grabbed her waist, and shifted her until she stood between his legs. Wrapping his arms around her hips, he tucked her belly against his chest. The gold in his eyes gave way to darkening shades of brown as he stared up at her. "How was your day?"

"Crazy busy." She touched his dimple, lost in his heavy-lidded eyes. "I really need to go in more often to keep up with the schedule."

"Nonnegotiable. I fucking dread the one day a week separation as it is."

No sense arguing it. They were leaving in two weeks.

He walked the fingers of one hand around her waist and inched up her thermal shirt. "Any memorable tats today?" His lips shimmied over her naval.

"Mm." She closed her eyes, shivered against the smooth texture of his mouth. "Some guy from Montreal asked me to ink the letters *S E X E*. One letter on each finger."

"Sexe?"

"Sex in French, I think." When he arched a brow, a laugh bubbled out of her. "True story, I swear." She pushed her hands through his hair and circled her thumbs over his scalp.

He closed his eyes and moaned. "I'm still waiting for my answer from this morning."

A thrill trickled through her. "I gave myself a tattoo today."

His head jerked back, and his wide eyes collided with hers. "Where?"

She shrugged, biting her cheek and squirming with the itch to blurt.

He searched her face and lowered his gaze to her neck, lingering there, heating her from the inside out. His eyes burned over her breasts, her belly, all the way to her toes, as if he could see through her long-sleeved shirt and cargo pants. He pursed his lips. "Remove your clothes."

Emptying her expression, she did, fumbling as excitement sparked her pulse. When she stood in only a pair of red cheeky panties, he ran his hands over every inch of her flesh, spinning her around and lifting her arms.

He looked at her panties, her eyes, back at her panties, and shoved them down her legs. With a nudge of his toes on the insides of her ankles, he spread her stance apart, hesitated, and sat up. "You'll give me your answer to my proposal, and you'll tell me where the tattoo is." His jaw tightened, and his chest lifted. "Go to the dungeon. Put your back against the tower."

Turning toward the door, she let her smile stretch so wide her cheeks ached as she dashed down the hall and into their playroom.

At the center of the room, a wood beam rose from the concrete floor and disappeared into the ceiling. She backed against it until her ass touched one of the two horizontal bars bolted to the tower. She positioned her feet at either end of the lower bar, buckled the shackles around her ankles, and rose to her full height.

His soft, steady footfalls announced his approach in the hall. She gripped the bar at her back, her breath rushing out in noisy pants.

Clad in only his too-tight-to-be-legal leather pants, he didn't look at her as he padded into the room. Her heart skipped a beat. Master Jay carried his authority with a confidence that quickened her pulse and fluttered her stomach.

Pacing along the wall of implements, he dragged out his decision, torturing her as he fingered every flogger, butt bruiser, whip, and cane. Finally, he removed the well-used leather belt, his favorite impact toy, the sandpaper long peeled away.

In three long strides, he stood before her, top button undone at his waist, belt dangling from his hand, masculine vitality heaving in waves from his rock hard body. "What's the answer?"

His timbre was growly and demanding. Holy shit, he was sexy. Impatience flooded through her, tempting her to capitulate so he'd fuck her already. "Find the tattoo, and I'll give you the answer."

He reached around her, opened the collar affixed to the tower, and secured it around her neck. He did the same with the shackles attached to the horizontal bar at her ass, strapping them around her wrists. "What's your safe word?"

"Huntress."

Stepping back, his eyes lingered over every trussed inch. With a flex of his bicep, he swung the belt.

Fire spread from each slap on her thighs. Sweat beaded on his golden complexion. His muscles swelled through his swings, and his leathers strained to hold his arousal.

Her own urging rushed through her groin, leaking free of her pussy and drenching her inner thighs. Sweet mother, she wanted him to peel off those pants and slam into her, fast and bruising.

He locked eyes with her, and the belt thudded to the concrete. Groping the waistband of his pants, he shredded them in the next beat of her thumping heart. Then he was on her, plunging his dick between her legs, gripping the bar for support as he thrust faster, deeper, slamming into her cervix.

Charged quakes zinged through her womb, stirring her body into a fast-approaching release. She teetered, hanging from the binds, the power of his hips banging her into the tower.

With a rush of exhausted air, she gave into the orgasm, shaking with the force of it. A moan ripped from her throat, and he smothered it with his mouth, biting her lips and curling his tongue with hers.

He pulled out, halting his own release. He squatted at her feet, eyes on her throbbing pussy. "Is it here?" His probing finger wouldn't find it, but she used the reprieve to catch her breath. His exploration moved deeper, and she grinned at the image of tattooing her own vagina. Unsuccessful in his hunt, he shifted behind the tower and spread her cheeks.

A ragged laugh burst from her chest. "You must think I'm a contortionist if you're checking my asshole for ink."

"Stubborn brat," he mumbled as he lifted her feet as much as the shackles would allow, bending her toes, checking her soles.

"You're getting closer." *Not.*

He stood, yanked on her hair, probed her scalp, and released her with a huff. "Fuck this. I don't need to ask. You're marrying me and that's that." He spun and tagged his pants from the floor.

"What are you doing?" Was he done? His erection disagreed.

Tugging something out of his pocket, he held it up to her face, pinched between his finger and thumb. A point-cut diamond caught the dim light, casting a glimmer over her vision. Black curling flames engraved the inside of the silver band. The design mirrored his tat, a symbol of their pasts, their future.

She sucked in a breath. "When?"

He trailed his fingers along her left arm, over the wrist cuff, and interlaced their hands. "I commissioned it while on the plane from New York. It's been in my pocket for a long time."

"Why didn't you give it to me this morning?"

"I didn't know where my pants were, and I was quite comfortable." He leaned his weight against her and captured her lips, his tongue rolling with hers in a sensual dance. "Marry me."

Without waiting for a response, he shifted toward her outstretched arm and uncurled her fingers. The drum in her chest was so loud she was certain he could hear it. With her palm open and facing him, he slid the ring down her finger and stopped.

His lips parted, and their eyes collided. She nodded, floating into his gaze, their dreams, her promise.

A smile blazed over his beautiful face as he looked back at her hand, at the word permanently inked on the inside of her ring finger.

Yes.

PLAYLIST

Punk Rock Girl by The Dead Milkmen
Swing Life Away by Rise Against
Paparazzi by Lady Gaga
Running Up That Hill by Placebo
Nothing Else Matters by Metallica
Drive by Deftones
Where Is My Mind by Pixies
Lebanese Blonde by Thievery Corporation
Waiting Room by Fugazi
Just Like Heaven by The Cure
Forty-Six & 2 by Tool

OTHER BOOKS BY PAM GODWIN

LOVE TRIANGLE ROMANCE

TANGLED LIES TRILOGY

One is a Promise

Two is a Lie

Three is a War

DARK ROMANCE

DELIVER SERIES

Deliver #1

Vanquish #2

Disclaim #3

Devastate #4

Take #5

Manipulate #6

Unshackle #7

Dominate #8

Complicate #9

DARK COWBOY ROMANCE

TRAILS OF SIN

Knotted #1

Buckled #2

Booted #3

DARK PARANORMAL ROMANCE

TRILOGY OF EVE

Heart of Eve

Dead of Eve #1

Blood of Eve #2

Dawn of Eve #3

DARK ALASKAN ROMANCE
FROZEN FATE
Hills of Shivers and Shadows #1
Cage of Ice and Echoes #2
Heart of Frost and Scars #3

STUDENT-TEACHER / PRIEST
Lessons In Sin

STUDENT-TEACHER ROMANCE
Dark Notes

BILLIONAIRE REVENGE
Dirty Ties

OLDER WOMAN / YOUNGER MAN
Incentive

DARK HISTORICAL PIRATE ROMANCE
King of Libertines
Sea of Ruin

ABOUT PAM GODWIN

New York Times, Wall Street Journal, and USA Today bestselling author, Pam Godwin, lives in the Midwest with her husband, cats, retired greyhounds, and an old, foul-mouthed parrot. She traveled the world for seven years, attended three universities, married the vocalist of her favorite rock band, and retired from her quantitative analyst career in 2014 to write full-time.

Her interests veer toward the unconventional: bourbon, full-body tattoos, and tragic villains. Equally peculiar are her aversions to sleeping, eating meat, and dolls with blinking eyes.

EMAIL: pamgodwinauthor@gmail.com

www.ingramcontent.com/pod-product-compliance
Lightning Source LLC
Chambersburg PA
CBHW020353310726
48979CB00015B/2584/J

* 9 7 8 1 9 6 6 5 3 7 1 7 5 *